AF228420

RETURN

THE AFRICA LIST

RETURN

Raharimanana

Translated from the French by

ALLISON M. CHARETTE

LONDON NEW YORK CALCUTTA

Seagull Books, 2025

First published in French as *Revenir* by Raharimanana

© Éditions Payot & Rivages, Paris, 2018

First published in English translation by Seagull Books, 2025

English translation © Allison M. Charette, 2025

ISBN 978 1 8030 9 495 3

British Library Cataloguing-in-Publication Data

A catalogue record for this book is available from the British Library

Typeset at Seagull Books, Calcutta, India

For L.R.

To my children

CONTENTS

Beautiful clear water on a high sea catching the sun, nearly to drown, the wind on the waves for the ripples of leaving, landscape of ore and ocean sublime, Hira sets his feet in the water, one after the other, slowly, moving through the thin rocks, almost blades.

Wanting this water, to dive into it, but to swim, he doesn't know how, not really, not going in for a swim. The water, crystal, barely comes up to his ankles. Another step and he plunges under, he'd thought it was a few centimetres deep, it was a drop-off, a sheer underwater cliff, a trap buried beneath suddenly furious waves, the surface calm.

Tossed against the wall, trying to grab hold, finger flesh slit on cutting shells, sliced, he realizes this is the moment, the waves send him to the open sea, then bring him back in looping rage, towards the rocks where he tries to cling, to no avail, the shells are too sharp, the waves lift him to the surface. *This lifting, is it from my own body, or maybe this is always how it goes?* When drowning, bodies float but panic sinks. He's already going under. And thus does the dead man fathom himself, it is now, today, *this is the way that I die, and my body will float*, he cannot endure it, if She sees that, his floating body, he dives under before the waves can throw him again, and underwater he swims, towards the cutting rocks, but it's like keeping hold of scalpels, he's desperate, *come on!* Blood runs, he sees it, no more breath to hold, he comes up again, he spots someone up near the fort, he wants to scream, he cannot. He drowns. A wave, he surrenders to it, drifting, head under water. A dark mass, he catches hold, climbs onto the rock, his lungs on fire.

A long time, sitting there, feet in the water that almost took him, he will not leave, he suddenly loves that place, that city, town, Algajola, which he had not known just two days before.

emerge

The Boat

Today, in this hotel room, at this desk, window onto the sea, late in this night—he checks the time, an hour gone, that other island, the ocean within him—by these songs he spreads through his veins, in front of these words he puts down as he pleases, onto paper, or his screen, he begins his story again.

Yesterday, as if a part of him had greeted death, a part of him was nearly apart from him. The high sea is only calm on the surface, there's that sun in the sky that knocks you down and plunges you into a beautiful stupor, he is still that child who lays down and shuts his eyes, the light dances through his closed lids, the light never stops dancing. He slowly reopens his eyes. He has to. He pounds that into his head. He has to. He opens his eyes.

Hira does not know if he regrets that he got out of the water. Yesterday. Already so far. Sitting on that rock, he'd let himself be taken over by the sun and the pounding of the waves that bring back and back again that feeling of being prey, being nothing to the devouring sea. He hadn't moved, feet in the water, the water that had toyed with him, squeezed him in its clutches of waves, and finally aborted him, to life, anew, into the current leading somewhere else.

He knows something has shifted. He's tired of his memory, and the things that carry him, and the things he carries.

He simply wants to live with her. When he saw her for the first time, in the street, She was in a transparent bubble, not walking but dancing. A full pink skirt and a shirt knotted at her waist. She was in a bubble. An actual bubble. Like the ones you get when you blow into those little circles. A real bubble that didn't pop. Then, he followed her. He saw where She lived. And the next day, he started over again. Without ever approaching her.

Night requires calm and solitude, but his memory, tumultuous, drives him towards recollections and away from her. Night falls on war, and you sleep. Night falls on crises, you dream. He screams the land. Land between lands of no news, no name, no existence. Night over disaster. Night over time. All unfolding but in truth he needs only a bit, a morsel of edible shrapnel to savour in his hammock, beneath some pyro's display that smells of flesh and cumin, yes, needs this bit that bursts the belly, a moon to gaze at from the ruins and to revel in from charred expectations, and the weapon set on the ground where he'll have laid down his fatigue. That's all he needs, to lay down the fatigue, but there's screaming in his head. Fire and its foolish dance. Grooves carved in paper and his veins a swollen ravine. He laughs. He does not die. He's from the South. There's cackling beneath his skull, loud cackling, very loud, very, very loud.

On the hotel balcony, he looks out over the place that nearly drowned him, a medieval fort set on a cliff; below, rocks coming up through the ocean's canvas, he is realizing that he still lives, still exists . . .

His first act of rebirth, for her, he writes:

We still have the boat that does not reach the sun.

Vertigo

His mother is terrified of water. A friend of hers had dived into a pool one day. There'd been a tool, left underwater. Sticking up like a lance.

Hira had not learned to swim. For his mother. He knew that every time he went to the pool—he or his brothers or sisters—his mother would relive that nightmare, in one way or another. So, he decided to stay home when it was swimming day. He will not swim.

Yesterday, clinging to that rock, he'd thought about that, his body floating in the sea and his mother's anguish, and his wife's, and his children's, he had refused, not for his life, but for his family.

He left the rock after a long while, retraced his path, in reverse: crossing the shallow water and the rocks poking up, returning to the sandy beach, climbing back up to the village and its fort, stone walls, and the boundless sea on the horizon, and stone, and more stone, he arrived at an open circle, paved, like an arena encircled by the sea, he stood in the middle, breathed in deep.

His father had scarcely got out of a coma, and he, his son, he'd set foot in waters he did not know.

Vertigo hit him, there in the middle of the arena, as though the world were turning, the arena becoming enormous, as though he were insignificant, that vertigo that seizes you and urges you to end it all, as though there were no more horizon left, as though nothing mattered any more, as though you just had to fall and accept that you'd no longer feel your legs.

He thought of her then. As he did every time he was in danger of falling. She was his sturdy base, She held him up. Writing devoured him to no end, even more so since he'd made himself its willing prey. It was up to her, always, to piece him back together. She, the one who never took time to take care of herself.

He waited for the vertigo to subside. For his legs to ground him to the earth again, to her.

Endless return, for a filled page to hollow out again, the ink deranged from having to go back over it again, screams and screams, silences to balloon, which will burst like a farce of party favours, he was astonished that he still had things to say, still had to justify why he would condemn this world.

Back at his hotel, he awaited the night, the lone place where he'd claim legitimate residency. Night protected him from the madness of days.

He can still see that day, the 14th of June, which he'd rather swallow up in forgetting, the day of his father's regression, two and a half months ago. Hira often travels, railways and landscapes, spaces to cross as quickly as possible, or as smoothly as possible, at the very least. But this trip was not like others. This one was the culmination of all the journeys he'd had to take since they'd abducted and tortured his father, eight years before, already eight years. Long. So long. He, with thoughts turned towards her, remembered that market and its empty archways, it had been night, and her words that he didn't understand, *kidnapped*, that he rejected, *kidnapped*, that he didn't understand, *kidnapped, your father has been kidnapped*, She said on the phone, he thought he was getting bad reception, thought that's why he didn't understand. He'd tried for the rest of the night to reach his father's phone, consistently getting a soldier, *your father has been secured*, and the following day he'd realized that his own father had been felled, been tortured.

Eight years later to the day—two and a half months ago, on that hastily taken train—his father was again laid low. Relapsed. Wounds reopened and life at stake. That day, he was racing towards him, towards his father, he didn't know, maybe towards a dead body, maybe, a body laid low, or towards a living body, which was still fighting, maybe. The railway, lines of iron on rain, grey cable lines melting into grey memory, and the whole journey renewing torture, the train was flying.

After several weeks in a coma, their father had come back out of
it. Hira was there with his brothers and sisters. Angela, the lastborn,
had been singing softly in his ear. Every day. Everyone joining in. They
didn't want their old man to go like that. No. Not after overcoming
torture. Not like that. Tita and all his cousins were there too. And
aunts. And uncles. Everyone was there. No one wanted him to go like
that. Not that way. Everyone whispering something to him. His sisters-
in-law teasing him. *Hey you, big guy, you're letting yourself be defeated
like this? No way! That's not like you at all! You're messing with us, aren't
you? Just pretending to sleep! Come on, you've got all your girlfriends here,
get yourself up and keep your tall tales coming!*

The patriarch came out of the coma. The folks at the hospital lined
up for a guard of honour when he was discharged, a long line. Hira
cried in secret. From joy. But also from weariness. He'd had enough of
all that. Of being confronted with his country's violence.

As soon as their father had the strength, he went back to the island.
Apartment living, no, that wasn't for him, no settling for crisps and
TV. He needed his land.

Hira hadn't tried to hold him back. It was better that way.

A Happy Child

His is a pallid figure, in this room, pacing, he doesn't go far, he haunts
what is no more—his childhood songs, in the distance, he stands, in
the gloom of curtains drawn, he senses the day breaking, he has a
choice, to stay in his night or come out and meet this new sun.

Flat dance of gnawing anger that pokes out through his skin, he is
missing the caress that scrapes the soul, he forages in the slow spiral
that pulls him down deep, he breathes, he returns to the surface.

He is confronted with this paradox, that his childhood was bliss in
the midst of his country's violence. How can delight cosy up to violence

like that, how can it be that only now does this violence hurt him so much?

He opens the curtains. He wants to be in the light to tell his story, not in that anger, not in that pain, not like this, not in these brutal rushing rages. He has made his choice.

In the beginning was the father, and from a far-flung childhood in the shadow of abuse, the father escaped, alone, an orphan.

As for the son, Hira, he would just like to write that unlike his father he was a happy child, living under dictatorship, obviously, in an impoverished country, one might even call it destitute, but a happy child. He would like to write from there, from that joy of having had a simple childhood and loving parents.

He returns to his bed.

From fatigue.

Back to the blank.

Born

He has not slept long.

He leaves his room to go out on the balcony. He sways 'neath the drunken wind and raises pathetic bits of pride out of his ruins. It is how he is proud. Still able to sway and laugh about it. Like everyone back home does! As long as you aren't falling, you're alive! He'd like to laugh. Crumples in his chest. Let him laugh before offending. Some sort of rage to intoxicate, and. Some sort of dormant violation, and. Time bequeaths him to silence, he laughs with heart contorted, the wind has no plans if not drunken damnation, he would gladly dive into it, with yawning pride, with unbound fear.

He settles in to write. The wind ripples his pages. He remembers the notebooks his mother gave him. Composition notebooks to put his poems in. He hadn't thought of that until then. That you could write poems in notebooks. He thinks of his mother again and the desire returns. To write.

He has to start the story over again, from where it all began.

Birth.

He likes it when his mother tells him that story, of his birth. He likes listening to his mother. He likes looking at her. When her laughter bubbles up and her eyes sparkle again from the rather unusual delivery.

It's as if he'd experienced it, his birth. He's been told the story so many times.

Hira, he had been there. And for the record, conscious. Conscious that he was being born. He, Hira, in that room that welcomed him, that old woman, blind, scouring the placenta. He, Hira, still soaked with the waters, he saw his mother rise, scour around in the old woman's place. He had a simple feeling of being in the world, his head upon his neck, his surroundings open. And the calm filling him. The proof of existing. Nothing and everything was a wonder to him. He, Hira.

A few hours earlier, they'd been at the hospital. He and his mother, his mother still carrying him in her womb. There was no one there at the hospital, it was a national holiday, Independence Day, the 26th of June, the hospital staff were in the parade at Mahamasina Stadium with the soldiers, with all the lifeblood of the nation. No one's born on a national holiday! What are you thinking, Madame, giving birth on a national holiday! No doctors in the maternity ward! No midwives!

Back to the house.

In the taxi driving them back, his head was almost out. His mother told him to keep waiting. Wait a little while longer. She climbed the stairs and had hardly laid down on the bed when he came out, eyes open already, not crying, calm, so calm. The old retired midwife had arrived, called by the neighbours. She was practically blind, unable to read the placenta. Hira remembers he had his eyes open, he got a sudden smack on his bottom. Air rushed abruptly into his lungs, it erased all memories and set confusion hanging next to the serenity from whence he'd come.

He isn't lying. Hira remembers all of it. He swears, he remembers his birth, the room, the blind old woman seen before any other beings, seen before any moon or sun, as though that woman's empty eyes still spoke of the even blacker womb from which he'd emerged, as though he hadn't changed worlds, womb black and old woman's veiled light, this has stayed with him, even now, those eyes coming through the day to scour the original black, the eyes do not alight upon the day, they come through the heart of shadows and curl up within.

He has not moved, in truth, since that day of being born. He is just a pair of eyes, plunging into darkness.

The Zebus in the Stars

He is walking to a beach. Dusk. He quickens his pace to be closest to the sun's bed. Sand beneath his feet, he takes off his sandals. He loves going barefoot. He heads for the rocks, dips his feet in the water. He picks a rock to sit on. On the beach is a family of travellers, gazing out at the sea. Hira has a sneaking sense of intruding on their privacy, but they pay him absolutely no mind. The woman, leaning back on her elbow, and the man, seated, they continue chatting with each other, the two children, two girls, they run and run, they laugh, one sometimes darting between the adults to escape the other.

Hira savours the beauty of the scene, the children's black hair windswept and tossed as they run and play. He turns away out of modesty, yet catches every bit of music from the shrieking children, of foreignness in the couple's language. The slow, lush sound of waves rises through the melody without smothering it. Now he looks afar.

The horizon is stretched out astoundingly taut, like a thin, dark line. Wide bands of clouds cut across the sky from end to end.

Horizontal. All in pastels. Blues, dusted with pink. The farther out you get from shore, the more the sea blots out the pastels. The closer the sea gets to the horizon, the more vivid the blue. Above the horizon, four placid boats, their sails lowered. The masts are the only vertical lines in the landscape, the sloping ropes seem to foster gentle curves, but they are still nearly taut. The boats do not move. You can't see the sun, just behind the small mountain to the left, just there, in the pink spreading over more and more of the sky and sea. Hira looks down at his feet dipped in the water. He starts in surprise, the clear water has also drunk the pink falling from the sun.

An intense pleasure washes over him. The water is cool. The pink becomes darker and darker, the blue turns black. The mountain is steadily more present, the sea more melded with sky. The horizon fades. The lights on the boats are the only sign of separation between the worlds. Like an implacable black and white, with magenta pink to contrast the rippling waves. Soon the pink disappears, the blue returns, deep navy blue, the boats are nothing but black cut-outs, each mast topped with a white light.

To the right, the city lights appear. Yellow. Red. White-sided houses. Shimmering columns of reflected light sinking into the water. Hira sees the sweet family is no longer there. The shadow of a tree traces within him its ordinary serenity, nature's gift, if you stop to contemplate it. He stays there for a long time. Cold sets in, gently. Looking towards the beach, Hira doesn't see much any more. He decides to leave, taking one last look at the sea.

On the open beach, he is suddenly among a herd of cows. He gasps, so great is his surprise. The male of the herd spots him and stamps directly, aggressively at him. Hira is scared but keeps control of himself. He says to the animal: 'All right, all right, I'm going . . .'

He walks towards the road, the bull pushing his back. He does not panic. He knows that to run would be more dangerous still. He has a sudden understanding of the beach as a shared space, how it belongs to different groups depending on the conditions and time of day, he is only passing through, wasn't respecting the customs of the place, and as he leaves, he speaks again to the bull: 'Forgive me, Raomby, I wasn't paying attention . . .'

Hira senses an instant understanding from the bull, for it stops pushing him. In his head, Hira bids him a friendly farewell: *veloma, veloma . . .*

He stops after getting off the beach. His heart is beating too fast. He stands there, on the side of an unlit street. He is at a bend. He looks for cars that might speed by. He crosses. There's a dirt path up to the hotel, a shortcut. He looks around and sees, in the underbrush, far from the path, an earthen embankment, he heads over to it, sits down, and leans back against it. He suddenly feels like he's back home, the zebus a normal presence, the wind that longs to caress his skin, not so keen on the barrier of his shirt . . .

He closes his eyes. He savours this time. He remembers that he's always been scared of zebus.

There was that great-great-uncle of his, Yaban'i Hira, on his father's side, a large, bald man, his head all shiny, who'd brought the whole brood out there, all of his boys. Hira was one of the smallest in that huge field stretching out of sight, with only the occasional plant poking up. Yaban'i Hira led them to a herd of zebus. The closer they got, the more afraid they were. Hira got behind his great-great-uncle, instinctively. The tall man told them not to be afraid: *These are our zebus, they are like our family, bequeathed to us by our ancestors.* Hira saw only the animals' hooves, the menacing clouds of dust they raised, and when he looked up, the huge humps on the verge of toppling over, towards him, and the horns, enormous, pointed, reaching up to the sky, he was scared of them turning against him. They left the pasture. Yaban'i Hira introduced every tree to them, all the important plants.

Hira wasn't really listening, the plants' names had no meaning besides how strange they were, he was just relieved, they weren't with those huge animals any more! He walked in his great-great-uncle's shadow, he thought him a giant.

Then the tall man told them to each choose a zebu. *It will be yours, the one that comes to you by rights, from your ancestors . . .*

He watched as his cousins whooped and hollered and dashed around the herd to pick out the strongest zebu, the best-looking, the most majestic. He was afraid to go back in. He heard an odd mooing, it came from the distance, away from the herd. He ventured out from his great-great-uncle's shadow to follow the mooing, in the opposite direction of the herd. There was a kind of natural hole ringed by a barrier that felt reclaimed by the wild, with bushes growing through the posts, and the wind sang, carrying the mooing that was trying to melt away—Hira had no idea that it was a cattle pen, holding a zebu in calf. The cow looked at him as if asking for his help to get out of the hole. Hira's heart swelled, he made his choice. His cousins had all chosen males, with black hides, heavy humps, a good size, their horns pointy and curved. When he pointed to his animal, there was laughter. He defended himself, said he'd heard the wind pulling the cow's lost song towards him. They laughed even more. His tall uncle let them be, and he pulled Hira close.

Much later, he came to understand that there, he had been chosen; there, he had been found worthy of the name people called him: Hira! And that Yaban'i Hira had taken that name in his honour. He, the great-great-nephew, had given his name to his great-great-uncle! Hira. The song. The song of the world. The song that holds out the first note and first intent for as long as possible. He doesn't remember when or how he'd figured it out. The others had chosen strength, power, and beauty. He had chosen fertility and benediction. He had chosen the song. And every year, when he returned to his great-great-uncle's house, the tall man brought him out to the herd, told him: 'Hira, your cow has birthed so many little ones now, and her little ones have birthed a male, a female, a male, a female, a female, a male . . . Give them a name!' He called them Dzao, Remainty, Ramèna, Gilamaso—blind in one eye. He remembers all of them, especially Gilamaso, a big sweetheart. His great-great-uncle passed away, no one brought him to the field any more.

Yaban'i Hira had foreseen for Hira that he would roam the wide world over, that here would not be enough for him, that he would extend his universe much farther than any other person in his family tree. That's what his choice had meant: 'You are from the city, you enjoy school, yet you chose the mother of the herd. You live in the din of the city, yet you heard the cow's song, that lost song carried back on the wind. You are of this place and you will be of the whole world, you will carry the customs. Your song, Hira, will travel over the world and tell of our own.'

Sitting against the embankment, Hira looks at the stars. He thinks of his zebus, whom he's not seen since. Are their horns perhaps stretching out on high? He reconstructs the constellations of zebus, great horns that give him another map of the sky, the galaxies redraw his cattle pen, there where the first cow bestowed his destiny upon him. He'd long thought that Yaban'i Hira had made a mistake. He hadn't chosen anything, it was the cow who had called to him, seen him. But what did it matter in the end who had made the choice, he or the cow? Surely it made no difference to Yaban'i Hira. The significance would be all the greater if the cow had picked him. Deep down, Hira regrets not knowing his great-great-uncle better. But perhaps that's how things had to be, for his own personal mythology to be built. The pieces of regret that spur you to invent possibilities.

The last image he has of his great-great-uncle is a huge figure, standing on a small hill, red earth all around, welcoming him with booming laughter.

Shortly after Hira had chosen his cow, Yaban'i Hira invited him for a walk. He remembers it as an endless walk and an unstaunched flow of speech. His great-great-uncle talked to him, he remembers that he didn't grasp the meaning of what he heard, he discerned only the music of his great-great-uncle's voice, and the song that floated from it. He noticed how the voice did not die away in the vastness of the land in which they walked, that the shrill birdcalls that tried to pierce through the voice did not kill it, that the wind that came to carry it off could also bring it back soon after, that the seeming weight of the murmuring sea was not there to bury it but to receive it. The faraway that eyes cannot touch, the faraway all flowing all over, was not to abandon it but to magnify it all the more.

Hira understood. Hira noticed. He still didn't know if the echo or his great-great-uncle had spoken first. He thought to himself how a voice is a strange seed. Once sown, you never know what tree, what plant, what flower or thorn it will produce. His great-great-uncle's voice seemed to be all of these at the same time.

Sometimes, they would encounter a man, a woman, Yaban'i Hira would stop for a moment, saying to them: Here, this is Hira, my grandson, the one who will go beyond the seas, his voice will carry farther than mine, farther than all of our voices together. *Oh! How true!* the man or woman would inevitably reply. *How true!*

Hira didn't grasp all of it. This 'beyond the seas' that was so often mentioned, it was amazing, how could anyone go there when its boundaries could not be fathomed? His own boundary was his great-great-uncle's stride. There he stayed, not losing sight of his great-great-uncle's legs, and the staff that he held in his hand, and the seams of his clothes that tapped his side. The tree just over there was already too far, Hira wondered how they would ever get back.

A desire to walk along the sea flitted through his mind, but Yaban'i Hira never took him there.

There, the tall man told him, *is where our ancestors' first zebu came from. Your great-, great-, great-, great-, ten-times-great-, one-hundred-times-great-grandfather, was looking at the ocean when he saw swirling eddies moving towards the shore. He was sure that it was neither the cruel blue shark nor the serpent of the deep, for they did not slice through the waves, he was sure that it was neither a daughter of the water nor some other spirit thing nor anything from the world of beasts, in that age man still lived among all those beings, but this was something that no one had yet seen, something that had not yet visited our world. Your great-, one-hundred-times-great-grandfather first saw the horns, perfectly white and curved, then the hump emerged, a heavy hump that seemed on the verge of falling but never toppled over, the head appeared, the star on its forehead—look closely, little one, look closely, our greatest zebus always have this star on their foreheads—the body followed, a massive body, the hooves carried it to solid ground. The zebu's curves are like mountains. The sky is vast, it may well go on forever, but it cannot curve or take form. The sea can try, but makes only waves or whirlpools. The zebu is form itself, the zebu is a piece of the land of Antara that broke free, a piece of the underwater land in the black ocean mist, look closely, do you see any difference between the curves of the mountain and the zebu? Your great-, ten-times-great-, one-hundred-times-great-grandfather got on the zebu's back and it took him up and down all this land. But you, you will not climb onto the zebu, you will climb into an aeroplane, and you will see more lands than your great-, ten-times-great-, one-hundred-times-great-grandfather did.*

Then Yaban'i Hira burst out laughing, a side-splitting laugh. And Hira saw then that they were back at the house. He said to his great-great-uncle: *Dadilahy, we didn't turn around and we got back home?* His great-great-uncle replied: *Ah, dady, walking straight ahead will always lead back home!* So Hira started running, straight ahead, just to affirm his great-great-uncle's words, straight ahead to the house.

This is what he thinks, in that moonless night, leaned back against the wall. Has he walked straight ahead? It seems as such. Has he got back home? He does not know. What is his home? He has no true answer. Maybe he'll never have a home. Maybe he will have to keep walking forever. The thought brings him sorrow. Not for himself. For her.

For he will never be home. Not completely. There will always be a piece of him. Somewhere. Outside. He doesn't know where.

birth

Antalaha

He was still a young child, sitting on a bed, bamboo walls filtering the light, a sunbeam, it was warm, it warmed his clothes, already cotton-soft, he felt good. A man entered the room, he looked at him with amazement, he knew him but was different from him, that was amazing, another person could be someone different from him, the man stretched his arms out to him, that was amazing, he felt good where he was, he had no need to be anywhere else, but something inside urged him towards the man, he went into his arms, it was his father, and his father brought him outside . . .

His earliest memory dates back to that scene, the amazement of being there, and the blank void before that moment, that was truly when he saw himself given to the light of day, by realizing that he was another, different from the place, different from the man stretching his arms out to him, he remembers the house, he remembers the bamboo walls, the wickerwork door that needed just a push to hit you with the glare of outside, breeze and birds, snaps and voices, the song of the pestle dropping on mortar, women laughing and children shrieking, dogs barking and other sounds in chorus, a very big world that demanded he leave his small warm place, he felt good where he was, just a wisp, just breathing.

Later, he saw one of his childhood photos, he was outside in the yard, a young child, barely walking, wide astonished eyes, reaching out his hand, he guesses it was towards his father who was taking the picture. That was in Antalaha, at the time still a village, between forest and vanilla crops. He remembers that moment very well: What was he doing there? Was somewhere else possible, even though in his cocoon of flesh he was unchanging? The outside, it was chaos.

And here is his father reaching his arms out to him, here is his father holding him. Time holds us, our fathers hold us, our stories hold us, but only our mothers truly carry us, carry the whole of us.

The Photograph

There's a studio portrait that shows all five of them. His two sisters, Vola, Nannie, his older brother Pat, and him a newborn, in his mother's arms, asleep. His mother posing not with a smile, but with statuesque poise and unadorned beauty. She wore her hair in a chignon worthy of royalty, with white gloves set off by her grey tailored skirt. The framed photograph hung on the living-room wall. His mother looked like the women in magazines, he realized that she was different from others, and she seemed Karana too, he looked at his eldest brother, he had straight hair, lighter skin, and didn't take after anyone, almost like a little Vazaha . . .

So he asked his mother: 'Mama, are you Karana too, like Papa?' She said no. 'Your father is a Karana métis, I am French, I'm a Malagasy métis.' And he asked: 'A French métis?' 'No,' his mother replied, 'a Malagasy métis.' He didn't understand the distinction, much less the term métis. His mother showed him the photograph of his grandfather, Paul Joseph. It depicted an old white man, in a suit and shoes, thickset, moustached, hair slicked and styled, bushy eyebrows, hands on hips, a broad stance, a wide and frightening smile—a Vazaha. He'd seen his grandfather before, of course, but he was never able to match him to his portraits. It was like he transformed into a white man when his picture was taken. He wasn't exactly sure whether the camera was magic or his grandfather was a magician. Vazaha in pictures and Dadilahy in real life. His mother was proud of her métis heritage: 'Look how beautiful we are, that's because we're a mix of many things, we're métis.'

'You're Breton on my father's side, so you are French, because Bretons are a French ethnic group, Antakarana on my mother's side, and so Sakalava, because Antakaranas are the Northern Sakalavas, you're Karana on your father's father's side, Tsimihety on your father's mother's side, you're Betsimisaraka on my mother's mother's side. And we've taken all the beauty from every one of these roots. In one house, we are the whole island. You're even a little bit Merina, because the Tsimihetys and Merinas are kin, and because you were born here in Antananarivo, the first of my children born here.'

Before he was born, his parents lived in Fénérive Est. His father found work at the University of Antananarivo and the whole family moved with him. A year later, Hira was born.

He liked it when his mother spoke Antakarana to him. He always thought his mother was singing. He'd answer in Merina. He would shift between different vernaculars and didn't always understand when, outside the house, someone would correct him on the way he spoke. He would quarrel with his friends over a word, over his accent. He'd go home to his mother and tell her about their quarrels. His mother would smile and tell him not to listen to all the people who tried to correct him. We're right, she told him, not them. We are rich in all our dialects, we are free to speak however we want, and we will speak however we wish. It was just that Hira had a speech impediment, he couldn't pronounce certain sounds, he mixed up *d* and *l*, *tr* and *dr*, he had a lisp, he was bada lela, slow-tongued, lazy-tongued. His mother always told him to place his tongue below his teeth, along the gumline. She put a coin on the tip of his tongue and he would have to speak without flipping it over.

His mother was the one who taught him to read and write. He wasn't going to school yet but already wanted to read. He wrote with both hands and it delighted his mother. He wanted to write quickly, as fast as his thoughts, but his hands wouldn't keep up. So he would skip consonants and only write down parts of a word. He long had trouble holding a pen correctly, like his schoolteacher would ask him to, it was hard for him to hold scissors—hellish. He didn't fare any better with knives. Nor buttons. Nor screwdrivers—he would always turn them the wrong way. His mother would patiently help him practise the motions.

He adored his mother, he loved being near her, but he didn't give himself permission to touch her. One touch from her made him tremble. Even her dress brushing up against him, it would completely debilitate him. And then he would dig in his heels and reject her affections. His mother teased him and laughed. That made him even more furious. He was constantly telling her that he was a big kid, he didn't need that baby stuff! And then he got back at her one day, in the city, he nicked a handful of buttons from the seamstress, his mother had refused to let go of his hand the entire time at the market . . .

The Children in the Bottle Gourds

He liked to run first thing in the morning. He liked the scent of Dadabe's coffee. Different from his father's. More roasty. Less sugary. He ran to buy bread, to be the first to arrive at the shop and wait for the deliveryman to show up with all the bread, still warm. He even got to pick out the bread he wanted from the delivery truck. He had to get three of them. Two for the house, one for Dadabe, their neighbour. Dadabe wasn't his grandfather, but near enough. He still called him Dadabe, and Dadabe answered him like he would a grandson. He rushed back pell-mell. He couldn't let the bread go cold. He had to go down the whole row of houses. Theirs was at the far end. He ran past

Anja's house. He took care not to stumble. He'd memorized all the gaps in the pavement. Sometimes, to go faster, if he saw that the garbage collectors had come by, he'd hop into the little canal that ran along the pavement and take off like a flash. He called it the 'canal track', he sped along, went past their house, burst into grandfather's first, put the bread on the table, then flew out the back door. From grandfather's yard, he slipped through a hole in the rush thatching to get to his house, he got home by breaking in! Then he got the hot-chocolate bowls ready. His father was already up. Heating the water and getting out the cartons of Nestlé. He loved when he brushed by his father and his father ran his hand through his hair. His father tugged on his mane of coils, the most Afro-like out of all the kids. Once the bowls were set on the table, he watched his father pour the Nestlé into each spoon, add the sugar, and the cocoa last of all. Then he poured the boiling water. That was when he could call everyone, and usually wake them up. He leapt upstairs and shouted: 'Bread's here! Time to eat!' In his enthusiasm, he sometimes pulled off his older brother's sheet, leaving him naked and furious. And he laughed. He laughed with such great joy . . .

His older sister, Vola, got him ready for school. He succumbed to the ritual with meticulous precision. His shirt was all ironed down, his shorts all buttoned up—those notorious buttons, they gave him so much trouble . . . His socks were all dry, his toes crammed all the way in. His sister washed his face and told him to make sure it was good and clean. Yep, all done! Time for hair! He hated that. Plastic combs could never stand up to his Afro. They'd break. Snap their teeth. His sister said he was so disco, then she pulled out a wooden comb that tore his scalp. Inevitably, his hair got tangled. His allergies made his scalp get all patchy. The patches would ooze overnight, and when he woke up, he always had itchy scabs. His sister forbade him from touching them. She scrubbed them with a wet cloth then rubbed in the coconut oil. He hated the smell of coconut oil. But most of all, he couldn't stand having the oil slick his hair straight down. He thought it made him look ridiculous. So, he ran his hands through his hair, mussing it up as best he could. Sometimes, secretly, he even went after the coconut oil with a fistful of dust or sand! He understood perfectly why the wild dogs rolled in the dust and then shook out their fur! All of it happened every morning. The ritual. Then they left for school.

One day, on the way home from school, after he'd already got to the top of the hill, he heard shouts and turned around, he saw a man on a bicycle. Back then, there weren't many bicycles in the housing development. The kids started to run behind the cyclist. They shouted. They clapped. The bicycle easily climbed the hill, it was unsettling. Some of the kids gave up the chase. Hira knew the man lived over by them. He raced towards the road—flat, towards home. The bike soon caught up with him. They arrived at almost the same time. He was fascinated by the spokes. Why couldn't his eyes see all of them? Why did it feel like you could only see one at a time? Jogging next to the bicycle, he took his right index finger and traced the spoke, following it around. Then, the accident. His finger caught in the spokes, the bicycle on the ground. The man got up quickly. Hira, he had a bloody finger and cried.

The man picked him up and carried him in his arms to Dadabe's house. He cried a lot. His nail had come off. Dadabe wiped away his tears and thanked the man as he left. Dadabe put on antiseptic and a bandage. He gave him a caramel, then solemnly and sincerely told him a strange tale about children who were placed in bottle gourds at the entrance of a zebu pen: *In the olden times of the ancestors, this is how we would ward off the fate of a headstrong child,* he told him, *you were born on a national holiday, Independence Day, seven years after Independence, seven of the sacred, seven of liberty, the seven cycles of life, we took you to the hospital, but you didn't want to be born there, in the white man's world, and headstrong child that you are, you brought your mother back home and decided that's where you would come into the world, without any help from anyone, right as the national anthem was played, a blind woman scouring the placenta, you did not cry, you had your eyes wide open, you came into the world and your destiny was too strong. True, you were not born under the sign of Alakaosy, but that makes you even more dangerous, as if you had cunning enough to hide your true destiny! Before, children like you were left to the zebus' trampling, we would place the newborn at the entrance of the pen and let the zebus out—if the child survived, their fate was lifted and a great destiny was assured for them; if they died, then they could not harm anyone. Later, the ancestors abandoned this custom and decided to only cut one finger off of those children, or one knuckle. Starting in the time of the Prime Minister to the Ranavalonas, Rainilainiarivony, Prime Minister and husband of the three final queens . . . Today, we don't do anything to them any more, it's forbidden by law. But look, you've done it all on your own in cutting your finger, you are wisdom personified, wanting to assuage your destiny so as to not kill your family, I bless you, my child, I bless you.* Grandfather gave him even more caramels. Hira hadn't really understood what had happened that day, but for a long time, he was haunted by the image of babies in bottle gourds set at the entrance of zebu pens. He left Grandfather's house with a bandaged finger. He was afraid of his mother scolding him but she comforted him instead. All she did was give him a hug and put him to bed. He fell asleep almost instantly, the taste of caramel in his mouth, burning pain in his finger . . .

Today, the index finger on his right hand still bears the scars of that accident. His nail is ridged and almost translucent, it always seems like it's coming off, the same finger that burns when the writing turns fraught, when he won't go any further, when he's forced to catch his breath before confronting taboos and writing it all.

discover

Crucible of Possibilities

In the days that bring him back, Hira tries to be happy, express the simple joy of beholding this world. But people are dying a lot these days. Hira observes the sea. Hira listens to the rebel wind. How much earth has the ocean seen entombing man? A friend's sudden death, not long ago, death from alcohol overdose, well, almost a relief, his friend passed after years speaking out against dictators and shattered lives, years of stomaching his life, his country, his continent, with alcohol. Then, another death, from food poisoning, not quite a friend, but someone who mattered, a professor, an elder. True poisoning? The only one at the table to have suffered food poisoning. The family did not dispute the official version: a foodborne disease. A state funeral for the great poet. Were his assassins among those who paid their respects? Hira cannot keep doubt from coming to gnaw at the edge of his mind. Paranoia turns up uninvited to the banquet of exiles.

The wind does not stop. Nor does the news. From his country. A stream of senseless stories. Violence upon violence. Hira is only that crucible of possibilities, that slip-sag of improbabilities. He becomes that empty well where words melt down and release their essence. He lets himself be suffused and starts to write again, adds to the draft in his mouth. He whispers the words before he sets them down.

He wants beauty to rule his world.

In spite of it all.

Hira remembers another elder: 'Listen, brother, listen . . . Dictators win when you drink from the bottomless well of paranoia, when you see the government's hand everywhere, when you presume that every incident in your life stems from your oppressors, I am paranoid, yes, I know that, but I will not fully concede it, because sometimes I'm right, the dictatorship is everywhere, and that is what makes it a dictatorship, it is everywhere it cannot be, but we put it there ourselves, behind the loo door, over our shoulders, in the flesh of our fears, in our shadows before us, in the thoughts inside us. So I am paranoid, yes, but at the same time it's untrue, I am under dictatorship, and dictatorships are not just repressive, they are a disease injected into individuals, a disease with no diagnosis, no cure, save revolution or violence. But I am weak, I could never take up arms, and so, I remain, paranoid.'

Hira has this sense of being in the world not to unwind the thread of his own life but to untangle words from the snarl of rage and memory. By clipping them out. Under void of time. Under blade of meaning. In the light of timeless beauty.

Sometimes, under dried tears, too often, he stands, passive, falsely passive. He knows he has set a destiny in motion. All that's left is for him to be plucked, for the fruit to be devoured and take seed again.

Sitting on the balcony, Hira takes the rough treatment, he did not dress well for this cold wind. Suckered by the landscape, the waves, the horizon, the rising sun, the heat that's taking its time, his scant flannel shirt. He starts back inside, two steps backward, stops. He thinks about the woman who had chosen defenestration. In ashes, today. Near. So near. She's just been cremated. Maybe, she'll be scattered along rebel seas. He imagines a high sea and brutal waves. A little wind and her beloved's arm holding the urn, saying his farewells. Hira will probably do the same. Be scattered. Outside the island. Outside of continents. Outside of men.

Brutal news.

People are dying a lot these days.

Abruptly he turns away from the balcony back into his room, why in the world is he thinking about people's deaths while remembering his birth? He hates himself for it. His own birth! On Independence Day! At nine o'clock in the morning! As the national anthem played, he came out of his mother's womb! Head up and proud. Eyes open. A child born with open eyes, what do they see? Born without a cry, what silence do they carry? Outside, the news spread like swirling dust. He hadn't known it then but all the strange things he was ever going to do would be accepted. He was a miracle child, the child of all, a part of everyone, a shared piece, born under Independence.

He looks at himself in the mirror, *you were born under Independence, it has always felt natural to bind up your destiny with your country's.* He does not see himself in that mirror, he sees a body, a man passing through, he has always been afraid of not having enough time . . . not for living, but for penning the span of his sight, the arc from his childhood innocence to the horizon that stretches out of sight, out of sight and mind, out of sight and reason, a pursuit with failure preordained, a work unavoidably incompletable.

He feels a little desire for triviality, a small regret of nonchalance, which he buries deep down in an icy chill.

The Wall

Suddenly he remembers this. He was four, maybe five years old, must have been five, he was at school. He was playing with the other kids. The school was a long, one-storey building made from plain red bricks. The children were running along the building, as if competing in a sprint. And then at the end, going back the other way, until they dropped. Hira took off with them, all he had was his resolve, he wasn't powerful or fast enough to be up front. He was watching the dust kicked up by his friends' bare feet. That was all he could see. Just the dust. So he kept going. He forgot how out of breath he was. He was carried along by his amazement that those little feet could raise so much dust, and by seeing some of them collapse, and by the shouts and laughter ringing out. The last ten standing had to line up against the wall on the west side of the building, the wall in the beating sun, burning hot. And then, panting for air, mouths dry, stick their tongues onto the red bricks. The bricks would suck moisture out of their tongues. Their tongues stuck to the bricks. The kids could feel the rough surface of their tongues, how the wall would pull literally all the water out of their mouths. They could never rip suddenly away from the wall, they'd hurt their tongues, they had to peel them off little by little, one bit at a time. Their tongues would also tear if they stayed on for too long. The winner was the last to detach themselves from the wall, the one who could resist their thirst the longest, and resist that feeling of losing their tongue in the wall.

There were ten of them lined up against the wall.

The older boys didn't participate, they chanted the name of their chosen champion. Hira was always one of the ten, never the first or second to finish the race, but always the last one to peel off his tongue. That was how he won. With patience. He accepted the momentary loss of his tongue, all he'd have to do would be work up a generous amount of saliva and slowly moisten the wall, enough to take back his due.

He looked at his opponents, their faces contorted on the wall, he listened to the older boys behind them, goading, frenzied, laughing, he felt ridiculous, almost exploited, he didn't like that game, he thought it was for babies, he shouldn't be there. He was a 'big kid'. He didn't play those childish games. And yet there he was. And yet he always won. Always, systematically won.

He had a nebulous feeling there, of his very survival being in play: he must not lose his tongue. He was somewhere else. As if he had some inner impulse telling him to observe from a distance. He knew, as his tongue was stuck to that wall, that his experience, there, in that instant, was just a moment, meant to disappear, with only the story to revive it from the scraps, that's what he told himself as he peeled off his tongue, that he would speak again . . .

He has never forgotten that red wall, and the tongue-prints of children upon it, his own scattered among the rest.

Crossed Out

Someone's coming to get him. He hears the sound of the car. He does not move. He is an offering. He lets himself be carried along. He does not go out right away. He waits for them to knock at the door. He waits a few seconds. They knock. He waits a few seconds longer. Then he walks to the door. He opens the door. He smiles. He kisses his hosts on the cheeks. Two of them, two women. He follows them. There's a part of him still in the water, drowned. He smiles but he's actually far away. He talks, he answers the two young women, he says yes he slept well last night, yes things are good. He is lying, he is not good. He is not lying, he's alive.

They arrive at the hall for his reading. He is welcomed again. Congratulated already. He gets set up, the audience is already there, the lights go down. His light is the only one left, the spark of his story. He reads.

Words aloud are not of the mouth, they are the body of breath and meaning, the body of tension and caress, they sculp scansion and lead the body to movements that Hira would never have normally known. The belly contracts and, like a birth, welcomes the words that are no longer there, having already been spoken, sent out. The spoken words, they abide, and make the space echo with the void from whence they came. The words are as much gone as they remain. Aloud. Past percussive lips. Past modulating tongue. The speaking mouth takes the mould of the word to craft emotion. Emotion is the child left behind by words expelled. And emotion takes form in turn, a body to bear the other words that are flowing, flowing . . .

Hira is already far away. Hira is within the images that he knows are impossible to render as they are. No word, no sentence is able to replicate the images in our minds. The art resides in the approach. Getting as close as possible. A vain pursuit, a thousand times renewed. A vain pursuit. Hira gets tripped up on the crossed-out lines. Hira always gets tripped up in the same places. The scratched-out spots on the page that get stuck in the stutter. Hira would like to listen, to learn what the words have made of his body.

Hira is sometimes at the break, his breath often held, the words become music, the syllables notes. Hira is the composer who does not know his score. The song reveals itself to him. Hira sets about dissolving all will from his being. Hira makes himself crystal, susceptible to shattering at the slightest vibration. Hira makes himself feeling. Hira is nothing but a fragile coffer for a mighty song.

In bare feet, his skin is free, Hira knows he would go even further fully nude, but he is not yet ready for that.

Hira is afraid of his own song.

A voice can lead so far away. All the way to damnation.

It takes some time for him to return. He clings to the applause to moor himself alongside the here. The applause breaks up the place where he might have faded away. He has no voice left at that moment. He would like to collapse now, but his body does not obey, his body retakes control of the space, and his bare feet know the ground to walk upon. The rites of reception save him from madness, from what others would call madness, he goes out in vast solitude, returns, continues the reception with unflappable calm, he goes out, he needs love, he is of this world.

The Scent of Books

At his house, when he was very young, he would admire his father's bookshelves, mesmerized, at every chance he got. He looked up and saw only books. Books and books and even more books. He remembers he wasn't going to school yet. He was drawn in by the scent of the books. There were so many of them, so many scents and so many books, part moisture part dust, scents that dissipated and scents that remained, heavy in the throat, or the ones that made your voice scratchy and hoarse, made you cough, or the ones that alighted on the tip of your tongue and slipped into your saliva, or the ones that went straight to your head to sow confusion, or ecstasy, or the ones that mixed with your own scent, wrapping around you like a second skin, or the ones that hugged less tightly and invaded your clothes, they were usually aggressive, acidic, chemical, more like how other daily household products would smell.

Hira looked up. He wondered if the colours were tied to scents, if the scents were tied to where the books were placed. The bookshelves were too high for him. He climbed. He hung onto the edge and hoisted himself up to stand on the first shelf. Suddenly a huge shadow swooped down over him. He was so startled his heart nearly stopped. He was in his father's arms, it felt like falling, unable to tell up from down, his father's voice was a thundering that he'd never known before, he discerned neither its reason nor rhyme. He could feel he'd wet himself. A puddle formed at his feet. He was gripped with powerful rage, against himself, against his fear, against his father who'd torn him away, and in that instant he vowed to read all of those books. Every last one!

Later he heard the story of how he would cry when his two older sisters left for school. How he followed them with his little bookbag. Vola would bring him back home and he would cling to her. She'd have to break free if she wanted him to stay there. He imagines his mother took him in her arms, or the nurse did, or the housekeeper. Because of that, his mother decided to teach him to read. So he would calm down.

He's been told all of that, but he doesn't remember himself, he only knows that when he started school he already knew how to read. How surprised he was to see that the teacher was only showing them their letters, and the children were only haltingly reading *a, b, c, d, e, f* . . .

Soon he started lining up with the 'big kids'. And he always got brought back to the little kids' line. It made him so angry. Why did he have to draw stick figures, houses, cars? What did he have to do with babies? There were round tables, with ten of them around each one. There were 120 of them in that classroom! Two levels of preschool, early and regular. And that was his greatest wish: to escape from the land of babies!

He was always excited about going to school, almost feverishly so. Every morning his eyes were peeled for the slightest movement, to make sure his big sisters wouldn't leave without him. Vola was in charge of getting him washed up and combing his hair, as usual. He let her do it, without even flinching. She made his hot chocolate for breakfast, dressed him in his ironed shirt, and his socks, and his shoes. He was desperately attached to those socks. Even when it was 40 degrees in the shade. Vola scrubbed him. He felt no shame in being naked in front of her, but couldn't bear it with his mother. Sometimes she'd tease him and give his wiener a little tug. He didn't say a word. She had him pick out his shorts, he really liked the ones with green flowers. Like his cloth hat, with green flowers on it.

Every morning was a festive occasion: leaving the house with his bookbag on his back, racing down the hill towards school. It was a steep hill, a whole road. The housing development, which had been built on the side of a hill in the eastern outskirts of Antananarivo in the sixties, just after Independence, faced away from the city and looked out over the plains that stretched away in rice fields and swampland.

At the bottom of the hill they had to go through the village of Ampahateza, a village of poor folks whom the development regarded with contempt. There was a large house, traditionally built, nearly in ruins, with a veranda around it, three storeys tall, and a huge yard. Hira was never able to associate such a large, wonderful house with poverty, he didn't really understand what it meant. He just saw the kids in the yard there wearing torn clothes, their noses encrusted with snot, with no shoes on their feet, but he did the same thing too, a lot, going barefoot and running around outside wearing clothes torn from playing so hard, but he told himself that he would never let his boogers dry on his cheeks!

Maybe that's what poverty is.

Not being able to wipe your nose. Not having a handkerchief in your pocket. A clean one. That your mother had ironed. And embroidered. With your name along the top.

Ampahateza was a charcoal producer, the children who played in that yard were also blackened with coal, they delivered sacks of it to the homes in the development.

Yes, maybe that's what poverty is, he decided, being charcoal-dirty. He hated being dirty. Loathed it, actually. But being dirty didn't come from dust, or charcoal streaks—the thing he could not bear was the smell. The clinging charcoal smell. The burnt smell.

At the far end of the village, just before the priests' compound, across from the nuns' cenacle, was the school. That was his house of worship.

They had a textbook, *Je parle, je lis, j'écris*—Speak, Read, Write. That was something he could understand perfectly. He spoke, he read, he wrote. That was a given. For him, speaking, reading, and writing all meant the same thing.

When he read silently, it was an act of speaking, the words had a voice in his head. When he set words down in his notebook, he had this distinct feeling of storing his voice's treasure. His voice as treasure. When he spoke, it felt like the treasure was being wasted. So, the boy became a man of few words. There was a kind of joy he felt inside, keeping the words in his mouth and then suddenly giving them as a gift, precious gems, cut with tongue and lips, in black ink, scratched onto the page.

There was another book they used, *Irango and His Friends*— Irango the zebu, Irango the Wise. Hira loved the illustrations and stories in that book because he could see all of it on his way to school, as opposed to the other textbooks that featured the lands and rivers of France. All he'd have to do was take a quick detour, and there, in Ampahateza, in the heart of the village, there were one, or two, or even more zebus, tied to a stake or grazing in the grass. Just like in the book. And the girls who collected water from the river and walked back with the jugs on their head! The water would often slosh over the sides and splash their hair. As for Irango the Wise, his jug was overflowing not with water but with his friends' foolish mistakes, which would throw them in the path of Trimobe the ogre, or waylay them by a lake of undines, and the undines would take you to their strange world and never ever bring you back to your family! Hira would look at people and wonder if this man here could be an ogre, or that woman there could be an undine . . .

There was a large rock in the village of Ampahateza, they said it was a man who'd turned to stone, an undine's doing, the man had gone so far as to eat salt, which was fady for his undine wife. There it was: fady, forbidden. Such an intriguing word. And in Ampahateza, there were fadys everywhere. It felt like a mystery, you had to mind every-thing, your surroundings, the ground you were stepping on, the place where your gaze landed. A small pathway could prove dangerous, there might be a chameleon passing by, perhaps the ancestor of some unknown clan who'd adopted its appearance! And if you were more finely dressed than the chameleon, that beast could unfurl its mon-strous seven-headed tongue and gobble you right up!

Often there were tombs, between the houses in Ampahateza, they buried their dead right in the village. The paths would wind between houses and tombs. It was fady to point your finger at the tombs, fady to spit on the ground, fady to walk on anyone's shadow, fady to go around an old man or woman shuffling along with their walking stick, fady to eat pork near the swamps, apparently some folks even had a fady of garlic!

Hira was stunned by all of those fadys, yet the word was absent from *Irango and His Friends*. That was the first word he saw missing from his books, *fady* . . .

wander

Florence

Hira, now, was he positive that this city was Florence? How had he ended up here? Was he sure that his wandering had actually happened that night? Hira would very much like to reinvent himself from new stock, pick back up at a better present. Would that be lying? Or silence? Or unremembering? Or expunging? Violence besieges him, carnage of evils of old. It cannot be a bad thing to leave evil behind you. He is walking. Florence. Florence. Roots beyond the ground, dreams, dreams, hallucinations, with lights ad nauseam, scattered yellows, innumerable glaring pikes. And the asphalt 'twixt rain and his clouded mind. He'd left his hotel. He didn't know what he was doing there. He had to walk. Just walk. The moment was all there was, he did not exist. That moment of walking. That moment of light in a city he does not know. He is passing through a lot of cities right now that he does not know. A few days ago it was Algajola. Now Florence. Or what he believed was Florence!

People were looking at him. He saw it. Them looking at him. *It's my skin, black.* He immediately forgot it. Them looking at him. The city was dazzling. He wanted to cry. From so many beautiful things. But he also knew. That his tears had another source, another reason. He did not understand. He hadn't been beaten. He hadn't been tortured. He hadn't experienced what his father had. But he could not lie still. On his bed. In his hotel. The weight of his body awakening rifle butts that thud into his chest, his arms, his back, his groin. Every sudden movement made him cry out in pain. He didn't want to open his mouth, so it wouldn't let in the barrel of the gun. His heart beat to the point of breaking. He struggled to calm himself. He would rather completely forget why he was there. Block out the intolerable sensation of suffering, though bereft of blows. He still dwelled in the sensation of drowning. He was still anchored to the sensation of torture. The drowning he could understand, he'd lived through that, Algajola, Algajola! But the torture, no. That hadn't been him.

He walked down a street lined with monuments. He knew he should stop. The beauty before him. The history before him. But he kept going.

On the other side.

Gucci.

Hermès.

With the rest of the brands that give cities a shine.

Suddenly he came upon a plaza. Humongous. And the front of a church all in marble.

He panicked. Lost. None of this was real. It couldn't be real. How could he be here after enduring such abominations?

Rocks and stone. Exalted by the grooves cut in, the lines traced in, the faces set into them. Try as he might, he could not recall the reason that had brought him here. Nothing had existed before this night, before the moment when he'd walked.

He went back to his hotel. He was shocked that he was able to find the way. He saw again those same eyes turning towards him. *My skin, black.* But perhaps it's not that, his colour, his blackness. He went back up to his room. The hallway was infinite. Long. Red. Narrow. The walls. And floor. And ceiling. Only the doors trimmed in white.

He opened the door to his room. All erased.

Amnesia.

A few days earlier, She had said nothing when he told her about his drowning. It's night now, with the silence where every motion foretells a sound, the brush of a hand like the promise of a caress, the bead of water on a rock like a song dropped into the heart. He wants to be like fallen leaves aiming to unfurl a carpet of down and a landscape of faded soft, pastel of their caresses, delicacy of their love, but in reality he is nothing but some whisper set on fire, panicking beneath the crackling that consumes him. He wants her next to him. She. Always. Her voice right next to him.

It is dark. Distance is dead and they are by one another's side. He speaks. She says nothing. She knows he could go back to his world at any instant. He closes his eyes, bends his neck, he'd like her to set a kiss there, a gentle warmth. He breathes. A bird squawks. Double-time. Insistent.

To inhabit the night is to dress in shadows, the naked silence renders them innocent, just lie there and take it, everything comes at night, ecstasy and return to self, skin in the wind skimming past, over the feeling that begins anew the dunes of self. From skin to sky, shivers are no more than fault lines to steal away the other's presence. Loving is stealing from the other, and returning the spoils. Clothing is useless, only a prison.

Here they are, with nothing separating them. In that night. In that dark. In that silence. He tells her: *So take me, I've taken you.*

She knows nothing will ever be the same as before. He wants nothing else but to write.

Wandering is not losing yourself, just eradicating your borders and putting every expanse within reach. Wandering is not losing yourself when you know there is a person there. Somewhere. To come back to. And look back at. For reassurance.

She is there.

He has left.

Granada

Lethargy, the energy run off somewhere without desire, the path does not inspire steps, so You set down your luggage, if luggage there is, still, You set down your body anyplace, the eyes do not comprehend the view, the inhale jumbled up with breath, words are too heavy in the throat and plummet down to the stomach like lead. You do not move. You try to slow everything around you. You cannot. So You close your eyes. You are what must be slowed. You must sleep. You sleep.

You do not see the time pass. It's dark already. You've come out of a place that You've forgotten. You go out. You flee the smells that stir. You conceal the hunger that recollects life. You walk, with no direction. Losing yourself has no meaning for you since the space does not change. You have no shelter within you. You're just a moment of waking. An accident of coherence. Eager to return to oblivion. To stop working the thoughts that keep inventing worlds for you. You forbid the words to rise from your stomach. You stay in the thirst to sour the path of speech. The words do not come back up, they prepare the fall, a mattress of torpor . . .

You do not speak this country's tongue, that's fine by you. You do not have this country's complexion, that's fine by you. You are not this country's colour, that's simply perfect, You can abstain from all effort for sameness and socialization, You can stay in the wild, not give your glances to other people's glances, not give your mouth to other people's mouths, You are just walking and treading the path of your perdition.

You have no care for yourself, your appearance, nor for people, their opinions. You have erased all that was you. You have erased her.

And You leave.

Predator of the space, You see lights—stunning!—up on the hill, You head towards them, it's the Alhambra. You head towards the fortress but You don't know how to get there. The houses funnel you down their narrow streets and take you back down the hill, it's as if no path could lead you up. Two women clock you. They look like they're having fun. Eyes that sparkle in your direction. You go over to them. They tell you this is the third time you've walked past them. Where are you going? You say You're making your way to the Alhambra and cannot reach it. They laugh. You laugh. Look, another Moor trying to take back the Alhambra! They laugh. You laugh. Come take us instead! You take a seat beside them. They order you sangria! They ask where you've come from. My hotel, You say. They laugh. No! What country! You start to say the name of a country. They immediately stop you. They want to guess. You say no. It's not that country. You say that You come from war. This world is at war. Always. You've seen soldiers shooting people. And bodies on the ground. And limbs in the scattering of indifference. They laugh and say that's certainly some way to seduce women! Leave it to a Moor, they're the only ones who will always talk about war! You're kidding, You promise. You smile a smile about this wide. You say You come from Tibet, You're a mix of Indian and Tibetan, a Zen/Hindu métis, zen, zen, zen. See, my father left Lhasa in 1966 after the violence of the Cultural Revolution and went to Dharamshala with the Dalai Lama, he met my mother there, I was born a year later. For the briefest of instants, they believe you, but your smile soon sets them straight. You're lying! OK. I was born in Japan, of a G.I. father and a mother raped after the atom-bomb defeat. Then, they're not laughing any more. You feel such deep sadness . . .

You're ashamed of your stupid jokes, of not being able to get past this issue of where You come from, of not being able to make up some imaginary country where all would be well, with no talk of war, no talk of poverty and torture.

You're ashamed of not being able to just talk up the beaches on your island, your gorgeous countrysides and the lemurs that are just too cute, your country's name that carries dreams, Madagascar, You aren't able to explain that that's how people in Tokyo saw you, as a child of rape, your being métis, your eyes with a slight slant, light skin and frizzy hair.

Over there, people had been overly considerate towards you. You'd figured out why once You discovered the stories about those children of rape, how they represented the shame of defeat, how they became outcasts and turned to violence too, and how a baseball player had changed everything, the son of a child of rape, the next generation reconciling with history, You look like that baseball player, the hometown archipelago kid who'd won it all in that arrogant US of A . . .

You leave abruptly. The women say no, stay! You head for the Alhambra again, glass of sangria in hand, You hear their laughter behind you, they're coming up with you. You knock back your whole glass, the lemon rounds, the fruit inside, strawberries or peaches or raspberries or who knows what. You swallow a gentle slow burn. There's too much in your mouth, too much fruit, too many flavours. You walk fast, intending to shake them off, not wanting to lose them, the two laughing women. You know full well that You have no idea how to get to the Alhambra, that the laughter You hear behind you is the trail of what You do not know. They're laughing because they find you funny. They're laughing because they can't believe You don't know the way to the Alhambra! They're laughing because You're so foreign in all this, so foreign to the way things are. They're laughing because You're freeing them from everything that's so obvious. The Alhambra is right there, just go, but You can't get there. And they like that.

You're almost running. Their laughter intensifies. They run too. With their high heels and throats full of mirth. It's a cobblestone street.

You slow down instinctively, afraid they might fall as they're following you. The walls of the houses are astounding. They have little gargoyles with long necks that bellow steam or smoke. The night is completely dark now. You pass a few kids with beer bottles, having fun. Some loud voices, maybe very loud, but You're in your bubble and only the women's laughter can really pierce through. You get to a staircase of stone. You climb up for a second, then You stop.

The two women catch up to you. They tell you that You're a mean Moor for making them run around like that. You bring your glass to your mouth automatically but there's nothing left. That sets them off in hysterical laughter. Practically crying. You watch them laugh, with fondness. There's the Alhambra, across the way. On a different hill. You've got further away from it! City fortress lit in turquoise and gold. So much beauty. The sky is inky black. The hill is inky black. Only the Alhambra appears, floating between black and black, city shadow and sky dark, the stars and other cloud colours gone. You turn to look at the women. Sink into an abyss of fondness. They wipe their tears. Come on, they say, we'll take you to our fortress. You set your glass on a low wall. The Alhambra is reflected in it. Upside down. It's gorgeous. They tell you that you're a child now, it's time to go! You follow them. You think they're taking you to the Alhambra but You realize very quickly that they're whisking you off into a whole new affair.

You get further away from the Alhambra. You take more narrow and winding streets. You notice villa gates and house facades. Twirling arabesques in beauty. Traced against the void. Spirals and scratch-outs. Transits of touch. Transience of light. You follow the women. They talk but You don't understand. Except for the laughter. And You laugh. Over the empty space of your hope. You hang onto their laughs to spend a bit more time in a place that doesn't look like you. You have been too engulfed by your country. By its miserable filth and the scandals it's brought you, the unending uproar of indignation, and the strain of revolting that at any instant can push you to the brink of explosion. You desire somewhere else. You desire oblivion.

No wind lifting on your horizon, only the marvelling on knotted roots, frail, almost furrows, some simple scratches underground, anticipating the wound, en route to the rift.

You don't notice that You've stopped in the middle of the road, You see the two women waiting for you, they're still having fun, You don't move, time is stretching you, dangling you in the void.

You wait.

They come back towards you, You realize You got stuck smack dab in the middle of the cobblestones. You laugh and suddenly You're off, sweeping your rambling companions along on a grand chase. And once You've got a more-than-respectable lead, You stop to wait for them. They tell you that the Moor really is a child. They catch you and twine their arms through yours. They carry you, nearly. They hold you. You, already riven upon nameless shores, this is just what You were waiting for. Deep down. To be used. To give in. They carry you.

Is the Moor drinking? Let's get the Moor drunk. You always watched out for witches at night, as a child, You dreamed of being snatched up by those who inhabit the secret, unspoken hollows of the world. Witches where You come from are statuesque women, with hips and curves to twist the very horizon, with hair that creeps to the very edges of lands possible, they walk five centimetres above the ground. Is the Moor drinking? Guttural voice and a red eye. They cannot let you escape them. You cannot escape them. They'll bring you where they will. They'll take advantage of you at the hour when the unimaginable occurs. And You can't do a thing. It's like You're paralysed. You can't tell this story. No one would be able to believe you. You yourself can't believe you! Is the Moor drinking? These witches have nothing statuesque about them, but this isn't the right time yet. These women enjoy decadent liqueurs and exquisite poisons. Like Odysseus, You demur, because You'd like to embrace the pleasure and dispense with the danger. Doesn't the Moor want to drink? The Moor will drink. Their laughter covers your face. You see only the night, smiling at life.

They open the door of a house. You walk through a room plunged into darkness. Cats, brushing up against you, between your legs. You're back outside. You're in a courtyard thick with greenery, the dark, and the strange. Small statues of naked women wasted by wind, breasts abraded, lips scored, hair eroded, and a fountain that spews only ivy and wild roses, a flow of plants, roots taking hold in the tangle. Abundance is often like that, the wellspring is lost in its branches, curves that coil and twist together to conceal the source. Your shirt gets unbuttoned. A hand strokes the uncovered skin. Your fly unzipped. Your dick taken out, already gone hard on you. Your trousers taken off. You get caught in your shoes. You take them off quick. And You watch the two witches take your clothes, laugh at you, and race for the house. You think it's a game. They're no longer there and You're alone in the courtyard. Naked.

Cats come to rub up against you. They come out from everywhere. The walls of the house become covered in fog, and soon there's nothing but that square of garden, the rigid women extend up into the mist, the fountain extends upward and towers ever higher, now the ivy and wild roses spill over, as if from a goblet, revealing the nectar concealed within.

The creeping plants—the cats?—play around your ankles, tickling, they come off of the walls to seek your skin, they catch you up, You pull back the fog that lies on the ground, You slip underneath, a standard turn of events, this is the path that will lead You to your desires. The view spreads open before you, a world of white, You roll in the quilting.

You breathe.

Breathe breathe.

You close your eyes.

It's all going well, going wild, it's brittle, it's precious, the cats' padding paws bring you other mists, other silences, the heat of your breath liquefies some surrounding translucent white, You hold back your breathing—a good idea, too, You don't want to chase away these engulfing mists, your breath is sporadic, stingy, each breath held to the next.

It is past time to wonder where You are, this land is already mad and your senses porous enough to accept the possibilities, it's warm, it's nice. Whispering winds, sometimes what reaches you are songs. Will the Moor drink? The Moor will drink. You drink your fill and You untangle your thirst from the incessant hate, your thirst is not for hate, your thirst is not for rage, your thirst is not for death, your thirst is for beauty, nothing more good Lord, your good and righteous thirst, in the songs that reach you, for another world, in the songs that You know are talking of another that, that could have been, yes, that.

We will drink the mists to fill ourselves with eternal roses, we will lap up the wind's curves to learn travels and turns, we will leave our certainties and beliefs behind, we will leisurely reinvent the looper moths ourselves, being born or dying or reborn, we will drink from cracks upon our lips split open by lightning, the space of an impossible time barely ever glimpsed, we will be the channel for the passing ephemeral, and . . .

And no longer will it concern us to think of being. Being has no meaning in a world where the possible is everything, we will be everything, tessitura of wind and flame, both empty and devouring, we will not abide full and solid bodies for long, we will circle them, caress them, enter them, and finally devour them and return them to the ephemeral that we are, while rivers take the form of our devouring and our embrace.

Evermore.

Mirrors that will not shatter, for reflecting only memory.

You relax your muscles, let yourself go, your skin is still a wall and the roots of the wind climb up like veins from far away, naked silence, adorned with song, at the hour of rereading the crackle, You fade into white stupor. Gem of notes and dress of voice, veils and evanescence, as a refusal to retrace soporific steps. Yet You feel no preference for the naked state of oblivion, the unremembered so well clad in cowardice, tears stream down your cheeks, in abundance.

There's nothing else You remember any more.

accept

Frankfurt

Maybe there's a seed of nostalgia that remains so that hope may grow. Maybe the seed of nostalgia finds no more soil and rots away in despair. Hira is in Frankfurt. Along the Main. Hira pulls the curtain in his hotel room shut. Black. From refuge to refusal is not a long distance, a thought bursts in, he snuffs it out. Why make the trip to a new city only to ignore it?

He does not sleep. He does not write. He is emptied of land, emptied of tale. With a desire so vast that he cannot tie it down anywhere on himself. Desire. He himself is nowhere. Desire to run away from it all but not die. As if he regrets that Algajola did not take him.

He thinks of that other time when he'd brushed up against death. He's walking, in Besarety, a teenager, through the dense market-day crowd where the cars edge past. A truck parked on the pavement, a pousse-pousse on the other side offloading sacks of rice, and then the walkway gets even narrower, another truck driving through, now step aside and let it pass. Hira keeps going, not spaced out, but showing off. Then he sees the mass hurtling towards him, he gets stuck, he presses his body against the parked truck as best he can, it grazes him, he hears the crowd screaming, they think there's been an accident, the other truck slams on its brakes. Hira has barely enough space to move between the two trucks, he gets out, he continues on his way, people flock around him, touch him, he's not dead, he gets slapped, he gets clapped on the back, he gets cursed, he gets blessed, hands ruffling his hair, rubbing his back, pinching him, elbowing him, people walk along next to him, he says he's fine, he's in one piece, he sees that he must reassure them after causing such excitement. He hears nothing more. There is a white veil before his eyes. He keeps going. The veil is a wall. A hard wall. He's never seen something so white. He freezes, instinctively. Questioning the reality of the ground and what stands before him. In an instant, the veil is gone.

There is a man in front of him, talking to him. He doesn't hear him. He sees that it's the driver from the other truck calling him crazy. He can tell by how the man's face is moving. He sees it on all the faces around him, all now sneering masks. He's not scared. Everything has slowed. Even the rush of anger inside him. As if he could hold off anything. He says nothing. He sets off again. The path opens before him, masks parting, people like puppets he can control with a look, except the puppets jeer at him, the puppets will only move from the terror he inspires. To keep hold of power, you cannot reassure. You must alarm. You must provoke. You must upset. Do that and people will fear you. Hira can't stand the idea. Of becoming powerful by withholding reassurance.

He winds up the memory, lies down on the bed. In the dark. He doesn't know what he'll be reading. He'll see. He will open his book to a random page. He knows every line. He stays like that until the phone rings. He goes downstairs. There's a car waiting for him. He is greeted with a bouquet of flowers. Red flowers. The door in the black metal frame is red. He walks into the theatre. The seats are red. He thinks back to the Ako Cinema of his youth, the same red seats, velvet fabric, the height of luxury to him back then, a theatre reserved exclusively for the rich, exorbitant ticket prices, stewardesses like in aeroplanes, or in

Spirou, they sold ice cream, chocolates, and candy. If there was a good film playing, his father always went for it.

He is given a brief introduction. He reads. A page and a half. Then the lights go down. The actor's voice takes over from his. He discovers himself in another language. He can't see the audience in the dark, he only sees the actor. Every so often he is illuminated. By a subtle light. In the ebbing of the actor's voice. He's acting, he tells himself. Making a spectacle of himself through the simple act of putting himself on display. He gives this time over to strangeness. A time for other people to craft their own images of you. Nothing he can do. So he slips away.

He thinks back to his father. Eight years ago, for an entire night, the only thing he could do was dial his father's number. His kidnapped father. Disappeared father. His country beset by violence. The weapons ruled. On the phone, the officer's voice. Your father has been secured. And then hangs up. Hira calls back. Again the same unrelenting voice. Your father has been secured. Hira tries to keep the voice on the line and ask for other details, he doesn't want to beg, he tries to speak calmly. The answer is the same. Your father has been secured. *Tapitra.* Over and out.

He reaches his older sister. Who tells him. It happened on the road out to Amborovy. A barricade. The patriarch pulled from the car. They say he was tied up behind a Jeep. And dragged like a dog. To the airport. Then his whole body bound and loaded onto a plane to Antananarivo. Apparently, Papa had said no, shaken his head no to his Antemoro friends, fishermen, zebu ranchers, farmers, who'd come running as word spread, ready for a fight. The Antemoros lowered their machetes and slingshots, they were facing Ravalomanana's army and a general.

Hira recognizes his father so well in that defusing, that reassurance, that refusal of violence. His father knew that it would only end in massacre if he didn't put a stop to their attempt to save him. A spiral of violence against his beliefs, against the speech he'd delivered on the radio just minutes before being stopped at that barricade. The President of the Republic had fled abroad. The provincial governor had left the city, and the prefect, and the deputies. The standing army had turned to his father, the only authority—the moral authority—that could keep the people in check. His father asked the armed forces to remain in the barracks and allow Ravalomanana's army to enter. Without firing a shot. Without resisting. For Ravalomanana was indeed the new power.

Hira listened to his sister, in awe of her calm: *This is what he wants, Papa doesn't want blood to flow. That's what he said on the radio this morning, we Malagasys will not fight one another! I can't believe they arrested him, it's unfathomable. Papa doesn't hold a political position, he hasn't committed a crime, on the contrary, he facilitated things so that there wouldn't be a confrontation between the two armies! And they arrested him anyway! I don't know where they took him. They put him on the plane. Tied up. That's all I know.*

Hira returns to the audience. There is applause. He thinks there's going to be a discussion. No. People thank him politely as they leave the hall. The actor comes over and says how moving it was for him to read his work. Hira barely responds. He's not really sure how he should behave. Or how to reconcile the tortured man inside him with what is happening in this moment. The present is like a foreign land. He's discovering it all.

Hira has not always been confronted with horrors. As a child, he had always gravitated towards the details, door to dreams and possibilities. Like that one day, the morning dew: Which daughter of the water was it who'd been curled up in the curves of the leaf?

Was it Yantso?

Hira liked remembering that, when he was telling Anja, the neighbour girl he was in love with, about how you had to wait for the sun in order to see the daughter of the water rising up again in hazy mist and ephemeral form. And he lay his small body down, beckoning Anja next to him, his eyes fixed on the dew that would surely retake the shape of an undine. Anja joined him. In the dew, colours and images, trembling timidity of life, the hazy blur of beings who are not of this place, flutterings from the other side of this world.

In Hira's hands, the little things, he liked bottle caps and marbles, pebbles and twigs. Hira dreamed. A twig in the wind is a scratch from the papango bird, stuffed with dust and then turned hard as wood, a twig! His friends, the boys, thought he was nuts. So he preferred to play with the girls. The girls listened. Anja listened. Anja was his first true friend.

Other kids would always come looking for them, to play, or do something else, they would leave and say goodbye to the daughter of the water, to all the beings they'd seen flitting away from the uncertainty of the eye. And they would almost hear Yantso's song enticing them to stay a bit. Just a little longer . . .

One day, Hira had picked up the dew and set it against Anja's lips. She told him he was being mean. She didn't want to swallow the water's daughter. But he said no, it was to turn her, Anja, into a daughter of the water. Just like Yantso. Anja was afraid. She ran away. He stayed there, puzzling over why she'd refused to be transformed. And then he thought that she was probably right after all, no one ever saw the daughters of the water, and it wouldn't be any fun to be only a drop nestled in a leaf, sucked up by scrub spiders and other insects, to be only a sliver of mist, crushed underfoot as children played and raced by.

He jumped up and started after Anja. But she was already absorbed in something else, a girls' game, jackstones or hopscotch or some sort of other inanity. So he went back to the boys. They always needed one more for a team, stop thinking, just play. And in those moments, Hira threw himself into the game as if his whole day depended on it.

The Screaming Child's Cage

He goes out that night. By accident. In the piercing distance a sound of pounding, of metal being honed, and closer, the wind like crinkling leaves, scraping over construction tarps. The Main stretches on without a sound, drinking in the lights of the city. Lights that spill out from either bank, and in the middle, the shadows pouring in like a long sip. He passes couples, arm in arm or holding hands, catching flecks of their happiness from their laughter. The museums don't close here. He is dizzy from so much memory. He barely sets one foot in a museum before going back outside. He drunkenly wends through works and exhibits. What could he feel there, if not the same rage or terror that grips him every time he thinks about his country's haste to move on, a headlong rush that would never keep memory in mind, a craving for the future that leads only to wolfing down anything and everything on offer, indiscriminately, frantic consumption, and immunity for the powers that be?

He wasn't there but he can picture the days following his father's arrest, the soldiers who came back in a truck, mustering together by the family's big mango tree and then taking off like barbarians, breaking into the house to pillage and set fire. They saw the books and piled them up in front of the house, books and documents, archives, rare photographs, audio recordings, films, they added petrol, the brush of a lighter, flame. The fire licked the leaves of the mango tree, the smoke carried memory away. Hira wasn't surprised when he heard about it, it was just that he didn't know how to tell his father.

He sees suddenly that he's standing before a Francis Bacon painting. Seated, screaming naked man, hung in a false striped mirror. Mirror? A mere rectangle looming from the unseen? Man? Woman? Skin that is not skin now but strips that reveal the flesh, abraded flesh, the eye, the eyes spit out onto the face like wounds, the hands, bereft of hands, the arms. He cannot bear any more.

One day in May, one day when he was in love, in secondary school, he was on his way home with a girl, the girl, and two of her friends, they were going through the zoma, they saw a child snatching a purse and racing off somewhere, to someplace in that packed-tight crowd that only he knew. Someone tripped the child, he fell and soon was no more than flesh to stomp underfoot. Hira watched it all as if it were a movie. Come on, his girl called, she was already gone, moving with the crush. Hira rushed towards it, the centre of the universe, he wanted to drag her out of there, no, he screamed, no, his eyes seeing too much, becoming wounds for having seen too much, the three girls were in the crowd, he yanked his girl towards him, but his hands bereft of hands, his arms bereft of arms, the futility of a scream to get out, a crowd, a world black at heart, heels and feet kicking the child, the smell of blood despite the market smells, the smell of mangled flesh despite the tar smell, then from out of nowhere, a man with a tyre, and another with a petrol can. Hira stepped back, terrified, not by the display but by how his girl was drawn to it, and her friends, and everyone there, drawn to death, the death of a child they would set on fire. Hira took another step back, he'd forgotten how to walk, how to go forward, he saw all of the people moving past him, he smelled burning tyre so fast, he did not want to smell flesh.

The child is there, in Bacon's painting, screaming, in a green cage from which he'll never be able to escape. Hira wants to throw up. He leaves the museum. Backs away. And then outside, through the entrance pierced with circles of light, he runs, as if lost, crossing the boulevard amid angry honking, this is a road, he doesn't know what it's called in Germany, the *Schaumainkai*, he wants to get down to the Main, down to the reassuring smell of all rivers, all streams, all flowing water. But he doesn't know the city, he doesn't know the pedestrian paths in these cities that have been given up to cars. He walks. Most of the night. Clawing back the forgetting. He contemplates dying. And returning. He thinks of her. How could a person want to die and return?

The Aravis Massif

He did not post the letter.

For her.

A letter telling her that he was going to leave. He's not exactly sure. If it would be to die, or just to disappear.

He did not post the letter. He can't bear the thought of it, her reading the letter, it would destroy her, break her into a million pieces.

He's ended up on the side of this mountain road. On the Aravis Massif. The next stop on his book tour. After the glitz and glamour of Frankfurt, now he's come out of this dingy cottage to look for the post office. In his sandals. There's only one main road in this village but he did not find the post office.

He did not post the letter.

It's on the way out of town, someone had told him. And he'd gone out. Maybe he was supposed to go the other way up the street? He saw a little footpath between two houses, into the woods. He took it. Going towards, perhaps meanderings, eschewing destiny that designates ends, upon capricious wandering or head-spinning steps without steps, by rivers along empty space or around tunnels without an arch, guarding against the hours and what hope will owe, taking no route but erasure, peony and whitest soft, refusing. He took it. That scant little footpath. It led down. Narrowing. Down to the fragrance of the woods.

He hadn't planned on anything like that. Like making his way further into that pocket of shade where the leaves were like lace imprisoning light, tree trunks like an erection of raw colour. It was amazing, how the merry leaves shimmered between colours while the trunks stayed of a single skin. He told himself he could disappear, right here, right now, like in his letter, that's what he told himself. Yet, drawing him in were the lies of fantasy, the waltz of wills in the freedom ball, the rush of no-rules, the melding of chance and desire.

He followed the path down. Fairly well maintained. Very soon he heard the song of water, the coolness of a river, the brush of a few flying creatures, not yet the enamouring dragonflies but lithesome butterflies that he did not wave away, not yet the damselflies painting delicate arabesques but those indistinct and elusive little wings. He found the water, a sweet little brook that hadn't yet filled its summer bed. Flat stepping stones to ford, extending the path into a trail, he took off his sandals, flitted from stone to stone, now on the other side. Like a child. A happy child. He ripped off a piece of the letter and gave it to the water.

Chance has no part of our lives, save that to which we close our eyes.

He will not post the letter.

And it will not be by chance.

He removed his thoughts. Continued. Exploring this trail. Leading up now. A staircase, maintained more or less. The steps getting more worn as it climbed. From raindrops or footsteps? Erosion or wear? He began to breathe hard, he hadn't thought it would be such a climb. He stopped for a moment, looked at his sandals. He'd brought them along from home, leather and thongs, for sand. They were holding up. He pressed on. It wasn't such hard work, all he had to do was begin. Place his worries on the ground and slip away into the countryside. Think only of her, and rip a few more pieces off the letter. Breathe. Jump in again. The effort is the only thing that matters, feeling his legs carrying him even higher.

First dead tree. Which kept the dry wind. The lizard lapped up breaths extracted. Some life moved away. Of whatever creatures disturbed by his passing through.

Second dead tree, long ago, he read the unanswered letters of forgotten tree bark, pages written or gnawed away by some woodlouse, trying to find meaning in the alphabet collapsing and symbols decomposing. To grasp the meaning, before the bare is made of the branch and the indecipherable of the bark turned dust. That is where he was going to post his letter, he knew, scattered throughout the woods.

He made the pieces tiny, practically dust.

Furrow as a legacy, here is one of those birds, coming out of a nest of light that the sun has set at the tree's base. Wind as a caress of leaves to soothe distress. Had he glimpsed the cache of the gods among the singing twigs?

He pictures his father, a child walking through the Analalava forests to get to school. Did he stop sometimes to commune with the trees?

Ruins. Between vestige and rebirth, the bird is king. The wind's thousand leaves tell only a compendium of new beginnings. He scattered some more pieces of his letter.

The trail no more than a memory for a while now, Hira slipping in between trees and dead leaves. His sandals, their soles too smooth, barely carrying him. Then he stopped in his tracks. The ground in front of him had caved in. The mountain kept climbing on the other side. He had a choice, to climb down the slope and back up again, or continue along the edge into the depths of what was now no longer a small wood, into the forest. He sat on a felled linden tree. A gaze thrown into the void will surely cling fast to dreams. He saw himself again, a child playing in the cavernous holes of eroded earth. He thought about his mother. He won't risk it, no. The ground was clearly, actively crumbling. Below, birches upside down, roots unearthed, pines on pines on pines. Bare rocks. Another scent from the earth, of rich soil. A bird alighting, and suddenly taking off. Fine dust.

He pictured himself back there, at home, by the ocean, not because it's his homeland but because that's where he feels the most peaceful, where nothing can shake him. Blaze of memories opened upon embrace of tears, *song alone is what drips on the rock, shells collect the notes, score written on the wave, and we will read the pages of the shores, it will be the story of the ones that wash up on nameless beaches, and we, we will have read . . .*

He stayed there for a long while, he would have liked if She were there with him. For her to experience this moment with him. For them to be the only ones in the world. He thought back to the day he kissed her for the first time. Up there. In the pavilion lodge that looks out over the hills of Ankatso and Ambohipo. He'd offered her his hand, She'd put her hand in his. So natural. As if that was how it had always been. They climbed the hill. His heart fit to burst. He kept watching the path, full of stones and snares. So that She wouldn't slip. So that none of the weeds would get caught around her ankle. They got up to the lodge and kissed.

Suddenly Hira was ripping up his whole letter, leaving it to the wind and dust to carry off his last desires. He left that place quickly. He felt thirsty. He saw some bilberries. He ate some bilberries. He moved on.

It is hard for footsteps to survive the awareness of walking, they revert to imbalance if you think about them. Walking involves forgetting the fear of falling, entails the knowledge that the ground will always be there, that the fall, if fall there is, will not be on the magnitude of an abyss. To take away the landscape is to take away the balance. Feet placed where? The nest of light, then, at the base of the tree, from which egg will coherence be born? *There was a bird, deep blue, who'd pulled water out of the rift, maybe it was indeed the abyssal bird.*

Third dead tree, from bark to slivers, slivers to dust, compendium of time passing, woodlouse paper shreds, is it still possible to read from a dead tree, its bare body? To grasp the meaning, before the bare of the branch comes around, exhausted, reading from the unreadable.

Walk.

So it matched the egg, the sand hatched from rock. Levelled silence, wind shredded by leaves, every motion comes across, every sound cuts through. Walk out of the wind blowing through the gorge, swallow the echoes catching voices. Here and there, that, it lives. One step, Hira is past.

In scuffed-up ground, the sun fallen down, cemetery of skin when bark is the nursery of earth again. And Hira went away, rustling with the death of trees and souls unheard. And Hira moved away under cracking roots, shoring up his alarm. He refuses to know what trees sound like in death. He traversed the wind that caresses birdsong, he split open that wind in kidnapping sound, and then he was part of the pack that pillages by the echoes, cloaked in the tumult of years, as a power ploy.

Hira remembered this story, told long ago, such a long time ago that he thought he'd forgotten it, about the bird who never landed. When the ground caught the bird's talons, they were transformed into roots, and wings tried again to take to the sky but beat helplessly against the air. Then the bird had only its vision left, lost in the infinite azure blue. That bird had spied the sleep of the gods. Condemned to stay that way, rooted to the ground. Powerless wings that kept trying and trying, for all the time that millennia will last.

Hira clung fast to the wind when the earth rooted him into its breast. Hira wanted never to land.

He kept going deeper into the woods. His sandals lost their straps, one by one. He removed them. He went towards the light, in bare feet. The trees began to space out. He emerged onto a clearing and found himself standing before a mountain. With houses higher up. A resort lodge at the top. Although, he would have to cross that field, the grasses came up to his hips. He hesitated. There was no other choice, except to go back the way he came. He put his sandals back on, for fear of thorns, he started across. He hadn't even gone one metre before the creeping grasses caught his sandals. Couldn't keep going like that. He removed them again, his heart thumping, for fear of snakes this time. He made his way slowly, so as not to disturb. Parting the grass first before placing a foot. Very slowly. He left the coolness of the woods. The heat was brutal. He felt the vertigo for a moment. Don't fall here. He kept going and reached the edge of the field. Barbs. A barbed-wire fence. He could slip between the wires. Barbed wire for animals. For a moment he thought they were electrified. He spat on them to see, to make sure. No spark. Then a quick brush. No shock. And then he went through.

Gravel dirt road.

His feet hurt immediately. They'd grown accustomed to the spongy forest floor. He put his sandals back on, knotting what straps were left as best he could. He told himself he'd go up to the resort lodge. The lodge up at the top. The climb was practically easy. The lodge at the top gave him a goalpost, bolstered his courage. It didn't take him long to get there. He just had to follow the hiking trail.

He barrelled up to the summit to the tourists' bewilderment. He was aware of it. A strange stranger in sandals. White summer trousers, a lightweight shirt, also white. And his wild hair, his Afro. His face undoubtedly showing signs of thirst and fatigue. He felt extremely self-conscious. He said hello. Got no response. Had he actually spoken the hello? His throat was so dry. He saw a water fountain. He went to it and drank. He noticed a sign next to it. He could only read the altitude: 2,164 m. He felt cold all of a sudden. He noticed that everyone was dressed warmly. Not in winter clothes, but warmly. And especially that they were all wearing hiking shoes or boots. He realized the place was some kind of an inn. He only had enough money in his pocket for a stamp to put on his letter. Everyone at the tables had stopped moving, staring at him in disbelief. He didn't believe it either. Not that altitude, no. He didn't know where to put himself, whether to sit or stand. He didn't know what time it was either. Everyone was eating, so it had to be around noon, or one o' clock. He'd left at eight in the morning. He thought quickly. He needed that self-consciousness gone. Everyone still hadn't moved, their jaws dropped. Suddenly he felt too cold. He realized he couldn't stay there. He set off without thinking, back the way he'd come. Going down would be easy, right? He just had to tumble down the hill!

He went back down the mountain, he got back to where he'd been, through the barbed-wire fence, he went back across the field of grass, he just had to follow the furrow he'd made on his way up, he got back to the woods, to the forest. And was lost.

He didn't recognize anything. It felt like he was going up and coming down, taking the right trail and getting lost again and again. He wound up in front of a stone wall. He tried following that, convincing himself there'd be people at the end of it. He walked along the wall for a quarter of an hour, but then it stopped, at an insurmountable boulder! He felt trapped. Like prey fleeing from danger, which had no other choice but to reverse its course back towards the very thing that was hunting it.

Hira hiked, slipped, got back up, slipped, he took off his sandals for good, they weren't any use any more. He saw deer tracks, or what he reckoned to be, and he followed them. Feeling like prey, or fugitive. Not knowing where to go. Descending, again. Climbing, again. Pause. Breathe. Laugh. Talk, by himself. Piss. He felt thirsty again. There weren't any bilberries this time and he wouldn't risk touching the other 'fruit' he saw in the foliage. He thought he'd found the right path, he took it. But the woods grew deeper still. His feet hurt. That was the worst part, that was hell. He began to sense the danger in being there. This was no longer just a silly whim. He hadn't brought his phone. He thought about the people who'd be expecting him. He had a reading at 8 p.m. He saw more deer tracks. He was about to follow them next when he stopped to think. A deer avoids humans, they'll go deeper into the woods. So, don't follow those tracks! He didn't have much strength left. And soon it would be dark. He must not spend the night here. He saw a large rock lying on its side, he climbed on top, laid down, decided to close his eyes for a bit. He fell asleep right away.

He was awoken by a spider on his face. The spider had spun its web in his hair. That made him laugh. He thought back to the teacher he'd despised, the one who pulled his hair and mocked him and said hair like his was a perfect nest for lice, or grasshoppers, a spider's nest! He'd got some strength back. There wasn't much sun left in the woods. He had to get out of there. He sat up on the rock. He listened. Looking, within nature's songs, for the sounds of men. He sat, for a long time, without hearing anything. Then, in the distance, the sound of a plane. He felt the sound vibrate the rock on which he sat. Almost undetectable, but he'd detected it. Clearly. Then, far away, bells clanking. Equally tenuous, but steady. He figured it had to be that time when the farmer would bring his cows back in. He stood, he thanked the vibrations in the rock and the miracle of hearing. 'The landscape of sound will save you,' he murmured to himself, 'forget what you see, do not look for a road in a landscape that tricks you with its games of shadow and light.' He stopped often as his own noisy footsteps smothered everything else. Finally he reached a dirt road. Which direction should he go? Down! He didn't want to climb any more. No, no. After an hour, the dirt road became asphalt, he came out of the woods, and right at the treeline, a house. And in front of the house, a woman, an older lady, stunned to see him emerge.

'Excuse me, could you please give me a glass of water?'

'Of course.'

She went inside, returned with a pitcher, a glass. She let him drink before asking her question.

'Where on earth have you come from?'

'Le Grand-Bornand, I have to be back there before 6 p.m. . . . '

And he briefly explained, to her astonishment, how he'd left to post a letter, and then, not finding the post office, how he'd followed a trail between a couple of houses . . .

Then, she just plain laid into him. What a reckless thing to do. He was lucky to still be alive. The old woman yelled, and yelled, and yelled. He made no reply, not a single one. That was what he'd needed. For someone to lay into him.

'You can't go back on foot, it's a two-hour drive from here!'

She called inside for her son.

'Take him back.'

He collapsed exhausted into the seat. Sleep. Deep sleep.

The letter no longer weighed him down.

vigil

May 1972

Hira had made up with Anja and her friends—he hung off a eucalyptus branch and swung from it till it broke, then dragged it around raising a cloud of dust in his wake. The girls shouted with glee and paraded behind him. He kept running, turning back every so often to look at them through the screen of dust. They wielded branches of their own to smack him with.

He laughed.

They laughed.

He turned and faced the furiosa. They lashed him in a chorus of shrieking laughter. The eucalyptus leaves frayed on his body, such a distinctive scent, so close to quinine.

He laughed.

And broke off to re-join the boys, hurtled onto the football field and intercepted the ball in mid-air, he dribbled and passed, becoming a player for whichever team had the ball, just like that.

The pursuing girls stayed at the edge of the field. The boys had got used to his escapades. He could just as easily appear or vanish in the middle of a game, chasing a ball off the field, throwing it to his team, and not coming back. Wherever the ball had landed, something else had caught his attention, a butterfly, a shard of glass, girls calling, sudden curiosity, some other feeling, a sliver of light to bend or stretch, he didn't know how to leave his thoughts unpursued, he didn't know how to leave his curiosity unsatisfied.

He went back and forth like that, between calm and a flurry of action. He was introspective by nature but always got fired up whenever he played. The boys considered him girlish, but soon saw that there were some games where they simply couldn't compete, particularly slingshots, and play-fighting with their wooden swords, their home-made bows and lances. The boys also soon discovered his usefulness. Hira's body was very slender, very practical for slipping through a gate to snatch fruit from a garden, very adept at climbing trees and hanging onto the thinnest branches, his legs never shook as he moved from one tree to the next.

In fody hunting, Hira had no equal. Whenever he managed to persuade his friends, he'd tell them they couldn't use their slingshots though, because he hated it when they killed the birds, so he spread bird-lime on a tree branch and sprinkled a few grains of rice on top, the bird would get caught, and then Hira cautiously climbed up. He couldn't make the tree move too much, or it would shake the bird free. His friends didn't know how to do it. They always wiggled around too much after they got onto the branch, losing their patience and balance. Hira could be very light and he had a steady hand. He climbed back down with the bird, emotion swelling inside him, and only then did he tremble, holding the small creature in his hand, feeling its heart beating, hearing its cries of distress. He showed his friends the fody, he liked catching a fodilahy mena better, a male, a red one—the females tended more towards green, yellow, and grey—and then immediately let it go. He didn't like it when his friends tied a string around the bird's foot and kept it captive. The string was never long enough and the bird thrashed about miserably. Invariably, the instant Hira's friends were distracted by some other game, he cut the string. And then he yelled that the prisoner had broken free! The boys all raced to recapture the escaped prisoner, hopping numbly around for a bit before it flew away. Hira yelled even louder than the rest, but only to make the fugitive panic and take flight at last.

Hira could fit in with the girls or the boys as he liked, he wouldn't get teased by anyone. He spent a lot of time with Anja. Within her eyes. Within her scent. They lay in the grass, their shoulders touching. One time, they kissed. Just brushed their lips together. They were scared of doing what grownups did.

They'd been lying in the grass like that when they heard an uncommon sound. A gunshot. It came from the university hill. All the kids stopped playing. More shots, pop pop pop. Then voices, carried on the wind. *Tabataba!* They began racing towards the commotion. Thronging with other kids who were running the same way. Adults barred them all from going any further. They stayed right where they were, fixated on the growing rumble. Hira had never heard such chaos. The entire atmosphere felt charged. Nervous and tense. The faintest shout escaping the hills felt thick with danger. But it was a lovely day. Clear blue sky, the sun sponging out the shadowy nests of clouds. They saw students flying down the roads and pouring out of the trees around the university, in a panic that was spreading without a word.

Hira felt pressure on his arm, it was Vola taking him back home. He saw other big sisters there for his friends, other mothers, adults, pulling away, getting the whole lot to safety.

That is his memory of May 1972: students fleeing before gunshots, and he being herded back into his pen like a little zebu . . .

The country was leaving neocolonialism behind for good. City Hall burned, and May the 13th Square had risen from its ashes. And there, young people will die. There, a dream of freedom will spark. There, a revolution will erupt. There, a new country will be born. A Malagasy country. A free country. A rich country. A rightful dream by all means, for the island that endured sixty years of colonization. That sacrificed its children in 1947. That had to make do with a bowdlerized Independence. There had to be more to remember, surely, but at the time Hira had been just a child, a happy child. History was much too large a place for him to think of giving it a single glance. Besides, he didn't even know what history was. He was living, and that was all. Today, he almost blames that child for being just a child.

For there was a before 1972, and an after.

Bamako

1.10 A.M.

Hira does not know if he's been feeling any better since he scattered the pieces of that letter in the Aravis Massif. He finds it difficult to breathe the Bamako air. Pollution. Too much pollution. Having to draw so deep for so little air. Everything comes to him slowed. Sounds. Images. Everything is breaking down. This sound does not match these objects banging together. That speech is not born of that mouth. There is no more movement. He sees only frozen bits of motion. That is his state of being. Disconnected.

He closes his eyes for a moment to try and revive something, anything, even a shudder. He opens them again. Even his hands, at the ends of his arms, do not feel a part of him. It would be a miracle to make them move. So he tries to turn them over. They're moving . . .

It requires an immense amount of effort to pull himself out of this state, every time. He is forever on the brink of nausea. He is afraid to lie down on the bed. He stands there for a moment, then strides out of the room. He takes the lift, doesn't look at the prostitutes waiting in the lobby, he leaves the hotel, he walks through the night. There are still plenty of people out. He goes down an empty side street. He senses he's walking away from the river. He goes back the way he came. He sees people looking at him. *My skin, not black enough.* He keeps walking, ignoring the looks. Goes, irresistibly, towards the river. Some kind of muffled song, surpassing the noise of the city, *Djoliba, Djoliba, river of blood!*

He crosses a long boulevard with cars tearing past. Headlights yellow. Asphalt black. And the marshy stretch before the river. He sees a bridge. He goes to it. Martyrs Bridge! Which martyrs? Fallen to crown a future dictator? He steps off of the boulevard and walks out onto the marshy stretch. He sees a sandbed ringed with tall grasses. He lies down there and closes his eyes. The silence, hope. And the dark, plundering the shackles upon lives. He falls asleep.

2.27 A.M.

Soul's refuge, some unremembering, or rambling through thoughts without narrative or rule. Hira wakes up. Or perhaps he dreams. What does it matter when sleeping on a bed of sand? The river shimmers despite the night. The bridge seen only by its shadow. The stars are not drowning, unlike Hira's eyes. He is not surprised by what he sees. From the bridge, one by one, the martyrs are taking off. Hira watches them with no reaction. Never any black on the riverbanks, the water is a mirror shedding light. The martyrs fly like birds. Hira gets up from his sandbed, he catches the wind breathing gently on his cheek and he too takes flight, slowly, his back pelted by grains of sand pining for the weight of his body. He leans into the soft wind and joins his companions floating above the bridge. *So then, you were massacred here by the umpteenth dictator . . .*

Yes, say the martyrs of the bridge, now let's go!

Hira.

Light breeze and the heavy weight of him.

Hira.

Heavy not from his body, heavy from his rage.

Light breeze.

Hira departs one land and prepares to lower onto other soils that will know him only as an exile, a stranger.

. . . fly!

Song,

Hira is a song.

Tell me what colour the night is when it dies.

Hira sees his body way down below. He hears the screams of so many other men, women, lying among the stray bullets of Martyrs Bridge.

Let's go, the martyrs of the bridge say to him again.

Hira has stopped dipping towards the land, he has stopped turning back. He hears the cries wishing good luck, have a good trip, have a good revolution. The cries are scattered by the wind and whip up such strange birds as they: *Oh night, the birds that at low moon flee the tumult of men, I am of you.*

Despair, the ultimate form of clarity, Hira keeps his eyes open and steps into disgust.

The breeze is light, still, but he feels the earth's heat waning. The wind brings him a feather. It is white then red. This is not his blood. It is red then black. This is not his night. It is black then turns red again. Hey, let him yell, didn't we leave feathers there, in May the 13th Square! But he's just here, Martyrs Bridge, Bamako. Elsewhere, it's Kasbah Square, Tahrir Square, Lumumba Square, Um-Nyobe Square, squares for the displaced of this world!

May the 13th Square, long long before, before he flew here, long long before, before he was an adult, he'd plucked out one of his feathers and laid it on the ground! The army riffraff, hadn't they stabbed it down, into the cobblestones, so it wouldn't fly off? Another, a bird of dreams and utopias, next to him, had done the same, plucked out a feather from his skin, laid it on the ground. Then the riffraff again, stabbing the feather! Then the feather again stabbed down into the cobblestones! Ten just like that. Birds' feathers. Illusory wings. Then a hundred. Then a thousand. A field of feathers plunged into cobblestones, no hope that grew from the rage. The rage did not sow flights. The rage had no place in the field of the possible. White rage then red. That was not the blood of birds. Red rage then black. That was not a night of free birds. Hira does not forget, they were birds who marched against beasts of iron and metal. Sputtering death, and the plunged-in feathers were expunged.

3.03 A.M.

Wings beating next to him, he turns to look. One of the martyrs, long feathers stuck into his fingertips.

Martyr

Greetings!

Hira

Greetings!

Martyr

No! Don't ask me!

I do not know why all the ones we bring to power become a dictator!

The martyr changes course and makes for the absent sun (no moon, stars, or other stellar contraptions logically able to shed light on his appearance—and disappearance), Hira says nothing, he continues threading through the wind in his flight. He feels a prickling in his legs. He looks down towards the continent. He sees the ogre's child throwing fistfuls of sand up at the night, stretched out like a canvas. The sand clings to the weave of the night. Grains that are soon stars. But Hira's not interested in that, he blinks his eyes, everything fades. The ogre's child screams in bitter rage. Hira's not playing games. Hira has an exile to carry out . . .

69

Stay the course and do not concern yourself with the absent sun, nor the stars of winds. South. North. East. West. The stars don't count. You are a starless traveller. Also the moon does not count. You are a moonless traveller. Also the horizon does not count. You are a horizonless traveller. You go you go you go you go you go you go you go you go you go you go you go. To the winds. And you can laugh and split your sides in a thousand guffaws! Laugh, my friend! Do not stop!

The laughter carries him. It is a force that lifts him from the inside and kindles his impulses. Laughter carries him. Out of those fragments of deliberate dancing. Laughter or wild dance to stir his animal nature. And he swoons. He's lost control of everything. He gives up the laws to any takers. It doesn't concern him. And he swoons. He will no longer show himself to the world. He gives up his image and bearing to any takers for the freezing. Laughter shakes and shoves him around. Laughter breaks down meaning and breaks up motion. Outside of all representation. Outside of all consideration. Laughter leads him to his wish to be lost. Outside of his journey. Outside of his view. Outside of all he can know. Horrendous world in which nothing matters any more, for in truth, nothing matters if we consider that we are just the sum of nothingness and insignificance, that this life is just a grand farce where we stuff ourselves with story and conceit. Dust we are, dust we will become again. That is the one and only truth we have. So he laughs. Weak as he is. He laughs. Poor as he is. He laughs. At that country he's in. He laughs. At that race he's in. Human. He laughs. At that body he's in. He laughs. At the guts. At the burns. At the trembling. And he laughs. Dismantling. As though his chest were ripping itself out of his body. Heart laid there. On the ground. Back breaking and bending. Over his reality. Over his condition. He does not stop.

Laughter leads to death.

3.40 A.M.

Hira falls.

Very fast.

Towards the ground where his body sleeps.

By Martyrs Bridge.

The earth as if streaked with waves and reflecting only the depth. At night, the river is all shimmers. A dark mass he can distinguish only by the sky mirrored within it. At night, the river is made of wind. He cleaves within it. He is caught swiftly, he is spat back out towards the heavens. He finds himself surrounded by a thousand other star eaters. *Look,* one of them says, *we all came through there, but you must not descend, you must never descend, you must never land, there is nothing down below, nothing for us, truly there is nothing for us down below! Once you have left your bridge, your cliff, the void must be erased. Look only to the heavens, think only of what breaks the horizon: the infinite space.*

They fly in a flock of star eaters.

It does not matter if they come from Marrakesh or Lhasa. From Gaza or Ouarzazate. They come from Lomé, Kiffa, Tahoua, Angyul, Yazd, Akadyr, Benghazi, Homs, Kamsar, Naro, Moroni, Agadez, Batroun, Businga, Mbandaka, Shamakhi, Rawa, Hillah, Gujranwala, Jaffna, Ürümqi, Numrug, Jabalia, Tôlanaro. They come from nameless lands. They come from nameless cities. They come from a nameless neighbourhood, a nameless street, a nameless alley, a dead end. Dead end with no memory. Unnameable. They themselves no longer have a name. No name to define themselves. No name to identify themselves. No name to betray themselves. No name to be subject to an identity. No name to be subject to a family, an ethnicity, a nation. They have only one language, the language of split stars and horizon. They have only one song, the rhapsody of migrant tailwinds. They make for El Dorados lacking conquistadors or gold. They make for Edens lacking fruit or gods. They fly and do not land. Ignoring lands and moons. Ignoring powers and attractions. For a homeland of no territory.

They fly in a flock of star eaters.

Down below are wars and massacres. Famines and oppression. Men kill one another. Men tear one another apart. And Hira and his friends hear their crimes. They hear their anthems. Their words immersed in the clang of weapons and caress of golden plates. Their words jangling along with platinum and silver as they fall. Occasionally, resistance will topple tyrannies. And the shouts of joy shake them, make them doubt. Then, some of them cannot help but look down below. They see hands waving, beckoning them to come back. They see signs of elation and invitations to land at last. All at once they become heavy and fall like a stone. They become men again. Confined to the earth.

The void sometimes on shallow speech, Hira tells himself silence, silence of wisdom, silence of decency or tact, the void is the ultimate dream for a creature in the clouds . . .

And he thinks: *Do you remember the child who skewered his own stomach rather than continue to live under the admiral's dictatorship? Do you remember the old man crying at the bus stop? The crowd who accused him of faking it, and him hurling about how they believed spit far more than tears? Do you remember the man staring into your eyes for one moment, with a prayer, a certainty—that he will be lynched, a stripe of blood on his chest and his eye ruptured already. You were on the other side. As if. Sower of death. As if.*

Hira hears them, his ghosts showered with mist and covered with dew, their souls dripping the black water of forget. He hears them buried under the dust of cruelty and injustice. Death is his inheritance. He is of the earth. Under droplets of rot and decay. He closes his eyes. A tear drops from him and he falls with it. He is sadness too heavy to catch the wind any longer. He sees a feather floating in the sky. The feather is black then white. It is not his innocence. The feather is white then red. It is not his sun that is collapsing in blood. He collapses.

5.01 A.M.

He opens his eyes. Sky without stars, birds, martyrs. His back feels damp now, the sand is not as dry any more. The water must be rising under the riverbed. He gets back up. Knowing that the water's song has been strangled in the noise of the city. He goes back to his hotel. Death of the word in his mouth.

6.30 A.M.

He cannot fall back asleep. He watches dreams with the ruptured eye, every glow that bathes him feels a slaughter. Sometimes need there is, a need to lose the meaning. His warning. All that follows will have no meaning. As goes the world.

He has not opened the shutters again, he has not let the day back into his room, he pukes.

Once he has poured out a flood of words.

Recounted for the first time how the gun's barrel had raked through his father's mouth. The room is black with ink. Wooden table, metal chair, paper for crossing out. He speaks. He speaks. And suddenly he's going to puke. Puke up all this shit. He pushes back from the table, goes straight to the bathroom, kneels down, and pukes up all his suffering.

He's forgotten how to walk, he drags himself over to his bed. He does not have the strength to get into it. He lays his head on the edge. Another contortion twisting his stomach. He pukes. Drains his insides. He struggles to get up, rinses out his mouth. He strips down, takes a shower, no strength to hold himself upright. He slumps slowly down the wall, he sits, the water pours over him. He welcomes the water to drown his tears and his rage. He struggles for breath. Unable to utter a cry. And still this urge to puke, even when there's nothing left.

He sleeps not in this world, will submit not, he stops up his words, he seems to be hatching nonsense speech, an island down the drain, Earth Day birthday (he cackles at his moronic rhyme, doesn't want a dearth of earth, easy rhyme and breezy mime), the words self-immolate on the ashy lamp, the decor can't stop being exotic, the river is drop-dead gorgeous, the postcard can't stop going postal, gorgeous, puked-dead.

The poem returns to him, *so it matched the egg, the sand hatched from rock*. He was born of misery, his shell rotten in being laid. He reproaches himself for such a thought. He sheds tears for his mother. As though he'd insulted her. Another contortion. Not even time to get to the bathroom, he has only time to turn and puke at the foot of the bed. He drags himself to the bathroom, rinses himself again. Returns with a towel to wipe it all up.

To him, the world is an open book with its wounds on display. Slumber comes only to those primed for illusions. His dreams pull him farther from sleep.

A vast abyss is the night for those who do not sleep. Better to jump straight in to not think of their infinities. Hira dives straight to its heart to forget the rest. It is dark in the solitude of dead thoughts. Hira tries desperately to not seek the light. It's unnatural. To not seek any light. It's unnatural. To not think when you're not asleep. It's unnatural. To add more night to the night. To add more day to the day. But Hira adds more night to the night and dives down to the heart of darkness. Hira adds more day to the day and dives down to the heart of blindness. That is where thoughts are most exposed. No light that shines, on no distractions. Naked. Seeing scatters the thought. Seeing distracts from despair. Hira's night leads him back to its blank.

Hira does not sleep. He is already renewing the absence and empty space.

9.00 A.M.

He opens his eyes and sees that his bed is smack dab in the middle of the road. Downtown Bamako. Or Antananarivo. Or Port-au-Prince.

Or Lomé. Or Dakar. Downtown HERE. He stands up, on the nauseous side.

The nausea is the show of contrasts and all-consuming scenery. HERE devours him with its gaping maw of *nouveaux riches*: sweet rides over potholed roads and splashy logos on dilapidated walls. The nausea is the show of contrivances that ignore one another accordingly, and error triumphant, and injustice triumphant. The nausea is the show of powerlessness and capitulation, fascinated to offer up ourselves, unresisting and unheroic prey. Not a single shudder of the limbs being consumed. Not a single flinch of the body being swallowed. The possibilities that await us are in sight. Mud and carved flesh get along extremely well. And therein lies the nausea: in the peeling of flesh from the soul. For, truly, soulless are the poor. Let them die of their wasted flesh, let them die! For soulless are the weak, with no soul, no point, no godsends, no useful wombs to pay or pop out golden eggs.

He does not move. He readies the spurt of nausea. And another contortion.

Nausea.

But he should not. Yell. Scream. The man who screams will attract the very scandal he condemns. A scream, at times, turns away the eye. A scream, at times, distends the emptiness. He should not. Should not yell. Should not scream. He defies the tranquil skies—the easy rhyme again, eyes to the skies, how unwise, the disguise for the prize! He'd rather abuse the absurd, he's overexerted, with so much unheard, an abscess that will not cede or cease. A scream is an abscess in the throat, a wound putrescent from indifference, that kills its creator first . . .

HERE, smack dab in the middle of the road, nothing is hidden. Riches and poverty alike. And what's more, Madame Poverty is glorified! She is naked! She is sensual! She is human! She is humble! With a smile on her face! Not like Madame Rich, that stressed-out bitch! Afraid of losing everything! Madame Poverty isn't afraid of losing anything at all! She has the riches of her soul, your Madame Poverty does! And a soul cannot be lost!

HERE, nothing is hidden. There are pearls and obesity on display. Hollow flesh and bones for gnawing on display. And those sweet rides that they run over beggars. And those asses that get drunk off power and force and whores. The opulence drips under the sun of starvation.

He laughs. Sometimes he laughs and forgets how to stop. He puts himself back in bed. Sleep on it, my friend, it counsels well, and sometimes the nightmares can be overthrown.

11.00 A.M.

He cannot die. He does not die. Other people die. He does not die. Other people die. He does not die. Not HERE. He'd rather drop dead than die HERE! Other people die. He does not die.

He does not die of the bullet that punctures his throat. And the bullet strikes true. For the hole to be inlaid. His throat needs a hole to let the screams out, the screams that stink up the very heart of him. And it will hiss out spent verbal shit. He does not die. And the bullet strikes true. To spread the golden powder of power. It'll disembogue the pipes of his knotted organs. It'll do him some good, that fair game stray bullet.

Thank'ee kin'ly, he spews himself!

Shadows, stealing into his room. They are many, these shadows. They stand there, upright, unstuck from the wall, struggling not to stick to the floor, squirming to stay upright. He recognizes a few of them, shadows of his friends. He does not care. He does not care. About that one, for instance, approaching his bed, stumbling and tottering in its shivery naught. He fires off into its ear that it is nothing but a beating wing of shade on a fleck of flickering, fluttering on a breath and unable to wrest itself from the dust, a faded grey falling fast into heavy ash. He has no room for compassion.

He does not die. He does not know why. A forgotten breath of winds? It is terribly dry in these stretched-out sighs. He does not care about the shadow of another friend, yet another in this soon-stuffed room, who had thrown herself out of a window one New Year's Day, or nearly. They all say to him '*Ciao*, veloma, *basta*,' we'll see each other again—*inshallah* in skies beyond, where words will no longer be knives. Words will just be poems of life, words will just be the next part of the trek where we whisper: *Have you ever seen the dawn prowling through the orchard of night?*

He shrugs it all off, and back to earth again, back to earth. He does not die. Other people die! He cries. All these friends who have gone!

See, shadowless, shadowy, showing up where the relentless rant on, he drags, lags, ambling and damning, abutting the rubble of some redundant slum.

He does not care. He does not care.

Nothing is hidden, none of this world. Nothing can be hidden, none of this world. Cut off the Negro's head, slag upon this earth! Too many ethnicities! Blow up the Afghan's head, and may democracy reign! Obscurantism will never fly! Go and bomb Gaza, serves them right, right in their nasty terrorist faces! Back to earth. Back. The crisis will pass! Man will triumph! The market will prevail!

He has a sensation of growing, filling the room. He spreads his giant legs over the crossties and crosswise of this world.

Men keep busy. Weapons sellers sell weapon slayers to scrape the books. It's an art! Of arms to heart! Sellers of grapes or plates, or maids, or renegades, they drink acid juice and the cows wolf down powdered meat.

Creeping up his ankles to seize the peaks.

Land sellers spout diatribes about borders and build walls around their precious little shacks. Taking shots in the dark to use up the ammo and fence the barrage. Saving children from famine and raping the mamas. For the eyes, they're sized up by the whites, and for skin, it's shot out by the black. And songs arise to praise the nations. It's all in sight, but cheating brains paint a much better scene. This one is a fresco. Hold still! The colours are ready. Blood-red.

Well may the sun be the sun, it knows nothing of night.

12.00 P.M.

Someone knocks on his door. He struggles to the surface. They talk to him through the shutters, tell him that his appointment is here. He's delivering some photos to the father of his photographer friend, Sam. His room reeks of sick. He drags himself to the window to get a little air. The stench of city fuel smacks him in the face. Tainted petrol. Tailpipe smoke. He cannot breathe a thing. He drags himself into the bathroom, takes a cold shower—apparently it's sweltering outside, he is shivering. Fever. He turns the hot water on. It burns him. He gets dressed and goes out to meet his friend's father.

An old man in a boubou.

Kind and gentle.

Who ushers him into his car.

Hira wasn't planning on that. He thought he would just hand over the photos, chat for a moment, and then go back to his room. But he reacts on instinct as though he were back home. You don't contradict your elders. He is the one who came on behalf of this man's son. And this man is treating him as though he were his own son. Now, Hira is just a son.

Across the city.

He can't bear the heat. As if the air has kept all the pollution in the city burning. He still needs to puke, but since he hasn't eaten since yesterday, there's nothing more to come up, except for saliva, so much saliva, like acid, he's certainly not about to spit inside the car, not about to ask to stop so he can puke at the side of the road.

When nauseous, never swallow saliva, he swallows.

He does not know if the old man notices the state he's in. He thinks at one point that it can't be very hard to notice he's in pain, but he'd like to believe that he hides his suffering well. He sees nothing but black smoke coming from tailpipes.

The old man talks to him, about things he doesn't remember a second later. Some stuff about football and education. Willpower and success. The old man asks about him. He talks about himself, but more about Sam. He knows that fathers aren't liable to show when they're worried. He says that Sam is doing very well and that yes, you can live off photography work in France. The old man nods his head and murmurs warmly. Hira thinks it's probably a blessing, a prayer, something like that.

The old man pulls up to his house and makes the introductions, they welcome him in like their own son. Hira isn't quite sure how he ends up in a room for a shared meal. Millet. Lamb. It is Eid al-Kabir, a major holiday, celebrating the strength of Ibrahim's faith when God commanded him to sacrifice his son. People are eating with their fingers. He hesitates. They show him how to do it, how to make a ball, dip it in the sauce, and bring it to his mouth, without leaving a single crumb in his hand. But he's not concerned about that. He feels ashamed of puking all night long, ashamed of his hand, the hand that had wiped his mouth over and over again. Besides, his stomach's not going to accept anything. He makes an enormous effort and prays that his hosts won't mistake his attitude for disgust. He scarcely begins eating and everyone claps for him, conversations break out again, all the tension released. His hosts speak their own language. Two girls take it upon themselves to converse with him in French. He notices that the old man isn't there any more.

At the end of the meal, they bring him into the living room. The old man is there. Next to his wife. They have him sit on the couch. Hira talks again. About himself. Then about Sam. He realizes the woman is Sam's mother. She takes fewer detours in asking about her son. He reassures her too, saying that yes, her boy can live off photography work in France. He feels like he's talking in a fog. They serve him little cakes. Several kinds of cakes. Several times over. He's had enough. He can't stop himself, he burps. And their eyes light up. He is buoyed by a soft inward smile. He'd forgotten that here, a burp means thank you for having me. His relief triggers an internal collapse. Sam's mother comes to his rescue and tells him to lie down on the couch. He soon crashes into a nearly blackout sleep. There's metal clanging, children shouting, women calling to other women, sheep bleating, laughter. And life making itself heard.

5.00 P.M.

A gentle hand wakes him. It is Sam's mother. A small pinch in the corner of his eye. He sees the time on the living-room clock. He is flustered. Perhaps he has overstayed. But he feels much better than when he arrived. He notices that someone took off his shoes and pulled a small blanket over him. He is very flustered, even more so. And moved. Deeply moved. He hears that they're heading out for . . . He doesn't retain the name of the town, the village. He says goodbye to Sam's mother, who tells him he can return as often as he'd like; from now on, their house is his.

Everyone comes outside to say goodbye, give him a kiss, there are children, lots of children, boys, girls, and the two young women from before, practically adults, Sam's sisters?

He climbs back into the car with the old man. They leave the city. The air is infinitely cleaner. None of that black smog that hangs over Bamako like fog. He feels much better.

They drive for almost an hour. Hira can't help but nod off occasionally. The old man has a pleasant voice, very soothing. He talks at length about educating the youth. Hira finds out that he runs a football club. He can't bring himself to ask him again where they're going.

The sun slips away but a strange light remains. Hira has never seen that, a setting sun that does not glow red.

Now they come to a village. There is only one tree, all of the moon's light seems held there, as if caught within the lattice of branches, captive. The tree is opulent and milk-white in the moon. Beside it, there is a small house. A young woman is waiting by the door. She's the same age as the two girls from the other house. Hira thinks that it's another of the old man's daughters, but he sees his mistake at once when he notices a small child running towards them:

'Papa!'

The old man picks up the child in his arms and introduces his second wife. It's much less formal. They have some tea.

They don't talk very much. They don't stay very long. The old man hugs the child again and they leave.

They do not return to Bamako.

They drive for some thirty or forty more minutes, down a bumpy road. They pull up to a house where another old man is waiting for them. Hira is cognizant of his own Westernization, for he's shocked that this other old man is there waiting for them! How come he's there waiting for them? How did it all line up so well? No phone. Or any other way of communicating.

The two old men embrace each other. Sam's father introduces him as the one who lives far away, the one who is returning . . . Then they talk, Hira assumes in Bambara.

What else can he do with two old men? It's not up to him. He is only a son!

The two men stop talking and suddenly turn to look at him. Hira realizes they know. About his father. What his father has endured. What he himself has endured. He is completely thrown by it. They talk to him in their language. He says nothing. He thinks only that they have their reasons for talking to him in a language that he does not understand. Their words give him incredible strength. Their words are questions. Their words are answers. Their words are silences. Their words are a rush of meaning. Hira does not open his mouth once. They talk to him for a long time, never pausing. Their speech sure and their eyes intense.

Once they've finished, Hira has only to follow Sam's father again, and both of them get back in the car for the ride back to Bamako.

The old man drops him off in front of the hotel but Hira does not go back to his room, he walks away towards a street, any street.

In the case of blast, hold fast to distended nights and collect what is left of self from the cracks. Song of fragments wedged in the defences of forget. Stopover of whispers, the sighs. Exile of screams, the wanderings. Set the words down behind teeth and never abnegate anything again.

Night compacted in silence, Hira says nothing, he forsakes no secrets. Night soothes him. Night stretching out to rebuild what is possible. In the discreet of mollifying words. In the delicate of impalpable walls. Hira knows what is making him sick, it is being of this world. The depths have his world at their disposal, there is no measure of his land save perpetual vertigo. Only the night brings him to the surface of the void and returns the measure of his body.

A twisted tree. Roots unearthed. As though baring origins, the sins of showing split earth and immodest dust skin. He scolds his steps for the insistent followers' path. In a corner of his mind, the billowy murmurs of coral as internal music, swiped away from beneath the roaring waves. Edge of desire, dress of excess, he has his moment in this circus of human beings clasping one another with slice and blade. He leans back on the tree and tries to recover control of his breathing. The rough of the bark traces back over the intolerable twists of his spine. He puts in the effort to stand up straight. He wants to go through this life as an upstanding man. He closes his eyes for a moment to feel the tree, he fits his back to it, the upright tree, and then slowly unfastens himself and chooses to leave that place.

Crowding, of voices and wares, of noises and scrap heaps, a murky border between road and pavement, dust, petrol, horns, colours spilling from every side, bodies and cars, tool shops and stalls, night does not stop the day in this city.

Looking at the ground, he flees from faces, he sees feet, bare feet, shod feet, sandals, black feet, sometimes reddened by dust, he sees car tyres, worn smooth, patched up, sees potholes in the street, he sees vendors seated on the ground, veiled in unending colours, and braids, and children laughing as they go by, sees his feet, his own feet taking steps, his nice shoes, he doesn't look at which way he's going, he just has to step off the pavement, a lot, to let other people go by, to go around the street stands, he knows that he's not passing unnoticed, his skin, not black enough, it doesn't matter, nothing matters but walking.

Soon he turns off the busy street, he sees a wide road of packed dirt. In the middle of the city! He takes that road. A goat is grazing on something or other. From that dry dust ground! On that unlit street. Only the moon, only the moon. He takes that street. Then another one. Another. Seeing only goats, a few dogs, and some children. Why aren't they sleeping? He's such a bonehead. It's Eid al-Kabir! Celebration and festivities. There is no night. He reaches something that looks like the city limits: a canal, with waste water, and goats again, nearly a herd. In the water: plastic, rubbish, empty bottles, crop waste, something like hay, he's not quite sure. Beyond the canal, empty land, even more than the city.

The stench is there, like a city wall. He knows that by crossing that line, he'd be lost. He feels a passing desire of no return but the urge is not strong enough to take him. He turns back, for her. But he does not know if living is enough.

read

Orange Crates and a Metal Barrel

Hira will never forget the day his father came home with the crates of books. The crates that were normally used for oranges. There were dozens and dozens of them. They had come by 'special delivery' in a white 404 that had been packed to the brim. In the front was the driver and his father. In the back, they'd taken out the seats, piled up the crates, stuffed the trunk full. The car rode dangerously low.

Slowly, carefully, it came up the small dirt incline to their house. The big kids were pushing the car, both a game and a habit—a lot of cars stalled there and the kids were always around to lend a hand—Hira was too little, he wasn't allowed to push, but he shouted encouragingly. The 404 didn't really need the help, but it gave the kids a chance to touch the car, cars weren't that common in the development, especially not a 404. The car parked, in reverse, just in front of the canal that lay between the road and the residential lots. Hira had a dog who would guard that border. She'd bared her fangs and started to growl, but Hira told her to calm down: 'Those are books!'

That surprised the other boys, they were disappointed, they'd thought the crates held oranges, they almost ran off again until they began to spot issues of *Zembla*, *Tarzan*, *Blek le Roc*, and more. Then the excitement was real, everyone started to help bring the crates inside.

Hira ran towards his house, his mother was facing down his father.

'You said it would be a few books!'

'Yes, a few,' his father answered, abashed, shamefaced.

'I don't have room for them here,' his mother continued, 'and you don't have any bookshelves!'

'We can stack them up over there for now, against the wall, where the bookshelves are going to go.'

Hira learned about it later. The French had left the country en masse in the months following the fall of President Tsiranana. We were applauding the Revolution. Singing the praises of Malagasization. Celebrating the end of neocolonialism. The French were losing their charters, more of their businesses were being nationalized every day. Professors had been leaving the university in a rush, entrusting or abandoning their libraries to Hira's father. Hira's father taught history and sociology. He'd started out as a research administrator when he'd first arrived in the capital, managing the nascent university library, then had taken advantage of the opportunity to continue his own studies.

The big kids were unloading the crates like it was a game. The 404 set off on its next journey. It had taken them all morning. And before long, there were stacks of crates where the bookshelves would go, all the way up to the ceiling!

'Now what are you going to do?' Hira's mother asked his father.

'There's always the wardrobe upstairs . . . '

'The wardrobe is for clothes.'

'It'll just be temporary . . . ' (Twenty years later, the books were still in the wardrobe.)

The smell of the house changed right away. It was there from the moment you walked inside, a smell of ink and paper, and other things Hira couldn't identify, a smell of water, paradoxically, water impregnated with soil or shells, coral or other oceanstuffs. It was so strange.

And smells of worlds unknown to Hira. Smells of travel. Smells of far away. And smells of men. And smells of cigarettes. Smells of other houses. Other spices that his mother didn't use. And smells of other countries whose names he could not know. Smells that were not of here. And a different light, when the sun beat down on the covers, when the glinting reflections raced to the opposite wall. And the colours. Red, a lot. Blue. Just as much. Black. White of the pages. And the pictures and illustrations. The promise of adventures and other tales. Hira was awestruck by the thick books that he could barely pick up. Encyclopedias. He had trouble pronouncing that word, trouble getting it out of his mouth: *an'si clopodila*. His father had him repeat it over and over: *encyclopedia*. Encyclopedia . . . *Encyclo, en . . . not an . . . cy-clo-pe-di-a*-pedia? what's 'pedia'? And then Hira never stopped asking his father his questions.

The bookcase arrived within the week. His father organized the books. Hira didn't leave his side for a moment. He stayed there, to make sure they got organized correctly! He was only going by size, the same sizes should go together! That was the only thing he'd been able to work out, but it seemed like his father was putting the books in a different order, more peculiar, more mysterious. In the end, there was a tower of books in the middle of the house, and no room for the comic books! The bookcase was never the plan for them, anyway.

'Let's put them outside for now, in the big metal barrel.'

That was the barrel his mother filled with water for their bath. Hira loved bathing in it, with the sun beating down on him. He would crouch down on the bottom and look up at the sun glinting through the surface, its rays yellow and refracted crystalline in the water. His mother's shadow came, he'd have to stand up again for her to soap him up and work through his hair. Then she'd add more bucketfuls of water.

His father got a floorcloth to dry the bottom of the barrel, but it didn't do enough.

'Go get me something else,' he told him.

Hira brought him a sheet, the sheet from his bed. His father blinked at it for a moment.

'All right!'

Father's head disappeared into the barrel with the sheet. Hira remembers his mother getting inexplicably angry. The sheet was done for.

They filled the barrel nearly to the brim. Hira was worried: How would they get down to the books at the very bottom? And were the books going to stay in the sun? And when it was time for their baths, his or his big brother's, how was that going to work? They weren't about to go in the shower, were they, with their mother washing them like she did for their littlest brother Tom?

Hira had started seeing his father as a god, he had an answer for everything, showed him this book or that, saying he wasn't the right age for it yet, but the time would come. Or his father would stand up mid-explanation to fetch a book from the barrel, *well, it's down at the bottom! Patience, son, you will get your own bookcase . . .*

And the barrel stayed outside, covered with a sheet of corrugated iron, with three red bricks on top. Hira remembers how the covers of the books just underneath were burning hot, baking in the sun.

Over the next months, Hira heard some strange words: Malagasization, Independence, neocolonialism, imperialism. The term 'Malagasization' was the most surprising, there was no question that he was Malagasy, he'd always known that, so why would he have to get Malagasized again? It was very perplexing, he didn't understand those adults, they were very clearly not Vazaha, not French, why would they have to be made Malagasy when they already were? Also, they'd had to start saying Malagasy, they couldn't say 'Malgache' any more like they had in French, and instead of Madagascar it was Madagasikara. Hira was part of the generation born after Independence, he had no concept of what colonization had been, ten or twelve years before. He was happy that he didn't have to say 'la France' any more, but Lafirantsa instead, it was much easier to pronounce, Lafirantsa. His father told him a French proverb, that *they were paying them back in their own coin*. Hira hadn't got the connection between the coin and the way he was meant to pronounce Lafirantsa.

We sang all the time. In the street. In school. Patriotic songs. Old Malagasy songs. And new songs from a young student group, Mahaleo. One of them, Dama, he was a student of Hira's father, in sociology, he came to their house a lot, like the rest of the university students, actually. They read books, had debates, their debates would never end. We brought out our traditional instruments. We were allowed to be proud of playing the kabôsy now. Valihas could take pride of place, our round hollow harp, and sodinas, our flute made of wood or bone or bamboo, and accordions, and lokangas . . . We listened to Rakotozafy and his Valiha Malaza, we listened to Rakoto Frah, his magic flute and hira-gasy, we listened to Mama Sana and her metal valiha, the groove of her marovany, and her voice that burst out of the depths of time and bored straight into your brain. The radio changed too, we could speak Malagasy, we told the story of our country, from our elders, from our scholars, legends, kabarys, ohabolanas, tononkalos from Randza Zanamihoatra, brazen declamations and improvisations from Dox, wisdom and noble ideals from Rado, we listened to other songs that Hira had never heard before, songs from the south of the island with rapid-fire lyrics, stunning a cappella choruses, words that he didn't always understand. It made Hira feel wonderful. There was joy in the atmosphere. There was the pride of being Malagasy, of everyone being Malagasy, north to south, east to west, and right through the middle. And one day, on that radio, he heard his father's voice. His father had started a programme: *Feon'ny Tanora*, Voices of the Youth . . .

Hira didn't know what a lasting impression this voice, his father's voice, would have on his life.

Dooda and Modern Times

People, bent double with laughter, Hira didn't understand them, nearly rolling on the ground, while he wanted to cry. The music. The static from the film reel. The dust motes like stars floating through the band of light made by the film, the projection. The big screen where Charlie performed, his jerky movements, tightening bolts, bolts, and more bolts, on that infernal conveyor belt, swallowed by the machine, tightening bolts, bolts, and more bolts, even trying to tighten the buttons across that large woman's breast. Paralysed, Hira, in fear, he was, in horror. And his terror was only intensified by the rest of the room. All those people, laughing at that man for whom he felt so much love!

His father, in the populist fervour of the Revolution, and out of personal conviction, had transformed the old Ampahateza church into a rec room where he screened films every weekend, nominal ticket prices, a paltry entry fee. First his father would view the movies at home, turning the living-room wall into a screen, setting the whole house abuzz with some extraordinary and unexpected new world. His first exposure to movies. At home. Then in the rec room. It was Zorro and his horse Tornado. Tornado, black as night. Tornado, black as his rider's mask and cape. Tornado, black as the shadows from which the hero suddenly leaps out, delivering justice and punishing evildoers. Tornado stark against the setting sun, there in the shadow of the hills! The house was also where Hira had met Charlie Chaplin's character, his beating heart, living with *The Kid*, jumping, crying, sticking together, seeing himself in that child. He never laughed, oh no! He only felt the tenderness of it, the emotion. When his father showed the film in the rec room, then, Hira's thought was naturally that it would move people to tears, but they only laughed, howling and slapping their knees. He was overwhelmed by a terrifying, chilling feeling. He couldn't imagine how anyone could laugh at the misfortunes that befell that man. The room held only monsters. He became quite literally petrified. He shut his eyes but it didn't help, the film lived in other ways, the sound, the music, the words, people's reactions, their constant commentary, the laughter flying thick and fast. Oh! Ah! Hee! Hey! And the shaking floor, shaking and shaking from people stamping their feet—they only had benches for the first few rows, the rest of the audience was standing. Hira couldn't tolerate the packed dirt floor any more, laterite red, more and more dust filling the room as people got more and more riled up. Hira was suffocating. From the anger and dust. And then from the heat. Then the sweat. And the mixture of odours and breaths.

So, he went to the back of the room, by the wooden doors, despite everything he couldn't bring himself to leave, he experienced the film through the crowd, how their backs moved, backs that shook, backs that rocked, curled over, straightened out, unmoving backs, it was as if the entire audience had become a single back with a hundred heads, a thousand arms, a thousand legs, what a nightmarish vision. He shut his eyes, his chest swamped with rage.

Something extraordinary occurred during one of those screenings. The heavy doors swung open, and in the sudden light, his sisters, Vola and Nannie, yelling, loud, panicked: *Teraka i mama! Teraka i mama! Mama has given birth!* Hira saw his father, springing up from the long table in the middle of the room where he'd set up his projector and chair, hightailing it through the crowd, which parted as one to let him pass. His father ran. Hira followed him outside, blinded momentarily, in the intensity of the afternoon light. His father was already far off. He followed as fast as his little legs allowed. He saw him off in the distance, his two sisters closer, stopping for a moment to wait for him, going on ahead, waiting. Steep slope, short breath, and, in the heat of the sprint, he chided the baby for not waiting two days more! Two more days and they would have had the same birthday!

When he got to the house, there were crowds outside. He wasn't allowed to go in. The baby was crying. People offered their congratulations on his new sister. He was happy. Impulsively, he said: 'Now, there are seven of us brothers and sisters.' Someone corrected him: 'No, there are six of you.' Crossly, he listed off his brothers' and sisters' names: 'Vola, Nannie, Pat, Me, Pacia, Tom, and the new baby in there.' Someone told him: 'No, Vola is your aunt!' He didn't back down: 'No, Vola is my sister!' And they said again: 'No, Vola is your mother's sister!' When he and his siblings were allowed into the house, he was just as anxious to see his new sister, Dooda, as he was to ask his mother about it, but she was clearly very tired, happy but tired.

The baby had light skin like he did. He got a surprising amount of satisfaction from it. He looked at all his brothers and sisters, Vola was dark, Nannie even darker, Pat was the lightest of all, like a Vazaha. Hira, people thought he and his sister Pacia were twins, Tom was dark, like a Karana. It was funny that they were all the colours.

Hira doesn't remember how long it took for him to come to terms with what he'd learned: that his sister Vola was actually his aunt. His mother must have confirmed it for him. It wasn't a secret, but he'd never thought that she could actually be his aunt! Vola was only nine years older than him.

His parents, especially his father, loved telling the story of how Vola had chosen to live with them: At the end of their wedding ceremony, Vola, only five years old, had followed them and declared that she would be their first child, they had readily agreed. And so naturally, when they moved to Fénérive Est a few months later, they brought her along with. That was common in his mother's family, a child could choose whom to live with.

How peculiar it was for Hira when Dooda was born—he gained one sister just as he lost another, and the one he had lost turned into an aunt!

For the first time, he realized that he could be a big brother, too, he actually already was. Pacia was only two years younger than him, and Tom, three. Pacia and Tom, the sister and brother who had scarcely existed in his world . . . He started paying a little more attention to them. He discovered a rambunctious Tom, who never stopped running or moving, a shock of smooth black hair, beautiful black skin, nothing could stop his audacious Tom. He discovered a Pacia who was often daydreaming, soft and quiet and always humming, so sweet, so delicate, an incredible mass of frizzy hair that would easily take on the colour of dust, just like his hair, light skin that flushed just as easily as his skin, but that didn't change anything, her little doll face was so annoying! And people still always thought they were twins!

He kept coming in to look at Dooda, he held out his finger to her and she squeezed it, it made him laugh, made him so incredibly happy. Then he'd leave again, hurtling downstairs to go pester Tom. And Tom scarpered off, every single time! Once, Tom fell down the stairs tumbly-bumbly. His father rushed over to make sure he was all right, Tom was already outside, Hira chased after him to bring him back, but to tell the truth, he was so scared that his father would be angry, it could have been his fault that Tom had fallen, he wasn't sure, and anyway, he was the big brother, his little brother didn't have to fall down the stairs, so if Tom had fallen, it was obviously his fault!

Coming home from school, quick quick, he had to see Dooda. If he was playing outside, he always found some reason to come in. And see Dooda. His memory is of a baby who didn't cry very much. He watched her take to suckling with utter delight. Then he went back outside. Inside. Outside. Outside. Inside. Inside. Outside. That was Dooda, a breeze for him to dive into and then blow right back outside through the open door.

The Opium and the Rod

Aside from his sister's birth, Hira's primary memory of that period is the film screenings. He was captivated by the colours that rippled off the screen, as if everything was being filtered through red. The air, red.

The sky, threatening, fast eclipsed by the sun, red. Clothing, so greedy for colours, ultimately glorifying only red. Even the actors' very skin, the ones known as 'pale faces', their skin had nothing pale about it. No, to him, the Indians weren't the Red-Skins, not at all—the men who called themselves white were red, instead. Hira wanted to step into the landscapes of those movies, to touch the screen and see it all in real life, those countries, those lands, those people, all so different.

He had known from early on that he was on an island, that he'd have to get past the sea, but there was something else besides the sea, too, you couldn't just waltz your way into white country. He didn't exactly know why, why you couldn't just go. He suspected it was some terrible thing. The people in those movies had no respect for one another, they never came to an agreement, they often killed one another, many of them acted like they were the most important people in the world. Hira wondered if it was like that in their white-man's reality, as well. He could understand why the Zorros and John Waynes existed. But he was also enthralled by all of that red, the actors' names, Burt Lancaster, John Wayne—because everybody loved John Wayne, but there was something off-putting about that actor, he didn't know exactly what, John Wayne was always in the right, and if not him, then his gun. Hira definitely liked Django better, the man dragging the coffin, the man whose hands were crushed under the horses' hooves, the man who hardly ever spoke, and who in spite of it all was able to defeat the bad guys, but Hira wasn't quite sure if Django was actually a good guy himself . . . Yul Brynner was his favourite, the formidable Yul Brynner, the man who never smiled. He couldn't figure out how one man could portray so many different characters: the king of Siam with Deborah Kerr, an Egyptian opposite Charlton Heston, an almost savage Cossack in *Taras Bulba*, a striking father to the indomitable Tony Curtis, a bandit, a hero. Of the seven magnificent mercenaries, Hira saw only him. He almost cursed Moses for bringing down the ten plagues upon Egypt and killing the pharaoh's son. The great Yul, his anguish spattering the screen as he held his son in his arms, dead, Hira in the rec room screaming, begging him not to get into his chariot, *the sea will close up over you!* But the great pharaoh went anyway. *Adiós, Sabata,* he whispered, *adiossa* with his accent, and Moses plunged his staff of commandments into the sea, parting it, then closing it again . . .

Hira did have a sense at the time, a vague sense of what was playing out, of how the white man was always the embodiment of order, justice, and good. Yul belonged to the civilizations that had to be conquered absolutely: magnificent but savage, magnificent but bloodthirsty, magnificent but merciless, magnificent but conquered, ultimately conquered, Yul Brynner humiliated by Charlton Heston in *The Ten Commandments*, burned at the stake in *Taras Bulba*, strict to the absurd in *The King and I*, Deborah Kerr meant to provide a good and proper education for his son, and for the great king Yul, to boot! It infuriated Hira, why should they have to follow white people's laws and customs? He would have slapped that Deborah Kerr governess across the face!

One time, before they left for the rec room, he asked his father: *Why does Yul Brynner always lose, aren't there any movies where he wins?* 'The Magnificent Seven', his father said, *he wins in 'The Magnificent Seven'. No, I mean where he's the main character!* His father got that small smile on his face that irritated him so much . . .

'Here, take these reels,' he said.

L'Opium et le Bâton. The Opium and the Rod. Written in black marker on the lids.

He'd read *The Blue Lotus* a few days before, Tintin's adventures in China, he knew the word opium, but what was the rod about?

'What kind of movie is this, Papa?'

They were already outside, his father carrying the projector and accessories. He set one of the spools on his head and held it with both hands. His big brother had the other two or three, because they always scheduled two showings, two showings for two movies, one at 2 p.m. and the other at 4.30 or 5.00 (at the whim of the projector).

'You'll see. It's about Algeria.'

He knew what the Algerian football team's jerseys looked like—they never did any good in the Africa Cup of Nations—but besides that, he knew basically nothing about that country. Except, actually: the Algerians were really good at independence! But even though he understood the meaning of the word 'independence', he didn't really grasp the significance of it. White people were so far away, in their unreachable countries . . .

Seeing the poster gave him quite a shock: saturated with colour, yellow, a dirt path between some hills, rocky ones like where he lived, men at arms, blue mountains in the background, and a helicopter flying over all of it, an army truck, a strange-looking tank, it was different from the Panzers that were normally in war movies, and a man lying in wait, ready to let loose with his machine gun. There was already a crowd in front of the church doors. People didn't know how to line up, they always waited in a big clump right around the doors. His father laughed, his strong voice rang out.

'And how are you going to watch the movie if we can't get by to set up the projector?'

The crowd parted. Hira followed his father and brother into the breach, and it closed up right behind them. Some folks tried to sneak up a little closer in their wake, other folks got upset and pushed them back indignantly. Hands were being thrown already. Hira couldn't take another step, he was caught in the middle of the crowd, with his spool on his head. His father and big brother had already got inside and closed the doors behind them. And there he was, panicking as if they'd abandoned him, not a sound would come out of his mouth. It was like everything froze except for the crowd rolling like a wave, now only one foot was touching the ground, he couldn't grab onto anything without dropping the spool. The door opened again. The wave poured towards the open entrance. His father was shouting.

'No! No! Nobody comes in yet! Where is my son?'

'I'm right here,' Hira yelled.

They let him through, or, more accurately, they extracted him from within the crush of bodies. He has a memory of moving forward without touching the ground, through a wall of sides and chests and arms, his hands still gripping the spool firmly on his head.

He went to his father the moment he'd been delivered from the crowd.

'Papa, what is this movie that's got everybody so wound up?'

His father was rushing to set up the projector, he still did not answer and instead asked both him and his brother to make sure there wasn't anything on the screen, make sure the seams were still holding. It was a big screen, made from three swaths of white fabric. Behind it was a ladder, which his father sometimes climbed to mend a tear, with a thick needle and thick white thread.

'All good.'

'Make sure it's clean.'

'All good.'

At times, or actually quite often, there would be a supreme display of excrement on the screen from the true masters of that place: the bats, hidden away up high, in the gap at the top of the wall. How did they hang up there, what was there for them to grab hold of, and why did they stay so quiet for the whole film, why weren't they scared of the music and the booming sound effects?

This time it was a gecko who had settled in a corner of the screen. The same one as last time, they hadn't noticed it at first, it was silhouetted in the light of the film, they watched it for the entire screening: motionless, then suddenly darting after shadowy dots and flashing images that it took for prey.

'The gecko's back, Papa.'

They tried to shoo it away but it was a waste of time, the creature was too high up and could easily avoid the pathetic swipes of their broom, and they couldn't shake the screen too much either, and everyone outside had been waiting a long time. The church doors were flexing with each impatient shove.

'OK, go ahead!'

That was always how his father would get the show started. OK, go ahead! That was their signal to open the doors just a little, to let people in one by one and have them show their ticket (they didn't have a ticket stand inside, people had to buy it in advance, or it only happened when his father had a few of his friends come with him, the same ones every time, but today they had to make do by themselves). Hira and his big brother were assigned the duty of holding the doors half-open, his father checked tickets. The whole process took a good ten minutes. Every so often, his father would allow a couple of people to squeeze in without a ticket. 'You, yes. No, not you, you didn't pay last time either, you, yes, you, no . . .'

Up until he decided that the room was full, or that ready or not, it was time for the show to start. Then they turned away any latecomers and closed the church doors, making sure to wedge them tightly shut because there would always be some who'd attempt to sneak in during the screening. Then the show could begin. The first several minutes were always suffocating for Hira, all the dust kicked up, the mingling odours, everybody settling into their places, kids slipping in between grownups, boys sidling closer to girls . . .

Hira and his brother had to stand watch at the doors the whole time, because people would frequently step out for any number of reasons, to go pee, get some air—the heat was awful inside the rec room—or smoke, and when they came back, sure enough, they'd have three or four ticketless hangers-on, taking advantage of the opportunity to slink inside. And Hira couldn't ever say *no, that's not the same person who went out to pee*, how could he contradict an adult or anyone older than him? His brother had found his own way to deal with it: he watched the movie.

Hira was expecting battle scenes and non-stop action.

. . . No.

It was just one man, leaving the city and travelling to a village, there were barricades, French soldiers everywhere. It dragged on and on, Hira was hot, his neck hurt from craning his head up towards the screen, he stared at the audience's backs, he went outside for a minute, came back in, went outside, came back in, there still wasn't anything happening and he couldn't even understand the dialogue, it was in Arabic, he was too short to see the subtitles, or if he saw one, he didn't have enough time to read it, he wasn't that good at French yet. So, as usual, he tried to follow along with the audience's reactions and commentary, but that day, it felt like they'd been pulled taut over silence, unmoving, almost unable to speak. Even the ones who would normally interpret (since many in the audience didn't know French) said very little. There was only one thing Hira could pick up from the crowd: 'They did that to us, too, in '47!' He didn't know what that meant, but there was a disconcerting quaver in the man's voice.

There were other kids there like him, they didn't understand it either, and decided to go outside to play. Cowboys and Indians, of course. He was always an Indian. A Cheyenne. He liked that word a lot: Cheyenne. Then they heard an uproar coming from inside the rec room. All of them raced back inside (the doors weren't shut tight any more, with the doorman playing outside!). There was a fight: in the movie, a river within a forest, an Algerian versus a Frenchman, then a larger group of French soldiers, armed. The Algerian lost. Hira figured that the action was finally getting started, so he decided to pay attention and follow the storyline, but he still didn't get any of it, except for the scenes where the French soldiers were speaking French. The rest of the time, it was back to Arabic, back to endless dialogue between the prisoner and one of the soldiers who was trying to be nice to him.

His friends pulled him back outside. They started playing again. One, hiding behind a tree, felled an Indian. One, popping up from an embankment, slaughtered a cowboy. That's how the game worked. Cowboys attack from afar, Indians kill up close.

After a while, they heard that uproar from the rec room again. This time, there was cursing. Hira went inside, his friends followed. One of the adults said, 'See him? That's the traitor!', pointing at a character in the film whose face filled the whole screen. Hira didn't understand the anger he saw on all of the adults' faces. There was a traitor in all the movies, it never got the audience riled up like that! Then, something awful was shown on the screen: prisoners sent down to the very bottom of a cellar, it looked like a rathole, a waterlogged hold, a grave for the living. Deep darkness. Utter silence. Then suddenly dogs, wailing, Hira was sure they were outside, it was how the village dogs wailed through the long nights of mourning. But this howling came from the movie, it felt so close, so familiar. Hira had never heard that before, not in any other film. Sounds from his own environment. Sounds from his own village. In that instant, the fiction became his reality. He saw people chained along the cellar walls. Being beaten, screaming. He turned. The screams were in the audience. The screams were in the film. Then it began. A rock flew at the screen. Then another one. Another. And his father said stop. But the rocks kept flying. The audience's sudden furore frightened Hira. Cursing, jeers. Booing. Some people spitting at the screen. Others, who had no rocks, throwing handfuls of dirt, scooping the dust from the floor, scooping the dust out of their resentment.

Hira had never seen that before.

Never.

Not in any other film his father had showed. Never.

He was very scared. A stool flew at the screen and ripped open the stitching. The screen didn't tear in half, didn't fall, didn't crumple in a heap, just had a gaping wide hole in it. Hira was horrified by what he saw onscreen, a woman with wounds all over her face, behind bars. Only one part of her face was on the screen, the other part was in the hole, on the back wall, bisected by a ladder.

All the ruckus startled the gecko, it scurried to the other side of the screen. Hira's father was standing on his projection table, trying to calm the audience.

Wasting his breath.

They kept shouting.

Protesting.

Hira heard his father yelling at the top of his lungs, the show was cancelled, everyone had to leave the room. He stopped the film. Clack! Pull the plug! Which instantly cut the stream of things being launched at the screen. People started fuming at one another. More shouting, more uproar. Shouting in protest, and anger. Hira sensed, rather than heard, his father's command to go open the doors. He and his brother and the other kids all went and pushed the doors wide open. The afternoon light plunged into the church.

The crowd pushed towards the exit. Hira neglected to step aside and found himself again within the wave, but this time he fell, people stepped on him, he tried to find a way back up, he made it to his knees but someone else tripped over him, the crush of the crowd was too strong, he couldn't do anything, he rolled up into a ball and covered his head. Time. With only laterite ground and heavy heels, and some steering clear, and some faltering but landing on him anyway. On his back. His head. His calves. Time. With only him, alone. And his scream that would not come out.

He felt himself being picked up like that. And he stayed like that. In the foetal position. The man set him down outside and asked if everything was all right. *No! It's not!* His scream burst out! He wanted to cry! His eyes were full of dust, it burned, he couldn't see anything, he didn't know where it hurt. All over his body, tracks from the feet that trampled him. He'd gone completely red from the dust. In his clothes. His hair. He'd even got dirt in his mouth. He spat several times. His tears fell, finally, promptly brimming with dust. The man didn't know what to say. Hira tried to run to his father. But he didn't get very far, nobody had left. They were still there, in front of the doors. Negotiating to restart the film. Hira was mad at them. Hira wanted his father to console him, wanted to tell him that everybody there had trampled him, but now all of them were blocking his path to those protecting arms!

He was suddenly struck with the memory of the children in bottle gourds, the story Dadabe had told him when his finger had got caught in the bicycle spokes: *Before, children like you were left to the zebus' trampling, we would place the newborn at the entrance of the pen and let the zebus out—if the child survived, their fate was lifted and a great destiny was assured for them; if they died, then they could not harm anyone.* His heart felt so heavy, like his chest was too tight. His stomach churned in sedition. And the tracks, he could still feel those feet upon his body! As if the footprints had been stamped into his flesh! He wailed, *no.* Only the man who'd saved him acknowledged his awful cry. The man was right behind him but he only wanted his father, he pulled away and hid behind a tree.

The crowd negotiated at length. His father acquiesced, but only with the conditions that they would help to restitch the screen, they wouldn't throw any more stones, wouldn't curse at the actors any more, wouldn't yell at one another any more. The people agreed every time: 'Yes sir, Monsieur Venance! OK, Monsieur Venance!'

The day had begun to fade. The sky was already red. The rest of the kids were still playing cowboys and Indians. Hira didn't want to any more. He'd retreated to a small grove of bamboo behind the church.

He lay on the ground, found a short stalk, tried to mimic a birdcall by blowing into it. His tears were still flowing, his mouth was full of spit, it was a sorry attempt.

When he came out from hiding, the sun was setting a magnificent red over the eucalyptus leaves. The trees looked so big! The night squeezed around the sun. And the trees turned to shadows and joined in, eating away at the vivid red. Everyone was still in the rec room, he went back inside. It had started up again about twenty minutes before. Hira knew it was close to the end, just by how thin the film was in the upper spool, there wasn't much left, maybe ten minutes.

Outside a building. A man's hands are tied behind his back. A French officer orders him to pick up a cigarette from the ground, his last cigarette, the man refuses, the officer threatens to execute other people if he won't do it, a woman is crying, the prisoner's mother.

The woman's wailing rent the silence in the room. Hira saw the audience with clenched fists and tears in their eyes.

The man starts towards the cigarette, the officer gives the order to shoot him down. Silent and cold as the machine gun crackles. And then, first softly, then growing, filling the air, the women's ululations.

Same as here, same as home, same as the women here do, from the film into the rec room, the women there picking up the ululations, a shiver ran through Hira's entire body, as if their singing was washing the footprints away.

The French soldiers, stupefied, unsure of what to do with these women, they step back. Then suddenly, behind an embankment, a man, crouching, taking out a gun, he's Algerian, he's the man from the poster, Hira recognizes him instantly, he shoots.

Emotions exploding in the room. Hira was frightened, he went out-side. Frightened of the rising violence. Not the violence in the movie, no. The violence washing over the crowd. Also frightened because he knew it was the end of the movie, everybody would be leaving soon, he didn't want to end up anywhere near the doors again.

He camped out across the way, basically inside the grotto of the Blessed Virgin that was cut into the rock.

A few minutes later, the doors opened, the audience quietly filed out. It was already night, the neighbourhood wasn't lit, they all made for the road. As Hira watched them leave, he knew that something had happened in him, he hadn't got trampled for nothing. He sensed something, some small thing that would stay with him for a long time, tied to that film, *L'Opium et le Bâton*. The rod, for him, was the trampling he'd suffered, he had figured that out, but then . . . what was the opium?

He went back to his father. The night shone inside the room. There was no lighting. His father was packing up the projector, cords, and spools in the dark, he saw him and stared in surprise, he ruffled his hair.

'Hey, you! You've been playing in the dust!'

Hira smiled so big and felt such joy in his heart . . .

lost

Pavilion Lodge

Even as a child, Hira had always understood the importance of a sanctum, somewhere to place his words so as not to lose them. Words are like an egg, as the proverb says, once hatched, they will make use of their wings. Opening his mouth, parting his lips, it felt to him like breaking the egg and freeing the wings of his words. He needed that sanctum of the word.

There was another movie in the rec room. He's forgotten the title and the whole story. He only remembers the end. A Western. Indians. Different this time. Indians who weren't portrayed as savages, as scalpers and heart-eaters. They were fleeing into the mountains after the massacre of their people. On foot or scant horses. Soon there were none save a father and son, a boy Hira's age. The father was dying. Wounded by a bullet. He told his son to leave him behind. The child refused and dragged him behind for a long while more, a sleigh of woven branches, a dismal stretcher tethered to the horse. But the father was no longer alive. Finally, the child resigned himself to leaving him behind. He gave him his burial of flames. Upon a flat rock he arranged the branches and laid his father, started the fire. The smoke rose into the air. Down in the valley, soldiers, cowboys, and traitors—three other Indians dressed in an approximation of the pale faces—they, the ones who had pursued the two fugitives for nights and days without rest, they saw the smoke. Their faces flashed with cruel joy, they whooped and hollered and galloped away in the dust of vicious pursuit. After one last tear, the child took the two horses and began to head further into the mountains. Transcendent in his suffering. And that was the end of the film. THE END. The child disappeared, and his pursuers filled the frame. With furious cries. THE END. But Hira could not accept that ending. The other children in the audience could not accept that ending. THE END. No. The child could not end like that . . .

Outside, the whole gang clustered around Hira, blinded by sun and tears. Normally, they went to play in the Catholic cemetery just outside the rec room, fasam-bazaha, the cemetery for white people and the like. And they often redid the film there, together, in the shade of a pine tree, each of them retelling it however they wanted. But Hira always took over by the end. Every time. He told the version that they all would have preferred, and whatever should have happened next.

That day, Hira flung his wooden pistol aside, the end of the film made him feel sick, he didn't want to be a cowboy any more. Instead, he picked up a stem of bamboo that was lying on the ground. His friends immediately followed suit and took off for the cemetery, like they always did.

Hira did not move.

No.

He couldn't tell the story there. Not in the white man's cemetery.

No.

He needed a summit, a rock sat up on high. He needed the flat stone from the film where the father's life had ended. He told his friends no. Not there. Not in that place. They set off again, in search of their sacred place. Calm and silent. They left the cemetery behind in favour of a large tree with roots pushing up from the ground. They could all sit there. There was a hollow within the roots for the storyteller to face the rest of them. But no. Not there. Hira muttered: 'Not here! We need to go up there . . . '

He was pointing up at Ankatso, the Vazimba hill. His friends stared at him in shock. We're not allowed up there! It's too far! It'll be sunset by the time we get there! We'll never get home before dark! The Vazimbas will steal us away and our mamas will yell at us!

'Up there,' Hira repeated, obstinate. 'On that rock below the lodge!'

Ankatso was the highest hill around their development. They were only allowed to go there on rally days. The cars would start down by the bridge over the tributary of the Ikopa River. The end was set at the top, after that lethal bend over the pass. Sometimes the engines would explode before they'd even made it up. For several months now, the star of the rally had been a red Renault Dauphine with rainbow racing stripes. (The race happened once a month.) Everyone brought a picnic, all the parents were there, everyone from the development was there: old, young, girls, boys. The road to the top was packed with crowds. A huge rock hung over the final turn, with a 'pavilion lodge' on top where people could go to get out of the sun. More a shelter than a lodge, really, but they called it that because it was made of solid wood and beautifully crafted.

On non-rally days, Ankatso would return to being the hill that it was, the Vazimba hill, the hill of sacred rocks. You couldn't just go there. There were spirits, dancing all around you. They were in the butterflies. They were in the geckos. In every thing that darted away, scampered by, and disappeared, the wind, the water, breaths, shadows. This was where they had settled, ensconcing themselves safe within the rocks. They'd been there ever since the kings had decided to leave Ambohimanga. And march against Analamanga, and rule the land, even if it meant exterminating their enemies. The Vazimbas had withdrawn into the rocks of Ankatso, the currents of the Ikopa, the marshes of Ambohipo, into the very dust of Ampahateza. From the peaceable people who had inhabited those places, they became spirits who haunted story and memory, haunted rock and water, spirits who lived on in the flight of a butterfly and the sudden appearance of a gecko.

Ankatso was the place, Hira was certain. The place where he needed to tell the story of what happened next for the Indian child, in the mineral of the distant and the mist of the unknown.

His friends hesitated. Hira looked them straight in the eyes. Explaining nothing. 'That is where I'll tell the story. Up there!'

A long stretch of silence. And then. A voice. *OK, we'll run!* They ran. They ran through the rice fields. They ran over the bridge. They ran a long straightaway down the road, to just before the climb. They slowed down a little, because there, right before the hill, was a Vazimba tomb, and no running, it disturbs the man who's buried there. They slowed down and walked, then once the tomb was behind them they started running again. Up the slope. Still in sunlight. The already weak sun. It was almost 5.30. In about forty minutes, it would be dark.

They made it to the top. Breathless. Lungs on fire. Throats dry. They hadn't thought of bringing water. Each of them picked up a pebble to put under their tongue. Unplanned. Unrehearsed. For staunching their thirst. Sun setting as they were seated on the rock. Now the story could pass through the shadows and descend over the land. A sanctum. The sun was vehemently red. A round and perfect disk. So, so close. Hira looked around the circle of his friends, and then began the tale of the child who was taken in by the mountain, whom the soldiers could never ever find. Never ever.

That was his first story.

A Story with No End or Borders

Hira told more and more stories, selecting a place for each one. He would only go to the rock in Ankatso for the great stories, the ones he'd been nurturing for several days, the ones he first told to himself alone, not seeing his friends for days, and then finally returning to them. He never had to invite them over or tell them he was ready. They would leave their games all on their own, their football or wrestling, swords or wooden horses, and follow him. And he would bring them wherever the story required. Until the sun began to set and their mamas called them more insistently.

He was having trouble with his teacher at school. He was shocked at how she couldn't understand that he could be listening and day-dreaming at the same time. He had told her so, but she wouldn't believe it. She didn't want him writing with both hands, either. He could. Left and right. His favourite way to write was actually upside down. With his paper turned all the way around and his torso practically lying across the table. Granted, with his tablemates, that wasn't something he could do all the time, it would get in their way—the class was arranged around tables of eight to ten students each, seven tables in all. He tried to follow the teacher's instructions, to keep his back straight, put both his hands all the way on the table, keep his paper straight, but then his writing would fall off the lines and slant perilously towards the bottom of the page. Then he would have to turn his paper slant-wise, or his body, or switch back to his left hand. But the teacher would always come around and smack his left hand with her metal ruler. He'd switch back to his right. She'd come around again and scold him for his 'chicken scratch'! Like the marks that a rooster would scrape into the dusty ground . . .

One day, she got fed up and yanked on his hair. He didn't say any-thing. He didn't do anything. She'd pulled so hard that Hira's head had hit her belly. Hira was startled. The teacher was pregnant. Hira's discombobulated reaction was to set his head back against her belly, to make sure she really was pregnant. Then she accused him of trying to ram his head into her baby and shrilly told the whole class that he was a wicked boy. Outrage, fierce defiance flooded over Hira. But he did not say anything. She told him to go to the corner. He did not. He stayed seated. Where he was. With the awful realization that he had started down the path of Evil. Disobeying an adult. That was the first time it had happened to him. But he could not make himself obey. It was beyond him. The teacher told him to hold out his fingers for the metal ruler. He held them out. She hit them. No whimper from his lips. No expression on his face. Save fascination at the fury she put into beating him. Beating him harder and harder. So hard that the nail on Hira's index finger flew off, the same finger he'd once injured in the bicycle spokes, the same finger that was supposed to be cut off from children whose destinies were too strong. Hira wondered how far it would all go, to mutilate his finger and temper his fortune.

The teacher, in a panic—or still angry, Hira could not read what was happening on her face—ripped a page out of his geo/history notebook and made him wrap it around his finger to stop the bleeding. Hira obeyed. The page immediately turned red. Hira tore out another page himself, and another, until the blood stopped flowing. Unsettling, to see the ink mixed with blood. Letters from his own hand, decomposing, but they did not disappear. Still legible.

He didn't go home right away. His best friend Mamy stayed with him. His heart was beating too hard. He wanted to scream but nothing came out of his mouth. They peeled off the paper scraps stuck to the wound. It burned. Mamy was very gentle with him. The last few scraps of paper, all steeped with blood, his friend brought them to his mouth. Hira was struck by the gesture. But he immediately understood. That's what blood brothers do! He looked at his finger. His nail was gone. So, he truly was a bottle-gourd child! He felt tremendous anger rising within him. His friend was seething, too. They were sitting on a pile of red bricks, and without any discussion, driven by revenge, as the blood brothers they were, each of them picked up a brick. They waited, brick in hand, for the teacher to come outside. On their feet. As soon as she appeared, Mamy took his aim. He missed, because the teacher had seen him winding up. Hira, however, did not miss his target, he got her in the leg. She screamed. They bolted. Fled.

The next day, a schoolyard rumour: the teacher had fainted right there, on the path. Hira was terrified. Maybe he'd hit her stomach, not her leg? Maybe she'd lost her baby? The teacher wasn't there. She was 'on leave'. He didn't know that phrase, 'on leave'. What did it mean? The headmistress called both of them to her office. She told them nothing, except that their parents were coming.

He didn't get punished. He was stunned. Punishment, for him, was a beating. His father came to collect him from school. His friend's father also came for his son. Hira stayed home for four or five days, maybe more, before he went back to school. The teacher had been replaced. He found out she hadn't lost her baby. The headmistress met with both of them, he and his classmate, before escorting them back to their class. She said that she sincerely hoped they had learned something from their suspension. But to Hira, suspension was not a punishment. How could it be a punishment to not go to school? Why would such great happiness be a bad thing? He had expected a more deserving punishment, as he had recognized the severity of his actions. What if he'd made the teacher lose her baby? A spanking felt only natural. A monster of a rollicking. Instead, his father had set a stack of books before him, saying simply: *Here* . . . His father had taken the books out of the barrel and bought him a little bookcase of his very own, a small credenza of rosewood that he had to sand inside with emery paper and wax outside with fat candles.

Hira, with a newly bandaged finger, had found such joy in plunging into the credenza, tracking down all the rough patches on his bookcase, polishing and polishing, to such a brilliant shine! Ten of the big Christmas candles went into it! Then he carefully organized his books and comics, by size first, then by colour, from bright to dark. There were many issues of *Zembla*, *Sheriff of Cochise*, *Texas Rangers*, *Atlas*, *Tarzan*, *Tintin*, *Zorro*—incredible! Myths and tales from Savoy. Myths and tales from the Basque Country. And Japan, and Babylon. And of course from Madagascar, the Éditions Nathan. Jules Verne novels, *Journey to the Centre of the Earth*, *Tribulations of a Chinaman in China*—'tribulations', that was an intriguing word—and even *Michael Strogoff*, he'd seen the movie of that one, *Dick Sand: A Captain at Fifteen*, and *The Mysterious Island* in three volumes—*Dropped from the Clouds*, the very title filled him with wonder, *The Abandoned*, and *The Secret of the Island*—and others that he would go track down from second-hand booksellers later, once he was older, in secondary school, once he was allowed to go downtown by himself. There was also *Moby-Dick* and *The Last of the Mohicans*. *The Adventures of Tom Sawyer*, *The Adventures of Huckleberry Finn*—that name, Huckleberry, he could never pronounce it, he'd sputter out *Chuck Berry Finn*! Books as big as he wanted to read. Illustration plates of wild animals and rare birds. Magazines from China, their drawings so refined, the pages nearly white, captivating. There was the white-haired *Bernard Prince* and his brave young companion, Djinn from the land of maharajas, defying *General Satan*, getting swept up in the *Storm over Coronado*, and even falling into the trap of *The Conquistador's Green Flame*, his favourite issue, and there was the boundless joy that he felt as he sat in front of all those books!

And he began to read, as feverishly as he told stories. From that day on, he never stopped. His father was always bringing him something new to read. Hira kept a lookout for him to come home for lunch, or after work. His father would be riding in the Méhari, he didn't drive, Hira would immediately pinpoint whatever he had tucked under his arm. The driver would be all smiles, too. Hira would run alongside the Méhari, he and his two brothers running together. Whoever'd spotted the Méhari first would be the first to read. Their father would let them choose, and also teach them that no one could claim ownership of a book. Books were for sharing. Hira never forgot that. No one could ever be master of a book.

Gradually, he conceded: he could not bring his storytelling spirit and book-filled brain to school. Telling stories was for outside, freedom of dreams and land of possibilities; books were for inside, home and self-solitude, his own private world; and notebooks were for school, for lessons, memorization, and obedience. It was all perfectly clear. Gradually, he conceded to be right-handed and show respect for his teachers. As the nail of his injured finger was slow to grow back, he came up with a new way to hold his pencil. Yes, he would become right-handed. Yes, he would stop writing upside down. Yes, his handwriting would be more legible. Using that finger. Yes, he would be a good boy. And he was a good boy. To prove that he hadn't wanted his teacher to lose her baby! But the teacher never came back so he could tell her, or so she could forgive him.

And then, when he was by himself, outside, that's when he made his peace with his left hand, picking up a long, thin stalk and tracing his chicken-scratch on the ground, twirling and whirling, delirious with dizziness and dust.

Then he gazed at the tracks of his scriptural dance and made up mountains of new stories from within them. Just for himself. Stories he wouldn't share, not yet. Lacking end or beginning. Merely stories, tales that wandered away and led him into the far unknown.

He liked that. To get lost in a story with no borders or end.

wait

Empty Pages

Sometimes the morning shows up in splinters of over-urgent days, in fragments of a sleep shattered too quick, impatient lives and excitement that just can't wait any longer, voices are born of waking, little is said without sunlight. The cacophonies don the light and reach out through your unconscious, You think the sun but it's just the sleep You've lost, some guys are arguing below your window, You're not familiar with the language and it crashes into your stillness, incomprehension is the dead end forcing you back to your realities, You abandon the un-Babel-ed world and the universe of dreams that has no appointed language, a car passes by in a loud growl, the days take their place abruptly in cities, no transition of the in-between, the borders restored, once there was the night where everything was possible, You are awake now, consciousness commanded to quick clarity, demanding immediate awakening, drowsing and dreams to be banished at once. She is still sleeping next to you, and your eyes are wide open. You know that if You move, You will drag her into callous awakening.

You think of countries where the muezzin calls to prayer at dawn, a sweet soothing song, a deep peaceable voice. You think of the childhood lands where birdsong slow-stretches the time of the days and the rays of the sun. You think of places where the real splits dreams with cock-crow and lifts you gently in rustlings aglow, You are awakened by the image of days and not their intrusion. Where waking was not rupture and breach but a soft screen to lay the sun before you, flowering, blooming, opening onto future lives, and You stretched up, ready to enter into light once more.

You do not move, for fear of waking her. But You know that in not sleeping, You'll only wake her. She never sleeps with you sleepless. So You try to go back to sleep. But You do not know how. The words demand you. The writing calls to you. Idle time urges you out of bed. And You get out of bed. As softly as possible. But She's already awoken. The touch of your skin, in leaving, has severed the union. She pretends She has not woken up. You pretend You do not know. You go to your desk, and You write. You are in your bubble. You have forgotten her.

At times, You are thirsty, your throat dry from being borrowed by silent symbols. You stand to get a drink. The day has barely begun. You like this time. You like this solitude. Right before the city hubbub spills in and intrudes. Car doors slamming shut. A motor starting up and driving away. Creaking hinges. Clanging metal. A yell far away, and then suddenly the background noise that is only natural to incorporate, and accept, and forget, succumbing to what is heard. It is the sound of the city. Ingested. Endured. You want to return to her but You have more to write, You have to write more. Your ghosts and terrors. Your doubts and pursuits. Your dreams and utopias. The world of endless imagination opening before you. Your words that must be forged now. Words to strike again and again, into lines that will sketch you and satisfy. Her novel, You know, is called *Wait*. Pages of nothing. No writing. Unbearably empty pages, erasing lives. You tell yourself that it's time. It's time to return now. But to you, an hour is just a minute, You have no awareness of time while You're writing. You ate up the time you could have enjoyed with her. She's already in the shower. About to leave for work. You did not feel her body waking. Again. She awoke next to empty space, your indent in the bed. You're there without being there, of course. Your body given over to the domain of page and crossing out. You've surrendered yourself to a fantasy that requires constant inking. The flesh of your wife, the meat of your writing—which of the two is your home?

She gives you a kiss. She leaves the house. You get back to writing. You say that You're thinking of her. And You're also writing for her. You are sincere. But You have dumped blank pages into the novel of her life, again. Waiting is always a part of ourselves going away, that we'll never get back. You cannot promise anything. An author's promise is but sweeping fiction. You don't know what to do. You are so very powerless. So, You get back to the only work You know how to keep doing, writing, writing. Writing more and writing still. She will find you there, when She gets back from work. And You are hungry.

Green, White, and Red

His father had given him a cloth hat, with white flowers and green leaves on it. Green predominant. A mellow green, the green of tender shoots. He also had some red trousers that he really liked wearing, some 'bellbottoms', he always felt as if he were tracing fleeting ripples on the ground. If he put on his white shirt, he was green, white, and red. Green hat. White shirt. Red trousers. Then everyone would say that he really was fêt'nat, wasn't he, and he cut a distinguished figure in the national colours. But Hira hadn't been thinking of parading around as the national flag, he just liked his hat and trousers, and the white shirt was a fluke. In all honesty, he wore his hat for protection, he had eczema on his scalp. But Hira declared that if that's what everyone wanted, sure, he could be green, white, and red. He was just living his life, heedless of the symbol he embodied.

One day he was playing by himself outside, he was leaning against the wall of their house, his father came up with a camera and told him not to move. He didn't move. His father asked if he would take off his hat. He took off his hat and waited for the click. He doesn't know why he has such a strong memory of it, to the point that he still remembers every tiny detail: the pounding sun that bleached out everything he could see, his sister Pacia hopping on one leg behind his father, her dress all white and her hair in a ponytail, hair that was verging on red in the heat, the ground, also red, barely stirred by the wind, high bars for gymnastics a couple of metres up on the wall, with a wild peach tree underneath just starting to grow.

He liked holding that hat in his hand, always his left, especially when he was running. He never lent it out, oh no, not ever, not even for it to be washed, absolutely not. How long had he had that hat? How many months, or years? He's not really sure. All he remembers is the first time he wanted to let it go.

One year, in 1974, that's it, 1974, one night, the night before Independence Day, 25 June, when everyone in their housing development had brought out their paper lanterns, along with everyone else in the country, back when they still celebrated Independence in community, fervently, back when they still sang, and danced, and went gallivanting across every neighbourhood and through every city unafraid of insecurity, unaffected by the bitterness that has come with the country's decline, they put him at the very front of the neighbourhood procession, and set the most impressive and beautiful lantern in his hands. And then people shouted: '*Ny anay fety naty e!*' *Hey! Ours was born on Independence Day!*

It was his birthday. It was the country's birthday. He was seven years old, the age of reason! The parade set off as songs began to rise. Hira could see his whole neighbourhood lined up behind him, all waving their lanterns, a long trail of colours and lights. It was incredible. Not because he got to be up front, but because he could see everything from where he was! A yellow line snaking back through the dark, faces traced in shadow and lantern light, clothes gleaming with each new colour in the shimmering dance.

He moved forward slowly, it was up to him to set the pace. Sometimes they came up behind him too quick, he was afraid of going any faster because speeding up would make his lantern swing that much more. He had to make sure the candle flame didn't jump out and nip at the paper, burn it all up. That would be a disaster, a disgrace for the neighbourhood. He kept hearing different kids crying—they'd burned up their lantern. Someone would console them and give them another one, something smaller, a backup lantern.

And when they crossed another line, there were greetings, songs in call and response, and from their column, to Hira it felt like from afar: '*Ny anay fety naty e!*' And the other line answering: '*Anay koy iny e! Samy iray tanàna e, samy iray firenena e!*' *Hey! He is ours, too! We all belong to the same village, the same city, the same country!*

Hira was not ready to understand it, but at that moment, he was no longer his own. Joy. For lights in the night. For songs. For smiling faces. But between all the laughter and excitement, the shouts and greetings, he could feel it: it was impossible for him to step out of the procession like the other kids. To race from neighbourhood to neighbourhood eating the candy, fritters, and biscuits that were all being served. Make some mischief, get up to no good! Make bangers bang! Shout at the top of his lungs! Kick other people's lanterns for the sheer thrill of seeing the flames licking at their hands! And then run away! Leave his rivals in the dust! Like kids do at night, on this night when the whole universe has come out to play! It was simple, really: he couldn't move from his spot. He had to stay there, for everyone to see! It was his birthday, 26 June 1974, he was turning seven! It was the country's birthday, Independence was turning fourteen! He could not remove himself from that equation. Instinctively, he sought out the soft cloth of his hat, he took it off, held it in his left hand. He wanted to hurl it away. So he held onto it, very tight. As tight as he could.

The Sofia Bridge

He didn't get rid of his hat until they were on a trip to Diego-Suarez. He hadn't planned it out in advance. It just happened. They were driving in a Renault Super Goélette. He'd picked out a spot behind the driver on a big crate kind of thing, just in front of the first row of passenger seats. He was sitting there. He could feel the heat of the engine underneath. He stuck his arm out through the driver's window, with the hat, seeing if he could catch air inside of it—a few days earlier, he'd read a Chinese tale about a genie who had trapped all the air in the world inside a bag, hauling it around on his back. Hira was enjoying the wind's resistance, how his hat billowed and puffed out like a hard ball, he stared out, at the green landscape, at the wavy haze of heat, he wasn't looking up ahead, he was watching how the world fell away, it might be nice for his hat to be part of that world, moving backward as he kept going forward.

All of a sudden there was a clank of metal, the Super Goélette had reached the Sofia Bridge, he understood in that instant, he got it, the excitement that swept over the passengers, the thrill in the air, the sound from the deck, a different sound, smooth. The bridge had just been inaugurated a few months earlier, Hira could recite all the facts about it, 810 metres long, 650 tonnes of steel foundation piling, 9,000 cubic metres of concrete, 3,500 tonnes of cement, and 1,100 tonnes of steel for the reinforced and prestressed concrete, inaugurated by General Gilles Andriamahazo, along with the ambassador of the Federal Republic of Germany, Alfred Vestring. The Sofia lay below. A river steeped in mist. He slowly let go of his hat . . .

He saw it, the green, floating like a leaf into the mist and the river. He had only a moment to follow its slow fall, and he felt a rush of delight bursting up within him. As if the falling hat was lifting him, raising him high above that river and its mist. The Super Goélette was already across the bridge. The moment had already passed. His mother had seen everything, she smiled a small, knowing smile. He would not be scolded. His sister Nannie had seen it, too. She was surprised, incredulous. But she didn't say anything either.

Later, on their way back from holiday, his father asked him: 'Do you know what Sofia means?'

No, he answered. I don't.

The Little Prince and the Glass of Coca-Cola

They'd stopped in Mampikony or Port Bergé, he doesn't really remember—was that even the same trip?—to see one of his father's cousins and his family. They were all thirsty. An unbearable heat and the dust that goes right down your throat, sun beating down, dry air roasting, blacktop burning under their sandals. Out front, and from inside, little kids were shouting: Hira! It's Hira! Hira was surprised to hear them shouting his name. Why him? His uncle and aunt came running like chicks towards a mother hen. Hira was shocked. Who had ever seen grownups rush towards a kid? Wouldn't it be more appropriate the other way around?

'Where is he?' shouted his uncle, 'Where is he?'

His uncle had never seen him before, but was only looking for him: 'Hira, where is Hira?' His mother brought him out from his brothers and sisters and pushed him forward. It was a celebration. They thronged around him. The children took his hands and pulled him into the house, chanting his name. Hira did not understand. It felt like they were focusing on him, only him. Hira tried to tell them that his brothers and sisters were there, too, they were all thirsty, but the thirst itself was preventing him from speaking. And his surprise and confusion. They led him inside. His mother, his brothers, and his sisters followed. There was a chair especially for him, a child's chair, but unusual in that it had been finely sculpted out of wood, intricate carvings that felt ceremonial. The chair was unique among the low stools that made up the extent of the very modest living room. They had him sit there, they brought him a glass and a little bottle of cold Coca-Cola. All eyes turned towards him. Captivated by his presence. He had to drink, for their gratification. He drank. Ashamed. His brothers and sisters were not entitled to a glass, they got the regular tin cups and had to make do on the stools. The Coca-Cola was the perfect thing to quench his thirst, absolutely perfect, perfectly refreshing, sparkling perfectly down his throat. But he did not understand. He could not understand why they'd put him on a pedestal like that. And he cannot rationalize it, even now. What made him, that child, worthy of such an honour? Was it just that he was born on a national holiday? He had never thought it was anything exceptional, it was just his birthday . . .

He missed his hat, for the briefest of moments, he could have used it to hide his face, or more precisely, hide himself away by covering his face, looking out at the world through the fabric, looking out at the world through that colour, mellow green, it was such a reassuring colour. He allowed himself to be on display. The family expounded upon all the ways that he moved, all his facial features, his hair, his clothes, his shoes. They found the likeness of a grandfather or great-grandfather. They said names he did not know. Long, drawn-out names. Strange names. And not just names, but monikers. He sat perfectly still to get them to stop joking around. Then someone loudly declared that oh, he had a truly princely bearing!

'You see? Tsimiharo! Andriatsimiharoaminarivo! Who does not consort with others . . . '

Hira didn't know who Tsimiharo was! Who that Andrian-something-or-other was. He did not want to say that long of a name. He assumed it was some grandfather and then immediately forgot, he was just angry, but he didn't show it. Why weren't his brothers and sisters entitled to their own glasses of Coca-Cola?

The Hooves of the Beast of Gods

He got quite the shock later on, back at home, when he discovered the myth of Ibonia, or Iboniamasiboniamanoro. According to the myth, the birth of Ibonia—Iboniamasiboniamanoro—was hard-won by his barren mother in an unrelenting battle against the obstinance of nature. She was knocked to the ground a thousand times, and got back up. She was thrown into the air a thousand times, and found her footing again. She succeeded in catching the locust of legend and immediately swallowed it. The locust curled up inside her belly and became a human foetus, Ibonia came to his mother's womb, and he stayed there for ten years, during which time he chose his future wife, already the wife of another, a cruel and terrible king, the cruellest and most terrible in all the kingdoms. And when the time came for him to see the sun, he instructed his mother to travel the world, so he could choose his birthplace. He spurned mountain high and ocean deep. He spurned mighty forest and fertile plain. In the end, he asked to return home. By the central pillar, near the hearthfire. He had his mother swallow a razor blade, for he would never come into the world head down, he opened his mother's belly and leapt into the fire. He was claiming his name, claiming his destiny.

Obviously, Hira was not that mythical hero, he had not told his mother to travel the mountains and plains, but he saw their quick journey to the hospital, he saw no warm and welcoming place on that most holy day, he saw returning home, the hearthfire and the blind old woman . . .

He hadn't made his mother swallow a razor blade, he had of course come out head first, but he had not cried of his own accord. And his eyes had been wide open . . .

He remembers an incident where his mother laughed about something he'd said as a child, it had made him really angry, he could barely even speak, he'd told his mother something like: 'There was no point bringing me to the hospital, you know, I didn't need anyone, and I don't need anyone now either, I'm all grown up.' His mother had laughed at him and he'd got upset. He had never felt like a baby, or a child. Not ever.

It was just, he had this feeling, like his life was controlled by omens and songs that came from faraway mouths, songs that came from unknown lands and a different reality. He refused to listen, he rejected them. He wanted to be free. Be his own person. And make his own decisions.

He knew his mother had had some issues after him. She'd got pregnant again right after he was born. The child had stayed in her belly. Died in her belly. Broken in her belly. Rotted in her belly. He felt guilty. He thought it was because of him. Because he'd rejected the songs. Because he'd rejected the words that came from someplace so far away, someplace he did not know. And even now, he's still not sure how he'd known that a child had died in his mother's belly. He just knew. That's all. But he was only a year old when it had occurred. And his mother hadn't ever told him about it . . . It had been hard for him to snuggle with his mother during that time. Her touch was too strong for him. Her scent was too beloved. And his mother was so, so weak. So white. So pale . . .

His mother had recovered. He got a sister. Pacia. Born premature. He watched this new sister. She didn't die, at least. He decided he would love her. Love her a lot. He got another brother, Tom, and then another sister, Dooda.

After Dooda, his mother lost another child because of him. They were on holiday, it was their first day. He was playing with his brothers and sisters, his cousins, friends, and neighbours. It was night, they had just arrived in his mother's hometown, the coastal city of Diego-Suarez, cool night, huge palm trees to rival the towering electrical poles, a wide smooth road, with no potholes, such a wide road, right in the middle of the city, he'd never seen anything like it in their capital of choked and rutted streets, where the street lights were always busted. They were playing kick the kapôka—that's what they used to call the Nestlé cartons. The kapôka started in the middle of a circle. One kid was the 'leper' who had to hunt down and tag all the others. Anyone who got tagged by the leper was a prisoner in the circle around the Nestlé kapôka. In order to free them, someone would have to dash in without getting tagged by the leper and kick the kapôka away to break the circle, then the prisoners could all scatter, and the leper would have to start their work all over again. Hunt them down, chase anyone they found, tag them, bring them to the circle, make sure none of the other players could get in and whack the kapôka away.

Hira was hiding under a brightly coloured bougainvillaea. He saw his big sister come out of her hiding spot and he dashed after her, hurtling into the road, not seeing the motorbike that knocked him down, ran him over, crushed his throat. He saw his mother running over in a panic. He saw his aunt running over in a panic. He saw everybody running over in a panic. Shouting and shouting. He wasn't hurt that badly. He saw the motorbiker panicking. The bike on the ground. He saw his big sister panicking. He saw panic around him, nothing else. Everything was happening in slow-motion panic. He saw all of the mouths screaming, shouting, but he didn't hear any sound. He was going gentle. He saw feet, he saw legs. Were they zebus' feet and legs? Was he at the entrance of the zebu pen? He was having those thoughts, that he was being trampled again, like at his father's movie theatre, his chest trampled, his throat trampled, but unlike back then, he could not protect himself or curl up in a ball, his body had stopped responding, everything hurt, the heavy weight of suffocation.

He was taken to hospital. He was put on the motorbike that had knocked him down, the motorbiker was alongside, walking, pushing the bike. His mother and Aunt Suzanne were filing along behind—it certainly seems to him as if that is how it happened, it felt like they were recreating the flight into Egypt, at night on those silent, empty streets, a child and his family making for a more welcoming refuge, he thought about his father, his father who was so far away, who wasn't on holiday with them. Yes, it seems to him as if that is certainly how it happened, he can't remember it very well any more, but that's not important, the feelings we keep from the past produce more than our lived reality. They reached the hospital, and right away he noticed that the doctor was only tending to his mother. His throat was swollen. He couldn't open his mouth, his hip hurt a lot. He couldn't swallow his saliva. It hurt. But the doctor was only tending to his mother. He got a room all to himself. He'd never had a room all to himself before. His mother's room was next to it, separated by a curtain. The curtain was night-red. That was how he'd perceived the colour, night-red. He fell asleep. He remembered that it was very dark in that room. Very, very dark.

Early the next morning, his aunt returned. She went straight into his mother's room. He heard their conversation. His aunt said: 'Yes, I enshrouded him on the roof.' *Enshrouded*? On the roof? That was the tradition for zazarano, children who came out too soon from the waters of their mother's womb, the foetus-child, his mother's lost child, lost from the shock of the accident, swaddled and laid on the roof, face up to the sky, untouched by the earth he would never know. Hira thought: 'My brother gazes upon the sun, he melts up into the skies.' Sadness overwhelmed him. He said nothing. His mother said nothing to him, either. But the thought stuck with him for a long time: that he'd taken two children away from his mother. The story came back to him, about the child in the bottle gourd, he accepted it in the depths of his heart. It had to be done for the children who were born under too strong a sign, they had to be crushed, their destructive destiny had to be taken from them, beneath the hooves of the beast of gods, in the same feeling of songs that came from so far away, in the expanses of homelands so very unknown. In the silence, he wept. He had taken two children away from his mother.

He thinks now about the tears that his mother will cry when she reads these lines. He knows what she will say: no, no, she does not mourn the children lost, she mourns knowing that such thoughts had ever crossed his mind.

Then, when his mother had Angela, Hira concluded that the angels were truly the ones granting them one last sister. Finally, there were seven of them, seven brothers and sisters.

Dadilahy

His chest and neck were bandaged the next day, once the doctor had examined him. He found the situation utterly bizarre, he felt like a badly bound mummy in the antechamber of a secret crypt, like in *Tintin: Cigars of the Pharaoh*. He couldn't move, the smallest motion was painful, straining to catch every sound from his mother's room, listening could hurt too, physically hurt, it broke his neck to bend his ear, he was forced to wait for the sounds to come to him, head tilted, like so, sometimes forced to hold his breath so it wouldn't muffle any signs of his mother's presence, longing for the comfort of knowing that she was all right. But he wouldn't want to completely stop breathing or stay still for too long, he didn't want to make his mother worry! So he was there, motionless in his bed, when the door began to open, slowly, very slowly. He couldn't really even turn his head. He saw the door open and his heart soared.

It was his grandfather, his mother's father, Dadilahy Paul Joseph. Hira tried to sit up and say hello, but his grandfather was already leaning down to him and running his hand through his hair, as he often did. And in Hira, that one caress became transformed, turning into a shower of tears and making his jaw seize up, as if sobs had come slashing through his very soul, slicing cold as a machete. It was heartbreak. Hira wailed and Dadilahy did not understand. Dadilahy had no idea what to do, he was painfully inhibited as it was, with nary a word of affection heard in his home. For a moment, grandfather and grandson both froze, startled. And then grandfather broke the unease, with a *hey marmay, you filthy rascal, you gave me a fright!*

Hira had always taken pride in being called a filthy rascal, even when it was to banish him outside to play. On the days when his grandfather was shouting at all of his grandchildren, Hira would stand his ground (although he could flee at a moment's notice) and stay in the room with him while his brothers and cousins scattered like frightened birds, it was fascinating to see how his grandfather's anger would grow, ferocious, he'd watch him coming closer and disembodying, shedding his Malagasy skin and transforming into a terrifying creature, screaming in a strange language that he could still understand. Dadilahy would come blazing towards him, but then, in just one more step, he would turn back into an ordinary man who could touch him, run his hand through his hair. Then Hira would know that it was OK for him to go help himself to an ice-cold Coca-Cola from the shop's fridge, or even a delicious Bonbon Anglais, the island's legendary limonade! His cousins could never understand how he did it!

Hira knew that his grandfather's true anger would only come out in French, usually when he was blitz-drunk, with his drinking buddies, well past midnight. His French would grow and grow, filling the room with a storm of insults and rage. Everything around him would stop breathing. The very silence itself would snap to attention! Hira had witnessed it more than once, while the rest of the kids were asleep and he was pretending to be. So, he was utterly bewildered when he saw his grandfather shuffle into the hospital room like a timid child, trying not to make a sound. Dadilahy ran his hand through his hair a second time, it made Hira's jaws hurt anew, so badly, but slightly less than the first time, again straining to hold back those surreal, icy-sharp tears. *Here,* his grandfather said, he put a five-thousand-franc note in his hand. *But you must promise not to tell the others. 'I promise, Dadilahy, I won't tell.'* His grandfather went next door, to his mother's room.

This touched Hira deeply because the year before, on that same holiday, one of his older cousins, Kamisy, had asked Dadilahy for five thousand francs to buy a very nice pair of boots, the latest fashion. Dadilahy had coolly walked over to the shop's register behind the bar, he walked back to Kamisy and set the money on the ground, a nice, crisp note fresh from the bank, not like the ones that already smelled like Friday market! *Step on that!* Dadilahy ordered. *Your boots cost the money on the ground, so step on that!* Kamisy, surprised and shocked, had answered, *'I can't!' Why not?* Dadilahy said, *you can stamp on your boots but not on their price? 'But Dadilahy, you don't stamp on your boots, you wear them!' Very well, my grandchild, if that's how it is, then wear these francs!* Kamisy's mouth hung open and he didn't answer. Dadilahy picked up the money with the same calm, slow steps, and went back to put the note away in the register behind the bar. Hira thought his grandfather was absolutely right. How could anyone ask for so much money, for something they'd be stamping on every day? Kamisy never got his boots.

Hira knew how impossible it was to ask his grandfather for money. The man was a market wholesaler, he had a shrewd sense of business and made his own rules. When Hira, or any of his other grandchildren were around, he declared that they weighed 25 kg and could be used to balance the scales. Hira would climb into the half-open sack and his grandfather would hang him on the scale, then fill the other side with yams, or rice, or bananas, or corn, or any other grain crop, broad beans, green beans, lentils, green lentils, black lentils, brown lentils, all kinds of lentils, plump ones or tiny ones—Hira was amazed at all the different varieties of lentils. Hira knew that he didn't weigh 25 kg, he weighed 23, but he always obeyed his grandfather and got into the sack as he was told. And if the customer ventured any doubts, his grandfather would start raving in his ferocious French and add another handful of the goods. Then the customer would guffaw, loudly, and peel some francs off their wad of banknotes. Seller and customer would seal the deal with a clap of their hands, and Hira could get out of the bag and come down from the scales. The customer would leave with their yams, rice, or lentils, but never with 25 kg.

Often, though, as the last of the sun was tilting down, as the silence and lost voices slowly began to steal back, in the secret of the coming slumbers, as the shop gradually morphed into a bar, Hira's grandfather would loosen up and come alive. He served the sacred drinks—cinnamon rhum at first, then betsabetsa by the end—and untether his tongue. Behind the bar, Dadilahy slipped into a strange act, his speech drowned within French, Creole, and Malagasy, thoroughly sunken under rhum. Hira acted as though he saw nothing, heard nothing, noticed none of it, caught none of it, he sat on the doorstep, let himself dwindle off into drowsing right in the doorway. The rest of the kids were playing further away, or eating kebabs, or roasted sweet potatoes, or cassava and bananas simmered in caramel and ginger and coconut milk. His grandfather's friends wondered why Hira always stayed there, on the doorstep, like a spirit between two worlds, why he rarely played with the other kids. Was he waiting for his invisible friends, would he goad them into haunting the here, incite their evil deeds? Then Dadilahy would scoop him up in his arms and swear at his friends, calling them all *kanay* has-beens, or a sunnuva *isalop* whore, told them they had gramma's *chouchounes* for brains, leave my *marmay* alone. And he put his grandson in his own armchair before going back to his friends. From there, Hira saw everything. It was a strategic location. You could see everything from his grandfather's armchair, anything that might happen in the shop/bar. The closer they got to the betsabetsa, the more stories Dadilahy told about how those French bastards had conscripted him in 1942 during the British landings. And when he had needed the French, where had they been, those *zon def* cowards, those *makoumés* who don'know nothin' about *bonbons la plim*. That was how Hira learned his grandfather's story.

Paul Joseph was born in 1906, nine years into colonization. His father, Neck Paul, an army infantry sergeant in the 1895 Expeditionary Corps, probably born in Plouhinec in the department of Morbihan, had met and loved his mother, Marie-Jeanne, a Betsimisaraka woman from Tamatave, in 1905, when the ship that was bringing General Gallieni back to France stopped over in Diego-Suarez and sent him ashore. Neck Paul fell madly in love with Marie-Jeanne before he left. He had just enough time to give her a child, which was Paul Joseph. He returned twice more, and left a child each time: Alice, the second, in 1911, nicknamed Dady Mangorohoro, trembling grandmother, and Henri, the youngest, in 1917, who was still called Henri Betsa because of his penchant for betsabetsa, the cane sugar wine, honey-flavoured and infused with citrus peels and wild fruit.

Shortly after Henri was born, Neck Paul disappeared. All the other times, someone had seen him board a ship for France, they knew he was leaving, they would await his return. But this time, after a day out with his horses, he simply didn't turn back up at the house. There had been no signs to foretell his departure. No word. No ships bound for France. He never returned. Left no trace. Perhaps he'd died. But his body was never found. His grave never existed. He never showed up in any other part of the island. He was never sighted on any other island in the region. Not Réunion. Nor the Comoros. Nor Zanzibar. Not even on the continent, not Djibouti, nothing. No administrative document ever attested to his disappearance. Nothing.

A few months after that, Joseph, aged nine, Alice, aged six, and Henri, a newborn, were taken from their mother Marie-Jeanne, because they were too white, they didn't really look métis. The colonial administration could not tolerate the idea of little white children living in a native woman's house. Thus, Paul Joseph and his sister and brother were declared wards of the state, sent to an orphanage, placed under guardianship, put in a boarding school, exposed as half-breeds, the lowest of the low in the colonial community, and when they reached the age of majority, they were cast out into the backwater. They were given a piece of land deep in the Ambibaka forest, opposite the bay from Diego-Suarez, to scrape out a living with the mosquitoes, lemurs, and bats.

Hira's grandfather had never forgiven the French for ripping him away from his mother, never forgiven them for later abandoning him in that forest with his little brother and handicapped sister—he didn't know what illness she had that made her rock back and forth, sit there all day long and only form snippets of words and phrases. In order to provide for them, he worked himself to the bone, ploughing, sowing, harvesting. He was moulded through his own labour and toil.

Once, at a large zebu market where he was trying to start a herd, Paul Joseph noticed Safy, the older sister of Volahira, both daughters of Dzoely Hira, a rich landowner and prominent zebu herdsman, but Safy had already been promised to another and was about to travel down to the great wide South, beyond Morondava, beyond the Tsiribihina River, deep into the lands of the Bara, a great herding people, down by Sakaraha. Volahira was offered to him instead, she accepted, they were married.

Did Paul Joseph know that he was joining one of the most important families in Antakarana? Dzoely Hira, son of Tsivosa, descended from the tradition keepers of Mitsio Island, where the great King Tsimiharo rests. They came from beyond the Comorian archipelago, they came from beyond African shores, they came from beyond Arabian shores. They had lived with Swahilis, they had lived with Bantus, they had lived with Comorians, they came from the great migrations that populated the lands of western Madagascar, and as they all began to put down roots, they preserved their ties to their origins, back to their dhows, back to their languages and the words they kept safe in their treasured manuscripts. The Sorabe of memory. The Sorabe that they carefully hid from colonials and other invaders.

Did Paul Joseph know that Dzoely Hira's wife, Siza, descended via a non-reigning branch from Andriamanetriarivo, the eldest brother of Andriamandisoarivo, originator of the Northern Sakalavas and consequently the ancestral clan of Antakaranas? Did he know that Antsoha, Siza and Volahira's village, where he'd bought his zebus, was the final stop before the tradition unveiling in Ambatoharanana, the Antakarana capital? A small, seemingly unimportant village, calm and peaceful, a village where there wasn't much that moved except when thousands of people descended upon it for Tsangatsaina, a ceremony where they reaffirmed their customs, a ceremony where they remembered their history, where they called upon the ancestors and all their allies once again, allies from the west, allies from the south. Whether from the highlands or the east, whether from beyond the horizon, from other lands or other islands, Siza's family unveiled several-hundred-year-old alliances. Through their songs. Through their prayers. Rombo. Tromba. Through the fact that the great ancestors had, and would, only descend among them, possessing them, the intricate path of trance, the metamorphosis of word, the incarnation of memory.

Once Independence came about, Paul Joseph and his brother turned down repatriation to France, they went back to the city, to Diego-Suarez, they set up shop in the heart of the central market and became its primary wholesalers.

Hira's mother had been born in Ambibaka, in the backwater—where the colonial administration had banished those half-breeds. Hira knew full well why his mother always said: 'Look how beautiful we are! Look! We come from the alliance between all of these peoples, we come from the best parts of them all. We come from desires, we come from their wanting to be together. The ones who call us half-breeds, do they have all the beauty of these intersecting worlds? It is a wonderful thing to come together. Look, look how beautiful we are! In your face are the lands of Ugunja. The lands of Pemba. And Maore. And Aden. In your face are the lands of Morbihan. In your face are the forgotten

Indian coasts and far-off Austronesia. In your face. In your skin. Sakalava. Antakarana. Tsimihety. Betsimisaraka. You are all of these.'

This is how Paul Joseph was French. French by French abduction. French by ripping a child away from a native woman. And this is how Hira is French. French by his grandfather who was left for dead in the backwater. French by his great-grandfather who left Morbihan and took to the sea for some reason, who knows why—colonizing, adventuring? And this is how Hira is Malagasy! Great-grandson of Dzoely Hira, the tradition keeper. Born on a national holiday. Independence Day! A celebration of self-restoration! And freedom! He wouldn't give that up for anything in the world, belonging to these two nations. No matter what the laws or opponents of dual citizenship say.

Today, as an adult, Hira doesn't say anything when someone remarks that he's pretty lucky to have French citizenship, isn't he? Lucky to have 'benefited' from 'naturalization', and he just wants to say: 'Every time you ask to see my papers, you don't know, no, it is not humiliation, it is the pain of a native mother whose children were taken from her, pain that I mend with my most gracious smile, it is the strength of the children they spurned as half-breeds, my grandfather and his brother and sister, who were never defeated, that you ask me to summon with these ID cards, I will show them to you, even show them off. French citizenship. My history. Your history. Every time you subject me to racial profiling, you don't know, no, my song resounds in the silence you think is submission, this song: *See how beautiful we are! See how beautiful we are! See how we are part of you and us both!* These papers, they are neither submission nor gratitude for France, these papers are the courage and lived experience of all my grandparents, how they learned to survive this racist colonial history. These papers are not rage, nor revenge, but simply a clear understanding of history, they are the knowledge of my rightful place in what is now this Republic. No one can dispute my place here. No one.'

It was plain to see that Hira's grandfather had never been a boot-licker, not to a white man nor any dominating figure. There was nothing he could not overcome. Keep going. Never stop. Hira remembers the times his grandfather would bring him along to that so-called remote backwater.

The way there was stunning, strewn with sand and pebbles, long boulevards of ravinala bursting with such vitality as to gorge you with vigour and sap, protruding roots laid out like wayposts and flattened stairs so your feet would not slip, a corridor of trees, antandronas, where the leaves drifted languidly down onto you, *the serpents make those leaves fall*, his grandfather said, *do not stop below them to try and harvest the fruit, the serpents will let loose the leaves, first one, then a second, and at the third they hurl themselves down, hard as iron lances driving into your skull.* 'But we're going through there, grandfather?' *Yes, and there is no danger as long as you do not stop, just keep walking. For by walking, we will never have two leaves from the same tree land upon our heads, much less a serpent, do not stop, child, never stop.*

Hira remembers the river they had to cross, the ford where they could shorten the distance with several jumps—never stop jumping, for with any stop on any rock a woman's hand would come up and catch your ankle to drag you down forever into the endless flowing river, and you'd tumble on forever and never stop, never, *never, not ever ever*, his grandfather stressed.

Almost as if it was forbidden to rest anywhere in that forest.

After the huge rock they were never allowed to lean against— because an evil spirit lived inside, a great dziny, forever imprisoned in the rock—and once the ford was crossed and the small rise climbed, the sugarcane field unfurled before them, and Dadilahy cut the cane into small pieces with his machete. It was the first stop they'd had in hours and hours of walking. Hira bit into the cane and sucked out the juice. What relief after the fear of plummeting snakes and the water woman in the river!

Next they had to cross the banana plantation, then more rice fields, and then Papa André, his grandfather's half-brother, was there waiting for them with his cart. Dadilahy introduced him first to the two zebus who were pulling the wagon, and then to Papa André, who never recognized him—*it's just, this kid, he's so big now*—and then, finally, bouncing around in the cart, they went up to the brothers' house. Dady Mangorohoro was there, the trembling grandmother rocking back and forth, so kind, all she ever wanted was a snuggle and a smile.

Volahira and Dady Maïnty

Hira got out of hospital, but his mother was kept under observation for a few more days. His throat was still swollen and his jaw extremely sensitive. He couldn't even try to smile, or make any expression at all. It even took effort to close or open his eyelids. Amazing how just blinking his eyes could make so many different parts of his face sting. So he forced himself to keep his eyes shut. Not napping. Not moving. They'd put him in his grandmother Volahira's room, an unusual room, no windows, no openings, no furniture or decorations, just roughcast walls, with nothing inside but a basic mattress and a plunge into pitch black when the door was shut. It was the room where she'd tell her grandchildren to gather round for stories on some nights, which she alone would choose. That was where she often retreated, where she secluded herself. Then they would hear songs, stomping feet, beating flesh, wood, metal, against a body, the walls shaking, strange rhythm of a dance welling up from the earth, they would hear voices, foreign tongues, and the songs, always the songs, was his grandmother really the one singing? Hira was always transported, the outbursts of marvel extracted from silence, which originate in whispers and then inhabit the whole of the heard world and break into echoes on the ramparts of the mind—reason rebuffs, fear that fortifies, flesh waiting with bated breath, the thrill of ages a stepping stone to the intimate unknown.

Another woman he barely knew had brought him into that bedroom, Dady Maïnty, whom he'd seen once with his grandmother coming out of that room, her salovagna barely covering her, sweat pearled across the whole of her dark chest, hair undone, like one possessed. Dady Maïnty set him on the bare mattress and lit the kerosene lamp, she undressed him completely and closed the door. Then, she massaged his hips, for a long time. They were hurting too, so much. Hira suddenly understood why he couldn't walk, why Dady Maïnty had carried him like a baby. He noticed that she wasn't using coconut oil, which had a smell that he hated so much. She'd brought in a Nestlé tin that was filled with some other kind of oil, it had a warm smell. There was a silver coin at the bottom that Hira didn't recognize, a piastre, silver of kings before our time, Dady Maïnty applied the piastre to different places all over his skin, then she spread the liquid across and rubbed it in with her hands.

Then, while she massaged him, she sang the story of the child who was trampled by zebus, unscathed, who tamed a long serpent and crossed the seas on its back. Hira was very frightened. In that dim room. Under that woman's hands. In her strange words. He couldn't really move with his aching jaw, he couldn't really talk, he couldn't really protest about being completely naked, but he understood from the very first word that came from Dady Maïnty's mouth that the child was him, he understood that the zebus were the motorbike. But what would the serpent be? Or this beyond the seas? The land of white men? What was this destiny being assured for him? Then Dady Maïnty placed the piastre between his two eyes and pressed down very hard, she massaged his eyebrows, his temples, and then his whole face. Still singing, soothing him, calming him. Hira took the song-ship and began to drift. Was the journey for real, or a sick child's dreaming? Hira never knew how to account for it, nor any of the many recurrences over the course of his recovery. Dady Maïnty massaged him, placed the piastre on his forehead, and he, he went away. Volahira, his grandmother, was suddenly there, in the middle of the room, watching him drift off. She told him to greet Adan'i Soazara: *Adan'i Soazara will be followed by Bora Andriana. Bora Andriana will be accompanied by Tondro. Tondro will introduce you to Dzoely Hira, your great-grandfather, my father. You mustn't forget anyone. These people are your family. Perhaps Dzoely Hira will bring you to the island of Mitsio, there to greet the prince of princes, Tsimiharo.* And leaving, Hira fell asleep, but his sleep was not in darkness, no, his sleep had never been in darkness, there were voices awaiting him there, lights and brewing storms, the unknown and familiar but a touch apart.

Hira stayed in that room until he was healed. Dady Maïnty fed him like a baby, he could only swallow little spoonfuls of steamed rice or pureed sweet potatoes. People were progressing through the dark room. Hira never saw them come in. They were just there. Standing abruptly, rigid and guttural. They were strangely dressed. They always, man or woman, wore one of the piastres, embroidered into their outfits or plaited into their long-worn braids, or they appeared with silver canes, jewellery all around their arms, white dust on their foreheads. Volahira never turned towards them, she was hidden beneath white fabric, her voice that was not hers came from under there, a deep husky voice, a voice that softened or hardened depending on the visitor, depending on the words and dances that the people offered. Hira saw all of it, now he could sit up on his mattress, he slept against Dady Maïnty who was tirelessly massaging him, stroking him, making him drink again from the silver plate. His throat was no longer swollen. His jaw no longer hurt, but he felt less and less desire to move it, to speak, or scream. He slept. And from the land of dreams, he knew not what to glean.

This is what his grandmother said when he asked her to teach him to tell stories: 'Learn first to stay silent and you will know how to tell stories: Words are drawn from silence.'

He knew he would have something to do with words.

through

Next to Her

Waking up next to her. Nothing is simpler. If sleep is faint absence, with dreams a possible pathway towards her, waking is complete presence, She, in first light, night changing to day in her eyes, Hira wants only for all to be renewed. As it is. She, next to him. An unfair desire, that which often has him leaving and her waiting. Well may he say it is for Them. To ensure their future. But the reality is there. She is present. He is absent. When he leaves, She gives him all of her, he takes it with him. She stays at home, emptied, body in wait, life suspended. When he leaves, he does not know when he'll be able to return.

Waking up next to her. He wants to promise that he will be next to her. Always. He is silent. It would be a lie. After he saw her for the first time, it felt like She was always there. She was there when he wasn't brave enough to approach her. She was there when he followed her at a distance. He placed himself in her path. He placed himself in her gaze. They did not speak to each other. But She was there. She was there when he put her on a pedestal and pretended to ignore her. Two years he made her unavailable. Two years he made her unapproachable. He didn't know he was already leaving. But She was there when he was chasing other loves. She was there when he was floating adrift off other shores. She could be nowhere else, once a smile connected them for the first time. One smile. Misconstrued. She had been thinking about something else. Their paths had crossed. By chance. And She smiled at him. He took the opening and dived through. As if they had always known each other. They were there. They were together. Their souls nevermore to be apart. She was there on that hill when they kissed, in the pavilion lodge where he had promised himself to bring her one day. She was there. And they loved each other. They were love's familiar scene, known so well. They were proof of two bodies joined. The earth had no sky if one was not there. The sky was empty if the other was away. She was there when he knew he was going to leave. Leave the island. Go into exile. Writing cannot endure suppression and dictatorship. She was there when his world was shrinking smaller and smaller, any possibility for him to speak coming up against fear, anger, and cowardice, hypocrisy and blindness. All he had done was collect his words under watch. He had seen. The street kids. The crumbled pavements. The rapes and assassinations on dark streets. The fat laughter from potbellies. The cynicism of the ruling class. He wrote, and soon knew that he would never get to choose his books. He saw it clearly, and he bent. He knelt on the ground, gathering tortured words. He rejected ugliness. But what does ugliness mean? He rejected violence. But what does violence mean? He could not look away. He had to write it all. And he had to leave. For the fallen words to fly again. She was there when he did not want to let her go. She was there with her womb in seed. And he left. Left for that beyond the seas, what his family had always predicted for him. He left without choosing when. Pushed out by censure and the danger of words he thought he'd just been writing for himself. He would not know in that moment that it was his first time leaving not a country, but her. He would not know that the *Return* would be not towards a place, but towards a love. She was there when he brought her to be with him, in the land of France and exile. He thought the issue resolved, thought they were reunited again, and thus he dived body and soul into the throes of the page, leaving once again, without realizing it, day after day. She was there when he drowned in strangled memories. Slavery. Colonialism. And the present-day corruption, where dictatorships are openly snogging democracies. Corrosive memories, memories denied. She was there when he left to relieve other pain, the unnameable deaths of 1947, all of the witnesses to ignominy for him to console, gather their words, record their stories, from Beparasy to Moramanga, from Manakara to Butare, from Mbandaka to Bujumbura. She was there, inwardly terrified, sealing off weakness, piecing him back together, helping him return, always throwing him the last rope and pulling him back up with her love. She was there. He took everything from her.

He often has the same dream: She is bringing him into a deep forest. He follows her like a child. Then She leaves him in the middle of the forest, and turns around. He watches her go away. He is lost. He panics. He waits for her to return, to come looking for him. But She does not return. Then he jolts awake. He wakes her up. He starts blaming her for abandoning him in the forest. She laughs. *It was only a dream, my love. 'No. This was not a dream.'*

Waking up next to her. Sometimes forgetting how lucky that makes him. Presence will make itself ordinary. Yet there is nothing more precious. The unknown yearns, deludes. The sun is the same but the new day will convince otherwise, it's so easy to say good morning, good morning, may it be so, truly a *good morning*. She says good morning. He responds with a child's beaming smile. Finding no words for a priceless treasure. And yet, he will get out of the bed, and he will leave.

He returned one day, from Kigali. In 2000. She opened the door, ready to rush into his arms. He shoved her back. *Don't touch me.* He still can't explain what he felt. He wanted to set fire to all the clothes he'd worn in Rwanda. Remove the dust of the dead covering him. He felt, not dirty, it wasn't that, but like the dust had burrowed into his skin, dust fallen from bodies unburied. He should have left his clothes in Nyamata. Stepped out naked from the communal-grave-turned-makeshift-memorial where the bodies were stacked on rudimentary shelves, just by themselves, without any protective glass. Where you brushed up against the hair of the dead as you moved between the piles, where your breath shifted femurs and mounds of other bones, where you had the brutal realization that you walked upon the dust of the dead. He should have offered his own clothes for a shroud. He should have woven the veils himself, the veils that carry towards repose. Unable he was, unable to bear that reality, the reality of genocide. The bodies do not disappear. They are there. Uncared for. Unidentifiable. Unnameable. Or perhaps, he thought, shouldn't he have stayed in that pit? Laid down next to them? Why was he alive? By what cowardice, what betrayal, had he evaded death? Even though he had not been on Rwandan soil during the genocide? What had the living done that this unthinkable event had occurred? Why hadn't the world given a damn while it was happening there, at the same time as we were drinking tea, having a shit, eating lunch, making love, riding the bus, sipping wine, taking the first drag of our morning cigarette? But the images. Explicit. Relentless. Or maybe we were just plain feigning in vain to not give a damn? Seeing and incapable? Finding any possible excuse? Seeing and sighing that *it's just a Negro issue*? And this was the world Hira was returning to, one capable of such thinking? He could not tolerate the thought.

But he did return. He climbed out of the memorial/grave. He did not stay in Rwanda, as other artists had. He never even went back. He was there. Standing before her. He forbade her even from touching his suitcase. She watched him strip down, the door barely closed, right there. And, naked, he emptied his entire suitcase into the wash, threw out all the books and papers and other things that had made the trip, he was horrified to see that he'd brought home a black doll with real hair. He didn't dare get rid of it, afraid of killing the soul a second time. Whom had the hair belonged to, whom in a country where so many women had been abandoned in gutters, forever defiled? He picked up the doll and set it out in plain sight, he offered it his dry tears.

He never put those clothes on again, and eventually She threw them out. And he refused to pick out any other clothes after that. So She dressed him. He would not take any clothes except from her. Clothes that She sewed. Clothes that She chose. Clothes that She bought. He refused to let anyone else cut his hair. He went back to his childhood Afro. He could not be anywhere better than in her hands. Hers. He gave himself over fully. To her.

He plagued his writings with everything he had not been able to write during his trip. He challenged his reluctance to enter that universe, which he'd always foreseen. The voices were assuaged now that he was accepting them, and they returned within him, more, always more, always coveting a body to speak. He made his decision, to live, and serenely receive the heritage of errant voices. He was born a second time in writing.

He had to care for his dead to assuage the living. The dead who had no burial ground. The dead who begged for this mercy, to not die again in oblivion. There was no other way through it, no other way but memory and forgiveness. Memory to acknowledge, and forgiveness to never ignore it again.

And to live together.

In spite of it all.

Genocide

Butare. The university. The hall packed to overflowing. And a series of men and women, one after the other, to tell the story of what everyone has gone through. Everyone in that country. Everyone on that Rwandan land. Everyone saw. The bodies on the ground, in pieces. The weapons that ruled. Rifles. AK-47s. Rocket launchers. Heavy artillery, anti-personnel mines, grenades. Spears, and bows, but also any household implements, knives, machetes bought in bulk before the genocide, pestles adorned with nails, axes, hammers, sharpened shovels, any murderous craze, any invention in the lust for death, no, not for death, for destruction, rape, evil intoxicate.

A woman tells her story.

Her husband, a Hutu, had refused to kill his children, the daughters of a Tutsi woman. They cut off the girls' legs, at the knee, they cut off the girls' arms, at the elbow, and the mutilated bodies were raped, in front of the father. Then they passed the machete to the father for him to finish off his daughters. He did it. Was there anything else he could do? Except put his children out of their misery? The woman was already lying among other women, severely cut and wounded. She had seen. They'd been brought outside the town hall to be massacred. And they all went, knowing full well what was going to happen. The Tutsis were first. Starting with the women. Hutu husbands were made to kill their Tutsi wives and children, for their own lives to be spared. Hutu wives were raped and hacked into pieces for marrying Tutsis. This woman stayed there, within the swathe of bodies, for nearly four days. She does not understand why she remained alive. At night, the dogs sniffed her, saw she was still alive, they went on, to eat the rotting bodies. Then she falls silent. The whole hall falls silent. An unbearable silence. A silence that will crush your chest. Another woman screams, long. A single woman. Out of all those people remembering their eyes, their own eyes that saw. That saw other atrocities, just as awful. Hira wishes he could have been there. Next to that woman. The screaming woman. Whom he does not see. The one among all those people who went through similar things. In that moment, when she saw her children being hacked apart and raped. Hira wishes he could have held a machete to finish her off, before she found out it would be her daughters' turn next.

There was a small wood by the university, of fir trees, and ferns, Hira was walking through it on his way to a restaurant. Something caught his eye, some fabric, he went to push the fern aside to get a closer look. And then he understood, it was the sleeve from some clothes, and in the clothes, a long bone.

That was six years after the genocide.

Remains, still lying about. And a hand pulled him back. The hand of a young man. Who brought him back to where he lived. His dormitory. And as they walked through the hallways, there rose a song: *Hey, Atome! Don't tell them! Atome, you who love to tell stories, don't tell them this one!* But Atome told him everything. His childhood in Burundi. His childhood in exile, where he was raised on dreams of returning home: '*Nd'aha nd'ahandi*, I am both here and there, here in Burundi, and there, *ahandi*, back in Rwanda, the ancestral land, shepherds' paradise, the soil blessed by gentle, fat cows, the land of incredible, beautiful women, the land of delicate, slow dances, heels that strike the ground and arms that split the air, heads bobbing, shoulders and chests shaking, *ahandi*, where the hills are green and the plains serene.' His parents had fled in 1959. After the first genocide. They dreamed only of returning. And his generation was going to make it happen. Returning. The President's plane crashed. And then it all began. Like everyone had predicted it would. Like everyone knew it would. That's why the genocide had happened. The victims knew they would be the victims. The executioners knew they would be the executioners. And the voices from Mille Collines came out of the radio stations and rushed down into the fields and Interahamwe throats. And the beautiful songs from long country traditions went into the mouths of the graveless gravediggers, the labourers paid only in blood and the intoxication of dismemberment.

It was a genocide rocked by a lullaby. Then Atome joined the RPF. He followed Kagame into the country. They saw the corpses piling higher the further they advanced. Into the country that had been called a paradise. Had been called a land of peaceful herds with its handsome, gentle cows. They saw international forces making passages to evacuate the *génocidaires*. In Gikongoro, they saw the French flag stuck into a mass grave. They went into churches with the dead stacked high inside. Their eyes were choked with looking. The dying smiled with hope, knowing that they were finally there. Sometimes, too often, they had to finish them off, the dying ones. So they could finally leave. What would they do with a life carved to pieces, severed arms and legs, belly open and innards nearly out? They reached Kigali. They stopped the genocide. Stopping a genocide when there were already a million dead? *Oh, Atome! Atome! Don't tell them!* But Atome told the whole story. Atome had been a child when he left Burundi. *Tell me, Hira, how will I be able to love some body now that I've seen so many bodies, so many hacked apart, dismembered? How will I be able to love a woman now when I've seen so many, so many women raped, so many stakes shoved up their vaginas and coming out their throats? How will I still be able to love another living being, a human being?* Hira didn't answer. He could only listen.

Just listen.

With his whole heart.

Atome led him up to another hill. *Picture this same kind of landscape, it looked like this, when I was in my village, I was with my parents' assassin. I asked him where he'd killed my parents. The assassin said, here. It wasn't there, I was digging for no reason. Over here then, he said, it wasn't there. It started to drizzle. The assassin was afraid of getting his feet wet. Suddenly he said, acting like he'd just recovered his memory, over there. And it was there. He'd run me around for an entire afternoon, only to confess all at the first tiny drop of rain. Is that all my parents are worth? The fear of getting stained by one drop of rain? Is that the value of a confession? The value of admitting the truth? I, Atome, am telling you this. I am telling you this. I do not want to not tell it. I am telling it. And I want you to tell it, too. To say what you have seen. To say that we're not liars. We didn't make it up. A genocide happened here. And all of humanity was complicit. France. Belgium. China. South Africa. UNAMIR. You must remember that year, Hira, 1994.*

Hira went back to his hotel. His skin had picked up the dust. He took one shower. Then a second. Then a third. Then. Then. Hira needed to leave that country. The dust did not go away. Hira felt love for all the people who had taken his hand and asked him to tell their story. Atome. Karole. Cyprien. Gatete. Aimable. Ishimwe. Immaculée. Diogène. Shyaka. Rugira. André. Nazou. The dust still did not go away.

Next to her again, not knowing what to tell her about his trip, he tried to hide between her breasts. She held him against her, and he fell asleep, naked. He kept telling her the story. From his half-sleep. From the abyss of his words. He recounted it all to her.

And he still has a dusting of the dust on his skin. The dust of death. The dust of memory.

Benandro

Months after he was run over by the motorbike, sitting up on the windowsill in Antananarivo, Hira looked down to the ground and asked his mother out of the blue: 'Mama, if I jumped, what would it be like?' He'd be killed or hurt, of course, that was obvious, but what about the freefall? What would that be like?

He doesn't remember what his mother answered. Had he just needed an answer? He'd dived right back into silence and distance. Surely he'd come down from the windowsill, surely.

He and the other kids, the clan of littles, were going out to play in the lavakas, the wide gullies that had been sculpted by erosion. He was the oldest in the group. He was the leader, the one in charge. He made everyone take an oath that they would not report back to their parents about going there, to the lavakas. They made their way over intermittently, so as not to attract attention. They met up at the bottom of the hollow, where the hill opened upward, and then went in deeper to reach the steep sides. They climbed up the crumbling walls, hands and feet bare, ground falling away at every hint of a step, they had to be light, had to know which places were the most solid, the most red, the parts that had the most laterite, and when the wall became cliff, the white dust nearly powder, sparkling silvery in the sun, they looked at each other, and most of them turned around and went back the way they'd come, locking their ankles and slowly letting themselves slide down the slope, and laughing, and shouting, in a billow of coloured particles, they'd end up down below, weaving between craters and divots, rolling into the chimneys that stuck out halfway up, turning the colour of the powder that spilled into what they called the White Sea, a little stretch where the earth was nothing but powdery heat that they could crush between their fingers, they would gleefully drill their legs down and burrow into it, over and over again.

That day, Hira was trying to go higher, up to where the wall was almost vertical for some thirty metres. No one tried to follow him. It made sense. Hira was the oldest. So, he was the model of bravery. Up there, he had to dig in with his fingers to find a hold, push in gently so the earth didn't give way, push in enough for it to bear his weight, the weight of a child. And that was how he made his way up, slowly, the younger ones cheering him on from below. His left leg, faltering from the start, suddenly started to shake, it was astonishing, as if it was no longer his limb, he looked at it, how surprising to observe that fear without actually feeling it. He was not afraid, no, and yet his leg was shaking. He focused, and the shaking subsided. Hira started to climb again. Then, he had to get his breathing back under control. No good. It was all over the place. He was gasping for air. The wall was too fragile, crumbling in his hands, crumbling below his feet, he let go of the wall with an enraged scream, roaring their mantra as he fell: '*Maty dia maty, ny fasana ve no tsy ho hisy!*' *Dying is dying, never may the devil take our grave!*

He was falling through space, too fast, and within his roar he heard everyone else screaming, all either riveted or frozen in fear. Hira crashed through more than a few chimneys before landing in the White Sea, on his back, the impact drove his whole body into it, buried him completely, he came up screaming, his mouth full of earth, eyes burning, some singe marks on his arms and thighs, the rest of them screamed in support, they howled for a long time, they howled like madmen, throwing handfuls of the white powder at one another and brawling like glorious wrestlers.

They could never go home in such a state, their clothes and hair and skin covered, the colour of sand and dust, their spit bloated with soil and sweat caked on their bodies, their parents would surely punish them. So they ran to Lake Mandroseza, through the little village at the bottom of the lavakas, setting the chickens and ducks a-panic, the dogs barking, they were afraid of the village children throwing rocks with their deadly aim, and even more afraid of one of the adults who lived there catching them up by their collar, afraid of being brought back to their parents like that, they crossed the rice fields, avoided the zebus grazing there, went past the first line of rushes and flood fields, they jumped into the water—although precious few of them could swim, they just let themselves sink, and then grabbed hold of the rushes that grew in the water, coming back to the surface with the plants that broke through the water, a forest that bent and pushed them back up, they returned to the shore, gave themselves over to the sun to be dried. And then, faces turned up to the daytime star, they giggled together, they talked, they mimicked the wild ducks' call, mimicked the call of toads that were never heard in daylight, mimicked the call of animals that didn't exist but lived deep within their throats, Hira thought about the legend of Benandro, sometimes he would tell them the story, many times he thought of it and decided not to share.

Story, story, here's a story, the mothers singing:

Leave not, O Benandro, do not go.
Woes there are,
And enemies too,
Storms there are,
And curses too,
Leave not, O Benandro, do not go.

But Benandro does go, despite all, despite the mothers' imploring, despite the fathers' imploring.

What need have you to leave, O Benandro?
Is not here the Great-Red-Hump?
Is not here the Great-Shining-Black?
Is not here the Peerless-Horns-of-the-Moon?
Is not here the herd that tends your soul?
Leave not, O Benandro, do not go.

But Benandro does go, not listening to any advice or prayer, Konantitra follows him, his slave, old servant. He walks far enough to disappear from sight, he walks far enough to throw off his shadow. He sits on the tallest of mountains, gazing down at valleys and plains, he sits on the unreachable summit, and all at once hurtles down. Benandro tumbles, tumbles, tumbles . . .

And the stones tumble with him, and the rocks tumble with him, and the branches he breaks, and the leaves and twigs he sends flying, and the stones and rocks tumble becoming skulls and bones, and the branches and twigs tumble becoming arms and legs, and the leaves and bark tumble becoming skin, the dust and sand tumble becoming flesh, the rain and streams tumble becoming blood. And Benandro tumbles, harms himself. And Benandro tumbles, kills himself.

And when the dust settles. We see entities, children, flayed, skin in ribbons, skulls showing, flesh pierced by shards of wood, arms and legs contorted. The children pick themselves up and collect Benandro's disjointed limbs. Konantitra the slave comes, she attests to her young master's death. Benandro speaks to her through the shadows:

> *O Konantitra, tell them not to make a sacrifice of the Great-Red-Hump,*
> *O Konantitra, tell them not to make an offering of the Great-Shining-Black,*
> *O Konantitra, tell them to spare the Peerless-Horns-of-the-Moon,*
> *I do not need my zebus to furnish my tomb,*
> *O Konantitra, tell them that empty shall remain my tomb.*
> *None shall weep for me, none shall mourn for me.*
> *Tell them that Benandro has gone away into the twinkling days and billowing dust,*
> *Tell them that Benandro has gone away from his own death, tell them . . .*

Konantitra returns to the fathers, returns to the mothers. The mothers cry. The fathers mourn. And we see other children climbing high, taking to the cliffs. Are they stone, are they branch? Leaf and twig? River blood and mountain froth?

Leave not, O Benandro, do not go . . .

Sometimes the children jump, they often disappear . . .

Story suspended in a moment of awe.

'Where'd they go when they disappeared?' his friends asked, *I don't know*, he said, *I don't know*, and was silent.

I will go there...

Sometimes when they played, as the dust rose, they looked down, they saw it clearly, a skull, tumbling to the ground and disappearing, and they fled screaming: *Benandro, Benandro...*

Kelimalaza

Hill after hill, very few trees, wind and light teasing the tall grass, a lone house, who knows, abandoned or left to time, visited from time to time, who knows, by an errant hiker, an adventurous child, like him, like Hira, some couple in want of shadow and secret, who knows, a shelter for lizards and geckos, and rocks, black rocks, as if scraped clean of the earth, red earth, laterite; sometimes, a trail, a line scratched across the surface, akin to a gash on a bare breast, the calm cut through by the railroad's roar.

Fleeting roar, a slowed arrow down the tracks, train cars and engine, nearly antique. And that was how Hira entered into the memory of 1947: through the landscape. He'd been one among many, just a happy child playing on the hills, all with their cardboard boxes, they would slide inside and hit the slopes, slick hillside grass, laughter, their laughter. And when they saw the train coming out of the tunnel, they raced down to wait for it at the tracks and then ran along beside the cars, the most audacious of them climbing up to ride for a bit, and then jumping off before the bridge, because the other side was beyond where they were allowed, the faraway, the lands of Ambohimanambola: Kelimalaza's domain.

Hira more often ran beside than climbed aboard. There was this fear that gnawed at him, a strange fear he couldn't work out, of getting crushed under the train? Missing the grab? Missing the jump? He truly could not work it out. All he knew was that he was no coward, and he always made it if he didn't think about it. There was something else causing a mental block.

These were the trains the colonizers had used to gun down the ones they called fahavalos, a term that had bizarrely been translated as 'rebels' even though it meant enemies. People who resist the invaders, are they fahavalos? People who want to keep the natural order of things, to stay in their homes, to remain free? Those trains had brought death. How did he know that? Who'd told him? No one had ever sat him down to pass the story on to him, in reality. He knew, his friends knew, they'd think about it or not, and he just started to wonder, that's all, out of his insatiable curiosity.

Hira stopped running, panting, he saw his brother and his friends, hanging on the train, and jumping, one by one, rolling down the side, laughing, the train went over the bridge, turned, disappeared.

Towards Kelimalaza.

Death was on the other side, in the other time, in the other age, during the colonization that people told them about so often, in the other country that theirs had been a little over fifteen years ago, a country they had not known, the one that had been battered, revolted.

Hira thought about it but could not envision it, could not imagine that country under occupation. He still wasn't able to decipher all the obvious remnants, not yet. The train tracks, colonial buildings, the French language, that was the world he'd been born into, all of it was part of his life. How could he envision the trains as one of the most powerful symbols of foreign supremacy? There are vendors and merchants in those train cars, with crates of fruits and vegetables, with chickens and turkeys, and sometimes sheep, there are country folk and travellers. And laughter, and smells. How could he envision that past? All of those people had experienced colonization? Which meant that all adults, all of them, had lived as subhuman? He was deeply troubled by the thought. None of them had been free! They'd been natives. Aboriginals! Indigenous! It was a silly word in French, *des autochtones*, it sounded like *zoo, tock*, and *tone*!

There was also another game that Hira played, along with his friends, they put needles on the tracks, it was supposed to make the train derail . . .

That's what the rebels had done, in 1947, people told them, the rebels took a humble sewing needle and laid it on the tracks and derailed the train. They tried it for themselves, they waited until the train was coming, they put their needles on the tracks, each of them had their own, spaced seven steps apart, sacred number seven, they took cover on the berm. The train went by, there was nothing left of their needles. Then, they put whatever they wanted on the tracks, spitting magic spells over eucalyptus stems, or a red cloth or a dead bird's wings or a red rooster's comb.

No good . . .

Maybe they'd have to go a bit further, defy the prohibition, and get closer to Kelimalaza's rise.

But they'd never dared, or rather never dared admit that sometimes they were there, on Kelimalaza's rise, a hill like any other, common, calm, and quiet. In times of peace, isn't Kelimalaza just any old piece of wood lying around on the ground? But in times of turmoil, he brushes up against you and boom, dead, right? Even if he doesn't touch you, you'll still faint, right, isn't that what people say? Sacred of ages past, Kelimalaza emerges to protect the earth mother, when war is inescapable. From a piece of wood, he becomes spear and lance. From a piece of wood, he becomes club and mace. From a piece of wood, Kelimalaza is a fearsome weapon. Even the might of colonizers has no effect on it. That is how the rebels resisted the French army, with Kelimalaza hanging from their necks, Kelimalaza with them as they struck. Kelimalaza was there before colonizers, the talisman of King Andrianampoinimerina who had united all of Imerina and nearly the entire island. Kelimalaza was there opposing the French occupation, fighting alongside the Menalamba, then the VVS, then the MDRM.

Kelimalaza has always been there. With no temple to be seen. Hira walked in that silence, and made sure not to snap any twigs.

In steel and wood, that is how the events of 1947 appeared to him. The might of steel and technology against the power of wood and talisman. The colonial army, he pictured like in war movies. The rebel army, he pictured like in stories and legends. He couldn't quite figure out how to put them both on the same battlefield. Bombs versus myths. Reality versus fiction. Two worlds that could not come together. He didn't really understand it. People said the rebels had lost, and yet the colonists had left, despite their victory and all the massacres they had committed! How could the colonists leave, when they had won the war? What, then, is the nature of Kelimalaza's power? Piece of wood, power of earth? Were the rebels right? That guns can never win against sticks? In Hira's imagination, Kelimalaza retained the whole of his mystic power, and so, in order for Hira to accept the story's fallacy, he thought of himself as a child of the hills, it went beyond explanation, how he belonged to those lands, he couldn't quite articulate it—those hills where nothing seems to happen are truly untameable, and that was where he came from, he came from that world, which could withstand being torn asunder.

Rano, Rano

Hira would often watch the train, he dreamed up stories about cowboys and Indians, stories that were true and not true at the same time. He didn't know where that boundary was, between lie and truth. The fact that these same trains were used to take prisoners east? That couldn't be part of reality! The fact that these same trains were armour-plated to bombard the villages around the tracks? No, he couldn't incorporate that into any possibility. His were such gentle landscapes that he could not conceive of them as being scenes of such cruelty and brutality. His mind could not accommodate that kind of memory, it could only be fiction, even if he did keep it in a corner of his mind, filed away as a chance, a rumour, a few dangerous words that challenged how gleefully he commandeered the hills as their playground. Was it possible that those places had been the lands of death, conflict, and violence? For real? Like in the movies where the cowboys slaughtered the Indians over a stirring orchestral score?

Hira soon got the answer to his questions, one day when an old man pulled back the curtains over the door to their house—the door was never shut, they often had visitors coming to see them, neighbours or distant relatives, friends, acquaintances, strangers who knew of his family's influence or generosity.

And so, that day, after their greetings, the old man sat down in the living room without a word and accepted a glass of water as his due. Then just as bluntly, he set down his glass and began to speak— or perhaps, that was all Hira's memory had retained, the entrance, the tall old man in a traditional Southerner's garb, and that motion of setting down the glass releasing a flood of words, such chilling words . . .

The old man told the story of being in M. in 1947—he'd said the name of the place, but Hira could only recall that it was somewhere around Manakara, he knew exactly where that was because that's where a lot of his father's friends said they were from—the man said he raided a French homestead with his friends, country folk like him, poor folk like him, simple folk like him, they hadn't waited for orders to come from the top, they rose up because their land demanded it. They set fire to the colonist's house, all the occupants ran outside, they slaughtered them, he was in front of a pregnant woman, he didn't stop to think, he raised his spear and sank it into her belly, he kept going to find other people to kill. Then, when he came back that way, he saw the baby was outside of her belly, as if coming up for air, and he fled, in shock, realizing that he was the person who had done that, he could no longer follow his friends in the rebellion. He refused to be part of it any more. As retribution, his friends accused him of being with PADESM, the traitor party, they assassinated his nephew.

The old man wept like a child as he spoke. Hira was stunned. Not by the man's story, nor by the cruelty of his actions, but by the anguish on his face, by the fact that an old man could be so sad, by the brutal change that came over his face, from the serene expression when he arrived to the pain that contorted his every muscle when he set down his glass and began to tell his story. Silence settled within the house. Shattered by the man coughing, such a dry cough. Hira doesn't remember anything else. 1947 had come out of myth and taken on this man's face.

Myth was the warrior with girded loins, assegai in hand, his forehead barred with red earth, braided hair rippling to his shoulders, talisman hanging from his neck—Kelimalaza or Matahola, bullets turning to water the instant they touched his skin.

Myth was when you were playing as an Indian, and if a cowboy spotted you, you had to shout *rano, rano* before he drew his gun! Then the bullets would turn to water, you didn't die, the game would continue on, to hand-to-hand combat, and you Indians always won at hand-to-hand. Those were the rules: in close combat, cowboys would fall. If Indians didn't invoke their magic, they would be taken down by gunfire.

Rano, rano, or the elements versus invaders. *Rano, rano,* or the earth's magic versus the colonizers' firepower.

Slowly, the old man's face replaced that of the invincible rebel. Moramanga, 5 May 1947: one hundred sixty-six men stuffed into three cattle cars, gunned down through the slats. The few wounded finished off on 8 May. Shot. Hira had a thousand questions. Why hadn't the magic words worked that time, *rano, rano*? Easy! came his answer, from the soul of a child. The prisoners had been inside the train cars, they couldn't see the soldiers aiming their weapons! They hadn't had the chance to recite the magic words! OK, but then why had the soldiers fired into the train cars when those men were already their prisoners? Easy! his answer came again. The soldiers were afraid that the rebels would turn into gusts of air, or snakes, or geckos or lizards, and escape before they knew it, they had to do something right away! Because the rebels had that power too, of shape-shifting. How else could you explain why the soldiers hadn't been able to catch them in the forest even with all their trains, and foot soldiers, and jeeps and planes and horses?

Hira didn't recognize the symbols of that massacre until much later—the train cars, 8 May, mass killings—once he had to grow up and understand, leave movies and myth behind, and start drawing connections between those events and other things that have happened in the history of the world.

Hira dreamed up a thousand different scenarios in order to confront the incomprehensible. He was never brave enough to ask too many questions, for he always saw how adults lost all sense of composure whenever 1947 was brought up. It was an almost obscene feeling, watching as their adult countenance vanished, to let the grief and weakness show through. He felt almost ashamed as their words went spiralling into fury or floundering. Most of his friends would just leave at that point, they wouldn't keep subjecting themselves to the old folks' 'crazy talk': men pushed out of aeroplanes, trains shooting down everything along the tracks, Senegalys hacking women and children apart, dead bodies thrown to the dogs, villages burned to the ground, herds of zebus slaughtered, men in the forest who turned into apes from having lived there for too long . . .

Senegaly

For a long time, Hira, like all the other children, would not go near an African. To them, every African was a heart-eating Senegaly! And their teachers would threaten to let in a Senegaly if they didn't work hard at school, right? Adults would call upon a Senegaly when they were acting out, right? A Senegaly like the one who lived in their housing development, the one none of the women would marry, the one who had no known family or relatives, the one who'd lived alone as long as he'd been there, the only person who visited the *tirailleurs'* cemetery near their school.

Hira and his friends were obsessed with him. He made them both scared and curious, they kept lurking around his place. The man would often sit outside on an old folding chair. The kids would yell *Senegaly! Senegaly!* and then run like mad as soon as the man looked up. The man always responded, *Malian, Malian.* They thought he was saying *Malin, Malin,* the Devil, as if summoning a demonic friend that would turn him into something even more terrifying.

Unbeknownst to his friends, Hira would sometimes go and spy on the Senegaly. He would crouch in the grass and crawl slowly, like a Sioux scout, up to a little clump of wildflowers, where he could see without being seen. He watched the man. The man didn't do anything other than sit on his chair, and spit his snuff, and close his eyes. The only time he left his spot was when the mofogasy woman showed up with her fritters. He bought five of them, always. Hira tried not to move, not to make a sound, tried to ignore the ants who were so fond of that place, tried not to panic when the bees came by to land on the flowers. By Wakan Tanka! A Sioux scout could endure anything and burn in the sun without a single complaint! And he was lying in the shade, what did he have to complain about?

Hira fell asleep in his position one day. He had arrived early, before the man had even come outside to sit on his chair, before the mofogasy woman had even started making her rounds. The dew had not returned to the sun, and the spiders were mending their webs in the unruly forest of plants. Hira had not moved for a long while, slipping slowly into sleep unawares. He was awoken by a sound. A small stone rolling by his face. He saw the man in his usual spot. He looked different. Almost happy. Hira felt the urge to stretch, resisted it. He tried to steady his breathing and fight off the instinct. But he couldn't hold it in for long. And then he saw a saucer next to him that had a mofogasy on it. His heart pounded. The man had discovered him! And once again, he followed the ways of the Sioux scout: crawl backward, don't stand up until you're completely out of the enemy's sight, and then you can finally run and jump on your horse. He had just begun to retreat when he suddenly realized that this saucer of mofogasy was a peace offering! He stopped, stunned. His heart pounded even harder! Or what if it was a trap? What if the mofogasy was poisoned? What if he ate it, would he not fall to the ground and be dragged off by the Senegaly ogre like a dead animal? But also, he reasoned, the ogre could have taken him out already, when he'd caught him sleeping! Why would you give a child a mofogasy after you'd got the chance to eat them first? Hira's hand shook as he reached out for the fritter. In that motion, he knew he was defying the prohibition. The one that said to never consort with a Senegaly. He wanted to know. His desire was too strong. To know. He quietly recited the gang's magic words: '*Maty dia maty, ny fasana ve no tsy ho hisy!*' *Dying is dying, never may the Devil take our grave!*

He waited for the poison to take effect. Nothing. He slowed his breathing to calm himself. He glanced at the man, who still looked rather amused. Still nothing. It tasted like a regular mofogasy. Hira crept out of his hiding spot to return the saucer. He once again strategized as the Sioux that he was: when raiding a caravan or stagecoach, plot a trajectory that allows for both attack and retreat! He sprinted as fast as he could up to a few metres in front of the Senegaly and put the little plate on the ground without stopping, he was already gone when he realized he hadn't said thank you. But he couldn't double back to say thank you now! His trajectory was perfect and he had to get back to camp! Besides, why would anyone thank their enemy for anything?

He went home, wanting to talk about it with his mother, but then decided not to. He stopped right in front of her with his mouth half-open. His mother asked him: 'Yes?' He said no. His mother asked him: 'He didn't eat you?' He was thunderstruck, and thought to himself: 'How did she know that?' He said no. His mother told him: 'Go check out the *tirailleurs*' cemetery.' He said nothing. Astonishment overwhelming him again. He went outside automatically. Because he always obeyed his mother. It was instinct. Not even obedience, really. It was a matter of course. The natural order of things. He tore down the hill to the cemetery at the back of the Catholic mission in Ampahateza, a little ways away, past the rec room where his father held his film showings.

He'd nearly made it and the Senegaly was already there, strolling peacefully up the same path. Hira froze in his tracks. He couldn't hide this time. The man was walking towards him. Hira waited, standing, unmoving. The man was next to him now. His smile was so sad and so kind . . . He stroked Hira's cheek. Such a large hand. Hira was surprised by how gentle it was.

'Malian, not Senegaly. From Mali . . . '

The man left. Hira knew this cemetery. It was the Catholic cemetery, actually, a colonial cemetery, the cemetery for missionary fathers, for fervent believers and deserving parishioners. Hira and his friends would play there. The graves formed a labyrinth, perfect for playing tag or hide-and-seek. They had memorized every tombstone. The ones covered in flowers, and the ones fallen to ruins. The tombstones with flowers were for missionaries and parishioners. The ruins were mostly the colonists. And relegated to the back were the graves of the *tirailleurs*, just behind the war memorial to the fallen, the fallen of France.

They never went there, oh no. Besides, there weren't tombstones there, just a series of small stone tiles overtaken by grass, and plain crosses stuck in the dirt. Hira stepped closer. So many plaques on the ground! Packed in so tight. Some of them cracked. It was shocking.

The graves being arranged that way. The graves being just blocks of stone in rows along the ground. Foreign names, with the soldier's rank and company, *born circa, died . . .* The date of birth was invariably *born circa*, and the date of death exact. Hira was scared. He suddenly didn't trust the ground he'd been walking on. What if he'd stepped on a grave? Because the graves were on the ground! He started shaking. Right before he bolted, he spotted the name Ibrahim. And as he dashed off, a ridiculous question gnawed at his mind: 'Why was it Ibrahim, and not Abraham? Why Ibrahim?'

Soon he had to slow down because the Senegaly ogre came into view, slowly strolling back to his house. Hira veered off towards the rice fields to go around the monster, so he wouldn't have to face his kindness again. A long detour, that led him back home. His mother was surprised.

'Back already?'

'Yes.'

He went up to his room and picked out a book. As he recalls, he understood nothing about the story that day.

upheaval

Björn Borg

Hira wore shorts a lot. His father had brought him a pair that was all-white with pockets on both sides: shorts fit for a tennis player! Like what Borg wore at Wimbledon! He'd never been to a tennis match, but he'd seen a picture of the champion. What struck him the most was the headband around his forehead. Did tennis players sport headbands like Apaches did? Borg and Geronimo, brothers in arms? Hira's admiration never went so far as to find a piece of fabric to wrap around his head, he adored the freedom of his hair being all over the place, but the shorts? Those, he kept!

One day, he'd been running, he was all sweaty. The father of a friend of his saw him and called him over. Hira went readily into his house.

'Have a seat.'

He sat.

'Are you thirsty?'

'Yes.'

His friend's dad went and got a glass of orange juice, came back, set it near him on a small low table, then sat in front of him. Hira drank to his heart's content. Without any warning he felt a hand on his thigh, the dad's hand. Suddenly it was hard to swallow his orange juice. The hand went up. Hira wasn't wearing anything under his shorts. The fingers touched the tip of his penis. Hira jumped up. The glass fell to the ground and shattered. Hira froze for a moment and then fled.

It was his fault, he thought, for breaking the glass. His fault for being impolite. His fault for running off. The dad hadn't done it on purpose. His hand had slipped, that's all.

But the next day, the next week, every time he ran into the dad, Hira crossed the street, he turned around, he hid, he did not want to believe an adult could be bad.

After that day, he didn't want to hear another word about shorts or tennis players, he told anyone who would listen that Björn Borg was actually an Apache! Björn Borg was an Apache, and Geronimo didn't wear shorts! To the extent that his mother sewed him a little Indian vest with leather fringe, covered in little pockets. And that was how Hira forgot about his friend's father.

The Lovers

In his bedroom, he read. In the house, only he and his mother. That happened a lot. His brothers played outside. As did his sisters. He liked it that way, the idea of being alone with his mother. Feeling her there without needing her to come and see him. He'd closed the bedroom door. He'd closed the window shutters too. He'd pulled a thick black drape all the way around the bunk beds—he slept on the bottom, his oldest brother on top, sometimes they swapped—so he could make a completely dark, enclosed space. Inside there, he stuck the middle of his comforter up between the slats of the top bunk to let it drape down around his whole body, like a tepee, he had plenty of room for minimal movement, he could breathe and hold his book comfortably. He hung his flashlight over his head. Now, the journey could begin. He'd picked out one of the books that his father had forbidden: *The Satyricon* by Petronius. He was endeavouring to read it all in Latin, glancing to the page on the right—the French translation—when he couldn't figure it out. He guessed at more than he got. It was fascinating. The shifting language. The images that sprang up between words he didn't know. And, through a few pilfered meanings, how the story was set in motion all the same. He saw lovers adrift on the ocean, intertwined, kissing, lips to lips, wrapped in the same tunic and cinched body to body, man to man, sinking down to the depths of love. Hira choked up, his hands couldn't hold the book open any more. He set it on his chest and let his tears sink in silence. He knew he would not be the same boy once he left his tepee and his dark room. So he stayed, for a little while longer. Until his tears dried on their own, until his mother wouldn't notice anything when he came out.

Auntie Tsontso

It was love at first sight when he laid eyes on her standing at the bottom of the stairs. A few days earlier, his mother had told them that Auntie Tsontso would be coming to help her out a bit, *she'll be staying with us for a little while*. Hira had been in his room when he was told to come downstairs and say hello to Auntie Tsontso, a taxi-brousse had just dropped her off at the house. Auntie Tsontso was one of his mother's cousins, he'd never seen her before. He had pictured her like all of his mother's other sisters and cousins: métis, light-skinned or slightly sun-kissed, the same familiar proud bearing, every one of them a strong woman. When he came out of his bedroom upstairs, she was already in the living room. He saw her. He didn't understand what was happening to him. A shot through the heart. He stumbled and choked. This woman was Black. Very black. With black hair. Very black hair. This woman looked nothing like his mother. She was large. With an incredible smile. And he plummeted in an instant. Into her eyes. Out of control. He staggered down the stairs. Auntie Tsontso wrapped her arms around him and he nestled into her bosom. He wanted to take a bite of her and get lost in her smell. In that moment, he knew that he was hers, from her bloodline. His roots were there. His Black roots. Regardless of his own light skin. He knew he was from the 'shores', as they say, and not from the highlands, as the outside world usually thought.

In the days and weeks that followed, he made Auntie Tsontso's life miserable. He refused to let her take care of him. He didn't wear the clothes she ironed. He didn't eat the food she fixed. He told her she was black as charcoal, said she had flattened her kinky hair. She shot back that the 'kinky-head' was him, actually, since his Afro kept on breaking combs. He was being duplicitous, Auntie Tsontso's hair was naturally straight. He didn't get how someone could be so dark and have such gorgeous hair. Often, he watched her in secret. She would be sitting on a low stool in the yard, to chop manioc or make curry, wash dishes in a basin, or otherwise just daydream, glancing period-ically at the kids playing nearby. Often she would only be wearing a simple kisaly next to her skin, the kind of sari that Northern women usually wear, a one-piece rectangle that covers the whole body. He would inspect her, and be flooded with a great surge of love that drove him to run to her—but then, without any warning, at the last second, every time, following some uncontrollable instinct, he would whack her squarely in the back. She never got used to it, never expected it. He fled, she yelled. She shouted at him, why would he do that. He screamed that he hated her. She thundered that he would be the first to weep for her when she was gone. She said he wouldn't be able to keep running away like that forever. She would always be there. With her love. No matter what he did.

Other days, he came to her. He said, 'Auntie.' And Auntie opened up her arms to him. He buried himself within them. And then bit her. But Auntie Tsontso would not let go. Her strong arms held him cap-tive. Hira could not get free. He yelled at her to let him go. But she did not let go. She told him that he was her child. So he surrendered to her again, and when he felt her loosen her grip, for a hug, some affection, he broke free and screamed no, no, he hated her.

Hira never went into his mother's arms. Being in his aunt's arms made him feel a sensation that he'd never experienced before, of being filled with fragrance and heady warmth. He couldn't do that with his mother. He didn't know how. The emotion was too strong, it would drown him. He tore himself away without meaning to, and ended up standing there, by himself, breathing.

Auntie Tsontso came over while he was reading. She asked him to read her what was written. She asked him if it was in French. He answered yes. She looked at him, impressed. *A young boy like you? You speak French?* He answered yes. *Read it, then.* He read. *And you understand.* 'Yes, Auntie, I understand it.' She was illiterate, and sorely regretted not having been in school. She laughed and said that they had taken her for a lemur when she came down from Amber Mountain and tried to register for school. But now, here's her child who can teach her how to read and write.

She told him stories about her village. Her region. She told him about how she went to the river to fetch water when she was young, and about how the men leered at them, at her and her sisters, her and her cousins, her and her friends. *They're worse than the crocodiles.*

She told him about how they had to go straight to bed at nightfall, but here, they had TV, they had radio, *here, there is no night at night.* She hated night in the countryside, and she hated seashore life even more, *that uncivilized backwater life.*

Hira protested that he was not uncivilized. *I'm not talking about you,* she replied. 'You said seashore folk were uncivilized, I'm seashore folk, like you, and Papa, and Mama.' *People who don't have school are uncivilized. People who don't know how to read or write are uncivilized, in a world that wants everything in writing, you live in books and you know so many things that even the oldest ones in my village do not. With books, you get lightbulbs, we only have stinky kerosene lamps. With books, you get taps, water comes out of the wall, you have to wash your hands before you open a book, so you get clean, just in sitting down to read a story, we have to go and fetch water from the spring, we have to wash in the river, we have to pee outside, wait until it's night so people won't see us, we don't have toilets in our houses, and you call that being civilized? Where I was, there aren't any children like you, those kids are all rascals and urchins, and these kids*—she pointed at the children playing nearby—*for them, that's the dream, not going to school, running around, uncivilized, they need a good thrashing on their backsides to get them going, but you, you'll go to school on your own, and you'll open a book, and you'll write.* 'I don't write.' *Yes, you do!* 'No, I don't write.' *But you do! I've seen you.*

She took out a balled-up piece of paper that she'd hidden in her bosom and smoothed it out: *Isn't this your handwriting?* He snatched the paper out of her hands and ripped it apart. *That's all right, you'll just write more, you write all the time, you're not uncivilized, you're not seashore folk.* 'Yes I am! I'm seashore folk!' *I've never seen a seashore kid pick up a notebook and write all by themselves like you.* 'Dzoely Hira did! He wrote!' His aunt went numb: *How do you know that? Dzoely Hira did not write, his words were dictated by the ancestors in him, and not in French either!* 'I just know, that's all, I've seen him write.' *You couldn't have, he died before you were born.* Then it was Hira's turn to be dumbfounded. He couldn't understand anything any more. He did what he'd usually do when he wanted people to leave him alone, he buried himself in his book. Speechless, out of arguments, but convinced deep down that he was right.

He never agreed with her about anything. Never. He told himself, *I'm seashore folk, I'm seashore folk,* over and over. She let it be for a little while, but soon started in on him again. *Read me some more, my light-skinned seashore child, seashore folk are uncivilized because people make them uncivilized, and you have never been uncivilized.* He read.

She told him about how she'd been married off to a man she did not love. And so, she ran away to the city. And so, she became a prostitute to survive. He stared at her: 'You were a prostitute?' *Yes, men love women like me, Black women with my huge breasts and long hair, you'll tell my story, won't you?* He felt tremendous anger wash over him. He wanted to kill every man in the world. *I have a daughter,* she added, *I haven't seen her in such a long time. She doesn't want to see me any more, she says I'm a whore. That's why I'm here. Your mama said it was to help her take care of you all, but I am here because your mama loves me very much and she's trying to help me escape from all that.* He didn't say anything. *I went to Diego-Suarez once when I was little, I was blown away by the city, it was the first time I'd been in a city. Everything was beautiful. Everything was clean. There were roads. And cars. There was music. And movies. At night, we danced. On Sundays, we went to church. And then I saw your mama. Someone introduced me to her. They told us we were cousins. She was beautiful. So beautiful. With her light skin, her ringlets and curls. Her hemmed dresses and pretty shoes. She was drinking tea out of a porcelain cup. I didn't know what tea was, much less a porcelain cup, I'd never seen a porcelain teacup before, never seen stone worked so fine. And then I saw her father, a Vazaha, a big bad Vazaha.* 'Dadilahy isn't bad,' Hira protested. *But I didn't know that when I was younger, the Vazahas in my village were all bad men, we had to go around them when we saw them out walking, you had to keep your head down or else they'd hit you, they took any girls they wanted, and when their parents raised their objections, they called in the Senegalys. When they blew their noses, they kept their boogers and snot in their pockets. Yuck. They used their whips in the sugarcane fields. I worked in the sugarcane fields, you know, I saw the Vazahas on their horses, with their whip in hand. I was envious of your mama when I saw her with that porcelain cup, she looked like a princess, she'd definitely never been in a sugarcane field before, not your mother, I never forgot the sight, and even though your mama is a Vazaha's daughter, she has always loved me. Always.*

When I returned to the backwater, I had only one wish, to find her and live with her. 'Now you're here with us,' Hira said, emotional. *Yes, now I'm where I belong.* Her eyes were filled with tears. Hira looked deep into those eyes and, as he was about to break down too, she kissed his eyelids and told him not to cry. She told him she'd rather have her little mister smacking and biting her. And she laughed. Hira got offended, hot under the ears, and he chucked his book at her face. She laughed as she left. Reknotting her kisaly around her breasts. Laughing her radiant, beautiful laugh. Hira has never forgotten that laugh. Never.

Radala

An island in the rice fields is the village that had given their housing development its name: Ambohipo. The name actually means *heart-village*, or *beloved-village*, beloved of the king, dear to his heart. At the end of the eighteenth century, King Andrianampoinimerina would come there to rest.

Ambohipo is across from Andohalo, the royal hill where the king's other hut had been built and near to where the queen's palace now towers magnificently. The first hut, the original, the most sacred, that is twenty-five kilometres away in Ambohimanga. Andohalo and Ambohimanga are considered royal hills, but not Ambohipo, the king went there to relax alone, with just servants and slaves.

There is a zebu pit, showing the memory of that time. They say that's where the great king reared his war bull and would often sit in the shade of the standing stone, which can still be seen in the village today. The place is still surrounded by some sections of tamboho, red walls, made of a surprisingly durable and impermeable material, now there's no one left who can reconstruct it.

The village was renamed Ambohipo-Tanàna, to tell it apart from the newly built housing development. Right after Independence.

To reach the development, the buses had to bypass the steep north face of the hill and go up the southern side. That forced them to drive by Ambohipo-Tanàna. The village wasn't hooked up to the grid, its population was extremely poor, the walls of its houses were still clay, and the roofs thatched. The villagers scarcely made a living selling rice and vegetables at the market. Their children could be recognized by their downcast eyes and the black dirt that clung to their clothes.

It always surprised Hira, the silence that would suddenly come over the passengers when the bus went past the village. Often, the driver would act as though he didn't hear the request for the stop: *misy miala e!* Or if he did stop, some of the passengers would have the nerve to moan and complain and insult him. The pretext in defence of the indefensible was the bus losing its momentum right before starting up the hill to the development, its motor would overheat and it would stall partway up! Hira found this an odd excuse, since the bus slowed to a crawl to go around the potholes before the hill anyway, and besides, there was the stop at Ampahateza, lots of people got off there, the bus stopped there all the time! Hira said nothing, he just kept seeing if he could make out the asphalt under the thick red earth. In the rainy season, this section was virtually impassable. Buses got stuck, smaller cars couldn't get through. Then the villagers would stop asking, tired of fighting. They got off at Ampahateza—at the foot of the hill, where the asphalt started. Hira watched as they headed back the way they'd come, they had to walk by the wastewater treatment plant for the development. That was where the city sewers ended. The treated water would go out to the rice fields, which incidentally were where the villagers worked. It gave off a pestilent stench, especially during the rainy season. Hira had heard some people in the development who revelled in how the village folk were living in their shit now, the age of kings was well and truly over! They scoffed and laughed. Hira was shocked, he went to confide his anger in Auntie Tsontso. She listened to him without saying a word. She heaved a sigh. A heavy sigh. He said: 'See?

The city's not better than the countryside! There's none of that in your backwater! No one dumps their shit in their neighbour's rice fields!'

By then, Hira had been convinced that not all adults were kind people, but since he didn't know how to articulate that, he kept quiet. He said nothing when the bus didn't stop in the village. He said nothing at the village folks' constant underscore of soft, slow, *misy miala* every time the bus's wheels dropped into a hole, pointing out the injustice and calling out the other riders. One hole. *Misy miala e!* The next hole. *Misy miala e!* The younger folks and kids in the village didn't even bother any more, they opened the door and jumped down from the moving bus. No point in asking for anything else.

However, the village did elicit a touch of dread: everyone in the development knew that long ago, during the king's visits, it had received the talisman Kelimalaza as a guest. And Kelimalaza would not tolerate jibes or laughter. And so the people in the village were also feared, hated, resented, spurned. When Hira walked to school, he felt a spirit prowling around there, a dangerous spirit, which could manifest itself at any moment, but they weren't supposed to believe in that, people in the development deemed themselves above it, the city's traditions had been growing stronger, and most paramount of all, school was abolishing all the ancestral beliefs—in fact, it taught that they were mere superstitions!—and nothing was truer than school, nothing else was supposed to count for anything any more. Kelimalaza was one of those thoughts that would only fleetingly cross Hira's mind, a fallacy that he would carefully avoid. Nothing could threaten the supremacy of school.

The Saint Pierre Canisius School (named after the author of the famous sixteenth-century German catechism) was run jointly by the parents and an order of sisters, under the auspices of the Ambohipo parish. The Church had taken note of the quality of the land very early on, well before Independence, and had set about annexing the majority of it, to the point where the villagers were left with almost nothing.

But Hira was much too young to be able to grasp that reality. The edge of the rice fields was a wonderful place for him and his friends to play. They built rafts and shoved them out into the forest of rushes. They found birds' nests and an incredible variety of dragonflies, they went fishing a lot and wouldn't catch a thing, they were much too impatient! Yet there were fish in abundance, some that would even leap onto their rafts! It was the only way they could ever get any!

They would never press further than Ambohipo-Tanàna, daunted by the prevailing silence, stricken by the feeling of emptiness that hung over the place. Their rafts would about-face without them even using their oars! And they would watch the village receding, with its streets where no one ever walked. Windows closed tight. Houses from which no smoke ever rose. Children that were nowhere to be found. An absence, inhabited only by a few chickens and errant pigs. Back then, Hira didn't know that the village children were working during the day. In the fields, for the best conditions. In the development's houses, for the best pay. And in the stone mines, further off on other hills, for the rest of them, most of them, in conditions that bordered on slavery.

The area was plagued by talk of curses. Lifeless bodies would often be found in the marshes, poking through the surface, or deep under the currents, heavy and stiff. Before Hira and his friends ventured in atop their rafts, they would spit on the ground, chew bitter leaves, the ancestors liked that, the chew, they would mock the catechesis, slander the priest, insult the sisters, it felt like the best prayer they could say. Hira relished the fear, he would've loved to know everything about the disappearances, to meet the spirits who carried the bodies away, he tried to track down the legends. His friends didn't care about the stories, they paddled and swam, gorging themselves on guavas or rose apples, just played! Hira's motivation was different: he liked his games better when they defied the forbidden.

At day's end, before the sun's intensity was lost, they dried out their clothes on the bank. Coming home with wet clothes would be flagrant proof that they'd been in the marshes, and it'd be a lashing for sure! The headmistress and the rest of the nuns were even harsher: 'God abhors that swamp. God sees all that you do. As God saw the sins of Adam and Eve, so he will see yours!'

One day, Hira was punished for asking the following question: 'If God abhors these marshes, then why are the minor seminary and the convent and the Christians' cemetery and the parish compound all here? Why does the bishop always take his spiritual retreats here?'

His punishment consisted of going to the convent for school, three days in a row: prayers, conjugation, more prayers, and endless tests by the Mother Superior on the life of Jesus. For his break, Hira had to water all of the plants, they were all over the convent! Then he had to gather the peaches that had fallen and resist the temptation. Not take a single bite, and recite the passage about the Garden of Eden. Accursed serpent! Accursed serpent! Open his mouth when he got back to the kitchen. Show that no, we haven't eaten a single one. Not sass the Mother Superior, not say that she'd taught them herself that it had been an apple in the Bible, not a peach, and certainly not this variety of Malagasy peach, it was a shiny round apple like in the painting behind the altar of the chapel.

In reality, none of it was very difficult for him, he quite liked the silence in the convent. He didn't really talk much as it was, neither at home nor in class, and solitude had never bothered him. Those three days were anything but a punishment. And so it was that on the fourth day, he showed up at the convent as usual, he'd forgotten that the penalty had been lifted.

The trainee nun let him in, she didn't know where the Mother Superior had gone. So Hira was standing there, in the middle of the courtyard, when he saw Radala coming. Radala was a madman, he and his friends would often run into him in the marshes. He was an absolute nightmare, surging out of the water to come and flip their rafts.

Radala was also the caretaker of the nuns' garden. They could never steal any peaches when he was there, half-naked, horrid.

And now Radala was right in front of him, Hira didn't dare move. Nor did Radala. They stood there, frozen, Hira had no idea for how long. The trainee nun did not return. The Mother Superior's whereabouts were still unknown. Then suddenly, for no reason, Radala took off. Hira started following him. Instinctively. Radala was heading through the garden behind the canonesses' building—the cloistered nuns that no one ever saw—he went out a way Hira had never noticed before, which led out to the marshes. Radala's step was sure, Hira almost had to run so he didn't lose him. Radala disappeared into the rushes and still Hira followed him. Hira knew that the mire was dangerous there, it could swallow you in a flash. His heart was pounding but his curiosity was so strong that he wasn't thinking any more. He saw, to his great surprise, that the trail led to an island formed by a small dune. No sooner had he set foot on it than he started sinking fast, he was caught in a trap, the mire had him up to his armpits, he panicked, he screamed, it didn't do any good, there he stayed, scared of sinking even more, but he'd apparently reached the bottom. Except, he started to suffocate. The louder he shouted, the more he suffocated. Then Radala returned. Hira stretched out his arms, Radala took his hands so naturally, it blew Hira away. Radala pulled him out easily and then left again.

Hira sat, stayed there, for a long time, taking off his mud-covered T-shirt and trousers to wash them in the water. He sat, naked, deep in the forbidden marshes, waiting for the sun to dry his clothes. After a quarter hour, they had already dried (or at least, that's what he determined). Now his only concern was hiding it all from his mother, he made up a whole story to explain why he didn't have his sandals any more, since they were, of course, still down at the bottom of the clay . . .

From that day forward, Hira never hesitated to ask questions of anyone around him about the marshes and Ambohipo-Tanàna. He gave ear to all the stories and legends people told about them, to beliefs, superstitions, traditions. He sought corroboration from his father, from the Mother Superior. His father was always keen to tell him about the village and its fadys, but the Mother Superior took his questions rather poorly. She unfailingly declared that they were all just *imaginary legends*, whereas the Bible alone was *truth*.

Hira started hunting through his father's books for any mention of the Ambohipo marshes. His father gave him history books, gave him all the volumes of the *Tantaran'ny Andriana*, Book of the Kings, where there were passages referencing Ambohipo and the talisman Kelimalaza. Hira began to frequent the convent's reading room. It only had catechism books and volumes on the saints! He didn't understand why those were the only kinds of texts there! Why wasn't there a single book about that place, where the convent had been established, after all?

One day, he finally found a book of tales collected by a missionary. A manuscript penned in that beautiful script of old, the pages bound with a thin sisal cord. He raced to the Mother Superior and said: 'If the legends aren't true, then why did this priest collect them?' The Mother Superior snatched the work out of his hands and forbade him from going into the reading room again. The victory, however, went to Hira.

Lifting the Tempest

And so the months passed. Hira spent less and less time in the marshes, played less and less with his friends. All of his time was devoted to reading. The instant that school let out, he ran back home. There was only one thing he wanted to do: read! Devour every book in his father's library! Auntie Tsontso looked out for him: whenever a kid came by, whistled, or tried to call for Hira, she would chase them away like a common black bird.

For his first communion, Hira had to go to catechesis. He was more than willing to go, because he really liked the sister who read them the Bible—he'd first begun to like her when he saw her at the market one day with Auntie Tsontso, she hadn't had her veil on, her hair spilled down her shoulders, so long, so black; she had slipped away, ashamed, beautiful as sin, and when he asked his aunt why she hadn't been wearing her habit, her answer had been evasive: that she wasn't any less of a bride of Christ for it.

Catechesis was held in a room at the parish: one large wooden table, some creaky pews brought in from the church, a few kneelers on their last legs, a confessional with a ratty curtain and a great big spider-web inside, and along the wall, most importantly, a bookcase, being swallowed by dust. He made certain to absorb all the lessons, so he could answer before anyone else and give the right answers, even predicting what the nun or vicar would ask.

And what he was hoping for came to pass, especially with the vicar. Every time he raised his hand to give an answer, the vicar acted like he didn't see him and called on a different child: *everyone must participate equally!* Then, he could stare at all of the titles that were lined up on the shelves. *Around the World in Eighty Days*, he had that one, or rather his father had it. Hira had read it. He'd seen the movie. He'd read the comic. *Queen Margot.* He didn't know it. *The Vicomte of Bragelonne*, another Dumas book. He didn't have that! His father had let him read *The Three Musketeers.* Not any of the other Dumas books. *Not yet*, he said, *when you turn ten. The Death of Satan, and Other Mystical Writings*, he shivered with excitement at the author: Antonin Artaud, all the way at the back of the wardrobe, behind Sartre and Beauvoir, next to Cendrars. His father had said he was a madman. Like Lautréamont. Killed by his madness. Like Rabearivelo. But didn't his father know that he liked madmen now, ever since Radala had pulled him out of the marshes? He peered hard at the shelves again: another title his father didn't have, he knew all the books in his father's library, knew where every book went . . . He kept looking: other titles, of no importance. His father had them! He resolved to start with Artaud. To raid the bookcase. And thus avenge himself on the Mother Superior who had forbidden him from reading.

At the end of catechesis, they had to practise their first confession. They would step into the old confessional—and face the old spider— close their eyes, and clasp their hands together in prayer. Hira recited: I stole a piece of candy, drank red wine, I even put sugar in it, I laid in the canal with some friends, I looked under ladies' skirts as they walked by, but Father, I swear we don't do that to mamas, we shut our eyes when they walk by, and besides, they don't wear miniskirts. Hira did not confess that he wanted to raid the bookcase so, so badly. By the end of the first week, he could recite every title it had. There were four shelves of about thirty books each, with periodicals tucked in wherever. Two of the works were particularly tempting: *Venus in Furs* by Sacher-Masoch, and the *Complete Works of William Shakespeare*. He hadn't heard of Sacher-Masoch, he had no idea what it might mean, it was a fascinating name, completely foreign. But *Venus in Furs*, simply because he had— his father had—a gorgeous book on the painter Goya that he loved, he particularly admired *La maja desnuda*, the nude Venus. His father had caught on and torn out the page, there was only *La maja vestida* left, the clothed Venus. Hira was furious! His father had dared to rip a page from one of his books—his books! And Shakespeare because his father was still saying that he wasn't ten years old yet, he had to wait. He had already read Rimbaud: *No one's serious at seventeen!* And he wasn't even ten! He needed Shakespeare. Desperately.

He decided to make his move after one of the rehearsals for their first communion, learning how to take communion the right way: open your hands, receive the host and place it in your mouth, don't bite into it. He volunteered to sweep the classroom. Granted. He asked permission to bring one of the kneelers home to repair it. Granted. The vicar had scarcely turned his back for a moment, Hira's hand knew exactly where *Venus in Furs* was. He hid the book inside the slot of the kneeler. And left. He got a mighty shock in reading it. He didn't get all of it, but he knew it was not meant for him. He knew he'd entered a world of adults, a world where sex had a fundamental position. He didn't understand why it was so important. He wouldn't even look at an adult for a while. He thought that was how all grownups acted! At home, he shelved the book with his father's *Complete Works of Julius Caesar*, next to Petronius' *Satyricon*. Books so old they were already crumbling to dust, no one was allowed to touch them—*fingers will ruin books, pages prefer your eyes*, his father said. Hira purposefully did shoddy work on the kneeler so he'd get scolded by the vicar, so he'd get told that he had done a sorry job and should bring it back home.

He had to wait a few days before the vicar gave him more chairs to reinforce. He took *The Death of Satan*. He took *Queen Margot*. He brought home pews, too—he hid books underneath, *Astragal, I Spit on Your Graves*. He brought home the votive and candle stands to scrape and polish them, *The Life of Jesus* by Renan, *Two Years' Vacation* by Jules Verne, a George Sand book (he didn't realize until years later that she wasn't a man). When he took his first communion, he bit into the host. There wasn't any blood.

After he and his communion cohorts had passed the religious exam to be altar boys, the vicar called them all into the catechesis classroom and pointed at the bookcase: 'Books are disappearing from here, I'd hope that in the future, you will prove yourselves better Christians.' Everyone knew Hira was the culprit. Beyond a shadow of a doubt. Everyone knew that, when he climbed a tree or went deep into the marshes, he wasn't playing Tarzan, or Zembla, or Robinson Crusoe, he was reading. He'd made a little secluded nook for himself up in the top of a dense, bushy tree. That was where he read his spoils. He did not turn himself in to the vicar. He knew he'd gone too far but he was still missing one book, in two volumes: the *Complete Works of William Shakespeare*, the Pléiade collection, translated by Henri Fluchère. Pages so thin that the letters seemed to come off the page, stick to fingers that were leafing through . . .

He waited almost a whole semester to pull off his stunt, the night of Christ's death, Midnight Mass, when he was scheduled to serve, during the Stations of the Cross. The parish was singing. The women had worn their best lambas, silken cloths draped around their shoulders, the men had worn their best suit jackets, their best ties, they were suffocating in the heat. A dramatic re-enactment had been prepared—his father had created it, he wasn't in on his son's plans—a huge cross that they had raised over the altar, hiding behind a black curtain, with a man on it. The parishioners didn't suspect a thing. The vicar read the crucifixion of Christ according to Mark, and the old ladies in the Chorus of the Daughters of the Virgin Mary began to weep. Already. The plan was to simulate the sound of a short-circuit and then kill the lights right when the vicar got to the passage about the tearing of the temple curtain, the moment when Christ gave up his final breath. The altar boys, him included, were going to knock over a bunch of pews and scream like crazy. It was perfect for carrying out his mission. At midnight exactly, his father triggered the device. The lights were cut, there was a bright flash across the altar and up to the curtain, they pulled it down to reveal the cross and the crucified man! More lights flashing through the church, pelting the cross. A scream rose from the worshippers. The altar boys shrieked as they'd been instructed—like crazy. Hira grabbed his chance, he left his place by the altar and ran for the classroom. Everything was plunged into darkness but he knew exactly where he was going. He heard the actor wailing: *Eli Eli lama sabachthani, my God, my God, why have you forsaken me?* Another blinding flash and the throng of worshippers roared again. Hira grabbed both volumes, he hid them snug under his altar-boy robes and knotted the cords around them several times. He got back to his place just as the lights were restored. The old women in the chorus were still weeping. The vicar signalled to the altar boys. They set off on the

Stations of the Cross. Here, a soldier piercing the sacred heart. Here, the lowering of the cross, and there . . .

Hira resolved to read *The Tempest* first. The next day, he went back to the marshes, lay down on his raft, and met Caliban . . .

stumble

Every Season

On the road is no one. The leaves fall, whirling and yellow. Like birds that are all wings in decay. In landscapes whose painter seems to be absence, everything is there but no one is, land of emptiness, no real flaw in the composition of the canvas, the only things missing are characters. He fights against ennui and sleep, he turns the music off, makes the drive a kind of meditation, becoming aware of all that is passing before his eyes, the road, obviously, and the shoulders, the cars coming towards him, the faces of people inside, the rumbling engine, the rumbling engines, the signage, towns driven past and colours that pierce the grey, details appearing in the eye that quickly recede, for the space is whisked away by speed, scarcely gone and already replaced by another. He moves, meanders, from her, losing markers, no matter, his warren is to burrow into her until he knows nothing else, not path, nor time, so long as She doesn't leave him somewhere, in the woods, without her. And split, She is the hand that cannot harm him even if She opens up his heart. Why does it feel like She's ripping out his guts when She takes her hand away from his skin? And this refusal/desire, so absolute, to not learn how to make do without her. Putting forth no effort to not depend on her. He does not dream of being free from her. He murmurs. *Freedom without punctuation . . . where does your sentence end, my love?*

In the furl of leaves, curled up on the veins, their leaves small, better to hold the bead and stream the sun and shadow, the surfaces vast and hold fast on a single contact of their skin, touching, it is opening worlds, how massive are these loves! Hira knows how lucky he got with her. Corkscrew willows where lives prevail, teeming small things where secrets flit, it is there, the dream to live and life to dream, and sometimes there are hardships and troubles to dump in the mulch. Dew of a kiss, drip-dries of sighs, scents of twining together, every season is for dropping leaves and the leaves will never be dead, bed of embracing, desiring reproduced. Hira will be winter and She the snow, they will be spring and the pinks, they will be autumn and the prevailing branches, they will be summer and the stolen sun, they will be the petals bestowing colour, they will be the pollen dusting flights, ephemeral butterflies will see a sturdy plant as they push their roots into steadfast earth, they will be young shoots, and old trees, they will be birth and rebirth. They will be fallen leaves or flower buds, they will be sap. For all time. Hira turns the music back on. The world rushes back in again. False reality. He switches the headlights on, night has come.

Malagasy

Hira spent his days in his tree, thick foliage hiding him from sight, the crown was sawn off but the blooming branches made a little cage for him to nestle into, he could lie down and not be afraid of falling. There, he read. He stacked his books on top of the hewn trunk, then he set off exploring his world. From the book's first page to the day's last light. He knew that a tree was an unusual place to read, of course, but it was the most peaceful place he'd found. There were always people at home, his brothers, his sisters, his parents' friends, and the neighbours' radio, all the sounds and everything else that made the world his house, or made his house the world. Up there, among the boughs and leaves, people would forget about him, but he would not forget about them, it felt like he could slow down the world to observe at his leisure. He could dive into reading, come back up, dive in again, come up once more. He could see all. Hear all. People walking underneath him. Who had no idea he was there. People far away. Who had no reason to suspect that he was in a tree, yeah, go figure. And none of that ever interfered with his reading. It would always take Tom's voice to pull him out of it.

'Hira! Hira! It's night-time.'

He'd keep on persuading himself that he could still make out the letters, he stretched towards the last of the sun's light—maybe if he couldn't read, he could write instead? But even his tree cast shadows to turn him out, and the cold settled in the same fell swoop. Hira thought that maybe, one night, he could try staying up there. But frightening his parents, the unthinkable defiance . . .

He climbed down. He didn't need to see his way down. He knew every branch of his tree. He would always jump from the second-lowest one. He'd land next to Tom, who was barely five, so small and already so audacious to come outside by himself at dusk. Tom would have peanuts or coco-melts with him, his share of their snack. Their father always brought some sweets home after work, or pistachios or other snacks, Tom was always thinking of Hira, he always had his big brother's share in his little hand. As they ate on their way home, Hira told Tom about the adventures of Tom Sawyer. Tom loved that.

They barely stopped to listen to the grown-ups, playing guitars and singing Mahaleo songs. Mahaleo sang the Revolution. Mahaleo sang rebellion. Mahaleo sang defiance. Love and insobriety. In strange voices. They were bad singers. Bad by academic definitions. Intentionally talking like drunkards. Like the hometown lads they were. They stirred the very depths. There were seven Mahaleos. Like the seven mercenaries. From the movie. Not like the other mercenaries, with that man. Denard. *Le Bob*. The *affreux* of Katanga. Bob Denard, who they heard was about to invade the island. Hira didn't know where Katanga was, nor what was happening there, the war, the atrocities . . . He knew this wasn't how it worked, but he associated the name of that place with akanga. Guineafowl. Akangas in Katanga, clearly the most perfect, sound, perfect-sounding logic. He pictured a land out of a story, or a movie, or a crime novel, adventure novels, comic books, a land where soldiers—colonists—would shoot at everything that moved, slaughter guineafowl out of pure sadism, or maybe, instead of colonists, ogres who would gobble women and guineafowl whole, feathers and small feet thrashing between their lips, screams from their prey abruptly severed, swallowed along with the bodies. A land like that, no, no, such a place would only belong in a cruel story. But it felt like Mahaleo were saying that those colonists were right there, actually, among them, in other skins. Blacker skins. *And we Malagasys, what are we doing?*

Hira would come home with his brother. Then it was time for dinner. Then they slept. Tom was still sharing Hira's bed. Hira liked seeing him fall asleep. Tom always fell fast and sound asleep. The next morning, they had school. Hira was supposed to hold Tom's hand so he wouldn't go running off. But Tom loved to run. They both ran, and didn't hold hands.

Many evenings, including that one, Hira noticed Vola coming home late, or not at all. If she did come back, in the middle of the night, she smelled of cigarettes. Hira heard her footsteps on the stairs. She tried to keep the wood from creaking, but Hira heard. Hira checked to make sure Tom didn't wake up, and Tom never woke up, no matter how loud the commotion. But that was Hira's instinct, looking at his little brother. Hira was sure their parents had heard it too. But their parents didn't say anything. Just a father's cough, that was all, a solemn promise of punishment. Night settled in the house. Rising croaks from the rice fields combined with howling dogs pursuing their mates, way off on the farthest of hills.

That night, Hira's head was echoing with one sentence: *Tsy hiam-boho adidy aho, mon Général!* Colonel Richard Ratsimandrava had just been given full powers that morning from the hands of General Ramanantsoa. One sentence that had spread by word of mouth on the morning of 5 February 1975. A sense of exhilaration, that they were experiencing a significant historical event as a country. But Hira didn't know what made it so significant for Colonel Richard Ratsimandrava to have full powers, what made it so significant for adults to act like they were acting that day. He just liked the name: Ratsimandrava, *One-who-does-not-destroy, One-who-does-not-steal-from-the-hands-of-others, One-who-does-not-walk-off-with-it, One-who-does-not-bring-an-end*—to a meeting, or a business, or a movement. Hira was mesmerized by the possibilities of meaning in that name. But Hira remembered how, as General Ramanantsoa was wavering between who should get the power, Ratsimandrava or Ratsiraka, the Southerners who came to their house said to his father: 'Does he not, in fact, destroy? Your Ratsimandrava? Has the country forgotten the rebellion four years ago, in 1971? In Tulear? Before the general uprising in 1972? Ratsimandrava had command of the police force that killed us there, three thousand dead. And your General Ramanantsoa, wasn't he an officer in the colonial army that tried to take out Monja Jaona? And now he's the one expelling the colonists?'

Hira tried to understand, tried to picture the three thousand dead. Counting: five hundred eleven houses in their development, two to four rooms each, about two thousand residents, adding the small villages in the area, but there aren't a thousand people living in the area, no, he had no idea . . . so if he lived in the South, he would already be dead, he, his little brother, his two little sisters, his big brother, his big sister, Vola, everybody, or else the Southerners were liars, they were always bragging about having herds of zebus in the hundreds, even thousands, but here they pulled pousse-pousses, or worked as night watchmen, or manioc farmers, or corn farmers, three thousand dead, that's a lot. Hira reckoned that those people were liars. Anyway, we Malagasys, we don't kill one another! White men kill Blacks. But Black men don't kill Blacks. Unless the Black is a Senegaly. But Senegalys are stupid. They do not act. They obey. They do not think. They obey. The orders from white men. Blindly. Senegalys are black not because they're Black, but because they bear all the darkness of white men. Truth be told, white men are black with all their barbaric acts, and Black folks are white with all their innocence under oppression and colonization! But this line of reasoning left Hira stumped, even as it spouted out from his head. And it stumped him even more when he thought about his grandfather, a white man! So why didn't he—a white man's grandson—look white? What was the deal with him being born on the anniversary of Independence in a Black country? And why, in this Black country, do we never stop talking about white men? White people are off in their own countries. And the ones that do come here, they're called Vahiny, guests, or 'foreigners' if you like, but the word 'foreigner' doesn't exist in Malagasy, so here they are, the Vahinys, warmly welcomed, smiles on their faces, sweets in hand, and lemurs their only interest! They're nice guests, what are they hiding that is so terrible?

He sat in silence with all of his questions, *Tsy hiamboho adidy aho, mon Général!* That's how the Minister of the Interior became President, 'Monsieur Ala-olana', *One-who-removes-problems*, from the name of a radio show he'd started, Ala-olana. Hira listened to the show regularly, and he fully understood the people's excitement as Ratsimandrava crisscrossed cities and countryside to present his ideas: decentralization, development through traditional village communities, economic autonomy through local production, Malagasizing the economy, distance from the former colonial state. Certain words kept coming up: fokonolona, fihavanana, fokontany, vokatry ny tany. Hira held onto one of them: *fokonolona, fokonolona...*

And then there was the other officer, Didier Ratsiraka, Minister of Foreign Affairs: he spoke in exceptional French, he gave long speeches to the OAU, he faced off with imperialists, he stood up for non-aligned nations, he wasn't under anyone's thumb, not American capitalists nor Russian communists! Hira burst with pride: such incredible officers, strong and handsome, and Madagascar had two of them! One sat in the 'Elephant's Foot'—that's what the Ministry of the Interior building was called, it had been designed to flare out at the base—he gave extraordinary kabarys, in the pure tradition of Malagasy language; the other travelled the globe in a fine ship and went toe-to-toe with every world power! He could match any orator of the French language. He expressed himself in flawless English, too! One ran the interior of the country, the other took care of the exterior!

Hira was also aware that his father's voice had moved into their radio set: *Feon'ny Tanora*, Voices of the Youth, that was his show. His father's voice was everywhere. In the little box. In other people's homes. It was strange for him to hear his father's voice with people he didn't know. Sometimes it would paralyse him, if he wasn't expecting it, like the time he'd been buying fritters from a woman listening to a radio she had on the ground. He'd heard his voice, his father's voice, the man who wasn't too fond of his son being in those kinds of places. It felt like his father was always there! As if Hira would never be able to avoid him. And when he returned home, there it was again, that voice, outside of the radio, his real voice, talking with other people, discussing, invigorating, exclaiming, going on and on, always, laughing, talking politics, always, even more politics. Hira went to rest his ears by his mother and Auntie Tsontso's chit-chatting.

Hira could see everything from his tree: the bus arriving, people getting off, and his father's tall frame rising a good head higher than everyone else. Hira knew that it would take his father a quarter-hour to make it one metre. Conversations were never done. His father leaned forward to listen to people. His father leaned forward to talk to people. They were rehashing what he'd said on the radio. His father explained again. Again and again. In Hira's mind, he had an image of his father always leaning forward. But whose voice rose. Rose up. It was as if the voice were capable of unfurling the silence around it, as if sitting upon a throne. His father wasn't yelling, that was clear to Hira. He did not have to exert himself to speak loudly. His voice filled the air while everything else stood still. And then his father moved forward, slowly. One metre at a time. Only when someone else was talking. His father could not talk while walking. He stood still. He spoke. His voice continued in his place. Hira heard it from where he was. From his tree. Carried to him on the wind along with everything else. Hira knew that it could take his father over an hour to get home, if things had already got started on the bus. How many times had their mother sent them, him or his older brother, to tell their father that dinner was ready? The shame of tugging at his sleeve, in the middle of the road, and telling him: 'Papa, the rice is ready . . . ' And how many times had his father rounded up everybody else: 'Come on, let's keep this going over a nice plate of rice!' And instead of bringing one papa home, Hira brought home three or four?

Hira didn't understand the point of all these conversations. He didn't understand why adults were getting so riled up about what was happening. All of the officers negotiating. All of the people in the streets. The shouts. The slogans. The songs. Saying that we must remain what we are: Malagasy. Hira was dumbfounded. He hadn't known there was a problem with being what they were: Malagasy. If they weren't Malagasy, what were they?

So Hira tossed and turned, playing Ratsimandrava's words over in his mind: '*Tsy hiamboho adidy aho, mon Général!*' *I will not shirk my responsibilities, General!*

Ratsimandrava

Hira was playing football when he got wind of the rumour. *Maty Ratsimandrava*. Six days earlier, the famous words had been spoken.

Six days earlier, the oath of office for the President of the Republic. Ratsimandrava was dead only six days after General Ramanantsoa had handed him full powers.

Hira was with his cousin Tita at the time. Tita walked with a limp. When he was a newborn, he'd fallen off the bed and dislocated his hip. He hadn't cried, and so no one had realized it until much later. The baby wouldn't walk. And if he had to, it was all tears and pain. Tita was a year younger than Hira. Hira admired his daring and his unwavering will. He admired his fire. He loved his voice. His eyes, looking directly into his and always up to the horizon. They were constantly talking. He was the only person who seemed to truly understand him, more even than Mamy, his best friend at school. When he talked about his pebbles and dragonflies, Tita always listened, he never laughed, never thought it was frivolous. Tom listened too, but Tom was still little, could he truly understand Hira? Sometimes when the two families got together, the mamas would exchange kids. Auntie Suzanne, Tita's mother, was the almost-twin sister of Hira's mother, they were only a year apart. There would be times when Tita wouldn't want to go home, so he stayed with them. It had happened to Hira before too, not thinking of going home—because he'd caught a whiff of some delicious spices, or because they hadn't finished their game, or because he had a story to tell that night, or because it was so hot that . . . All of them were valid reasons, and so he stayed at Auntie Suzanne's house and she just had to let her sister know, or one of his brothers or sisters would, or a cousin, who would tell his mother when it was time to eat, *no, he stayed at Auntie's house.* The actual count was done around the table, then the mamas knew who was eating at which house.

Hira and Tita followed the current events like a Western. Their games weren't about Apaches or Cheyennes any more, but instead the general, the colonel, the major, the captain, the officers, and the Bluecoats. Hira, Tita, and all the other kids, including Tom, lined up according to their respective ranks. Tita had chosen Frigate Captain

Ratsiraka because the rank was so intriguing. There wasn't a frigate captain in the cavalries that attacked Indian camps! They wondered what a frigate was. When they found out, Tita was beside himself, he said he'd seen one before, in port when he was in Diego-Suarez, the city where their mamas had grown up, he'd spent part of his life there too. Yeah, he would be the frigate captain! But when someone pointed out that he was more like a pirate with his wooden leg, then a fight broke out instantly. Tita was a force to be reckoned with, regardless of his disability. Hira jumped in to pull them apart. He hated fighting! Since he was the oldest one in the group, he quickly got the better of them. He had been named general in their game. But soon, he became colonel. Because in real life, *General* Ramanantsoa had handed power over to *Colonel* Ratsimandrava! Power had been demoted! The head of state was a colonel now, not a general! And so, on the very same day that Ratsimandrava became head of state, Hira became a colonel too, so he could still be the leader of their pack! So Hira repeated before his friends: *Tsy hiamboho adidy aho, mon Général!* On their field of play, of dust and sun: *I will not turn my back on my duties and responsibilities, General!* And there they stayed, for a long time, at 'tention!

They didn't believe it at first, when they heard the rumour. Ratsimandrava couldn't die after only six days! Then they heard he'd been assassinated, near Andohalo. In Ambohijatovo Ambony. At the roundabout going down to Faravohitra. In the city. They decided to make their way there to see for themselves. But should they go as Indians or Bluecoats? They had a vague sense that the Bluecoats were being pulled apart at the seams, so they'd have to be careful, plus, their mamas wouldn't be best pleased about them up and going into the city, and never, not in a million years, would the bus drivers let them aboard for an expedition! They held a war council and resolved to travel as Sioux. On foot. They would veer around, back behind the trees, through the bushes and backroads.

They quickly found out that banking on discretion had been the right choice. They saw three trucks of soldiers sweep into the development. Soon, the soldiers had set up a barricade on the road and a checkpoint for people coming in, and would not let anyone leave. Cars were turned around, men same as women. Hira analysed the situation and, with joint approval from Tita, they decided to go through the lavakas, the ones they called the caves.

Sneak in silence. Walk with steps that leave no trace. Breaths that make not the slightest breeze. Movements that suffer no hurry or haste. They set off. They slipped into the 'caves' as they'd never slipped before. One by one, no scree skidding loose. They had no need for speaking. Hira felt strong, filled with duty and responsibility. He couldn't afford to make any mistakes, or do anything wrong. Tita was walking in his footsteps, Tom, all their friends. But they would have to leave the 'caves' eventually, and take the road into the city. They had got around the first barricade at the top of the hill. Now they were in Andohamandroseza, they would have to make it across the road. They had the rice fields and the tail end of Lake Mandroseza in front of them, so they'd have to get back on the asphalt if they didn't want to trudge through the muck or swim across the lake! There was another barricade there, even more imposing. With tanks! It was the first time they'd seen a tank in real life. What should they do? Tita did not want to go back. Hira hesitated. There were tanks, after all, and he was the oldest of all the kids. And one of those kids was his little Tom! He could feel that this wasn't a game any more, wasn't a movie or any tale of legend. They had to go home. Their mamas were probably already looking for their brood. And as the eldest, he would get the most unforgettable walloping of his life if anything took a turn for the worse. But could a Sioux retreat? Could a Sioux listen to his mama? And could he, Hira, break the oath he'd made six days earlier? *Tsy hiamboho adidy aho, mon Général!* I will not turn my back, General, I will not run away, I will face it head on, General!

They could go a different way, but they would have to cut across to the other side of the road, run into the rice fields, climb out by the village, go through the woods and bamboo forest, come out at Ambatoroka Major Seminary. From there, they could make for Ambanidia, track south across the village, then go up the Andohalo steps, up to Andohalo itself, practically at the foot of the Queen's Palace, and head down towards Ambohijatovo Ambony, then they would finally reach the sharp bend, he would have to be the first down the slope, where the colonel's black Peugeot 404 had been riddled with bullets! Hira looked at his gang, they were scared to death and still they nodded. Hira whispered their mantra, *Maty dia maty, ny fasana ve no tsy ho hisy!* At my signal! Together they leapt onto the road. There was a flurry of activity from the soldiers who were posted a few metres away.

'Halt!'

And then a gun fired into the air! All the children froze in their tracks. They regrouped automatically. They were shaking. Someone had shot at them! They had caused a gunshot! Some of them were already crying, they'd peed their pants! Hira's heart was hammering in his chest, he noticed that Tom's hand was in his, he saw Tita standing tall over his lame leg. It was his pre-fight stance, Hira recognized it. That gave him incredible strength. He stood tall as well. He thought about a scene from *The Fall of the Roman Empire*: *we are in the arena, the lions are coming . . .*

An officer and some other soldiers were running towards them. Hira recognized the officer's rank: a lieutenant. Not some mere corporal who was only fit to bellow orders at a training exercise. So, this was serious. Very serious indeed.

'*Ho aiza?*'

The lieutenant's tone was clipped, and very cross.

Hira answered him.

'We just wanted to go over there.'

'Where, over there?'

'To play in the rice fields . . . '

'Absolutely not. You will return to your homes immediately.'

The lieutenant softened his tone as he noticed one of them shaking like a leaf.

'Where do you live?'

'Up there. In the development.'

'Up there?'

The lieutenant got angry again.

'Were you let through?'

Hira did not know how to lie.

'No, we saw it was being surrounded, so we went through the caves.'

The officer took out his walkie-talkie. They all stared at it, they'd never seen a walkie-talkie up that close before, either. It melted some of their fear, hardly any, but still . . . The lieutenant gave orders to make sure the 'caves' were also 'secured'.

'No one leaves the development! *Na zaza na lehibe!*'

When they heard the word zaza, they shivered. *Child.*

'You will return to your homes, you will use the road—there, you see? You will go up the road, the normal way, we will have you in our sights, you know that bullets can make it to the top of the hill, don't you? Go on up, now, and no running. You will walk at a normal pace. You will go back through the barricade and then you will each go back to your own house, you will not come outside again until further notice! There's a curfew in effect!'

He gave one more order through his walkie-talkie and said he was sending the children over.

'Now, get going!'

They wanted to run but remembered what the lieutenant had said, that bullets could reach the hilltops! Never before had it felt so gruelling to walk. Never had any hill ever been so steep. They didn't dare sneak one look behind them. They felt the barrel of the gun at their backs. They didn't dare talk, either. As though the tiniest word could blow through the barrel and force out a bullet. They hardly breathed. One of them almost said something, it might have been Njila or Ndrianja, he can't remember any more—it probably wasn't Ndrianja, because Ndrianja was younger than Tom, he was too little, he couldn't have been with them, so he's not sure why but in his mind Ndrianja is the one who let out a breathless moan. And suddenly they heard gunfire. They froze in place. The shots were coming from far away, the other side of the university—the hill they were climbing was by the outermost buildings in the university complex. Hira couldn't feel his leg any more, Tita seemed to be limping more heavily, and Tom, always the rebel, had let go of his hand, he was up at the front. Still they walked, still they did not run, above all they did not run. The gunfire continued further on. Njila, Ndrianja, whoever it was said it was coming from Ankatso, someone else was crying, insisting that it was actually coming from their development, they were going to die, they shouldn't go home. Hira drummed it into them: yes they should, they had to! *We can't stay out here in plain sight, we have to trust the lieutenant.* Hira felt like he was in a movie, in one of the stories he made up for his friends. That sentence stuck in his mind for a long time, a piece of fiction to replace the shock of reality, *we can't stay out here in plain sight, no, we have to trust the lieutenant.* They kept going. The gunshots did not stop. As they got closer to the top, they could pinpoint where the shots were coming from.

'It's over by Fort Duchesne, near Antanimora.'

Fort Duchesne was a garrison behind the university. Njila said that Colonel Brechard was down there.

'No, he's a general.'

'No, he's a colonel, because he doesn't like General Ramanantsoa, he wants to be general instead of the general.'

'Is this a war?'

Hira said no. 'In a war, everyone dies, and we're still alive, and there are still grasshoppers all along the side of the road!'

'What are you talking about grasshoppers for?'

Hira didn't know what to say. Aside from the gunfire, everything felt so peaceful, there was still sun, still wind, a light breeze, and the grasshoppers, yes, still there. War wasn't that. They'd made it to the top. The barricade opened. Hira noticed which armbands the soldiers were wearing. They said FRS. The Republican Security Force. The FRS let them through and they whooped with joy and scattered back into their own houses.

Weapons ruled the whole day long. Hira looked out the window from his parents' bedroom. Next to him were his brothers and sisters, each pressing their faces up against the glass in turn, searching for whatever there was to be found: a human being to match with the gunshots, any sight of this 'war'. But they didn't see anything. Just deserted streets and houses shut up tight. *Tsisy raha. Nothing! Tsisy n'inon'inona. Nothing at all.* When it was Hira's turn, he saw the vapour that was misting on the glass, steam from their breath, steam from their stress, because their papa wasn't there. They kept watch for his return. Hira hadn't seen when he'd left. Soldiers had got the orders that morning to collect their father. They'd taken him away. Hira couldn't figure out the connection between his father and what was happening, especially the gunfire. His father used the mouth of his body to speak, not the mouth of a gun or a rifle. He didn't have any guns anyway! Later, Hira found out that he'd been brought in under the orders of a high-ranking officer who was advocating for calm and restraint, his father spent hours talking to flaring tempers, students, ragtag groups who were ready to duke it out now that Ratsimandrava was dead, appealing to young people over the radio, on his show, convincing everybody that violence was not the solution. Later, Hira's father would tell him that the officer was General Gilles Andriamahazo, who in the process was named head of the Military Directorship that imposed martial law. Gilles Andriamahazo had fought in Germany during World War II, and he never would have wanted anything like that to happen on the island. Which was why he brought together eighteen officers, representing every force in the country. Which was why he did everything in his power to keep the island from igniting. He was the de facto leader of the country for five months before ceding power to another officer in the Military Directorship.

Hira could plainly see that their mama was worried. Beneath her calm exterior, she wasn't hiding her anxiety very well. The FRS was shelling Colonel Brechard's GMPs. It wasn't just gunshots any more, now there was heavy artillery that made the walls shake. That was alarming. If the walls were shaking here, what were the bombarded walls like? His father had screened war movies before and Hira thought back to the images of soldiers marching through the snow, being bombarded by Nazi planes, the French title was *Marcher ou mourir*, Walk or Die, it took place in Russia, the dead blanketed the ground, blood froze on the soldiers' faces. Hira was scared of the FRS. To him, the acronym sounded like efa resy, 'conquered already', it brought to mind soldiers who had nothing left to lose, who would slaughter everything in their final battle. Not so long ago, people had still been talking about May the 13th Square, about how the FRS committed a massacre by firing on the protesters. The FRS was everywhere!

Then, planes and helicopters flew over the development. They were all heading towards Fort Duchesne and Antanimora. Hira was listening to the radio, as was his mother. The radio said that rebels had taken control of the Antanimora camp, they'd liberated the prisoners from the adjacent prison. Everyone was to stay inside their homes. There was a curfew in effect!

Hira did not understand. Why had the country collapsed so suddenly into violence? Everything had seemed bright and beautiful to him before that day. He loved the sunset over Ambohipo, when the daystar bowed to shadows, a glowing red ring being eaten away in the rising of croaking toads and the clamouring of unseen creatures, he liked the silence of those parts. The gunshots, more sporadic now, had changed his landscape.

There was a curfew, and such an uncommon silence, and dogs who would not stop howling. All night long.

leave

Rotten Country

Setting: A public square of packed earth. Three or four military trucks. People dispersing. Returning. Leaving again. Usually in silence. Sometimes in a fit of anger, swiftly suppressed.

In the background: A sound like a whisper, like fear, like disbelief . . .

Scene: The soldiers. In the dusty square. In their playground. The soldiers, hauling off one of their fathers. A father that could have been his. The soldiers chain him to one of the long benches bolted into the truck. The father spots them watching. He shouts, Get out of here! The father stands. A soldier cracks a hammer over his skull.

That day, Hira knew he'd lost something: the beauty of believing in grown-ups, the comfort of letting adults carry him along.

That day, one of their fathers, a respectable man, a lehibe, a grown-up, ray aman-dreny, father-mother, parent, had been cussed out by a young soldier, his head struck with a hammer. It was beyond reason. That anyone could raise a hand against a good man. It was beyond reason. That a tool, which was meant to nail things together, could be used to hit a papa.

Action: Hira was petrified, he didn't know what movie he was in any more, he didn't know how to tell stories any more, how to make anything up, if he should tell his friends the story of this movie, some-where up in Ankatso, or more nearby, under the shade of the church pine trees, if he should build the suspense, he felt lost, like everything had gone rotten.

President Ratsimandrava's death,

Rotten.

The shooting that had followed, the dead, the disappeared, the rounded up, the chained together, the laughter of the ones who believed they'd been victorious, military and civilian, the shouts of triumph, the radio that suddenly railed against the enemies of the nation,

Rotten.

The words that were coming to tell the story,

Rotten.

The blood that he saw on the beat-up papa's face,

Rotten.

The words from the soldiers' mouths,

Rotten.

This country, such a beautiful country, which had collapsed so suddenly into this violence,

Rotten.

He went home, he got some paper, and he wrote. His first time writing with a pit in his stomach. His first time writing beyond just himself. His first time writing for a country he no longer recognized. He could not write in Malagasy. It had turned so rotten. He wrote in French. That felt rotten too, but it hurt less and the words were easier to accept.

Today, Hira does not recall what he put down on that paper, neither words nor story. He remembers only that he promised himself he would never show any of it to anyone else. He remembers only what paper he wrote on. It was a newspaper page from *Lakroan'i Madagascar*, The Cross of Madagascar. He didn't want people to be able to read it, not on a white page, nor a blackboard, nor the wall, nor the ground, he hid his writing between the lines of newsprint. He went back to his left hand, to make it even more unreadable.

He did that for a while, he wrote in secret. He said less and less. When his friends came around asking him to tell them the story of a movie, he would go, but he knew that was something different. Movie-storytelling was his gift to other people, movie-storytelling gave him a challenge, he had to pay close attention to his listeners so that he wouldn't lose them, so they stayed immersed in the story. Storytelling was speaking for others, not speaking for himself. So, he went back to his room, he wrote, he hid his writings under the mattress, behind a painting. One day, he peeled back the wallpaper, wrote behind it, and then glued it back in place with his saliva and a bit of sticky rice.

One time his mother came into his room, his heart plummeted, he hadn't heard her coming, he hurriedly flipped his paper over. His mother acted like she hadn't seen anything. He relaxed. His mother left. She returned a few moments later. She'd brought a notebook with her. She said to him: 'Here, this is our secret, you can write in it, no one will read it, not a soul.'

He took the notebook. He wrote.

A poem of love for his mother.

He didn't want to write for this rotten country.

He felt like he was leaving on a long, long journey, and he could not see the end.

TSIA

Hira liked to wake up at dawn. To feel the evaporating damp, the brisk wind that grips your lungs and makes you breathe deep, your mind surprised by the chill and responding with intelligence, sailing wide awake and clear-headed. He stepped outside, was quickly greeted by his dog Milou, a good girl with a pure white coat whom he'd stolen from the Four-Rooms neighbourhood, the rich part of the development where all the houses had four rooms—back then, it was a luxury! He and his Three-Rooms gang had launched a false attack, and while most of them were facing off in the streets and the gaps between buildings, Hira raced in and snatched the pup from her mother. By the time the Four-Roomers figured out their ploy, it was too late, Hira was already long gone, back at their basecamp. The Four-Roomers organized their own raids several times to get the dog back, but they were rebuffed every time, or they didn't find where the dog was hiding out. Hira never tied her up, he had taught her to crawl into a drainpipe every time something like that happened. Milou had stayed and grown up with Hira. Only once had the Four-Roomers succeeded in taking her— they'd committed treachery, everyone had been at school, and two at a time, they cut class and sauntered over to get her back, but later that day, Milou returned all on her own. Later on, she even snarled at them, they'd wasted their energy trying to bring her back. The Four-Roomers got tired of fighting and threw in the towel. The dog had made her own decision. Hira was her master and her friend.

And so, every morning at sunrise, Hira went out to run with Milou. That was how he saw the car. A black car with tinted windows, a driver in cap and uniform. And it parked by their house. The back door swung open and a man stepped out. Hira recognized him immediately, despite the pale dawn light. It was the frigate captain, Didier Ratsiraka. Out of uniform. Another man stepped out at the same time. Hira didn't know who that was. Together, they strode quickly up to the house, and Hira saw his father greeting them even before they'd knocked on the door or announced their arrival. They went inside.

Hira warned his dog not to make any noise, because she'd started growling at the driver in the car. He brought her through the backyard and, for once, leashed her to the medlar tree, telling her not to bark. Hira trusted her. Milou always obeyed him, even though he was young. Hira slipped softly through the kitchen door. The shower was across from there, Hira slid behind the curtain, back up against the wall, sitting on the ground, and listened. He heard only the frigate captain's voice. That was unusual: until then, no voice had ever dominated his father's. Hira was stunned. No voice had ever been the only one in that room. There were always many voices having conversations, going back and forth, being raised or lowered, but now, his father said not a word. He listened. The frigate captain went on and on until suddenly, he stopped. The first silence, broken by a question to his father: *Eny sa tsia?* Second silence, a very long silence, until Hira finally heard his father's voice: TSIA.

NO.

Third silence, lifted quickly with the sounds of chairs they pushed back, the door they opened, the house they left. Hira dashed out the back again so he could see the car leaving. He saw that Milou had almost got free from her leash. He barely managed to throw his arms around her neck and keep her from barking and chasing after the two men. She didn't want to obey him and tried to squirm free. Hira held on tight and didn't let go until he heard the car doors shut. Milou growled and ran towards the car, but it was already driving away. It disappeared around the buildings, with the little white dog in hot pursuit. It was 5 a.m.

Hira went quietly back into the house. His parents hadn't noticed he was there. He caught fragments of what his father was saying, anger bursting out, his voice cracking: 'That fool is trying to walk all over us! I will not join his party!'

Some days later, on 15 June 1975, the frigate captain was appointed President of the Supreme Revolutionary Council and head of the government. Hira realized—to some extent—that his father had made a powerful enemy by telling him TSIA, for in the months that followed the appointment, the same voice he'd heard at his house posed the same question to the entire nation: 'ENY sa TSIA?' 'Yes or No' to the new Constitution? The 'ENY's took it handily, and on 30 December 1975, the Second Republic was established: *Ny Repoblika demokratika Malagasy*.

His father joined forces with his Southern friends in the Vonjy Iray Tsy Mivaky party, In Unity, Our Aid: One Madagascar, Indivisible . . .

Hira didn't know then that his father had been the first to take a stand, before anyone else, against the future dictator.

TSIA.

Revolution

A few months later, a structure was erected in the middle of the dusty square. Tranompokontany, they called it. The community house. Where the civil registry was issued. Where foodstuffs were rationed: rice, oil, sugar, or salt. Hira saw Anja again, by the structure. Anja, who didn't talk much any more. Anja, who they didn't see much any more.

Revolution, they kept hearing on the radio. Revolution . . .

That square, where it was now forbidden to play, where they hauled in the traitors to the nation. Traitors for having sold rice! Oil! Sugar! Salt! Only the state cooperatives were authorized for that. The socialist revolutionary cooperatives! The traitors had to stay there, on their feet, tied up, waiting for the soldiers' truck to come and load them up.

Today, Hira remembers, Anja, he remembers. He remembers your father in particular. You were beautiful, Anja. You were sweet. Your mother cried like a madwoman as she followed the soldiers. Your father bowed his head. He looked down at his hands. Chained together! The crowd grew in your wake, saying not a word.

More dust. Red dust lifted by the breeze . . .

Hira remembers your mother, Anja, he does not forget. She was a tall woman. And she was bent, broken. Like a stalk of bamboo. Clean break, sharp split. Crippling. Raw. People distanced themselves from your family. You didn't go outside any more. But did anyone come looking for you after that? To play? To dance? You, who often danced beneath the moon at twilight. With the rest of them. With hands clapping, with laughter keeping time.

Hira would often pass by your street—to get those abhorrent doses of quinine from the Red Cross, or to prowl around stealing cobs from the neighbouring corn fields—and his thoughts went out to you, he begrudged your father for daring to commit such an act! Daring to sell rice and oil! You, Anja, you were his heart's first ache . . .

How could that story work? Before, he could have told you about the undine trapped in the dew. Before, he could have told you about the dragonfly in the night that transforms its wings into magnificent clothes, revealing itself to be a woman of infinite beauty. Before, he could have told you all of it straight from his mouth. But ever since that time, he has known that less beautiful things exist in this world. It is his share of the loss—for everyone in the country had lost something. Even if other people didn't know it, Hira did, he was painfully aware of it, so painfully aware.

It was around that time that he started going to roam the hills alone. Coiling up inside his feelings. His small steps took him up to the hilltops. Short of breath, his chest on fire, the gusting wind sheared through him as if through an old tree. Blossoming again. Head swimming. He soaked uninhibited in the vast solitude of that place. He found himself. He was not of the world being formed. He was not of those unceasingly hailed revolutions. He was not of a world where the eyes alone lived. Eyes that stared and did not understand. Eyes that only reflected images in gossamer, or a bright glare. In his mind, he was not of his parents' world. He was not of his brothers' world. Nor his friends'. Nor anyone else's. He was of that world where magic was the twin to reality, where stories became alive, where lives became a story. This new world was slowly killing his.

He understood it all too well. His world was retreating, concealing itself in silence. The solitude was so vast, and now, it was all his life was. He longed to dissolve into it and not remember any more. For it was all forgetting, endlessly undone. He was stunned by time passing, why did nothing ever stay? He felt like he'd been made from whole cloth, he had nothing to change. So then why was everything around him changing? Hira could obviously see that even his body was developing, but he had such an acute awareness of his presence in the world. He *was*. He understood that verb: *to be*. But the verb did not exist in his native language. It was a paradox. To see himself in a foreign verb, from a language that he couldn't quite bear to place in his mouth, not yet. He was, and he grew every day in studying the world around him. He often likened himself to a mango pit: if he was the pit, then life and time and the world were the flesh ripening around him. He reasoned that death would be like removing the soft fruit, planting yourself somewhere else and becoming a tree again. Living beings are just the fruit, the dead become the roots and trees.

He lay down in the tall grass, disappearing into a mass of ferns. No one saw him, nor guessed he was there. Sometimes people passed by. He stopped breathing, stopped moving. He knew he was like the grass-hoppers and all the other insects clinging to the grass. There. Without being seen.

From the church at the top, the development stretched down the hillside. He could see the buildings in your compound, Anja, slumping down every tier towards the rice fields and the traditional homes in the surrounding villages, clay walls and thatched roofs, red laterite of the low walls that date back to the kings, humble relics of the past that are still standing, here and there. The villages were called Ankatso, Andohaniato. Further east was Ampahateza and Ambohipo-Tanàna. And beyond that, Ambohimanambola and the Ikopa River, winding away like a long snake and its railroad double. Sometimes, he walked that far. You never wanted to go along with him, Anja. Never. But Ambohimanambola was the limit of what he dared explore. Beyond, the hills closed around Alasora, and then the roadway led out to the province of Tamatave. He was stretched out on his stomach, hands under his chin, chewing on a wild anise stalk, dreaming of lands farther off, the sea, the shores, the beaches, when one day he noticed a multi-coloured plastic bag. He crawled over to get it, stuck his hand inside, found a sticky nothingness. He pulled his fingers out, red with viscous blood, blood of a liquid-child, flesh of a clandestine abortion.

He ran, off the hill, through the woods, crying, stumbled through railway ballast, almost fell in the rice fields around the tracks. He washed his hands in the river water, for hours. He crouched on the bank of the Ikopa, washed his hands, then climbed up to the railway, sat down on the track, spread his hands in the sun to dry, then went back down to the river, the washwomen mocked him, they sang a song for him about the little boy who never thought he was clean enough so he decided to go to the white moon, next to his adoptive mother, the moon's wife, and he vanished forever, now he only twinkles, some-times, his buttock agleam with milky skin. Hira did not listen to them, he called silently for you, Anja, but you did not come. He tried to forget the liquefying foetus and its tepid putrescence, and did not leave until much much later, when one of the washwomen told him that his mama would start to worry. *Go on now, your hands are clean.* That sensation, eternity, time unmoving, it was the first time he'd felt that. It was the first time he'd wanted things to change, wanted to move on, but there was no moving on: there was still the foul warmth of rot on his hands.

When he got back home, he was shocked and confounded that no one knew what had happened to him. He wondered if you were aware of it too, Anja. As if it would be only natural for you and his family both to know everything that happened to him. His mother gave him her usual kiss, told him to go wash his hands. He ran off, elated. As if those words had been all that he'd needed. He picked up the soap. Scrubbed for a long time. A very long time. He went back to his mother and showed her his hands: 'Yes, child, they're clean!' His heart leapt with joy. They were clean. Clean.

Hira began to visit the hills less often, leaving his brothers and friends to get drunk on berry liquor and savour the ripe scent of blueberries. His brothers went to the hills and brought the fruits back by the bagful, to crush and poke a hole in. They sucked on the bags like wine-heavy breasts. And waved him over. And urged him to drink his fill. He stared at them as if they were suckling from the liquid-child. As if they were prolonging the fetid drainage of dead flesh. He answered them sharply: 'I don't drink!'

The leaves in those hills rustled, masked the violence unfolding around them. Oh Anja, you who had felt that violence in your father's arrest and disappearance, was it truly the fruits of an abortion that Hira had found in the plastic bag?

Organ trafficking, he would later think, foetus trafficking, child trafficking.

Vazahas rip out hearts, Vazahas abduct children. Do you remember, Anja? All of you in the development would scatter at the sight of a single Westerner. Their smiles were those of madmen, their eyes thirsting and bright.

Still, your fear of Vazahas was nothing compared to your fear of the spirits who filled the Ankatso hills. People in the development always cautioned you not to infringe any of the customs and prohibitions that concerned the village: it was fady to point your finger at their tombs, fady to put a foot wrong as you tread their ground—what did it mean to put a foot wrong? It was a terrible fady because you didn't really know what that meant, to put a foot wrong, every step you took became suspect, but most of all it was fady to utter the word that might vex the spirits. What word? You didn't know . . .

All of you kept silent when you went through the village, barely skimming the ground for fear of a wrong foot. It was always a huge relief to crest the top of the hill. The village ended right where the incline grew steep. At the very top, you turned your eyes to the east. Even more hills, stretching away. Far as the eye can see. Horizon creeping over the blue mounds. Earth's infinite reach into vertigo.

It was also around that time that Hira started to push his solitary rambling past the Ambohimanambola swamp, all the way to the rocky hill. That hill was Ngita, as you called it, Ngita-of-the-kinky-hair. To get there, you had to go through the rice fields and embankments, to the fallow land where a few skinny zebus grazed, and finally the swampland where the rushes concealed the depth of the water. The ground gradually softened to a slippery mud where plentiful aquatic plants intertwined. That was the start of La Ngita's realm, where you had to remember to make an offering. Hira usually laid down a candy shard, crystallized honey or sugarcane, water set in sweetness or rock that your mouth could melt. Here, they said, La Ngita had succumbed. Ngita with the kinky hair, a Vazimba queen who'd been conquered and expelled by the new princes with light complexions and smooth hair. The water had carried her body and laid it on the other side of the dead leaves. The whole of her body vanished below the mass of vegetation. The day went away. The night fell. The morning dew soaked the leaves and crystallized: a sacrosanct tomb of quartz, a blessing of rock and stone. Today, through the rock, you can still make out the veins of leaves, the breath of wind that transformed their jumbled heap into a twisting motif. Leaves fell on the tomb still, more leaves, more days, more nights. They say that the tomb extended over seven layers in all, and as many towering rocks. And so, La Ngita became the hill. And so, the entire hill is La Ngita's domain. Hira climbed only with a racing heart, his mind tormented by that queen and her strange destiny. Anja, you know it too well, you would never defy the story and put your foot wrong there. The hill was only a pile of rocks, dizzying debris of minerals where the sun came to collapse. Hira stretched out, his belly an offering of touch, of memory. There, he cast off his skin, the skin of a child, and stepped into the flesh of a poet. The child was dead, and its corpse none other than the poet.

Anja, he wrote poems to you.

taken

The Revolutionary Women

His mother brought him along to a mass meeting of the Revolutionary Women. It was the first time that Hira had seen such a massive room, it looked even bigger than the Rex, the movie theatre in central Antananarivo. There were other kids there, other sons and daughters of Revolutionary Women. Everyone wore a red scarf knotted at their neck. Then they sang the anthem of the youth. Then they sang the anthem of the oppressed. Then they sang the anthem of non-aligned nations. Then Hira learned a new word, *azimuth*, as in 'all azimuths', all-around, full-on. From that day forward, the nation had to be firing in every direction, striking from every angle. Not to kill, but to forge connections and liberate themselves from colonial oppression and French rule. All azimuths, to compel a just and balanced relationship with all countries of the world and all ideologies of humankind. Hira was positioned up by the stage with the other children, he had just won a trivia contest—he'd been answering what he thought were preliminary questions just a few hours earlier, he hadn't realized it was already the final round.

He looked out at the crowded room, packed with mamas. Auntie Tsontso was there, tucked way in the back, so proud of him that she wouldn't stop crying. It was confounding to Hira. Why didn't she spill the same tears when he answered one of those big questions at home, or when he got high marks at school? He'd done the same thing here, and she was crying?

All at once, the crowd stood up and broke into thunderous applause. Stepping into the aisle was the wife of the new President of the Republic, Céline Ratsiraka. Followed by several other women, about fifteen in all. Hira's mother was in the third row behind the First Lady. Beautiful. Always so beautiful. She'd swept her hair back into an elegant bun and wore a marvellous dress. Pastel flowers, and her red scarf. The Revolutionary First Lady waved at all the children. Hira got to see her up close because he was the last in line, being the smallest and youngest one there. Céline Ratsiraka paused in front of him, asked if he was the son of Marie, it was always funny to hear that, yes of course he was, but it always sounded like the son of Mary when people said that, and he was not Jesus. Marie was just his mother's name.

'I heard you were born on the 26th of June?'

'*Eny tompoko.*'

'Then you are a Revolutionary child for certain.'

'*Eny tompoko.*'

The Revolutionary First Lady stroked the top of his head—his Afro had been cut the day before, his hair was all plastered down and he hated it, now he looked like that numbskull from Les Surfs who'd stripped the protest out of 'If I Had a Hammer', who sang that if he had a hammer he'd hammer stuff day and night, if he had a hammer he'd want for nothing else, by the love of his father, his mother, his brothers and sisters! If Hira had a hammer, he'd cast it deep into the swamp so that no one could use it to smash in papas' heads any more. At dawn, before leaving, his mother had washed him herself. She'd daubed him with perfume—he hated wearing perfume, the same perfume as his mother. Vola had come to his rescue, laying it on him that he shouldn't be a melon-head, and that any time someone asked him a question he should just answer: '*Eny tompoko.*' Hira abhorred the phrase. He knew perfectly well that it wasn't meant to be taken literally—'Yes, my master'—but instead considered a standard reply. Even though tompoko did mean 'my master', even though Tompo did refer to 'God the all-powerful master and keeper' before whom you grovel and lick the soles of his feet, that was no reason to feel like a slave. Vola gave him a kôfy on top of his noggin, a gentle thwack with her middle finger curled up like a stone: 'Got it? Again!' '*Eny tompoko.*'

A young woman in traditional dress came up behind the Revolutionary First Lady.

'For you, our contest winner, here is a Revolutionary prize.'

It was a large red parcel with green ribbons. Fairly heavy. The women went up to the stage and began to speak, one after another, his mother still in the third row. His mother talked about children's health, anti-malarial quinine schedules, disease prevention through hygiene— scrubbing the entrance to the house, making sure that little ones have clean hands, not just before they eat but as soon as they get home from school, thoroughly washing lettuce and greens—and a reminder to bring children to the Revolutionary Clinic or the Red Cross once a week, no need to wait until they get sick, just remember to bring along your Revolutionary Booklet and record the weekly check-ups. 'Soon, the Revolution will set up these clinics across the whole country, everywhere, out to the farthest-flung corners of the island. Colonization makes these public claims to the world, claims of bringing health to the people—is that really the truth? Where are the medical centres they're so proud of? Where are the hospitals? And the rare ones that do exist, who do they benefit? From now on, every Malagasy, whether rich or poor, from the central highlands, the south, north, east, or west, will receive attentive care from the Revolutionary State. So these things are spoken, so they will be done. *Ho ela velona anie Madagasikara Malala.* Long live our beloved Madagascar!'

Hira, and all the rest of the children, had been standing for the entire meeting. Nothing else held his interest after his mother's speech. The large parcel he'd received was weighing him down. It was out of the question to open it in front of everybody at the meeting or set it down on the ground. Hira had been given strict instructions to not lean against the wall but instead stand up straight, tall and proud, like a Revolutionary child should be. He struggled to hide how exhausted he was, but the red scarf was starting to choke him, and his arms could no longer take the weight of his gift. He was really thirsty. They'd just made it forbidden to drink Coca-Cola, the imperialist beverage. Hira wanted to have some so badly. It wasn't that he hated Caprice limonade or anything, but he just liked Coke better. Caprice was made by the La Star distributor group, which the state had acquired a stake in, much like it was nationalizing all of the country's largest businesses. All thirsts now had to be quenched with Caprice, the most refreshing of all the Revolutionary limonades. It was a lesson that Hira had learned by heart: 'Only through the Malagasization of the culture and economy will our country truly be independent.'

They were brought home in an official motorcar. Hira was squeezed between his mother and Auntie Tsontso. His mother explained that his father was now a very important governmental figure, he was 'Number 2' in the Vonjy Iray Tsy Mivaky party and chief advisor to the Minister of Foreign Affairs.

'He'll be going to Mauritius and the Seychelles tomorrow, to make the Indian Ocean a region of true peace, camaraderie, and solidarity, he'll ask the Americans to take their weapons and leave, he'll ask the French to take their battleships and pull out of the zone, he'll ask the Russians to stop roaming around the area with their submarines—he's going to negotiate for all of that, together with Mauritius and the Seychelles!'

'Is he going to Réunion, too?'

'No. Réunion is a slave to France.'

'Then we should liberate Réunion.'

His mother explained that from then on, he was no longer allowed to leave the house by himself, same for his brothers and sisters. There were people who wanted to sabotage the Revolution and they might go after the leaders' children.

'Trust Ralita, he will be your driver and bodyguard.'

The driver glanced back and nodded. Hira took the opportunity to speak up.

'But Mama, I don't want Ralita to drive me to Revolutionary Women any more.'

'Why is that?'

'I'm sick of saying *Eny tompoko!* and I hate all those lips kissing my cheeks.'

Auntie Tsontso burst out laughing and Hira's mother gave a hint of a smile. That was so frustrating, he was being very serious. His mother didn't bring him along any more, unless he wanted to go. He went maybe three or four more times, he's not sure. At any rate, with all his brothers and sisters, his mother had plenty of options to keep her company. And Nannie, the oldest, was always keen to go. Already a Revolutionary Woman in the making!

Hira opened his parcel. It was the *Complete Works of Kim Il-sung*. In twenty-five volumes. And tied together with the first volume, on the very top, a *Boky Mena*. The Red Book of the Malagasy Revolution.

Rasoa Marguerite

Hira had met his paternal grandmother Rasoa Marguerite before, but this was the first time he had seen her at his own house, in their home. She was so small. So simple. So rustic. She pretended not to be amazed by any of it. Not the hot plate. Nor the iron. Nor the telephone, which terrorized her. How could a voice be in there? Hira explained that it was like the radio. 'The voice is inside of it.' 'No,' she said, 'it's not the same, you don't have a conversation with the radio, but with the telephone it feels like people are right next to you, but they aren't actually there. You can't be present and absent at the same time. How are you able to hear people on the other side of the island, or across the seas? Tell me that!' When night fell, she was reluctant to turn on the lights. She said that there was always some way for them to see even without sunlight, *The moon shines, and the stars, and when there's no moon or stars, then you have speech and perspectives that can show you things. And if not, then ha! You should sleep.* She huffed at the tap for spilling water out unnecessarily. *A handful of water is more than enough to wash your face, three or four more to wash your whole body. The tap wastes so much water, where does it all go?* Hira explained all of it but she was never convinced.

Rasoa Marguerite always brought them cartons of brown sugar. Flutes made of brown sugar, whistles made of brown sugar, cigarettes made of brown sugar. Little brown-sugar cars. Hira loved it, and as he was sucking on his cigarette, his grandmother told him that finally she'd been reunited with her son, and he'd given her such wonderful grandchildren. Then she talked about other things. In Tsimihety, which Hira could barely understand. Whenever her daughter-in-law came into the room, she would stop talking and shut herself off. Hira thought there was something going on between the two of them, even though his mother was being even kinder than she usually was. Rasoa Marguerite was always throwing a fit. None of the new dresses were any good. None of the food had enough piment. None of the blankets were warm enough for the cold land of Antananarivo. It boggled her mind to be handed a fork: 'This spoon has been ripped open! The rice will fall right through!' What did they want her to do? Eat like a little kid and make a mess? 'That's how they fed my husband shards of glass!' she muttered. Looking at Hira: 'Your grandfather!'

Hira always left the room when he saw Rasoa Marguerite shaking her head to everything that his mother offered her. Hira did not understand. One day, around noon, she made a big scene and threatened to leave. She packed up her bag, rejected the suitcase—'A coffin that white folks want to make us carry during our lifetimes!'—and started off by herself. Nannie was going to go after her and beg her to come back to the house—she and Rasoa Marguerite were like two peas in a pod—but their mama held her back: 'She won't get far, Mampikony is 700 kilometres away, and your father's coming home soon, he'll see her on the road, he'll bring her back!' Twenty minutes later, there she was, leaning all her weight on her tall son, who even carried her over a broken gutter slab. Rasoa Marguerite was beaming, and Hira's mother simply smiled. Hira thought that he could go down the road like that too, and his father would surely find him someday. What a move by the old dame!

One night, she told Hira this story. *Out by Port Bergé, there is a village. Lemaitso. In this village, there is a boa constrictor. In this boa's stomach, there is a precious stone. In this precious stone, there is a green light that makes the area around it glow. And in that area, there are animals for hunting. Every night, the boa vomits up the stone, it illuminates the entire forest like a green moon. Then the boa sets off on the hunt. Nothing can escape it. Nothing can resist it. Crocodiles cower on the river bottom, hiding in the very heart of the mud, but the green light can pierce the deepest mud, and the boa dives down. The mightiest of all crocodiles is swallowed up in a single gulp. You are far, far away, by Mampikony, my village, you see the forest pulsing like a heartbeat. You are far, far, far away, by Mandritsara, your grandfather's town, this light twinkles softly like a star on the ground. No one has ever located that stone. No one has ever laid hands on it. The stone is extremely valuable. You could be richer than the richest king of all the kings of the Earth, all you have to do is cover it with a hat made from the hide of Lesambilo, the handsomest of all the zebus with forehead stars, the mightiest of all the zebus with tumbledown humps, the blackest of all the zebus with black coats, then the stone's green light will not get out from under that hat, the hat with nary a crack, the hat of the night of nights, then the boa will not find the path back to its lair and will die at the first light of day. Vazahas have tried to locate the stone, they saw the green light in the forest and tried to get there in a helicopter. The helicopter fell. The explorers' bodies were never found.* Then, enigmatically, she concluded: *But I have found my own precious stone again.* And, to Hira's stupefaction, she added: *In the hands of your mama!*

1976

On Friday afternoons school let out early, and Hira would race to church to play the piano. He'd got hooked on Ray Charles and the blues. A fascinating show had come on the radio, a man named Latimer Rangers retracing the journey of American Blacks through song. Hira played the music by ear. Then, very quickly, started improvising. He'd never taken piano lessons, no one had showed him how any of it worked. His only audience was an old woman, Rafotsy, the church's caretaker. Rafotsy didn't care about his music. She grumbled when he got there. She grumbled when he left. There was only a short time for Hira to play between the end of school and when the priest showed up. The priest always kicked him out, he disapproved of Hira not try-ing to learn the liturgical music. Hira didn't like religious music. Eventually the vicar put a padlock on the lid of the keyboard. Hira didn't know what to say. He hung his head and started home. And then he ran into his father coming out of one of the Four-Rooms houses, residence #1 in a development of five hundred and eleven. 'He's going to have to move,' his father said. 'Soon, we'll be living here.'

They were going to leave Three-Rooms for Four-Rooms. Hira was happy, to a certain extent. He loved his neighbourhood, it felt like he was betraying all of his friends and joining up with the enemy. He couldn't stand the Four-Roomer snobs, and now he would be one of them. Plus, they would be taking ownership of residence #1—the residence that had been given to the first President of the Republic, Philibert Tsiranana. Could there be any greater sign of snobbery? Residence #1, President Tsiranana? Hira's father brought him back to Three-Rooms and told him, as if it were the most natural thing in the world, that he'd no longer be working as chief advisor to the Minister of Foreign Affairs because he'd 'been resigned', along with the Minister he'd advised. They'd both had the audacity to go against President Ratsiraka on the Mahajanga situation. His father said nothing more than that. Hira had no idea what the Mahajanga situation was but wouldn't dare ask his father. When he got home, he went to ask Auntie Tsontso. His aunt closed her eyes for a long time, gave a heavy sigh, and told him not to think about it any longer.

Hira snapped.

'How am I supposed to stop thinking about something I don't know anything about? Tell me what's going on and then I can stop thinking about it!'

'You're too young. Although it was a child who started it all. It wasn't the kid's fault, but God in heaven, everything happened because of what he did.'

Hira didn't learn anything more. Outside, Tom was shouting for someone to come fix his slingshot. Hira went over and tried to stop thinking about Mahajanga. Hira worked on convincing all his friends that they should aim their slingshots at streetlights instead of birds. For two reasons, actually: because the streetlights didn't move, and then if they shot out the bulbs, they could play kick the kapôka after nightfall. Tom took a few shots but he didn't have the patience for it, he liked riding bikes better, and vines strung between a pair of trees, he liked adrenaline, jumping off of huge rocks, climbing up the walls in caves. Hira thought about the Mahajanga kid again. What could he possibly have done?

That night, he went back to his father and broached the subject.

'Papa, what did he do?'

'He didn't do anything, he was just being a kid. In Fifio, none of our houses have latrines inside, our neighbourhoods are still very poor in Manjarisoa. You know where Fifio is? No? It's just an empty space, a lot of kids play there. The little boy had slipped away from his older brothers and sisters, he went poop right outside the door at a Comorian's house. The Comorian got angry and smeared the kid's face with the poop. The kid was a Betsirebaka child. You can't do that to a Betsirebaka child. It's fady. But it's fady for everyone, we cannot blame a young child for going poop wherever if we do not have latrines in our own homes, if we do not teach children where and when to go. There was no reason for the man to do that. The Betsirebakas demanded redress as is the custom, one or two zebus for a sacrifice, and prayers to the ancestors. The Comorians agreed. But, we don't know why, other Betsirebakas rejected the agreement between the two families. Other Southern folks decided to turn on the Comorians. The man who'd smeared the child's face had been arrested. People went looking for him at the police station. The police refused to hand him over. So the crowd forced their way into the station. That's how the massacre began. The police were stretched too thin. Reinforcements came the next day. But there were certain things. Law enforcement could not shoot at Malagasys. But we Malagasys, we killed many people. Truly, so many people. For two days and one night, we killed anyone from the Comoros, from Anjouan, Grande Comore, Maore. Houses were set aflame. Children, women were hacked into pieces, Betsirebakas surrounded the city, in Morafeno, L'Abattoir, Manga, Tsararano, the Comorians couldn't escape, the bodies were thrown into a mass grave, in the cemetery in Tanimasaja. Yet, they are our relatives. We have had children with them. We have married their wives, and they ours. You could call them a sister ethnicity. But we massacred them anyway. I went there with the Minister. I did a flyover with the Comorian ambassador. Up above

Analalava, he pointed down: "Look! That's my neighbourhood, I was born there!" He was speaking Malagasy, speaking like us, he is one of us. I wrote the report and the Minister approved it. The Minister asked me: "You take responsibility for this?" I did. The Minister signed the report. The President read it in front of us. He didn't say anything. He looked at both of us, the Minister and I. "Allegedly, there were fewer deaths." That's what he had heard. I replied that there had probably been many more. The President signed the report, which meant that Madagascar acknowledged the facts before all the nations of the world. But I knew he was also signing a declaration of war against the Minister and I. We had killed our brothers. We had to compensate them. But could that truly be compensated? We had to have a trial. To try those responsible. How can we say that we condemn colonial massacres if we do not take responsibility for our own acts of violence? How could we forget so soon? My report was sent to the UN, which issued a condemnation of the island. We should have acknowledged it immediately. We should not have delayed, but everyone had been satisfied with the report. After the massacre, in agreement with the Comorian government, we sent over ten thousand Comorians back home. We said "back home", but these people are not Comorian, they are Malagasy, like us, and have been for several generations. Many who boarded the Sabena plane have never seen the Comoros Islands. Many of them do not speak Comorian. What will they do there? What is this gift we have given the Comoros, just after they have gained their independence? It's only been a little more than a year, and we throw this at them? The further inquiry that I had recommended in the report never happened. And when the Minister and I pushed for it, on the grounds that those who had died were also ours, they were Malagasy like us despite having Comorian origins, then lo and behold, we were "resigned". Now I'm the director of SEIMAD, I've been appointed to head up buildings and zoning even though I have no experience in that field, I'm a historian, a sociologist, my area of expertise is international relations, or domestic affairs, or youth, or culture, but they put me here, to silence me. They told me that by authoring that report, my work was complete. It's out of my hands now. But I'll show them, I can do good work at SEIMAD, too.'

How many times had Hira seen kids doing their business anywhere they wanted? A common sight. Almost natural. Were adults just that crazy, that such a minor thing could lead to a massacre? The Comorians were saying two thousand dead. Malagasys were suggesting about a hundred, maybe two or three, the executioner does not count the dead, we know that.

Hira's father set his housing plan into action, to build thirty thousand units per year. Houses with toilets. So little kids didn't have to poop wherever. Houses with water and sewer hook-ups. Houses for folks in poverty, which they could own outright after a period of twenty or thirty years, depending on the rent structure. He put architects to work. He created jobs for gardeners, for maintenance workers, for watchmen. He provided incentives for property managers. He reorganized all the relevant departments. He built student housing in the 67 Hectares, a stretch of terraced rice fields that had turned into a neighbourhood and kept the name ever since. And quickly turned the student housing over to the residents. He built units in Diego-Suarez, Tamatave, Mahajanga. He built lecture halls at the University of Ankatso. And as the student population exploded, he had 'prefabs' brought over from the Soviet Union: temporary buildings that unfortunately have lasted until today, forty years later, still pending government funding for more permanent structures.

Hira didn't know if he felt happy or upset when the Caterpillars showed up in Ankatso. The bulldozers felled the pine forest where they usually played in just a few days. But it didn't matter, they soon found a new game: every gang in the development came to face up against the Caterpillars, they rolled underneath them like in the movies where invincible Soviet soldiers roll under Nazi tanks. The machines moved slow. The challenge was to jump out from the side of the road and slide under the cab. Hira did it three times. More than anyone else. After a while, the drivers didn't stop driving any more, they were perhaps just careful not to suddenly turn the steering wheel, they crawled along straight ahead, moving and levelling all the dirt.

Hira watched as the 'prefabs' shot up from the ground in Ambohitsaina, the common name for the University of Ankatso. Every night, the engineers came to their house to consult with his father and deliver their status reports. It was very strange for Hira to see his father giving orders to white people, even if they were only Soviets.

As for the Comorians, Hira didn't think too much more about it, except when someone would ask him if he didn't happen to be from Anjouan, perhaps. Weirdly, he always answered: 'No, but I'm from Mahajanga, like my father.' Whoever it was would get flustered and walk away. Did they know what had happened in Mahajanga on 19, 20, and 21 December?

Later on, Hira learned that it had also been a Malagasy king who sold Mayotte to France: King Andriantsoly, on 25 April 1841. Who cares about that? Here on Malagasy soil?

DGID

His father experienced regular 'disappearances'. He would only reappear two or three days later, brought back in a black car, shown all the way to his door by the driver and the bodyguard. The two lackeys wore fancy shiny black shoes, they would not say goodbye as they left. They were DGID. *Direction Générale des Investigations et de la Documentation*. Research and Investigative Services Management. Run by the nefarious Raveloson Mahasampo. He was married to the Revolutionary First Lady's sister. Every time his father 'went away' like that, his mother would meticulously apply her makeup, wear her nicest dress, call for Ralita, and they'd head out in their stalwart 4L to see

'Céline', the leader of the Revolutionary Women, and incidentally her friend. 'Céline' would talk to 'Didier'. And Ratsiraka would give the order to release the big mafiloha—the hard-head, his father's sobriquet in the presidential palace. And if 'Céline' couldn't do it, his mother would go to see a man called General Trozona, the 'whale'.

His mother told all her children they were never to go with the DGID: 'You'll recognize them! They're always in a black 404 with tinted windows. They wear nice suits, and nice shoes, and they're extremely polite, you must never go with them.'

Hira'd had enough of Ralita. Always there to remind him of what his mother had said. Always there in his beat-up 4L. Hira was in Year Seven. He liked the freedom of having several teachers, escaping the tyrannical reign of a single instructor. He liked the schedules where no one started or got out at the same time, unlike in primary school. He liked all of it, but there was one thing he was ashamed of. Being the son of a director and going home in an old 4L whose passenger door didn't shut any more. He had to hold the door under his arm. The 4L would always stall partway up the hill as it was climbing to Andohalo. That was where he, his brother, and his sister attended secondary school, near Minister Sibon Guy's villa. An incredible serviceman, quite handsome in his white naval uniform. Sibon Guy was from Diego-Suarez just like his mother, a very close friend of his mother's. There were some nice cars parked inside the residence. And Hira saw all of it, every time he went to school. They had to drive past there. No way around it. Hira didn't understand why his father only had that lousy 4L, and why they didn't live in a villa but instead had stayed in Four-Rooms—granted, in *Number One* (the gang had bestowed the English name upon it), but Four-Rooms all the same. There were seven of them now, seven brothers and sisters, plus Vola and the various cousins who passed through. And Vola herself had just given birth to a red-faced baby girl, Freda, a lot of people in the development thought that Freda was Nannie's daughter, or their mama's youngest, Vola was much too young to be able to take care of her daughter. Hira was feeling more and more cramped. He often needed to be alone to write. So he'd run off after class. He'd give Ralita the slip and go sit by the cliffs in Ampahamarinana, where the queen that they called cruel had thrown Christians over the edge, enshrouded in a wickerwork mat. Hira waited until the sun set over Lake Anosy's black angel, until jacaranda purple melded into the dark of night-time leaves, night-time leaves or the wings of the last birds on the lake.

Coming out of class, at four o'clock, Hira saw a 404 parked in front of the school gates. The car door opened for him and he saw black shoes. His mother's words immediately popped into his head but the man said that Ralita wasn't coming today, that they would bring him home. Hira jumped in the car without another thought. It was the first time he'd been in that kind of 404. Leather interior, an unfamiliar scent. It smelled of new. Hira had the sudden realization that the 4L gave off sweat and rust, it stank of petrol and exhaust, the 4L carried outside sounds and smells inside of it, if a mango vendor went by, the smell was in the car, a cracked slab of concrete over the gutter and the shit was in the car. There was none of that in the 404. It had the same smell all the time. It was pleasant. The same sound, too. Silence, actually, with only the gentle hum of the motor. The driver saw how surprised Hira was. He put on the *cassette radio*. Astounding. Hira had known that it was possible to listen to the radio in a car, but putting in a cassette tape, he was completely blown away by that. The 404 was gliding along the road like an iron smoothing a shirt. Not a single bump. Hira wondered if it was the same road. He looked. It was the same road.

The car slowed down in Ambatoroka, near the French secondary school. The bodyguard turned to face him.

'You see that house?'

'Yes.'

'That's the house your father doesn't want you to have.'

Hira could not find an answer.

'You know who lives there?'

Hira knew. The man whose office was across from his father's. He did not answer the question.

'Your father's deputy director lives there. His *hierarchical subordinate.*'

The bodyguard said 'hierarchical subordinate' in French. Hira didn't understand what *hierarchical* meant. He remembers it softened the blow of what had been said. Hira hated when there was a word he didn't understand, he would always race for his *Petit Robert* if he didn't know. But here, he couldn't. They kept driving.

There was a road that wound around the hill before turning up to Ambohipo, the same road that led to Ambohipo-Tanàna and Ampahateza. But before reaching Ampahateza, it went through the embassy neighbourhood. Hira knew the area well, his gang often went over there, to the large estates, to steal grapes or pester the owners' pedigreed dogs. They braved the barbed wire on the walls, broke the alarm systems and outside lights with their slingshots. They didn't break them to break things, they were just playing Fantômas, or Arsène Lupin the Gentleman Thief, that was all. It was more extreme than cowboys and Indians because here, the alarms would actually go off, the dogs would chase you for real, and you could genuinely eat all the exotic fruits that you'd never find in your own yards, no joke, grapes and raspberries and other things that were way more exciting than mangoes and lychees! And as the cherry on top, the watchmen would shout at you, honest to goodness, at the top of their lungs that were the white folks' slaves!

The car slowed in front of every house. Hira knew each one by heart.

'There's the house your father doesn't want you to have.'

Hira shut his eyes. He cried. He cried angry tears at his father. He cried from being mad at his father. He cried from feeling something that he'd never wanted to feel: he resented his father. He'd never ever harboured any animosity towards his father. It had never ever happened to him before. Not ever. And that was why he cried.

'Go on, cry. Your father will never get you that house.'

But Hira knew. He wasn't crying because he hadn't got a big beautiful house as a director's son. He wasn't crying because he felt any hatred. He was crying because he had just felt something so awful and ugly. The bodyguard had sullied the beauty that flowed within him. He loved the love from his father. He loved the love from his mother. He loved all the love that he had. His brothers and sisters. His Three-Rooms gang, and even the Four-Roomers. He loved his world. Even, when everything was said and done, Ralita and his stinky old 4L.

He thought about his mother again. He quit crying at once. 'We are dignified people,' his mother liked to say. 'We were distinguished before the Vazahas came and colonized us. We continued to be dignified and distinguished even when they treated us as children, servants, and slaves. We are Antakaranas. Never conquered by any other king. Hold your head high. Always.'

Hira stopped looking at the villas they were showing him. The driver and bodyguard got the message, they didn't make any more stops. They dropped him off down by the market.

'Take this,' they said, 'what your father has never wanted to give you.'

They gave him a stack of green banknotes. Hira had never seen that kind of money in person before but he quickly realized they were dollar bills. He'd seen enough Westerns and American movies to recognize them. He took the money and got out of the car. He ran home. Didn't stop to say hello to his mother. He raced up the stairs three at a time and hid the bills under his mattress. He came back downstairs like nothing was the matter.

'What are you hiding?' his mother asked.

Hira did not know how to lie to his mother. He told her the whole thing. His mother knew everything before he got to the bottom of the stairs.

'The bills can stay there,' his mother said, 'the mice are fond of dollars. Don't tell your father about this, it would hurt him too much.'

'Yes, Mama.'

Around the same time, Sibon Guy died when a military plane crashed. As did Prime Minister Colonel Joël Rakotomalala, as well as Colonel Rakotonirainy. Hira's father was appointed ambassador to Italy. They had their passports made. Auntie Tsontso was floating on top of the world. She'd got out of her backwater. Now she was going to Rome. She kept asking Hira to get the encyclopedia and read her the pages about the Eternal City. She insisted on watching *The Fall of the Roman Empire* over and over. '*No . . . We're really going to live there?*'

One night, Hira heard his mother say to his father: 'It's best if we go, he can't keep saving you here, he's tired of not killing you.' 'Yes,' his father replied, 'I'll take it,'—he was supposed to have been on the same plane as Sibon Guy, but he'd been delayed and never got on board.

Farewells at church. Suitcases packed. Furniture given to neighbours and relatives. Blessings given by grateful folks. Hira was amazed at the line of people who came to bestow their blessings upon his father. His father told all of them to take their bags of rice back home! He wouldn't need them, not in Italy! And he laughed heartily: 'They eat noodles there, not rice!' The country folks didn't understand: 'They eat noodles, like the Chinese?'

A week before their departure—Hira had seen the tickets for *Alitalia*—his father suddenly changed his mind. *We won't be going.* Another politician, who'd been appointed ambassador to the UN, had died of a foodborne disease. Supposedly, white folks' food hadn't agreed with him . . .

Return

Words Unrising

His wings, slow on the softly rending mist. Still. Dreaming of lightness. Shadowfall of white, then what is the extent of the mist? And so Hira would be the bird that leaves to peck through chrysalides of light. Shadowfall of white, the mist has nothing of darkness but its density. Still. A dream of lifting ephemeral, of what leaden weight is this over-strong desire, rending? Pole leans against the peat bottom and silently propels the small chaland. The guide does not speak. Nor Hira. They slide along the mirror of the Brière. A marsh where, the legends say, the lands were turned over, now the forest is underwater, original cities, worlds. Above, we are but usurpers who have confined the spirits below the currents. The city is already far behind. By the silence. Hira cannot push aside the thoughts that root him down in pain. Not when his books bring him, again, always, to the violence of that island, the violence of this world. He simply wants to live. Return, return! To the child he was, gorged on the beauty of this world, filled with wonder at the bees' arabesques or how birds in their flight write but leave no trace. He simply wants to no longer have to think about pain that is not his. To live with her. Live with his children. Not condemn them to waiting eternal. Waiting for him to return from his writing. Waiting for him to cast off what haunts him. Waiting for his eyes to return to them.

Waiting for his voice to wrest itself out of the silence and cast off the sand-burdened bog of murmurs.

Songs remake the space. A piercing call from the south. Sudden flutters. Winging afar. Twittering unbroken, from either side of the shore. One note rising from a drop. One note slipping from an embrace. Drifting away to nothing. They went on, Hira and his guide.

When the mist, fleeting, comes loose from the sky and reclaims its dreams from the marshes, dreams of flowing and water, the sun comes in like a blade opening an old wound to render unto the earth that which belongs to the earth, render unto the sky that which belongs to the sky, night conflates spaces and brings low and high together, the mist would rather die, Hira saw the ashen harrier in the blotting out of dawn and in the mirror suspended in the rising east, a shadow unreachable in the dazzled glare of day. His eye is captive already, having ravished the scene offered up to him.

A captor eye has no spoils but the joy of having seen. The world, already beautiful. What should be changed of the sun setting over the horizon? What should be changed of the dragonfly skimming the marshy waters, time hanging from its motionless flight? What gardener would come to prune the blossoms of our desires, our desires to be wholly captivated by what the eye has seen? A captor eye takes no spoils but the imprint of beauty. The hand strains in obeying its nature, the nature of flesh: to commute all encounters into flesh, body on body, flesh on flesh, bone on bone, matter on matter.

What of the world should be changed if not man?

Between hand and eye, the want, desire, dream of touching, the step towards possessing, dream of power: We have seen, we will have?

Between caress of sight and caress of touch, what of the world should be changed if not this desire, this hunger to possess?

Words woven twixt eye and hand . . .

A border says: Here is everyone's property, here is what hands may or may not touch, what the eye should or should not see.

Desire metamorphosed, language is born from chrysalides of reflection. This is what Hira would change: that he could weave scraps of words with the thread of seeing to speak the world, and hang the work on the urges of touching and appropriation, and return to only that state—of admiring.

Return . . .

The spectator is late to disentangle man from nature. The spectator forgets that they have become all of this at once, from here, from there, a leaf stitched over the ripped-open sky, a flake of water hemmed by the very heart of the dust, all of this at once, a little earth, a little sky . . .

This is what Hira would change: man. Hollow venture or essential dream . . .

Stuck are the sighs without blowing desires, ocean of men, they conceal the silent, mask meaning's refinement, ocean of men, waiting requires silence to dive into the ocean of men, do we even belong to ourselves near the ocean of men? Stuck are the hums near this cacophony of men, ripples of metal, droning of iron, rasping of rivets, the slick of the chills, is it screaming, this silence fabricated, is it screaming, men's greasepaint, men's mask, is it screaming, is it screaming, this silence that was only of us? Twigs under dead leaves, speaking is but an accident, a foot crushing the egg into cool earth. Do we even belong to ourselves so near the ocean of men? Sand to grass, to a display of disintegrating, to a flaw of cacophony that floods and flows over with every fresh wave, is it screaming, is it screaming, this movement, so slow, towards our songs? Stuck are the sighs, Hira's only overview is of those who take a moment to pause. Is it screaming, is it screaming, this ocean of men? What does it scream? What does it scream?

The sun opens out Hira's slow wings, eyes are there even then to pursue him. Dark coming of the day, in what dream could Hira have so destroyed his freedom? Was it really so vital for him to speak that he would gouge out his life? For all the years that he's been writing. Since the day his mother gave him that notebook. More notebooks came after. He would wait for his mother to notice he'd finished one so she'd bring him more, more notebooks. He never waited for long. His mother always knew. Perhaps his eyes. Perhaps his silence. Perhaps because he was there, at her side, and not in his room, on his bed, scrawling away. The notebooks became books. And book after book, Hira has rooted himself into solitude. For his world is not here. For his world is not this one. Not this ugly world. Not this world of war. Of poverty. Stupidity. Absurdity. Men who do not stop killing one another. Men who do not stop bringing everything back to their fleeting lives.

Hira thinks about his father's childhood, again. No, that is not for him to write. His father knows how to tell stories. His father knows how to write. Hira realizes that he's been trying to protect the child his father had been. But that childhood is past. His old man isn't a child any more! Hira is surprised that he hadn't seen the obvious! And, in terms of his own youth, Hira knows how lucky he was. As he had the first time he'd read his father's diary—a massive seismic quake, with aftershocks still lasting to this day. A diary written at the age of twenty, hidden in the back of the wardrobe where his father's theses and case studies had been filed away. In it, his father told of the good fortune that he'd had in meeting Hira's mother. Good fortune that could only be understood through his neglected childhood, orphaned by his father and taken from his mother.

Hira endeavours to look only at the landscape opening before him: the small black boat has spilled its shadow into the pool speckled with solitude, nothing moves unless it is time unending, nothing twitches unless it is the ruffled huffs of the brash bluebirds. People from around here, they say that this is where the woman lives, the woman with white breasts and golden hair. The small black boat does not rock, the water around it is dead quiet. Leaves take the plunge without wind to bear them, there to decay uneventfully. The hush of waiting, for that time when the white-bosomed woman will again let down her cascading hair and drive the shadow back to the depths of the water. Then it will be said that the pool is golden, and that the sun rocks gently in its small dark boat. The bluebirds will snare the night as the white-bosomed woman sings a tune without breath or break . . . Which is the child to be born?

Near the nights that are night no more, near the days that are day no more, when cracks open warily to softness and trembling comes from sorrow no more, from no suffering, no terror. Skin is skin no more. Flesh is flesh no more. Stone is a bone of earth and bark is a skin of wood. Water slips over peaks, breasts prick under caresses. Mouth is for words and tongue no more, is for senses alone. None-but-night to enter the day. None-but-day to retake night. When peaks wed peaks and valleys hollow out from other valleys. When water meets other waters. When doubt drifts off and rests hand upon belly. The wind's tresses are breath, intermingling with sighs upon powdered desires. Kisses are opening to other kisses and the earth is flesh. Wings are white on mist of white. Nights are of the night no more. Days are of the day no more. Mist is born of a wind so sweet and slow, will you come here next to me?

Hira thinks of her. Which is the life to be reborn?

As recompense for the scratches on our hearts and flesh, we will take these reckless pleasures that chance upon our lives, these pleasures do not know they are pleasures, these pleasures do not know they are succour and elixir, we will take them, the stray kiss of destiny, we will take them, the real gifts of dreams. As symmetry for the breaks that open us to pain, we will trace back over the cracks and crucibles in our flesh from whence gladness had come. And we will render pleasures unto pleasures. We will render caresses unto caresses. We will render dreams unto dreams. So that scrapes may finally join fissures, from whence new buds will come. So that pleasures remain pleasures. So that caresses remain caresses. So that dreams may float again and scatter-sow freedom. For our flower of love. For life to continue. Again and again. You, my love, will take what life sets before you, you will take what desire gives you as an anthem of joy. That, you shall take; me, you shall keep.

Horror floods over Hira: his father had lost his childhood, then gained his adult life with his mother, whereas he, Hira, has sacrificed the better part of his own adult life trying to rewrite his father's childhood. He has taken twists and turns, tried to understand the context, colonization, oppression, dreams of independence. He has examined history, examined archives, examined witnesses, he has confronted the realities of dictatorships, why was his father so well versed in politics, why was he perpetually the opponent, why had he never allowed himself to be corrupted? Why had Hira always had the feeling that his father was driven by something else besides his love of family? That he served his country more than kin? In spite of all the affection he showed them, in spite of all the attention he gave them, it had always seemed like there were other, more important things at play. Hira thought he would find an answer in the childhood that his father had always partially obscured. Abused as a child, now this elder would not suffer to see other children abused, any young people mistreated, tormented. Hira came up against silence. Hira wrote. Stories of violence. Stories of injustice. Stories of rebellion. Hira is a whole life in front of the page. Hira is not that in front of her. There is always the part of him that wants to return to the page. She can only keep him for the space of a moment. Those hours, hunching over the page. Those days, combing through the past. Those nights, awakening. Those years, going back over the details, returning to the faintest trace. Rewriting what was already written. And when his father finally did agree to tell the story, through his own mouth, through his eyes, outside of his pain, Hira was floored to realize that he had known the story from the very beginning. Ever since he'd opened that diary when he was a child, his father's diary, there, among all those drafts and manuscripts, those letters and archives amassed over the years. He'd known since that day, but that day, he'd been a child, he hadn't known what he knew. And his father had already told all of it, through his own life. Hira has spent so much time watching his father live . . .

Hira is tired, he sees that he has reproduced his father's folly. Trying to change the world and leaving something within his own family unfinished. Hira asks the guide if he can lie down in the boat for a moment, the man nods, yes, here, we are outside of the world.

Dreams cascade, and may decay. Peat rich with desires, the urge laid in earth, wings below the earth, once there was a bird whose wing brushed away the outlines of countries. Already are flights little more than journeying over lands that are foreign henceforth, islands are born, worlds pull away. The bird fell asleep and, decay by decay, was buried beneath the mud. It is there. In the peat.

Words unrising.

Outside

Thus Hira is, on the verge of scarlet hours in which tarry ruse to consort with the wicked and cry on the edge of desire, when men come forward with prayers and honey on their lips, souls of white and full transparence, Hira reclaims the original bile from all he resents, non-presence in the world, and his faded engravings, scarcely traced. Hira lands to carefully reread the mock suns that are filling hearts. Hira sees them, these men of a thousand betrayals, silent and inviting, seeking out any rustles of their own good fortune, a favourable future to be forked over bare-bones, Hira seeks refuge in silences and stones. Outside. Outside of men. Outside of turmoil. Outside of words. Hira sees them, these men in the hands of night, close to the doors of rock where they will end up as hearts of stone. Hira is the bird of pallor flying over guilty thoughts and irrepressible desire, flying over uncontrollable want and dreams of power. Hira is in the black blood of those who do not see. They do not see because they do not look inward. Hira slowly sighs his song. He would like to heal from having seen too much.

Sores of the flesh, sawdust of thoughts, wound of the world, dregs of the throat screaming, screaming. Hira has seen too much of this world. He hears her, She says to him: Do not force the world to sound as you desire, the forges of voice where sense, where anger, where comfort, the forges of voice where meaning, where madness, the furores are colour, are hunger, are succour, are . . .

She looks at him, She falls silent.

Anger and blood, dregs of the desolated throat, where anger, where comfort, where meaning, where madness. Are colours of desire.

She says again: Sores from sitting upon desire. Desire. Desire. Wounds are the lips of pain, my lips' only pain is the absence of yours, I stretch out, you are the briar with quivering leaves, spraying me with your petals.

Hira throbs on blows that are not meant for him. He does not listen to her, not to her. But what indifference hardens us, that we forget these blows, even aimed at others? What impulse drives us to watch these blows, even aimed at others? A fascination with harm? Eye's morbidity ensnared within the spectacle of violence?

Hira is on the gash of the gouged-out voice, up against the soul's nakedness and on the painting of blood, on the gouge, on the incision and the scar, on the fault line, on faces. He rises. The display remakes his lies from bare.

Where all blows are soft.

Dregs of the throat, words in decay, Hira stores up sawdust from the larynx beneath the turmoil of meanings. He stores up. Stores up. Scratches of sounds, he hoards, hoards, he hoards.

From bare, dream of the forge, forge of bodies, pounded, hips, bodies pounded, lips, bodies pounded on the axis of wailing and screams.

Round world of sounds, dig down into desire, drown, Hira displays his mouth. She says to him, do not force the world to sound as you desire, for you I have forged screams to clinch and cries to enclose, for you I have forged tears to harden and fury to coarsen, fits of rage and falls of wrath, laughter inbred with hysteria and laughter rotting ecstasy, you're laughing, you're laughing, look at me, love me, that's all, simply come here, come back.

Hira's air runs out in the last gasp of writing. She is the only way out. Her. Her. In her.

TTS

The fetid export, export, into the disaster of fetid lives, the export, and the shot in welcome, the export, slut on sight, he has. Shot. He has. The export, going by, the skirt does count, sexual har-rights-ment, by shots, she's going by, the slut, in trailing lives, the slut on sight, going, going, to snap his breath, he stinks in your honour, he stinks of you, and nearby, tracing, near touching, a fetid groove, as claw and souvenirs of throats entrenched and anything engorged that counts for him, the skirt, he'll grab a slip to squeeze the slut, as gaping jaws for puking, and, the export, not important, going, he's still got fumes, swollen with the slut's sweat, every one, body gone, slashed, the export, the Station over squirm of bodies swollen with sweat, with fetid, false, ruse, and avowals, he is tired upon sight of bodies and bailed laughter, he summons up shots and breaches in flesh, arms outsprawled and belly up, he screams, export, export.

In the beginning was the father, far-flung childhood in the shadow of abuse, he fled. This was during the time of colonies. It is hard for Hira to recount the flight, the surrender to steps that lead to uncertainty.

Often walking slowly, refusing to run, he surrenders himself to chance, he does not flee, he gives in, and sells off, fetid, the export, in rage and refrains of what was, of what is, of what will be, meaningless time, the shots without borders and the blood river, he's visiting this country and the words are foreign to him, transient land, the slippage is within the realm of meaning, and men are talking with crags in their throats, he stumbles there, and calls his bluff back onto his shoulders.

Perhaps lives and days should be kept separate, he doesn't have the strength to go through it all again, it should, perhaps, be gone through again, the selling and the rape, the sweetness child on the dragonfly's back, it's his from childhood, and then his old man from hall to hall, the crier's voice and the word of madness, but he is tired, tolerance is tiring, and the insult so strong, he doesn't know, doesn't know, he doesn't, that this station, another, this train station with blood-soaked stakes, in this, his country, in this adolescence now, his, this other station with blood-soaked stakes, Soarano, a head on a stake, he went back home, he said to his mother, he's here, she said, you're here, yes I'm here, I forgot the way, he added, she did not answer, I don't know how I ended up back at home, and the shot that I got, and that man's wild eyes, red, the pike broke through his naked chest, red, the jeep barrels past, the man fled, he ran towards the steps, the uproar is in the city, and smoke is in the city, and death is in the city, the shot is for me, it does not kill, it writes time that is dead.

He will never be dead.

Hira, from living in a blast that will never be heard, from haunting a pair of wild eyes that will never find rest, forever fleeing towards an exit that does not exist, he lives in a life that has no way out, he lives in a stray bullet, left in the memory of his disasters, ruins of his recollections, Hira is on his feet, he is sixteen, he sees it perfectly, he sees himself before the forgetting and blankness that later arose, people are holding burning newspapers with clothespins, the road is a slight incline, crowds are teeming, feet spill over the asphalt and cars slowly slump along, it was there, at Pochard, the clothing thrift market, it was there, the smoke, it was there, the uproar, it was there, the tide that had carried the smell, charred, flesh and rubber, tyres and flames and black smoke on the dirty black skin of a street kid, and another, and again another, and one more jumping from a window of the burning Pochard, and the crowd rejoicing *'olé olé'*, and the lighter flashing onto petrol and tyres, bodies, a child's head, arms blackened with soot, soot from their fat, soot from their skin, Hira, he was there, his feet that had led him there, he did not understand, his eyes that were watching, he did not understand, not what he saw but his own presence there, and the scream of puke he'd stuffed back down to yell with the crowd, we butchered in the days of TTS, street kids swapping back and forth between slayer and scapegoat.

The export, in rage as against him, he has no slut to dream up but his life, he does what all men do, brings everything back to a woman, loads all the pain onto her, so he's got the slut, the slut and the slut, and the slut again, every one, she's going by, he wanted to puke, the crowd was yelling, he stepped back, the export, fetid, in rage against him, he turns to face the girl, he makes her a slut, in rage, the skirt does count, he lifts it, the girl doesn't even notice, he tails her, she forces through the yelling crowd, thrusts in among the honking, she asses out, a round, and the smell of the scoured husk, tattered shreds of sex deflowered, dangling threads of a fleshless climax, the pain is vivid, the rage on the framework of a look, the export, fetid, she steps away, she brings him away from the massacre, she sits, crossing her legs, she tries on a shoe in the middle of the whole mess, of shouting and screams, of smoke and smells, of panic and thrill, he looks at the stones, and the sculptures for adorning gravesites, traps for tourists and white *zoreilles*, the vendors pack up their wares, the crowd gets bigger and bigger.

Suddenly he's burbling one of Rabearivelo's verses:

For his children he would bring back games made of stone and metal scraps, for his children he would bring back games made of wickerwork and raffia, made of everything he'd despised when he was younger, wounded by little toy cars, sharp scrap metal, free pox and scabs thrown in, wickerwork toys rotting in rain and sun, a home for fleas and other insects, proof of our poverty when compared with the plastic toys *made in France*, shiny and benign, sturdy . . .

Memory stuffed down, Pochard is no more, he forgot everything after the girl with the shoe, he ended up back at home, he said to his mother, I'm here, I don't know how to find the way any more, she did not answer him.

Pochard is no longer there, razed, erased, wiped clean away. Today, it's a fabric and handicraft market, imports and local, China and back-water, exported in the tourist's bag.

Full-of-life-and-laughter-and-haggling-and-colours-from-this-and-that.

Cottons and silks, jeans, thongs, and sneakers, fakes, knock-offs, bootlegs, dreaming of wealth and the Western world, fetid, on top of the street kids' butchered bodies.

That day, a kung fu group had decided to clean up the city. A raid against the street kids who were swarming around the market. Kids or teenagers. TTS. Teenagers or young adults. TTS. Thieves or beggars. Rapists or victims. Rounded up, set loose, or set free by the city.

Druggies. Paid for every misdoing. At Pochard, people said that they were gathering their spoils, that they were holding hostages there, the women and children they'd abducted. That the government was protecting them, the police were covering for them. Merely to break up strikes and exploit them. They were terrorizing the people. With help from the government. Help from the dictatorship. The TTS.

The kung fu fighters took to the streets.

Knives and blades.

Fire.

Lynching.

And the market crowd had themselves a grand ol' time.

Hira does not know if he will remember everything one day. There's a blank white veil, it shows that something's missing, missing from his life, a moment where he did not exist, a span of time where everything has faded, next to that girl and her shoe. It stops there. Dead.

Kung Fu

It was a few weeks before the carnage. Hira had just got out of school, he was with his friends, three girls, they were going through the Analakely market, over by the Albert Camus Cultural Centre, when all of a sudden someone knocked into them, past them, a boy about their age. In the same instant, a woman behind them yelled: '*Mpangalatra e!*' *Thief. Thief.* The boy was running, somebody just had to stick out their foot, he fell hard, the woman's purse spilling out next to him. Suddenly a voice cried: TTS! The crowd surrounded the boy and pummelled him with their feet. Hira found himself in the melee without knowing how, with his three friends, he saw one of them kick the boy in the face. Hira backed up, pulled his girl by the arm, *Come on, let's go*, she laughed.

Had Hira been part of the free-for-all? He had no idea. He was shocked to be standing there, shocked by the boy getting struck and stripped, shocked by the blood mixing into the asphalt. More people came over to partake in the lynching. Hira had lost sight of the other two girls. He was holding the last one tight by the arm. And in the chaos, he saw a man coming through, politely asking to get by: '*Azafady, azafady, omeo lalana!' Excuse me, please, let me through.* The man was carrying a tyre, the masses parted, another man swept along behind, with a petrol can in hand. Hira instantly understood. Everyone understood, in a euphoric rush of violence. His girl wanted to see: *Let go, you're hurting me!* He let go, she disappeared into the crowd. Hira backpedalled, eyes still riveted on the action, transfixed. He couldn't see the little boy on the ground any more. He was at a loss. Felt guilty for running away like a coward. No, no, he repeated, over and over. *This is sick.* He'd barely made it back twenty metres when he smelled tyre and petrol. He saw the black smoke and was hit with a shockwave of the roaring crowd. He could pick out, mixed with burning rubber, the stench of roasting meat.

Hira did not forget. No, he knows the images are there. But there's a blank white veil over it all.

The kung fu fighters had been disbanded, but riots were breaking out all over the city. Pierre Be's followers were sons and daughters of the people. The army stormed the streets. And fired into the crowd.

A few days before the bac exams, there had been mass arrests of kung fu students. Hira had been in class. The door opened. A lieutenant came in. With ten other soldiers at his heels. They went straight for one particular student. Sahondra. They took her away. Hira would never see his classmate. Ever again.

The riots went on. At the university. When the secondary schools let out. The crowd grew by the minute. The army was already waiting. Hira was yelling with the rest of the teenagers. Hira was shaking. Not because he was afraid but because he was hesitating. Sometimes, he would see a blade beside him. He didn't want to be with the murderers.

But there were AK-47s in front of them. Which was the executioner? Rifle or blade? His body was spasming. He was close to tears. His stomach in knots from so many contradictions. He couldn't wait for the army to throw tear gas and everyone to scatter with burning eyes.

On the first day of exams, at Rabearivelo Secondary School, downtown, there was talk that suggested a boycott of the exam. The students couldn't decide what the best course of action was: take to the streets or go to their exam rooms? Then Hira saw soldiers closing the gates. The students had been caught out. The roll call began, directing everyone to their assigned room. None of them moved. The roll call started over. Suddenly there were more soldiers, taking up positions all along the walls. Hira heard them release their safeties. Click. Click. The trap snapped shut. The roll call was done, for the third time. The students moved. Hira heard his name. He got in line outside his exam room, like everyone else. He wanted to cry. Tears of anger. Tears of hate.

Their only proctors were automatic rifles. One in front of the teacher's desk, handing out their booklets. One behind them, blocking the door. And a third that patrolled back and forth, from one side of the room to the other. Philosophy. Topic 1: What is freedom? A caricature of the current state of affairs. Topic 2: Analysis of a speech by President Ratsiraka. Delivered in Havana. Hira selected topic 2 and began dismantling the arguments made by the now-admiral. His days of admiring the frigate captain were long gone. Very long gone. Hira didn't get his bac, of course. He'd sabotaged himself. He'd conveyed his rage in every essay—French, Malagasy, history, even English. Flunked. He, the intellectual . . .

His mother tried to reason with him before the second sitting. He wouldn't hear a word of it. Not a single word. He did the same thing as he had the first time. But he received his bac. By one point. Salvaged by a passing mark from a couple of the philosophy and history teachers who could read his rebellion.

A few months later, the military laid siege to the kung fu dojo. It happened at dawn. While the city was still asleep. Soldiers stormed the dojo. Pierre Be and his followers repelled the attack. Then a tank was brought in to bombard their haven. That had never been seen before. Tanks that shelled their own people. Pierre Be's body was never found. Nor his followers who fell there. How many dozens? How many hundreds? Hira does not know.

He hated getting the bac.

Ruins and Wonders

Hira is like the bird that never lands. When the earth catches its talons, it changes them into roots, wings beat helplessly against the air, and soon the bird has nothing left but its gaze to lose away in the azure blue. The bird had seen the slumber of God.

Dreams, as roots that hold us down, beneath fertile ground of desire, of living, so evanescent in day, frail imprints fixed to infinity, of this space where life, tapered down, forever stretches and strains, far, so far from reality, as roots that keep us upright, hope, as infinitesimally small as it may be, a little fire in secret vows, a little fluttering that springs up from nothing. As for the reeds, Hira knows not: spears stuck into the ground, or stalks escaped from the depths. His talons are for him to cling to the wind when the earth anchors them in her bosom. Hira does not land. He is the bird.

Hira did not choose his country. Nor the day of his birth, nor the circumstances. From his very arrival, he was to be the son of all. Hira landed for just a moment. The island rooted his talons at once. Hira had planned to leave again, to reach the horizons, but the island shares its borders only with ocean and drowning, there Hira remains, eyes that cannot ignore the madness of men. Hira does not land. He knows he could fly for days on end, he will never get back to his world. In fact, the more he flies, the more he will come to understand that his world is ruins upon ruins. He began to realize it the first time he saw an elderly couple begging at the bus, and the conductor shoving them aside. Hira said nothing. It was the first time he'd taken the bus by himself. He was going into the city, he'd just started secondary school. Then he saw kids panhandling. He'd seen that before but thought they had parents, at least, like the poor kids in the villages, Ampahateza or Ambohipo-Tanàna. Poverty had begun to take over. The world was becoming less and less beautiful, in spite of the stalwartly gorgeous landscapes. There was a game that Hira played: he looked up and saw the hills, sunsets, plants, trees, it took his breath away, he looked down and saw the sewage and lepers on the ground. Hira wanted to go back to those hills, fly above them, be in those landscapes, but his feet and legs were down there, with the poverty. So, he would often keep his eyes on the ground, far from the dreams that made up his being.

Hira thought of the child he had been, the one who declared he no longer was, the child who stopped playing and shut himself away to read all the books his father had, the child who shut himself away to write in the notebooks his mother had given him, more and more every day, the child who thought he didn't have enough time to write every-thing he wanted to write, so sure that he would die young.

His world turned truly upside down one day as he came home from secondary school. He wasn't a child any more, no, he only had one year of secondary school left, and he knew that someday he wouldn't be doing anything else except writing. There were books on the ground, his father's books. There were books in the gutter. From the bottom of the front steps, all the way up to the front door. There was furniture outside, clothes on the ground, everything thrown out, blocking the pavement, in the neighbours' way, all jumbled up, piled up like it was junk. They had been evicted.

A few months earlier, at the end of Didier Ratsiraka's first five years in power, his father had urged their party leader, Razanabahiny Marojama, to seek the presidency. Hira had been at the heated party meetings. His mother made tea and coffee, Hira went to buy baguettes, Nannie and his big brother buttered and served them. Or Tom would be tasked with going to buy mofogasy, the pillowy little cakes were very popular with that crowd. Razanabahiny, a polygamist, would often be at his third wife's house a few blocks from them, they could have meetings there too, Hira always found a way to slip in without anyone noticing.

That day, Razanabahiny had refused to declare his candidacy, he argued that the President of the Republic deserved another chance. The Southerners immediately sided with him. Hira marvelled at their consensus. These were tough men, they weren't afraid of a debate, yet they had fallen silent as one, respecting their leader's will. The small parlour was suddenly divided. Behind his father, all the Northerners and Westerners, the ones from Diego-Suarez and Mahajanga. Hira's heart was pounding. Was the party about to splinter, the *Iray tsy Mivaky*, One Nation, Indivisible? Hira's father drew upon all of his talents to sway the party's leader, but none of them budged, Razanabahiny refused to answer him, retreating instead into a silence that spoke volumes. Not a cough, not a single sign of any hesitation. Their positions were clear.

Hira's father walked out of the room, followed by all of his men. Hira ran ahead of them to warn his mother. He knew they would continue the meeting at their house. The tea and coffee were ready for them when they arrived. The dam broke. Hira's father let them talk. Nobody was listening to anyone else. They all urged his father to split off from the party. They fell silent to hear his answer: 'How can we have any legitimacy if we betray our party's very name, Vonjy Iray Tsy Mivaky, In Unity, Our Aid? The whole country was divided by the colonists, we were set against one another, Seashores against Merinas, Sakalavas against Tsimihetys, Antemoros against Antandroys, Betsimisarakas against Bezanozanos, etc. They made up the whole thing about eighteen ethnicities, and even though we knew that, even though we knew it was a way to divide us, we dived right on in, so eager for our masters' favour, we tore one another apart to get the biggest share, we were a colonized people, we were conquered slaves, and the colonizers were able to stay here for sixty years, sat upon our squabbling, enthroned upon our weaknesses. What would any of our struggle mean, if we were to split off now?'

A very brief silence.

One of his father's supporters, an officer, rose to his feet. Even out of uniform, his bearing was distinctly military. 'You know as well as we do that Ratsiraka does not listen to anyone. You know as well as we do that he has already betrayed the Revolution. Have you already forgotten how Ratsimandrava died? Have you forgotten how Sibon Guy died? Have you forgotten how Rakotomalala died? We can't prove that he killed them, of course, but if you just observe him, spend a little time with him, you can tell that he dreams of ruling alone. This country will not make it through this, not with him at the head of it. You speak to us of colonization, the fear of division, to be sure, but we are independent now. It will take more than just a few years to fix all of the problems engendered by colonization—we are divided, we are resentful, there's the issue of ethnicities, the takeover by the Merinas, the challenges of decentralization—but let us see what is possible for us to save now, today, to create a future for our country. Marojama would leave the government in the hands of one man, and that man is a madman. That man promises us a Revolutionary National Front, the unification of all political parties to restore development on the island, but he only works for his own interests, for his own party, only for AREMA. We cannot afford to let this happen. And I also know that the army will not stand for it. You must run in Marojama's place. All of the North, all of the West, all of the East will be with you.'

Hira's father asked for a day to think.

'We will come tomorrow for your answer,' the officer said.

End of discussion.

All of them left.

The following day, there was no question in Hira's mind as to his father's answer. He gave no grand speech. Just one sentence: '*Lôso atsika zalahy hè!*' *Let's do it, friends.* There was no passionate outburst, no flood of emotions. They started developing their communications plan. How they were going to run their 'propaganda', particularly in the regions where their party had strong support.

Later the same day, they received word that Marojama had announced his candidacy, rallying the party together and placing a particular emphasis on the allegiance of Hira's father and all of the regions, the northern and western and eastern regions, and of course the south and south-east—his own. It stopped Hira's father and his friends in their tracks; however, they still believed that they had won over their party leader, it was just a little surprising that he hadn't kept them abreast of his decision. The party did not split, the Vonjy remained Iray Tsy Mivaky, One Party, Indivisible. From the north to the south.

Hira's father became quickly disillusioned with the 'propaganda'. Marojama's candidacy was just for show. He contributed nothing, except for a few TV appearances and radio spots. He styled himself as the opposition. Made people believe he was one of the President's greatest challengers. But in reality, he never took any action.

Hira's father and his followers travelled the length and breadth of their regions. Hira always wondered how his father could make himself heard by those huge crowds without even a megaphone, and he regularly declined a microphone, he would always captivate his audience with his powerful voice. The Vonjy party won the majority in the big cities, Diego-Suarez and Mahajanga and Tamatave. But the results kept coming in. The capital, countryside, rural areas, and smaller towns did not go in their favour. 'Cheating!' several of them alleged, but they had no evidence, and no way to investigate. Their party didn't make it to the second round. AREMA faced off against MONIMA, the great Monja Jaona's party. AREMA emerged victorious from the second round with more than 80 per cent of the votes.

After the presidential elections, Marojama was given additional powers, and AREMA asserted more and more control over the country. Everyone had to fall in line. The frigate captain had tipped over into dictatorship. Soon, he would name himself admiral. In a country without a navy! Hira's father didn't last long. The dictator had his revenge: Hira's father was sacrificed by his party leader, and he lost his position at SEIMAD overnight. They were evicted immediately thereafter. Hira watched his mother. She seemed to be such an unshakable force despite the stunned look on her face, or the humiliation, actually, the shame of their status being thrown to the ground, into the gutter, with all the neighbours—the whole development—watching. More than any fear of them being homeless and unemployed.

'Come along now, let's get all of this moved to the church.'

So, they all got to work, brothers, sisters, cousins, friends, carrying their belongings up to the church, about fifty metres away. All Hira cared about was the books. In fact, that was his responsibility. It was already enough work to carry the wardrobes, the beds, or the fridge. Hira commandeered Tom and their whole gang.

They stayed in the church for one night. They slept there, at the foot of the altar, it was so strange, so uncommon, to sleep in a place of peace and love, knowing that you'd been evicted from your home. Hira did not feel forlorn. His father even began to sing. In his powerful, rich voice. They laughed together. There was a surprising kind of joy. In having a whole church to yourself, and the incredible feeling they drew from it. But they had to find a solution fast, for Sunday was not far off, the worshippers would throng to the service, and the congregation could not see all their things piled up in the choir, they could not see their downfall.

The next day, their father scrounged up a truck, and they all went to stay with their cousins, their mama's sister's family. In Ambohimanarina. It was weird. They were used to going to one another's houses, they were used to being together all the time, but to turn up like that and put their furniture where the garden tools and equipment were usually stored, that was deeply unsettling.

Their cousins' house was enormous. There were three rooms on the ground floor, which were only used for bits and bobs and flowerpots. They put their furniture in there. The books took up almost the whole of the second room. Hira stacked them as if he were stacking oven bricks, with help from Tom, Tita, Aristide, a more distant cousin, and Daro, their mama's little brother—the same age as them! They formed a chain to pass each volume down the line one by one. Hira had insisted very strongly on that. No way could they be carrying several books at once. Because he had to organize them by size. It was a sacrilege, he normally sorted them by genre, but here, he had to take the sizes into account so the piles wouldn't collapse. Largest on the bottom, smallest on top.

Hira climbed higher and higher onto the piles as Tita, Tom, Daro, and Aristide kept ferrying in the texts. He was slowly building a labyrinth. They could walk in between the stacks of books, each one nearly two metres tall. Tita exclaimed: '*Ha zalahy!* Where in the world did all these books come from, your house wasn't even that big!' But Hira knew where they'd been. There was the double wardrobe, packed full. Each shelf of books went four rows deep, all the way to the back. Twelve shelves in all. A large bookcase in the living room. A smaller one they'd put on its side, incorrectly called the little bookcase, because it only came up to waist height but it could hold almost twice as many books as the main bookcase, and more books on every wall of the house, more and more and more. Under the stairs, in dressers that should have had clothes instead, underneath his parents' bed. In all the bedrooms. Hira had been in cahoots with his father to bring home even more. Time and time again. His mother had pulled off quite an achievement in making the books invisible, by hanging mirrors everywhere and cramming fantastic little curios into any open space! 'Well,' she said, 'at least that's something!' His father couldn't very well say: 'Oh darling, I'm going to move this figurine so I can put some books here!'

Hira, Tita, Tom, Daro, and Aristide didn't get everything put away until nightfall. Hira stayed a little longer to make the final tweaks. He was kneeling on top of a stack to wedge in the last books, he had to stay crouched over, his head was hitting the ceiling! He got tired and lay down for a moment. And then he laughed: Scrooge McDuck slept on his piles of gold, and he, Hira, was sleeping on his piles of books! He was still laughing when his uncle came in.

'Well, now!'

Amazed for sure, but also, he had a typewriter in his hands.

'Here, child, this is for you. We found it tucked away in a corner.'

His uncle gave him the typewriter. Hira was flooded with joy. Joy to rival the shock he'd felt when he'd come home from school and seen all the books in the gutter.

That night, he slept on his paper ramparts, hugging his typewriter to his chest. And then more nights. Reading. Reading more and more. Typing on his typewriter. He wrote the first seeds of his first stories there. But, of course, he didn't know that yet.

Ramanana

Six months they stayed with Tita's family. Six months during which their father was turned away everywhere he went. He applied for a position at UNICEF and got an interview. The dictator vetoed it. He tried to go back to teach at the university. They couldn't find the file from his leave. It was a very difficult time for Hira. He read. He wrote. He could not be away from his typewriter. He was consumed by rage. He ate little. He held to strict silence. He waited for hunger before writing. And then, once the dizziness took hold, he wrote. He knew that once he'd made it through that phase, then came tremendous euphoria, cool clarity, glorious detachment, as if everything were moving in slow motion, as if he could take it all into his hands, observe it all in his own time. He no longer threw away his drafts, no longer lost his notebooks. He no longer waited for his mother to supply him with writing pads. He was dealing in white paper now, each page slid reverently into the typewriter. Now, he had 'manuscripts'. He changed out the ink every week. He walked everywhere and saved his bus money to buy ribbon and paper. He would get back to Ambohimanarina at night. He had the shadow of his paternal grandfather beside him, Ramanana, who smiled, didn't say much, walked along with him. In the depths of fallen nights, it made the walk feel safer. In the silent neighbourhoods. In that time of insecurity when the streetlights no longer came on. Sometimes it felt like Dzoely Hira was there too, walking alongside Ramanana, and even—although he couldn't always recognize him—Adan'i Soazara, blending into the people walking past.

Ramanana, 'the rich man': the founder of the lineage, strictly speaking. Before Ramanana was the wall of things not said, the fog of memory, for too long a deafening wall, built by history, the country's history, the story of an impossible genealogy. Before Ramanana, the name had been written in another tongue, another tale, in another lineage that had disowned him. Hira declared his name in defiance of unremembering, a small trickle of water in a dark current that diverges sharply to seek other beds. Like his father had done. Like his grandfather had done. Writing the next chapter himself so as not to be buried by his past, creating his own escape for the rushing wind to blow him out from the den of inertia.

Ramanana had been a rich colonial administrator, writer, translator, and trusted advisor to a district official, on the west side of the island, rich with thousands of hectares, son of the Sokats, a family from the Indies. Ramanana had given himself that name. Ramanana. Had taken a local name. For that was still possible, to choose a name yourself. It was still possible to see yourself in a destiny. Ramanana felt that he belonged to that island. Born on that island, and India a faraway land. Much too far. Ramanana married Rasoa Marguerite, formally and forever divorcing from the Sokats. For a Sokat did not marry a Malagasy. A Sokat did not marry lower castes. A Sokat did not intermingle with the natives, colonized and inferior as they were. Ramanana ceased to be a Sokat. And thus he cut himself off from that tree, to plant another instead. One swift act that took him away.

The only trace Hira owned of this grandfather was one photograph in black-and-white: Ramanana posing in the courtyard of a colonial house, seated on a chair, with two men standing on either side of him, two Malagasys, in Western dress, all in white. The one on the right clasped his arms behind his back, the one on the left placed a graceful hand on Ramanana's shoulder. His grandfather wore an elegant black suitcoat, perfectly pressed, flowing trousers made of the same material, shiny white shoes, a crisp white shirt, tight collar, a black tie patterned with stars (Hira thought so, at least, he didn't know why it would be stars . . .). Straight black hair, cut short. Hands set one on top of the other, on his thigh, his posture calm and serene. He had black skin like Black Indians do, black as the deepest night, profuse eyebrows, an aquiline nose, deep-set eyes like soundless wells, a pencil moustache, well trimmed. A long neck that seemed to sprout out from his shirt. Squared shoulders set off by his long, lean, thin body. Ramanana had clearly been very tall. Even sitting down, he came up to neck height on the man to his right.

Hira would sometimes, discreetly, watch his father. His amazement unspoilt still, to see the resemblance between the two men. Their peace, especially. The peace on their faces. The photo of Hira's grandfather had been imprinted onto his mind, the image had always been with him. A door onto his history. The wall of unremembering. The story of his father's family stopped there, at that photograph, in front of that wall.

For a long time, Hira knew nothing else about that man. He could not go any further back in his genealogy. As if nothing had existed before that. Nothing but a photograph. Ramanana had died young. At thirty-two. And left nothing of his life story behind. Only the photograph, and a ledger of accounts in his exquisite handwriting. Only a heavy silence. And those calm, deep eyes. Hira had always felt like those eyes were looking directly at him. Like he was somehow connected with that man. Not only as grandson to grandfather, but as two points that were destined to converge again, to retell the old secrets together. He'd always been possessed of that certainty. It was entirely self-evident. He knew his writing was going to lead him there, to the place where memory died. He understands that now, now that he has pried his father out from torture's claws. Now he can ask his questions. Without it causing pain or suffering. Now everyone understands that the story must be written. And that is why he's been writing since childhood, for that transmission, for the breath that is passed from generation to generation, for the breath that is sometimes taken by other things that happen, by history. For the thread that is strung between the dead and the living.

The circumstances surrounding Ramanana's death were unclear. From pneumonia, they said. Following his imprisonment, they said. Ramanana had been in colonial prison for financing nationalists, he died three months after his release, they said. They also said that perhaps he'd been poisoned. By T., his half-brother. A mixture of cigarette ash and ground-up glass, poured into his coffee, they said, Rasoa Marguerite said. But why would he have drunk a concoction like that? The only sure thing was that afterwards, T. moved into Ramanana's house, availed himself of his possessions, tried marrying Rasoa Marguerite too, but she fled, leaving behind her three-year-old son, Hira's father. Hira's father, soon abused. Soon beaten, again and again.

Humiliated and made to eat goose feed. T. stayed in Ramanana's house. Until his death. Upon which he asked forgiveness of the abused child, who had become a man.

Hira's father, son of wandering, did not rediscover his origins until the end of his adolescence, an adolescence branded by unremembering, by a yearning for fulfilment and self-actualization. Regardless of family history, regardless of the colonial landscape.

Hira turned towards this elsewhere, the town of Mandritsara. The name had always sounded strange to his ears, Mandritsara, literally *The-Place-of-Sound-Sleep* . . . '*Aiza ny tanindrazanareo?*' An intimidating question that people asked him all the time. An ordinary question for the island, it came up casually in the middle of a conversation, all the time, like a dead twig carried on a pleasant breeze, but it lands in your hair, and you brush it away just as casually, you speak the name of your ancestors' land . . .

Your ancestors' land? Which precedes the question: *Your family tomb*? Which precedes the next question: *Where will you go back when you die*? And the unsaid, looming large: how legitimate is your presence here, *you are not from this place* . . .

Tanindrazana? One question could dredge up the entire family saga. When he was a child, he never knew how to answer that question. Eventually, he stopped answering. He got the question a lot, because he was light-skinned. But with his light skin, his hair was not straight but curly, an Afro. At first glance, people would take him for a Merina, and then realize that he was different. Blurt out the question. He always knew when it was coming, the surprised look that would hijack the other person's face. Once, at the beginning, he'd spontaneously answered *Mandritsara*, and the woman had burst out laughing: *You sure it's not Befandriana?* Befandriana, another town near Mandritsara, literally *The-Place-with-Much-Sleep*, or *The-Place-with-Many-Beds*. Angry and hurt, he choked and turned around. He fought hard not to break down and sob. He ran away and turned the choking into a triumphant war cry. Later on, he came up with a new trick, he answered *Mahajanga*! Capital city of the province of the same name—where Mandritsara was, in fact. That went over better. People dreamed of Mahajanga. A change of scenery. The sea. The shores. But he knew all too well that it didn't fall under the exact definition of the word *tanindrazana*.

Tanindrazana, land of the ancestors, land of the tomb, the land you came from, the land where you'll be buried. Origins and end. Life having been just a crossing; the other lands visited, merely a passing-through. Leaving the land of the elders, and then returning. Origins and end. He didn't have an answer to either question. Origins or end. What could he say? That his ancestor, Ramanana, was Karana, Indian. Was from Mandritsara. Could anything have made him Tsimihety, the predominant ethnic group in Mandritsara? Then would his tanindrazana be in India? But then why wouldn't Ramanana have chosen an Indian name? Hira did not understand. Why didn't this ancestor have any other family that his descendants could meet? Anyone else who looked like him? Origins and end. Hira did not know what to do with his body after his death. People are interred in their ancestors' tomb, and he had an acute sense of not having any. No ancestors, no land, no tomb . . .

He has always thought: *Why would I share the burial place of a man I don't know, about whom I've been told so little? Why would I have myself entombed in Mandritsara, a town I've never been to?* He decided that he would be buried in Ambohipo. He was born there. He could see himself there. He also decided that since he was born on 26 June, Independence Day, that meant the land of his ancestors was Madagascar, so he could spend his death anywhere on the island, because he was the island!

He had never gone to Mandritsara. His sister promised him he had. The family had been there once. But Hira had no memory of that. There was nothing. Nothing at all.

Hira walked. He was not in a hurry to get back. He bought a cone of cassava, nice and hot. He loved that. Cassava steamed inside ~~of~~ banana leaves. Then, he went straight back to his cave, back inside his literary labyrinth, back onto the bed where he worked and read. He lay down and read. He sat up, and wrote, typing away at his typewriter.

He could see his mother losing more weight every day, he couldn't bear the look in her eyes, as if she'd gone mad.

He was helping his father and his two brothers to fix up their child-hood home, the Three-Rooms house, the place where Hira had been born, which they had left shortly after the Mahajanga situation. But they weren't making progress. They didn't have enough money to build the wall any higher. They didn't even have enough money to eat. They were eating corn flour mixed with water. They were eating chayotes they had grown in their yard: steamed, as a salad, ground to a paste, their papa had even made an abysmal attempt at frying them. Their father had spent most of their savings on the bloody wall. Their mother wanted a wall around the small yard. To hide how destitute they were. To restore their status. Every day she asked how the wall was coming along. Their papa gave the three of them instructions, the three brothers, he put his hand at his hips and said: 'Tell her the wall's up to here!' And the three of them, to their mama, they said, yes Mama, it's up to here. Each of them placing a hand at their own hips. They were not the same height, of course, so their hips weren't, either. And their old man too, like a complete fool, set his hand at his own pelvis height, which was much higher! So, their mother lined them up like the Dalton brothers in *Lucky Luke*, tallest to shortest, from their father down to Tom, with him and his older brother in between.

'Now then, how is the wall coming along?'

And again, as one, all four of them put their hands at their own hips.

'That's good enough! We're moving tomorrow!'

The following day, they were back in Ambohipo.

You Must Not Die

Hira did not stop writing and reading. And somewhere around then, he reencountered Pujol's story. Pujol had just died. In prison. Incarcerated for illegal trafficking. For selling rice. For selling oil. He had been a friend of Hira's father. Hira was at the bookseller's and saw a two-volume set, *The Tunnel* by André Lacaze, an Édition Julliard. 'Lacaze' sounded like *la case*, which made him laugh: *la case* was a hut, so there was a hut in the tunnel! That was the kind of silly free association he would use to buy his books. It reminded him of the street kids in the Ambanidia tunnel. For them, the tunnel really was their hut! He took the book. Without reading the back cover.

What a bombshell. The camps. Exterminations in real life. Horror made human. In two days and one night, he finished both volumes. He stopped only to get a drink, get some food, gulp it down. And he remembered the story Pujol had told him, he finally understood what Pujol had passed on to him, in his way.

Pujol was a French Jew who'd come to the island in the sixties. He had been a prisoner at a concentration camp. Hira never recalled the name of the camp. The name was too difficult for him to recall. It was probably Mauthausen. There, Pujol laboured. And the word 'labour' took on the most tragic of all its meanings.

Hira had been too young to understand what Pujol was telling him. He had been ten at the time, maybe eleven. He's forgotten how the man came into their lives. One day, Pujol had arrived, smoking his pipe and holding a painting under his arm. A Versailles scene, two lovers, a girl sitting on a rock and a boy breathing in the scent of her neck, an endless garden, deer and stags at the edge of a pond. The colours were strong, vivid. Too strong? Hira judged the landscape rather accomplished; the humans, not quite. The deer were all right; the stags' antlers frankly exaggerated. He certainly wasn't a 'real painter', Hira concluded. His mother, however, was ecstatic. It was for her, the painting had been done for her!

Pujol had just got out of prison. Hira's father had done everything he could to get him out. Because *really! It's not a crime to sell rice! I've had my fair share of rations, I won't stand for it!* Pujol could be very loud when he wanted to. Hira had never grasped the severity of the word 'rations' before, until he read André Lacaze's book.

Pujol had noticed Hira's interest in stories. He saw how the child stopped doing anything else when he began to tell his tale. Pujol arrived very early in the morning. He didn't live in the development. He often came in a taxi. It was astonishing. Why was this man even there? Why did he come to talk to his mother about flowers, gardens, deer, rivers, colours, the horizon? Why at one point did his mother break off laughing and say, 'Ha! Pujol, you're a big ol' liar! None of that is true, it can't be!'

What could not be true?

That Pujol had crossed France, Germany, and Austria in a train where people had been stacked on top of one another?

That they'd had neither water nor food for the entire journey?

That he, Pujol, had climbed atop other bodies to get to a crevice in the side of the train car and lick the dew set there by the dawn, that he'd stayed there in hope of more dew, or at least to breathe in the thin stream of air rushing through the gap, he'd stayed there, trampling people, he didn't know whether they were dead or alive?

Hira didn't believe it either. No one tramples the dead. And why would they have been transported in such awful conditions, anyway? For what purpose?

And there was Pujol, telling the story as if all of it had really happened! Those kinds of things couldn't be true!

Hira came closer, he was intrigued by his tattoo. Pujol explained what the numbers meant. Hira didn't understand any of it. The Germans had done that to him, apparently. Hira had heard about Hitler, of course. He'd seen the Charlie Chaplin film. He'd seen images of the man, orating in front of an enormous crowd. He'd been amazed.

No. In awe. It was like something out of an epic film, except black and white, and even better than that. The blocks of soldiers were perfectly square! Looking at those men—so orderly, so rational—Hira couldn't see how they possibly would have acted like Pujol had told him. Like psychopaths.

The old man had been rounded up like so many others, he hadn't thought the journey would be that long, he'd left with only his toothbrush and tricoloured toothpaste. They had arrived at the camp. They had been sorted. He got put with the labourers, he saw the smoke coming out of the chimneys. He understood without understanding. Hira couldn't figure out what that was supposed to mean, understanding without understanding. And when he asked Pujol, the old man only smiled, taking out his metal nail to clean his pipe.

Then, he told Hira that he had learned to paint there, in the camp.

'Ha!' Hira blurted out. 'I knew you weren't a real painter.'

'Oh no, my boy, I was a real painter, that was even how I made my living! I painted for the kapos, and then I painted for the Nazis, the officers, the ones who could raise one eyebrow and send you to the gas chambers, or leave you on the ground to freeze to death, in the cold and the snow, naked. I conserved my toothpaste, the three colours, I mixed each of them with other material, dirt, I rubbed wood against stone, I chewed leaves and spat them out to extract their colour. And I painted these deer, these landscapes. And the kapo would give me an extra potato.'

Hira couldn't believe what he was hearing.

'A potato?'

'That I'd eat in secret.'

'You wouldn't share?'

'Sometimes I did, when the hunger hadn't made me forget everything else. But I was hungry all the time, I had been reduced to my stomach. I was no more than that. I became hunger. And hunger does not share.'

Pujol made dozens upon dozens of paintings for the guards. For a potato. For an extra piece of bread. Then he went out to labour with the rest. Outside the camp. Hira forgot what Pujol had been forced to do outside the camp. He had been reading *Asterix in Corsica* around the same time, and it altered Pujol's story in his mind. The Corsicans had been sentenced to forced labour, and they just lounged around on the ground, whiling away the hours, even napping, they would lay one cobblestone for the Roman road and then go back to sleep, howling at the Romans if they tried to make them get back to work. Hira pictured Pujol like that. It made him laugh a lot.

One day, Pujol showed him his metal nail.

'See this nail?'

'Yes.'

'This is what I used to mix the colours. Sometimes I also used it to paint. I couldn't lose it. I couldn't afford to lose it. But the Germans had prohibited us from keeping tools with us. So I hid it however I could. When we came back from labouring, the Germans would strip us naked and frisk us down. You know where I hid my nail?'

'In your hand?'

'No.'

'In your mouth?'

'No.'

Suddenly Hira got it!

'No!'

'Yes!'

'Up your . . . ?'

'That's right! Up my—'

But Hira had already started cackling too loudly to hear the rest.

'Ha! Pujol! You're a big liar!'

And Pujol smiled, scraping out his pipe with his nail. He'd become a regular at their house. Hira went outside to play, shaking his head. That man was such a good storyteller, he had almost believed him!

One day, the night caught Pujol out, he'd stayed on too late. There were no more buses, hardly any taxis. He said his goodbyes and headed out. Hira hadn't been paying attention when he left and was about to go up to his room when he spotted the nail. His heart dropped.

'Pujol forgot his nail!'

He grabbed the small nail and dashed outside to chase after his friend. It was a moonless night. The streetlights weren't working, as usual—but Hira might've had something to do with that! Hadn't he and his friends made a game of using the lightbulbs for target practice? Hira could see the glowing red dot of Pujol's pipe in the distance. He couldn't see anything else. Except for a little of Pujol's face. He looked so far away. So far! Hopefully, Hira wouldn't drop the nail! He'd never find it in the dark . . . He squeezed it tight in his hand. So tight that it was embedded in his skin. So deep that he felt like it would stay in his hand forever. He caught up to Pujol.

'You forgot your nail.'

'No . . . I did not forget it, because you have it in your hand right now.'

And he accepted the nail. He stroked Hira's hair. That was the last time Hira saw him. Hira only knew that he'd gone back to prison, he would never stand for food to be rationed through the state co-ops.

At the time, Hira couldn't believe that Pujol had left the nail behind, on purpose, for him. He had not tried to understand it, but the question had stayed in the back of his mind. It was only once Hira had read André Lacaze's *The Tunnel* that he figured out why he had never forgotten the imprint of the nail in his hand, why it was such a powerful presence. He understood what the old man had been saying.

Pujol had not forgotten his nail, no, he had left it for him, to leave its mark forever upon his palm, his ballpoint pens and all the rest settle into it so naturally . . .

Often, while Hira is writing, he rubs an imaginary nail. There is a space there, in his hand. When the absence becomes too strong, he'll go hunting for some sort of hard, thin object, anything that can fill the void left by a small piece of metal. Often, Hira realizes that he is painting with his words, that the pen in his hand is memory's guarantor, the guarantor of all survival, for a single life saved is all of humanity preserved. Hira, he is not afraid of thinking such things. Of giving such weight to an activity that is, all told, powerless: writing. That is what he learned from Pujol. You must not die. Simple as that. You must not die.

Mahajanga

1.10 A.M.

Hira is coming to settle the memory and pain. He is in the room where he was born. In Ambohipo. Antananarivo. In a few hours, he will set off on the journey to return to his father. Out in Mahajanga. He has hired a car and two drivers to get to his parents' city. Two drivers so they can take shifts, so they won't lose any time. Because Hira only has two days and two nights for this trip. Coming such a long way, ten hours of flying, ten hours of driving, to stay such a short time! But it's just as well. This time. A priceless gathering. Hira's been planning this trip for several months. The chance to do it, and the time. An invitation to Mauritius and a possible stopover. His parents are waiting for him. Hira feels the tension in his veins.

The night seems to be so deep. It's the first time in weeks that he tries to fall asleep by letting go of the pressure, tries to tell himself it's OK, he can surrender to sleep, fully and completely. But he doesn't feel like he can. Not yet. His father is waiting for him. Has his father maybe grown weak again? Might his heart stop beating, just like that, without warning? Might his wounds reopen, become infected? Hira tries to calm down. After all, he is happy. Happy to be here where he was born, to lie down under the same roof where his parents had lived, and he too, of course, but can we really think of the house where we were born as ours, once we become adults and experience so many other things, once we have built a new home, with our partners, our children? Still, Hira does find that sense of calm again. Of protection. But he also knows that this is just the natural inclination of a son for his parents, it in no way reflects his current reality. Today, he is the one taking care of his father, not the other way around. He thinks about his father's life, his father's story. Immense pride overwhelms him, mixed with sadness. They lived in this house. This is where his father truly began his adult life. His father had come from a place more distant than the provinces, more distant than the shores. His father had come from an abusive childhood. Hira does not want to think on it any more. Time to change the subject, he thinks. Change your life . . .

He feels the presence of his father's books around him, nearly the same smells, nearly, but more decayed, a musty book smell, damp, a sick book smell, the smell of books that have been orphaned, left without eyes to see them. It's been a long time since Hira left the country, left these works behind, it's been a long time since the patriarch left for another city, that other city, Mahajanga, a long time since he left his library behind.

Not long after that unpleasantness with the dictator, his father had decided to move back to his home region, to Mahajanga. Hira had just got his bac, so he had to stay to pursue his studies, just like his older brother, his older sister, already at uni, but his father left. He didn't yet have the means to transport all the books. He would have needed to hire a second truck for that. So, many of them stayed there, locked away. Hira had actually picked out which ones should go and which should stay. Then, he carefully closed up the wardrobe. No one has touched it since. In nearly twenty years . . . Hira's system is still there, to keep the wardrobe fastened shut: pieces of cardboard wedged into the door hinges. The locks had popped off ages ago. Actually, Hira had broken them off himself to get at the forbidden books, back when ol' greyhairs was still trying to monitor what he was reading. Hira remembers it very clearly, he had just passed his entrance exam for Year Seven, he had just received his first diploma, the CEPE from primary school, he figured *enough already*, he was all grown up now, *what kind of father forbids you from reading?*

Hira thinks about the rest of the books that no longer exist, the ones that died, out in Mahajanga. He'd been told about how, just after his father was arrested on the road out to Amborovy, the soldiers had come onto the family's homestead. Two military trucks. They'd loaded up the furniture, clothes, and curios. Everything. Except the books, which they piled up in the middle of the yard, they poured petrol on them and struck a match. The books flared up and the flames licked the leaves of the mango tree. Then they set fire to the house. And left.

Hira can picture that scene very clearly. It plays over and over in his mind. A fire of blackened pages, the letters seeming to float through the air and then crumble into ash. Letters that are not printed, no, not in the ashes, they're left caustic, unreadable, smouldering, and filled with rage.

This is a nightmare he regularly has: he is walking to the exact spot where the fire was, letters are burning the soles of his feet, he tries not to fall because, in the dust where the ash lies, sentences are starting to be written. He must push aside the ash but keep the dust. Then his father appears. Hira makes the fire disappear with a nod, so that his father won't notice anything. His feet are still burning but he acts like nothing's wrong. He walks beside his father, forcing himself to stand up tall, the letters turn back to ash. He makes an enormous effort to not turn around. To not see the ash eating away at the dust and wiping out the sentences that had barely been reformed. He prays that some of the letters would have had enough time to seep into his feet, into his flesh. And he wakes up. With a feeling of such regret in his chest . . .

The fire, the real one, the house burned down, Hira kept that hidden for a long time while his father was still in his cell, locked in a battle against death. Walls mattered less to Hira's father than books, mattered less than documents, less than the manuscripts amassed over more than thirty years of research. But Hira was also aware that any fire could break out at any time, you couldn't be part of the island's history without facing flames and anger.

Hira had heard the story of the arrest from his cousin Alphonse. The patriarch had just left the radio station after broadcasting his appeal. He climbed into the car, Alphonse was at the wheel. They set off for home. On the road out to Amborovy, a barricade. Alphonse said to him: 'Baba, barricades!' 'Keep driving,' his father said. 'It's a real barricade, Baba, it's the militia!' 'Keep driving,' his father said again, 'we have nothing to fear.' They continued on, slowed at the barricade. The militia leapt into the road, they shouted that it was Zokibe! It's him! Zokibe was one of his father's monikers. They dragged him out of the vehicle, got him on the ground. Alphonse took his chance to flee. A bullet whistled by his ear. He ran as hard as he could. He didn't see anything else after that. He hid in the mango trees, didn't dare to take even a quick look around, didn't go back to the house until afternoon. And there, he saw soldiers outside, he walked right on past as if nothing had happened, as if he was just a neighbour going by . . .

Hira found out what happened next from witnesses, people who'd been on a bus stopped at the same barricade. Zokibe was on the ground, they'd trussed him up with a nylon rope. Blue. Green. Why did the colour matter? The tiniest detail can grow to such excessive proportions in these types of crazy, volatile situations, nothing is innocent on a violent stage. Other people told him how the militia had hitched Zokibe up behind a car and dragged him all the way to the airport. But that didn't add up, because Zokibe hadn't shown any wounds consistent with that. Some folks even claimed to have been in the same aeroplane that had transported their elder to Antananarivo, and that the soldiers had suspended him upside down in the aisle of the aircraft. How could that be? A man hung by his feet from the ceiling of a plane? Those people had definitely never flown in an aeroplane before! It was like a movie that no one had understood, yet they were all trying to explain the plot in their own particular way.

One thing is definitely true: Zokibe had been driven straight from the barricade to the airport. There, the general of Ravalomanana's armies hurled abuse at him. Zokibe saw that all around, there were people coming to save him. Petty fishermen who worked off the Amborovy beach. They'd rushed to the airport after hearing word of the arrest from the bus passengers. They revered Zokibe for pushing them to organize a union, to fight back against the concessions that Japanese boats got, and the other ones with flags from who knows where. With a shake of his head, Zokibe said no. It was their slingshots versus machine guns . . .

Zokibe let them carry him onto the plane, still bound by the nylon rope. Blue. Green. Why did the colour matter? Why? Blue or green. Nylon or sisal. The nuance leads you down the path of truth.

The blows began to fall at the Antananarivo airport. In the van that accepted delivery at Ivato and brought him to Fiadanana, the police camp. Rifle butts slamming into his temples, his chest, his knees, his shins, his feet. The barrel in his mouth. Rotated. Rotated around. Mangling his teeth and upper palate. *Now talk! Talk!* And the ridicule. More unbearable than the abuse. *Now talk! Talk!*

Hira stops thinking about it. He should sleep now. Some small noises are coming from the roof, a bird, a lizard, the wind tumbling some seeds it took from a tree, or the sheet metal creaking, from age, from heat, just because, to prove it's alive. Strangely, there is still one image haunting Hira: of himself, carrying a huge sack of books on his back, walking down a dirt road, the sack is heavy, the sun is pounding, he sees stars before his eyes, he doesn't want to put down the sack, not even to rest, doesn't have the strength to reshoulder it if he stops, the sack holds the books he's bringing back to his father. It is no dream. He really did that. A few months after the move to Mahajanga, when he went to spend his school holidays with his family. He took the opportunity to bring some books with him in a huge rice sack, stuffed full. He'd slipped in a couple of shirts and a pair of jeans on top. From the taxi-brousse station to the house, it was a bit of a walk . . .

2.27 A.M.

This black, of dying night. Human solitude, insomnia. The world scattered all around the being. No space more important than where this body lies. The rustlings rearranging to remap the distance around. Croaks. The rice fields—lower now, nearly levelled, replaced by housing. A barking dog, another answers. East-West. A child who cries and then quiets again. Quite close. A newborn neighbour's dream. A rooster's crow. At this time of night! Hira expects some closer answer in response. No. Nothing. The fowls do not escalate. No other raging against the night. That feeling of slipping back into childhood, simply by being back in your parents' house! And yet, all changes! The development morphed almost completely into a shantytown. Insecurity so rampant that no one will raise chickens any more. Roosters give themselves away by their crow. Thieves only have to bend an ear to know which pen to pillage—and the house adjacent, while they're at it.

Hira has a small sense of regret, the regret of no longer being a child. This silence and darkness, turned commonplace. False silence. False darkness. A child's perception makes every detail extraordinary by its simple presence. From which absent sun comes the light that filters through the roof? Darkness and silence have always felt like ogres devouring the world. Silence captures the quarry. Darkness rips it to shreds, wolfs it down. Without a sound. The moment of waking was always remarkable for him, escaping the ogres. He would start by clearing his throat. Then move his body. Rustle his sheets. Breathe louder. Then he would pop his eyes open and cast his gaze far and wide, over all the lights of the dawn. And he would smile. The smile would drive the ogres away. Then, he would yawn. And then stretch, finally. He'd won!

Hira lets out a long sigh. He has sat up in bed. His rough drafts all around him. He'd been trying to conflate time and memory. But today is today, a matter for the living! He: also living. Living this life, his life. Living on top of ruins that he has failed to leave. What is the nature of this pain? Why are scars still sensitive for so long when life is there, good as always, simply waiting to be enjoyed? Others suffer, too. They do not write their hurts. They do not ruminate over them. They don't keep looking back. Hira has an opportunity to live a normal life. That's all. Just a normal life. But no, instead he writes himself to death. It's not normal to write.

He can't help but think about the days that followed his father's trial. Eight years ago, it was. When the judge delivered the verdict, Hira had given in to intense anger, *two years suspended*. The following charges were made: *attempted assassination of the head of state, inciting ethnic hate, threatening internal state security, disseminating misinformation, sabotage and destruction of public goods, torture . . .*

All that was missing was murder and genocide. In the moment, Hira hadn't registered how absurd it was: two years suspended, for all of that . . .

The trial had barely lasted twenty minutes. The evidence from the prosecution consisted of a video clip seven seconds long, one sentence that his father had read during a TV broadcast, a sentence that his father had read as a reporter, a sentence that someone else had spoken, a sentence saying that Mahajanga was independent, a sentence from the regional governor declaring the secession of the province. During the broadcast, Hira's father had condemned the declaration as unconstitutional. And reading that declaration had become proof of his guilt. The court clerk had nearly fallen over himself to press stop on the remote, so intent not to let any other sentence play, the whole room had seen that his father was holding a letter, that he took off his glasses after reading it . . .

Hira was on his feet with everyone else when the verdict was read. On his feet.

He'd leapt from his seat when he heard the sentence. He'd only registered the word 'guilty'. People immediately started coming over to tell him it was OK. One friend, a court lawyer, put his hand on his shoulder: '*He only got two years, it's a suspended sentence, he's getting out of prison, that's all that matters, calm down, we'd been predicting ten years, you won.*' His father was taken away, and Hira was told to be back at 2 p.m. to sort out the paperwork.

He needed to breathe, get out of there, he went out into the main hall, there were so many people, there was so much injustice in that room, in that court.

Someone else came up to him, made their way directly over to him through the crush of bodies, someone he didn't know: *they found a middle ground, don't appeal, it'll be better for everyone . . .* Hira didn't answer, like he hadn't understood what they'd said to him, he left the court building, pushed away another concerned friend who'd been waiting for him on the steps outside. He walked along the avenue, crossed the street without looking for cars, they honked but he didn't give a damn, he made for Lake Anosy, he kept walking, walking: *no, we won't appeal, you just got your father out of hell, if you appeal he'll go back to prison until the next trial . . .* He couldn't do that.

He turned around. He made some phone calls. He called his mother, his brothers and sisters, his phone tree of friends who'd been supporting him from the start. His mother would come on the taxi-brousse that night to be with them. Anger gave way to immense relief, and immense pride. He had done it! His decisions had not killed his father! His decision to stop paying up, his decision to stop giving in, his decision to defer the human rights deliberations until later, his decision to not let the trial become a media event so the State could have some way of saving face! And it had happened. They didn't get a dismissal or an acquittal like he'd hoped for, but his father was free! Two years suspended . . .

What is justice in a lawless state? Hira didn't have an answer. Deep down, he understood. His father had said something unacceptable, in the most basic sense of the word, in a country that was terrified to hear its own history.

Truth cannot be heard in times of fumbling blind. It seems so obvious to say that every region should have some autonomy and not have to depend on the national government. But when the national government gets conflated with the dominant ethnicity, when the fear of being divided gives rise to a fear of autonomy and decentralization, then those words, those declarations are unacceptable for all those who have not forgotten how the colonial state did everything it could to pit them all against one another, *divide and conquer*.

To speak of autonomy feels like opposing the unity that had been years in the making. To speak of decentralization feels like criticizing the capital. To speak of federalism feels like endorsing division and tribalism. This is the lasting trauma of colonization in this country, the fear that it could break apart at any moment . . .

So yes, his father had said something that could not be heard in a country that had been so profoundly impacted by colonialism, where the mere mention of the term 'ethnic group' could put the whole country on edge, lead to tensions and even violence.

Had his father's words come too soon? No, that is the fate of words that must be said, the words that burn the ones who give them voice. His father knew that sooner or later these issues would return. This country cannot live like that. All that power in just a few hands, in the capital. Hira knew that by saying so, his father would always and forever have to clarify his point of view. The capital does not mean the ethnic group in the capital. The capital is just a place where all the power has been concentrated. Not the power of any particular ethnic group, but the power of a handful of men and families who ultimately are only representing their own interests . . .

The day after the trial, his mother arrived. His father was eating breakfast at the table and made the effort to stand up. Despite his weakened condition. He returned to his wife.

Hira can see his parents embracing again in the dim living room. Silent, intense emotion. He slipped out of the room, holding back tears. He heard them whisper their love, felt their soft voices. A sentimental swell in his chest. He'd done it, he'd brought them together again! He knew how much his mother mattered to his father. Oh, he knew it so well.

But is Hira aware of just how much his own wife matters? When he is away so often. Writing. Travelling. And if he does realize it, what is he doing? Spending so much time in a story that has already ended, already been resolved. His father isn't in prison any more, and still Hira feels traumatized. Listening only to his own sorrows in the end. Hira has been caught in a trap. But it is a more awful trap for the one who shares his life. Who had never asked for this. Never wanted an absent husband.

6.01 A.M.

The car will be there in half an hour. Return. For a long time, he thought it was going back to his father's childhood. No. Return. Back to his own life. His own family. Settling his old man's childhood, of course. But return to himself. Return to her. Be the happy adult that he must be, since he had a happy childhood! Despite the dictatorship. Despite the shifting tides of his father's politics! Despite the controversies around his books. Return.

He slips quietly into the bedroom that is no longer his. He is stubborn in thinking it his, but it is no longer. A wall has been knocked down to extend the house. Instead of the window, wide open to sunlight and sounds, there's now an entrance to another room, a long interior room, always submerged in darkness. He thinks of her. He thinks of his children. It is time for him to return to them. All these years, thinking only of his father, all these years living only to write the old man's childhood. His own father's story, which had been tangled up with the history of the country. Difficult. Violent.

After Hira's mother was reunited with her husband, she couldn't stop touching him. His head, his arms, his chest. She asked him if he was okay here? There? Here? His father's skin bore a number of bruises. Black spots that Hira had noticed, too. Hira felt redundant. Not needed to understand his mother's hand returning to his father's body and finding that not all of it was familiar, parsing out the wounds, the injuries, the silences. He would have tried to do the same, because his father hadn't told them about any beatings—was his father even aware of all the times they'd beaten him?

Looking at his parents, Hira knew that only his mother could guide his father along the path to healing. That role was not for Hira to fulfil, just like it is not his role now to tell the story of a childhood filled with so much harm. He cannot go back in time to comfort the child his father once was! That role was for his mother to fulfil, and what's more, she already had, his mother always had, like she had at the beginning of their story together, when the woman had been the man's rebirth. Why couldn't Hira have understood that, for so many years? Why? What was this obstinacy, which drove him so hard that he wouldn't listen to any-one? Why had he dug in his heels so much when She had said the same thing: 'Returning proves fatal if it is not back to yourself'?

In his childhood home, however, Hira knows that he has lost his neighbourhood, his birthplace, his homeland. He's from there, of course, but also from somewhere much farther away. Where? He doesn't know exactly. It's not a place. Not a country. He's not from a land, he's from his father's childhood, like all children who are planted in one place but then suddenly their roots are revealed to be from somewhere else, he's from the story of that childhood, the story containing all of the fractures and displacement, a story that will soon come to a close, his old man is finally, completely ready to let it all out.

Hira knows that his place is not really here, in a culture where the lands of ancestors are idolized, the tomb of origins, tomb of the clan's forebear, the first forefather of a great family. Ultimately, he is not bound to any lands, nor any tomb, even if such a tomb does exist, even if the ancestor's lands are there, in Mandritsara, out there in that one particular place in Tsimihety country.

Hira does regret that he's never seen Ramanana's house. He regrets it very much. But it's not over yet. This is not over yet, now that the tale is freed to assuage all things.

9.12 A.M.

The car came to get him as planned. At seven in the morning. They've been on the road for two hours, and have only just got out of Antananarivo proper. Hira is feeling strange, he doesn't say much, neither do the two drivers. They're not drivers exactly. They're business partners who hire out their cars. Hira didn't ask how many cars they actually have in all. He feels as though he's in a trance. Likely the sleepless night. Curves and bends rocking him gently. Place after place. Familiar. Hira needs to go back through all of these places, needs to visit them again, as if for one last time, a farewell, to childhood, to a story begun, a story that he did not—or could not—carry on.

Hira unfurls his song of silence, safe from bitter sorrows. Will he alone spread his song over these once-monotonous hills that now buzz with new builds? Construction as far as the eye can see. Sumptuous villas and estates. Rock mines with open pits. Makeshift houses. Projects abandoned, gap-slabbed walls, still encircled by barbed wire. A smattering of modern ruins. Plastic bags in trees. And SUVs that overtake them, flying past on these very narrow roads.

A wisp of memory, like a mist whose parting is the sun. He hears a small bang. It's nothing. The habit of fears and memories repressed.

He stops thinking. All is calm. Road and more road. Twisting. Starting to climb. Rocks, hills that are forever bringing stones to the fore, and men, and more disturbances.

He closes his eyes.

Her. Her.

He opens his eyes.

He'll finish with this whole business of suffering, and finally be back with his love. Return. This country may not be at war, but it does share borders with sharks: the dry is sand or rock, shore or reef. Hira has his own borders with his countrymen: empty borders, for he no longer thinks of himself as being from anywhere. The sun runs him through. It hurts where the pulse of light sticks in and spurts. The logic of time passing that unravels affections. Part of things still, and body whole. A place for glooms and fissures thought. Unavowable desire to leave. Trace of anger. Seeming nothing. Laughable land. Walking on contradictions. All of these places were from a beautiful childhood . . .

Never had this sense of losing a land.

There is no more land, there is no more land. . .

Nothing will be like it was before. He looks for other words, other ways to say it. *Nothing will be like it was before.* He cannot find any. *Nothing will be like it was before.* His childhood bound up with Antananarivo. He grew up in these hills. Communing with the land. The air. The sound. The language. He was from this city. Now he will be no longer. He feels like a stateless man. Ripped away from his hearth. His father had tried to give him an enchanted childhood, he and his brothers and sisters, and he got an enchanted childhood, bound up with an enchanted city, but putting down roots does not always produce a tree aligned with the land. This is how he feels, deeply rooted but outside the land. And the anguish he feels is greater still. His roots took hold in this environment, and it does not know him. The happy childhood did not provide a land for the adult. They always say that roots are grown in childhood, but his childhood is a dream, stuck in his memories. Now that he is grown, nothing corresponds with any of the images in his mind. Almost nothing. Everything has changed, profoundly, and he has no place here.

Hira looks at a picture of her, stares for a long time. Love is a nomad's land where looking grows the roots. This is his land. In the reaches of love. In her eyes.

I brought you my horizon gloom,
The lands traversed in days without you, rains falling on stiffened
    shoulders,
I brought you the stones collected under my soles, the dust stuck to my
    dried-up lips,
The tumbling pebbles when my heart had gone off to beat the flurry
    of return,
On the way I will pick refreshing fruit,
Both pomegranate
And prickly pear,
I brought you some songs from afar to whisper loves' exile in your ear,
I brought you both my heart and my being.

But hasn't She already suffered too much? Has he not already killed her? Hira is reluctant to talk about her. Reticent to make her easy prey for the writing. He brings the chapter to a close. He looks outside. No. He does not look. Curtains. He slips away. The landscape outside is a curtain that falls on his thoughts. He nods off. He wants to be filled with dreams of her.

11.00 A.M.

Dream of umbra uncoloured, Hira's head spins before so many darkened havens. Unfolding his memory over the creaks of doors that struggle to close, he hovers on the fold, hovers on the threshold. How?

To tell the story, to race down the shame upon lungs startled high, wedge up the rage on the body enfrayed . . . To scream, the silence? The prone shadow's groan, fold upon the creaks, he does not right the whorled shadow, just the opposite, he leans on its paralysis, and its soul above. Craven the tone taken over his clearing throat. His minutiae. His usual debacles. But nothing happened. No death is taking him, while those who kept a tight hold of their shadow have disappeared, the ones who stayed rooted in place.

Ochre walls and ochre tracks, daub on either side of shoulders, Hira does not right the fold, he tilts over towards silence. Whether you are used up or burned out, you take it, music of your cracking bones, you know it, that's where it comes from, the kneecap twisting or the ankle that . . . you know.

Songs of memory for the days that resemble night, songs of memory for the nights that assemble with days, songs of memory for days to craft from the past, for nights that pass into later's unremembering, through to tomorrow where yesterday means no more than today, Hira is no more than moving towards the least heavy, a sense of refusal that comes from the void, he brushes up against faces and stirs a few nerves to shivers, memory when indifference and duplicity don their masks. Hira is from the horde of dream-stealers, Hira is from the horde of voice-revellers, Hira is from the horde of story-delvers, Hira is, Hira is no more, Hira lives no more, Hira lives, Hira exists no more, Hira exists. Hira is the drove on the shadow's back, Hira is the shadow on the dark's fold, he is from the horde of dream-stealers, he is from the horde of voice-revellers, he is no more, he's after you, he lives no more, he loves you, he exists no more, he exacts you, Hira is of the horde of choir-stonecarvers and great skin-drums, Hira memorializes by sending roots through the void, he is, he's not after, he lives, he's no livery, he exists, he does not exist. He is. He makes bare. And once the seeds of self-compassion are sown, he will take the way of the wind to leave and leave no trace, he does not know the plant whose husk he stripped for his memory, dead skin for his story, he does not know the root whose vertebrae he extracted for his back, but once the seeds of self-compassion are sown, he will leave, he will leave, he will leave, he will leave. The eye tires from being shown too much, known too much, fed too much, read too much, he will leave, letters of the wind and alphabet of forgetting, upon dance of time and tiny trance.

Hira dreams only of writing profound but life took his body for crossing out. He is scrawling. Recent history has dumped him into its violence. He cannot stop putting ink to paper in constant hope of recovering the wonder of childhood. Small sprig of memories running through him, any wind carries. He'd left his homeland at twenty-three. A censored play, barely complete. Needing to leave of his own accord, so that he would not implode.

He had never dreamed how much he would lose control of his life. He had left her alone once before, She who would become his wife.

On the same road, going the opposite direction, when he'd been with his parents, one night, going back to Antananarivo, his parents had objected to him getting married already, *later, yes, later, not with such haste, better, more beautiful, more lavish, you're much too young, too young, and also you're about to leave, you don't know if you'll still settle down with her, life lasts a long time.* But he told them that She was the one. He knew it. *You don't know her, and you say She's not the one?* She was the one. He had never—not for a moment—expected his parents to object. He thought he was giving them good news. But the shock was plastered across their faces. His parents felt like they were losing their son twice over, with his departure in the wake of the pressure from censorship, and then this marriage that had blindsided them. Hira's blood turned to ice. *We're not saying no, let's just give it time, we'll do it properly, in a year.*

But he would be in France in a year, he didn't know what was going to happen there. How would they plan any more lavish of a wedding in a year? They'd barely started to get back on their feet after moving to Mahajanga. Hira could not argue with his parents. He just lost hope. Inwardly, he said no, no, *you're wrong. You were both also very young when you got married. Mama wasn't even eighteen!* But that was different, they argued, it was a simpler time, and we were in love. *But I'm in love with her, too.* Of course, but we're going to do your wedding properly, we'll do the proper planning, we'll make the announcement to her parents. We will come with you for the discussion. We'll ask for their daughter's hand.

Hira conceded, his tears stuck inside. He knew they were wrong, but there was no possibility of going against them, it was this paralysis he'd never felt before. In all his life, he'd never fought with his parents. In all his life, he'd never been told off by his parents, not once, or maybe that one time, when he was three and climbed up the bookcase to smell the scent of books and his father had swept in like a cyclone. The paralysis prevented him from ever standing up to them. He didn't know how to stand up to them. He didn't know how.

That very night, they went to do the 'marriage proposal', but it was mostly to delay the union. Hira had already begun the administrative processes there in Antananarivo, so he had to go cancel everything at City Hall. Hira thought of her. She had not asked for anything. He was the one, in the desperation of leaving, who had given her a child. He'd known that if he didn't pull out, there would be a child. He had not pulled out. He didn't want to leave. He didn't want to lose her. How could he leave, and leave her behind? Leave her like that? He'd clung to his parents' promise. Yes, they would do it later. More lavishly . . .

And so, on that same road, going the opposite direction, on that night, he'd laid his head on his mother's shoulder, not said a word, one tear had run down his cheek, a tear of farewell, almost forever, in the deepest silence of his sorrow, he could sense the ensuing, inevitable distancing, he would belong to her, he would not belong to his mother any more.

His father's voice that had always captivated him, confidently announcing a beautiful future union, was in reality decimating a beautiful existing love story. Her parents acknowledged. Devastated for their daughter. Deeply hurt. Hira saw. It was blindingly obvious. She was there. He saw her ruined. He could no longer bring himself to look at her. He made a vow in his heart. *I will bring you there. I will send for you to be with me. I will not abandon you. Distance is nothing. I will return.* He did not see how his parents would find the means for their lavish wedding. Not in a year, no. He did not see it, and his father continued speaking.

Hira left. He left the island. His absences began there. He didn't know it. And for her, her waiting began there. She did know it. The lavish celebration did not take place. The child was born, a girl. Hira returned. He'd decided not to wait on his parents to get married. His parents hadn't made any arrangements. Lacking money. Perhaps the will. His father was still mired in political troubles. His mother was still unsure of how to let go of her son, how to welcome the new daughter. They did not attend the ceremony. We're hurt, they said, not objecting. His old man was off somewhere, on some tour. Hira did not make a fuss. She would be Him. He would be Her. That was all that mattered. She was sunken so deep into sorrow. He felt so powerless to pull her out. He had nothing but promises, the promises of an absent man. He went away again. Left her, married, with the child. He couldn't send for them to join him until a year and a half later.

Leave . . .

Speak the island and end up in the middle of an ocean of ink and words to save from the swell. Like the child emptying the ocean with a tiny spoon. He was. Like the child not knowing that the riptide likes to give and take back. Hira has been lost since childhood. He was that child, lost from trying to speak an island unmoored. Without her, he would already no longer be here. Not in body. Nor in writing. His mother had been the source of his notebooks, yes. But She was the current that ran through all the books he wrote.

I will return, he whispers. I'm coming. Just let me finish this story.

The landscape.

Absolutely enormous.

1.45 P.M.

Around lunchtime, they stopped in Maevatanàna, the city they say has the highest temperature on the island—people say that, but Hira's been to other places around the country that were just as hot. Fill up on petrol. Get a drink. Stretch your legs. Have a snack. Hira headed over to 'his lemon tree' and plucked off a leaf to put under his tongue.

He always does that in Maevatanàna, a ritual, ever since a family trip when he was wracked with a headache and nausea from the high heat. He and his older brother were supposed to fetch cold bottles of Fanta and Coca-Cola for the car.

Hira couldn't follow his brother, he saw the steps outside a large hotel where a lemon tree provided some shade. He staggered over to it, resisting the urge to be sick, and under the tree the cool air smacked him square in the face, upsetting his head and stomach even more. Fragrant. Violent. As violently good as the nausea had been violently bad. Just as he was sitting down on the steps, he saw a wicker basket full of leaves. He went to take one, thinking they were leaves from the lemon tree. He got a smack on the hand straightaway. An old Muslim man with a white beard was chewing his khat. Hira realized his mistake.

Not a sack of lemon leaves. No. A sack of khat.

The old man simply pointed up to a branch hanging above him. Hira looked up and picked off a leaf, put it under his tongue. He breathed in through his mouth to swallow the aroma and stave off the nausea. He waited there for his brother to return, hands full, too full, holding four bottles, the two Fantas under his arms and the two Cokes in his hands. Hira didn't have the strength to offer to carry one or two for him. But his brother could tell he was feeling sick. Bro's no dummy, he held onto his bottles!

They made it back to the car. Their mother had got out the metal cups, three or four of them, his big brother poured, and everyone took turns drinking. Hira liked Fanta best, in theory, but he wouldn't be able to keep anything down. Plus, his mouth was already busy inhaling his leaf! When they got back on the road, Hira got more and more talkative while everyone else in the car was wilting. His brothers and sisters looked surprised. Hira showed them his tongue and the leaf underneath. *Because I took some drugs!* 'That's khat from the old man!' his older brother exclaimed. Nannie, his older sister, looked at their mother: 'Mama?' But Mama just smiled a small, impish smile . . .

Hira loves remembering that smile. The lemon leaf had parted the clouds, a sunbeam for both his body and his mind. He thinks of it often during the hard times in his life. And by some miracle, the fragrance returns. His mother's smile. Their shared secret. And how stunned his older sister was that their mother didn't do anything! Then Hira can carry on, heart full and spirits raised.

Hira returns to this day. Maevatanàna. A pitstop. A break. He sees the two drivers chatting jovially, they clasp hands, *Let's go, boss!* They set off again. Hira knows that after the blazing furnace of Maevatanàna, it starts to get easier. They drive for two more hours and then the city of Mahajanga comes into view. The drivers whoop and holler, they think they've made it. The smell of the sea exacerbates the feeling. They've never been here before. Hira does not tell them that they've got another hour and a half to go. At least. The city is there, in plain sight, but the road is the master of time, you must first be absorbed by its twists and turns. The heat returns. Surprises are standard. Breakdowns frequent. Police are enterprising and bribes to be expected. All of it's bound to put the brakes on any self-respecting trip, in this land of moramora, *easy now* . . .

Hira turns onto the family homestead with a peace that he has rarely felt in his heart. His parents are there, standing beneath the mango tree, where the books were burned not so very long ago. He gets out of the car. A little girl comes up with a sijavo prepared for him to drink. She's Tom's youngest daughter. Hira takes a long drink, gives the half-emptied sijavo back to the child, and hugs his parents at last.

9.00 P.M.

They sit on the patio. The father tells the story the son already knows. But he tells the story free from pain. Tom, Nannie, Pacia are also there. The older brother and the two youngest sisters missing. The father tells the story of his childhood in such serenity as the son has never seen in him. He begins with Ramanana, the Karana, originally from India, the rich man, with holdings as far as the eye could see, the colonial administrator, and his desire to feel wholly Malagasy, his marriage to Rasoa, albeit no one had asked her opinion on the matter.

Already living in Ramanana's house was another woman, from the highlands, another child, Bertin. Ramanana wanted to be fully accepted by the people in his region. So, he had to marry a local. This was Rasoa. Which infuriated the first wife, effectively reduced to a mistress. This was during the thirties. The child was born without the mother having any say.

Ramanana was banished from his Indian family. Because he married a Malagasy woman deemed to be from a lower caste. Ramanana provoked the wrath of the other elite, rich colonists. Because he married a native. Ramanana tried going even further in his pursuit of Malagasy identity. Clandestinely financing nationalists who were working towards the country's Independence. Colonial bigwig by day. Nationalist by night. He went to Indochina under the pretext of the fabric trade. Myth has it that he met Nguyễn Sinh Cung there, who would later become Hồ Chí Minh.

Ramanana died suddenly, when Hira's father was only three years old. He remembers the coffin sitting alone in a small, empty house. There hadn't really been any family to sit with it. What had he died from? They had probably known back then. But Hira's father, no, never. Hira had asked his grandmother Rasoa one day why his grandfather had died, he remembers it very well. Hira must have been ten, he has a specific memory of it because his mother had been thrown off by his sudden question, she was still wrapped up in an argument she'd been having with his grandmother. It wasn't nearly enough to rattle Rasoa, *your grandfather, he was imprisoned after his last trip to Indochina. He was being punished for meeting with communists. The Vazahas beat him in prison. The Vazahas didn't give him any food, or water. Then when he was very hungry, they gave him food meant for the dogs and pigs to make him sick. And they beat him again. They left him lying there, on the mud floor of his cell. Then they released him from prison. Your grandfather was very weak. He'd developed pneumonia. The Vazahas told his half-brother, who was not rich, to give him rice that had been mixed with ground-up glass. That way, when your grandfather died, his brother would get his riches and his wife.*

'You?'

'Yes, me! Your grandfather's brother, T., did so, and your grandfather died a few months after being released from prison. He got all his possessions, but I left, I ran away. That's why I had another husband, and other children.'

This version surprises Hira's father. No, no. Ramanana hadn't been in prison. He'd fallen ill. What kind of illness, so young? In his thirties? But Hira does not get an answer. There is a silence. Accepting that no one knows the truth. Father continues. Son calms his thirst for details. The important thing is not the story itself but that his father can retell it, or relieve himself of it. The fatherless boy is left to the mother under the tribunal's decision, but the child must be given back to the half-brother of the deceased upon his sixth birthday. The half-brother will administer the property until the child reaches majority age, for what is a native woman in the time of colonization? Even one married to a French citizen? Could she inherit her late husband's riches? She is illiterate. She'd been taken from her village to be married to that man. Now she has this child. And now the man she did not love is dead. She does not want the riches, and much less to marry the child's uncle, or be eternally subjected to the other woman and her son. No. She left, bringing her child home to her village. There she found another man. Quite quickly. Too quickly. For soon the child got in the way. The unwanted child. They called him the dead man's son. He was entrusted to his grandparents, Dadaha and Dady, Rasoa's father and mother. *The child was raised on beef and the freshest cow's milk.* At age six, in accordance with the tribunal's decision, his uncle came for him, sent him off to school with his brother Bertin. The first beatings date from that time. For a lesson poorly learned. For a mark falling short of the uncle's wishes. Uncle lines him up against the wall and lashes him, sends him to bed with an empty stomach. The days that follow the beatings, when the child is leaving school, he sees other mamas, he wonders where his mama has gone. As for his father, he knows that he died. Isn't he called the dead man's son? He knows because Dadaha, his grandfather, always told him that T. was not his father. His questions would always get the same answers. T. was not his father. But he does not understand. Why do they have to beat him all the time? His uncle. His half-brother's mama, and her mother too, an old woman, cruel towards him, affectionate towards his half-brother. Where is his mother? Why had he been ripped away from his grandparents? Why does he live in such a big house with people who think only of abusing him?

Hira's father does not stop. It's a beautiful night tonight. The mango trees imbue the family land with a deep power that has always affected Hira. A perfect complement to the energy that radiates from his father. Telling his son everything. Passing it on. Now. Here, a few metres from where the books had burned. For so long, Hira has dreamed of this moment. For so very long. Ever since age ten, when he'd begun digging through his father's archives. He couldn't have known that the words would only come when the books had perished.

One fine day, my mother turned up with a small girl, she was very dark. Her name was Marianne. And that day, I was allowed to go with them to see my grandparents. And I stayed with them, for several days. Finally I had a mother. Finally I had a family, a little sister. But Marianne got sick. They took her to hospital. She died there. My mother gave me back to Dadaha and Dady again, in their village. I was the child who brought death. She'd lost a husband, my father. She'd lost a child, my sister, my half-sister. But I didn't understand any of that, all I could see was that I was returning to Dadaha and Dady's village, with the cows and bulls, back to the place before the beatings, back to paradise. Not for long. T. came to take me back. When I saw him coming, I hid out in the rows of corn. Everyone was shouting for me. I didn't move. T. spat furious threats and then left. My grandfather brought me back to Mandritsara the next day, and took me back to T.'s house. I was given my daily dose of backhands at once. I saw my grandfather look back, then stop himself and walk away, hanging his head. I felt lost. My grandfather was abandoning me. And, I had lost touch with my mother. The hell began again. Even worse, because I was starting to realize that the lashings were mainly for me. Because Bertin showed no trace of abuse like I did. He lived a comfortable life, he was well fed. Whereas I was starving.

Nannie heaves a sigh. Hira knows the enormous empathy she's always had for her father. Nannie was the first one to tell Hira to drop the whole thing with their father. *You're just twisting the knife. Don't you see how Papa suffers, when you ask him all those questions?* But it was so long ago. But it was stronger than Hira. He had to hear the story from his father's mouth. Yes, he knew all of it. But it would only be encased in truth from his father's mouth. Why? He was sure that there were some pieces missing. It wasn't clear. There were too many different versions, from other people.

One day, I was told to bring a meal out to the 'gisa', the geese, pure white rice. Wracked with hunger, I stuffed a handful of it into my mouth. Alas for me, T. was lurking nearby. I paid dearly for the minor act. Kicking, slapping, punching. I fell in the mud and still the beatings came down. He did not stop, I don't remember when he stopped, as if he never did.

When I was nine, there was a serious accident in Mandritsara. An officer in the French army took his own life, because he'd caught his wife with a private. He went to the munitions storehouse and blew himself up. The whole barracks caught on fire. And all of Mandritsara scrambled to take (and I do mean take, not plunder, because taking from colonists is not stealing) anything they could: furniture, linens, beds. I hadn't moved from inside the house. T. tore into me and forced me to go. So I took off with everyone else.

When I came back, I had a basketful of sardines and some other tinned food. Because I was hungry. Oh, I was hungry. This displeased T., he took out his switch and beat me as he screamed: 'You never think about anything except eating. This is all you bring back? You're a thief!' Unsatisfied with the switch, he pulled off his belt and struck my head: I got the buckle in my right eye. I still have the scar from it. I started to panic, I scrambled to my feet and ran away.

It was raining outside. I skidded around the corner of a house and got my foot caught in a telegraph wire. I fell hard into a canal and lost consciousness. Later, when I came to, I stumbled around and arrived in front of my grandmother's door—she had a house in Mandritsara, too. She took me in her arms and called for help. The president of the neighbourhood came and called the police. My grandmother pressed charges against T. There was a doctor at the trial. He testified that yes, I had been beaten and was malnourished. The tribunal granted custody to my grandparents from that day on. And so I lived in the company of those two angels.

Hira had never known those two angels.

With grandfather living in Antobato with his second wife—Maman'i Zafamo—and grandmother with us in Mandritsara, we would go to Antobato on Friday evenings to stock up on rice and 'kitay', our firewood. Sunday evenings, we would ride our wagon cart back to Mandritsara. And then, one night when I was sitting up front, I nodded off. Bumping down a hill in Madio Tsy Fafana, I fell off headfirst and the back wheel crushed the length of my left foot. I've had a slight limp ever since then.

At fourteen, I breezed through my CEPE certificate exams. At fifteen, I was accepted into the Regional School in Analalava. Before I left, someone told me my mother would be coming. And then, a beautiful woman did in fact arrive. I threw myself into her arms, taking her for my mother. She shoved me away savagely. 'Iza ity maloto be ity. Zaho tsy mamanao.' She was actually my mother's oldest sister. But that had profoundly impacted me. And then, when my mother showed up a little while later, I didn't even blink. It was a sad thing: just like children who no longer believe in Santa Claus, I no longer believed in Papa or Mama.

My grandfather sold fifteen zebus to pay for everything I needed for Regional School. Uniforms, fees, and travel costs. My mother went with me. She was very proud that her son was going to Regional School. But in her, I saw only a distant woman. I felt nothing towards her. We passed the medical exam before we left, and they gave us our TAB shot.

In Analalava, we were welcomed by Mamakely Manandrazana and her husband, who worked as a nurse. They were very nice. We'd arrived on a Saturday. The first day of school was the following Monday. On Sunday evening, we went for a walk on the beach with some friends. It was the first time I'd seen the ocean. And to be 'grown-ups', we bought cigarettes. And to be like everyone else, I drew in a big breath of smoke, and that was it. My head swam, I couldn't feel anything else. I was dead.

I didn't understand my mother's agony until later. Every time she was with me, there was death. First her husband. Then her daughter. And now, as she was making the effort to bring me to Regional School, me.

For I was actually dead, and they'd made arrangements for the funeral vigil at the hospital. Mamakely was very devout, so the sisters and priests and all the Zanaky Masina Marie women took shifts to sit in vigil. My zama—Mamakely's husband, the nurse—was doing his stint on Nosy Lava, he provided care for the convicts on the island, too. They were waiting for him before burying me so that he could administer the formalin, the facility didn't have any other nurses for it. You have to understand, this was under colonization. There wasn't a whole lot back then. Hospitals were nowhere near as big as they are today. The third night, my zama arrived. They prepared the syringe. And he had to inject it.

Me, though? I heard singing, crying, praying. I thought I was in church. Then someone took hold of my arm, probably for the injection, but they yanked their hand away and shouted: 'Tsy maty, velogno.' Then the singing stopped, and I opened my eyes. Everyone backed away. They seemed afraid. I looked around. I saw lit candles. Flower wreaths. The vicar and altar boys. I closed my eyes again. Then someone said: 'Aza mitabataba, everybody out!' Then the vicar came close and spoke to me.

'Venance, can you hear me?'

I had a world of difficulty trying to enunciate.

'Yes, Father, I can hear you.'

'Can you move?'

'Yes!'

And I raised my right arm. I was amazed. I had a rosary between my fingers (you all know the one). Zama came over, as well, and took off one of my bandages. It had kept me from opening my mouth, I realized why I'd had such a hard time speaking.

'Can you stand?' he asked me.

'Why not?'

And I got to my feet, but then I fell back onto the bed. Someone gave me a drink. The doctor arrived. He didn't understand, he'd already signed my death certificate and authorized the interment. I saw Zama handing him both documents. The entire hospital was at my door. Then I fell back asleep. But I'd had my 'Lazarus, get up and walk,' and I'd stood back up and I'd walked. They took off my white robe, but my shirt and trousers had already been burned. The clothes I wore that day were very tight, just temporary, too small for me.

My recovery took three months. The cigarette, that was because I was allergic. That's why, Hira, your head used to ooze pus when you were little. Those patches on your head. That's why my children and descendants must be cautious about allergies.

My mother had left, again. I said nothing. But my heart still sank to the bottom of my chest when she left. Of course, it was out of the question for me to start Regional School then. I'd have to retake the exam the following year. So, I attended the religious school. During that year, I thought about entering minor seminary. The sisters got everything taken care of, and I was admitted to the minor seminary in Ambanja: student no. 17, bed no. 13.

But my vicar kept telling me: 'Venance, you can't be a priest. You have another calling. Sit for the Regional School entrance exam again. And we'll see.'

We did as he'd said. I couldn't go to Ambanja without his signature, anyway. And so I was accepted to Regional School for a second time. The headmaster's name was Mari, exactly like the French word for husband. That made me laugh a lot. But it would have been dangerous to make fun of the head of a Regional School back then.

Before the school year started, I had to pass another medical exam. The doctor asked me several questions about my death. I couldn't answer any of them. What was I supposed to say? That I'd been heading for a bright light, and then realized I'd forgotten my bookbag? And that was when I'd heard the songs and prayers? And felt my zama's hand on my arm, about to inject the formalin? As I turned to head out, the doctor noticed my limp. He examined my foot and asked if I'd been in an accident. I told him the story about the wagon cart.

His prognosis: 'The only way you'll keep your foot is if you play sports.'

And so, I became one of the country's greatest athletes. I was the national runner-up in the 1500 metres, I was Madagascar's pole-vault champion, I played basketball, I was on the national team.

Throughout those years, I'd never stopped wondering about my father. I only knew his name. I'd never seen a picture of him. I'd been told he was Karana. He was rich. He was powerful. I would often walk by my father's house. Mandritsara isn't that big, I couldn't help but walk by it. I saw T. and his children sometimes. I said nothing. They lived there. In my wealth.

I was sick of colonization, too. Sometimes, I saw people in chains because they couldn't pay their taxes. I'd been sensitised to all forms of oppression. Every injustice summoned up my uncle's abuse. Every injustice summoned up the fact that he occupied my father's house. And the colonial tribunal had sided with my uncle. He was the administrator for my father's fortune. He administered nothing. He used it for himself, and if he could have killed me, he already would have.

1958. I'll skip over everything else, it would be too long and too difficult for me to tell. Madagascar became autonomous. 'Do you want Independence? Take it on 28 September!' And we had, we'd got autonomy—it was practically Independence—on 14 October 1958.

The Regional School—being a colonial school—was closed in the wake of autonomy, so I left Analalava and landed in Diego on 28 October 1958. That was my first time in an aeroplane.

I wasn't exactly welcomed with open arms back at my zama's house, it's true, because they already had four children at home. I was the fifth.

But my zama still enrolled me in the religious school. The fees had to be paid. After six months, he refused to keep shelling out the money. I faced expulsion. But by that point, I'd proven my athletic prowess.

Everyone already knew that I'd been Madagascar's junior champion in pole vault. So the priests couldn't expel me, because training was already underway for the national championship. What could they do? They couldn't take charge of me, either.

One day, I was cutting a friend's hair in the schoolyard when the headmaster came through. He stopped to watch me for a few moments.

'When you've finished, come to my office.'

That's it, I thought, I'm getting expelled. What will become of me now?

When I got to his office, he had my payment register in his hands.

'You're a good barber. Would you agree to become an even better barber by doing all the priests' hair? In exchange, you wouldn't pay any school fees.'

That's how I was able to complete my studies there, by shaving their heads every week.

The year after, 1959, was a very significant year for me. As I was walking along the seaside, I saw a very pretty young woman. I walked over to ask her what she was doing there. She answered, but I didn't understand what she'd said to me.

'What's your name?'

'Marie.'

And she said nothing more.

'You're not going to ask what mine is?'

'I already know it. Everyone knows it,' she retorted in her Creole accent, 'you're Venance.'

Because that was the year I'd become the pole-vaulting champion of Madagascar. I was a minor celebrity in the city.

And that was the beginning of our shared life, with two at first and then later with ten. A life filled with love. A full life. I'd found a LOVE. A Mama for my children, a mother for me. I'd met THE woman.

As for the rest of my life, my children, you already know everything, you've been through it all with your Mama and Papa.

Hira smiles. A warm, enormous smile that he cannot contain inside. He wants to go back to the beginning of the film. Like when he was a child. Tell the story again. Over and over again. Start over again with his father's voice, in a thousand different ways:

My life,

31 August 1939, my life began. At first, my father, Ramanana Albert, wanted to give me the name Valentin Roger. But my maternal grandmother was against it. No! My grandson will not be named 'Mivalantay'. The doctor had to do the whole birth certificate over again. The next day, when the priest arrived, he brought us all the news that Germany had just invaded Poland. The Polish army was leading the defence, commanded by General Venance: Wincenty Kowalski. Consequently, I was given his name: Venance Roger . . .

Hira knows this is no trivial thing. The father receiving a resistance name on the day World War II began. And he, the son, born on a day of national celebration, of Independence . . .

10.52 P.M.

. . .

She

This is a discontent wind, forever passing over the same slice of sky, as if trying to reform the fold of time, this is a wind that comes, and recedes, it seems like the sea, but it is not the sea, it seems, driven from far away by a mysterious force. It comes prepared to wreak havoc, but leaves again at the very last moment, we feel no danger, the wind is just there, steady, as if hung in one specific place, outside the bodies of men and women. We'd like to talk of her, next to this discontent wind, the words that come and, no, do not say enough about her, and, no, would rather take off in search of other sensations, the words return, and are still not it. Her caress is what we have to take from the wind, a wave that forgets not one bit of her skin, next to her is where we should exhale the breath that was sighed so far away, tell and retell her the words inhaled, inspired by love, words that will consign themselves only in kisses, we'd like to kiss her, but She is still far away, we kiss her.

She says, you never love me as much as when you are gone . . .

We tell her again: 'Towards the again, you'll see both the again, in the insatiety of holding you, on the shores of insanities where anchoring myself to your flesh is no longer enough, I need the androgyny, and carrying your body in my body and carrying your trembling in my trembling, however infinitesimally small the motion would be that moves you and would fully topple me, in a sensational fall where the only way out would be returning into your soil, into the again and again of your body. To you, one of these other days, on one of these tears to be deducted from destiny, in the sureness of suns that will open out once again, for another shore pertains to you next to my languor, there have I sketched out my dreams of feeble clashes, strange gutterings, and mild frights.'

We look at her, She is all the more fragile listening to you, hanging from your promises, life would need to take the place of writing, kisses take the place of the mouth.

'This is a nameless shore. This is a depthless shore. This is a stockless shore. And sands that speak only of you. And winds that erase only my dances. Of strange gutterings and feeble stirrings. Of mild frights and bits of trance. I bid you be there. I beg you be there. I bid you be there. I murmur it to you. My languor and my feeble clashes. All the waters of my soul ossified at your desires. It is the other shore of your hours. Time lost in beholding you freely. Time lost in saying nothing more

*to each other but return. And I return to the dream of
you who made me your future. I return. And forever,
I remain. Yours.'*

She is there.

THANKS AND ACKNOWLEDGEMENTS

The translation of such a rich, raw, and truly remarkable novel owes its existence to an entire tapestry of creative and deeply caring people. The translator would like to thank:

- Jeffrey Zuckerman, for his ever-present support and encouragement,

- Rachael Daum, for her edits and constant enthusiasm,

- Sebastian Schulman, for helping us both just do the thing,

- The Quicksilver Collective, for seeing me through the whole journey,

- The Translators Aloud team, for providing the very first outlet for the very first part of the translation,

- Translation House Looren, for the space and time (and the Alps),

- The retreat space at Saltonstall, for the space and time (and frogs),

- The Art Omi Writers and Translation Lab cohorts of fall 2024, for listening,

- Annette Bühler-Dietrich, for her comradery,

- Bishan and the whole team at Seagull, for their faith and trust,

- Michèle Rakotoson, Naivo, Johary Ravaloson, Mose Njo, Dwa, Marie Ranjanoro, Bao Ralambo, and so many others, for everything they write that deepens my understanding of everything else,

- Jean Luc, for all that he has shared,
- And finally, my loving, patient, compassionate family, for . . . everything. I couldn't do any of this without you.

This book is dedicated to the late Ernestine Lawler, who taught me not to shy away from the hard things, and showed me the strength that is found in remembering our history.

Allison M. Charette, December 2024